# *Deadly Conversations*

A Novel by

D.C. McLaughlin

*This book is dedicated to the spirit of Sekhmet who inspired me and was my fiery muse, to my husband, Drey, who has always believed in me, to the first people I trusted to read this tale, Kennedy, Morgwen, Beth and Ellen, and to my aging black kitty Aldonza who sat on my lap throughout the editing process with just a few meeps of protest.*

# ACKNOWLEDGEMENTS

First, to my devoted husband who was there from the start, reading drafts and providing historical advice on dates and weaponry. To my cousin Beth, my friend Morgwen, friend and co-worker Ellen for reading the first draft. Thanks Kennedy and Lily for inspiring two very beautiful characters. Additional thank you to Kennedy for book cover design and photography. Thanks also to Stacy and Avdi for raising such intelligent, beautiful and blissfully nerdy kids!

Thank you Morcades for referring me to Laura Lussier my first editor. Thanks to Connie Scharon, "Year of the Book" classmate and author of *Enchanted Lover* for editorial assistance and encouragement.

Thank you to Demi Stevens of Paul Smith Library for creating the program "Year of the Book" to educate would-be authors about the publishing process. This program was pivotal in getting this book published. You gotta LOVE libraries!

A big thank you also goes out to my boss, Dr. Elizabeth Preston, for first telling me about "Year of the Book" and then approving my days off to devote to meetings and events for the program. Your support was greatly appreciated!

And last but certainly not least, thank you Mom and Dad and my sister/author Gwen. Yes, vampires are not your thing but you still supported and encouraged me, and fostered a love of reading from a very early age. None of this would have been possible without that early foundation. You are as much responsible for this book being written as anyone else. Thanks for never giving up on me, even through months when I felt all my creative juices were dead. They weren't dead, just slumbering in a coffin waiting for the setting sun.

# PROLOGUE

The room smelled of blood.

Mykhalo staggered to his feet, drunk with the rush that fresh blood brought. Time always stopped for him right after a kill. The world around Mykhalo moved in slow motion while the emotions inside of him spun and jumped in a wild, chaotic dance. He gasped as the new blood swam through his veins, infusing him with strength and power, sating his insane hunger and at the same time drowning him in the memories of the person he had just fed on.

The problem was he was part of them.

The feelings that came threatened to overwhelm him. He held his head and tried to shield his heart. But the rush of blood strength was stronger than the bonds on his emotions. The flood of powerful feelings was too great. He was drowning under their torrent. He felt his heart would break. He looked about the room, desperate for some way to slow the barrage on his feelings.

A baby grand piano beckoned him from across the room. And then the keys were under his fingers, cool to the touch but soothing and welcome to his jumbled state. The contrast of black and white gave his mind something else to focus on. He closed his eyes against every other sensation and thought of a single note. He was well practiced in the art of music. Muscle memory took over and a stream of melancholy notes flowed outward.

He played what he felt. The music translated the myriad of dark thoughts racing through his mind and heart into a tune low and sad. The notes rang out soft but clear into the silence of the room. The feelings tumbling about inside him began to slow. He squeezed his eyes shut forming grooves into his perpetually forty year old face and played on until the notes grew louder reaching into every corner of the darkened room.

He played his grief, his sorrow, his loneliness. Here he was in this same damned position, crazed with turmoil while the blood of a dear friend raced through his God forsaken form. He had killed another friend. The reason didn't matter to him. He knew what he was.

It still didn't make the ache in his heart hurt less.

The victim's words echoed in Mykhalo's mind.

"It would be a mercy killing," Bill Gibson had told him just moments before. Mykhalo gasped and his eyes snapped open. He remembered his reply, laced with anger and dread.

"Not to me!" Mykhalo retorted. "How many times have I saved your life Bill?"

"I've lost count." Bill said with a smile.

Mykhalo's fingers trembled as his mind relived what had just happened. He continued to strike the keys and the piano continued to sing. His thoughts came slower. He forced himself to face the memory.

"We all die." Bill had said to him.

"Not me." Mykhalo growled with anger. "That blessing is denied me."

"Maybe not," Bill said softly.

Mykhalo glared at him, pacing the room like an angry lion in a cage.

"Please," Bill pleaded with him. "See reason. Mykhalo I'm dying, slowly, painfully."

Mykhalo turned his back on him and shuddered. He did not want to do this. But at the sheer mention of what Bill was proposing, to end his life, Mykhalo could feel the change within him taking place. His hunger and his teeth were growing.

Bill heaved a great sigh which turned into a spasm of coughing. Mykhalo couldn't look at him. He waited until his friend eased and he was able to speak again.

"I've lived my life. I've survived a war that claimed many of my friends. I came home, married, raised my children to adulthood, built a home and a family for myself. It's all over and done with save the dying. And I will not leave this earth a doddering idiot who can't even see to his own bathroom habits."

Mykhalo shook his head. "If you want to commit suicide, why don't you just use your gun? Why do you need me?" Mykhalo said.

Here Bill reached out and grabbed his arm.

"Because I don't want to be alone! Mykhalo, I trust you. And I know that you won't blab this to the police. You are a person that is invisible to society. That's why."

"You trust a vampire?" Mykhalo said softly. "Do you know how reckless that is?"

Bill smiled.

"I think we would both agree that as a vampire, you are unique among your kind."

Mykhalo tore his arm free from Bill's grasp.

"I don't want to kill you, Bill" Mykhalo resisted. "Please don't ask me to."

"It won't be killing. It will be releasing me. It is the one gift I want. You've saved my life so many times. Now I'm asking you to take it."

The insane hunger inside of him was growing.

Mykhalo said nothing. He refused to look at his friend.

"Please. It's my choice. I want some dignity to my end."

"It's not dignified!" Mykhalo insisted. "It's horrible and brutal!"

Bill had only laughed.

"I've lived through horrible and brutal when I was young. Now it takes too long. I want a quick end." There was a long silence between them. Finally Bill said the one thing he knew Mykhalo would understand.

"I miss Carol."

He was speaking of his wife.

His hands fastened on the windowsill, fingers digging in like claws and he hung his head. Mykhalo stopped in front of a window which overlooked the back yard of Bill's tiny little house. He remembered what it was like to be in love. It had been a long time since he had felt this way. For centuries he had guarded his heart against loving any woman in spite of his desire for a relationship. He knew too well how dangerous it would be for him to give in. He might kill the poor girl.

Yet Bill Gibson never had to worry. He didn't need to. He was just a mortal. He had married and raised a family.

And two years ago his wife had died.

"I want to see her again. My life hasn't been the same without her. Please."

Mykhalo's shoulders had slumped as he sighed.

And he relented. He gave Bill the release he so desperately wanted.

Mykhalo squeezed his eyes shut as hard as he could. The brutality of the act was still too fresh. He could taste the skin of Bill's dry wrinkled neck in his mouth as he buried his fangs deep into his throat. He could smell Bill's sudden fear at the pain and feel his old hands grasp at him trying to fight him off. And he could remember the taste as his lifeblood rushed in a red torrent into his mouth and down his hungry throat, slaking his monstrous thirst.

And now Mykhalo had to deal with the aftermath.

The piano keys sang under the expert dance of his long white fingers. He felt tears spring to his eyes. He blinked several times. Vampires never could weep real tears, only blood.

He bowed low over the keys as he coaxed a more dramatic melody out of the great instrument. He tried to concentrate on the notes and the tune only and just let the music sweep him along in its rush of power and pain.

It didn't work.

Two days ago Mykhalo had picked up the phone from his home in Germany.

"Mykhalo," Bill had said. "I need you to come to the States. I have a couple of things to go over with you."

His brow furrowed as he remembered the conversation and his fingers hammered on the keys in reflection of his emotions.

"Why do I have to hop a plane?" he asked not understanding. "Just tell me now."

Bill sighed in exasperation on the other end.

"Because you won't be convinced if I tell you over the phone."

Mykhalo snorted in disbelief. He shook his head as he remembered and the piano's keys laughed at him under his fingers.

"Try," he dared. He could picture Bill shaking his head on the other end.

"All right. But you're not going to like it!" Bill told him. "I think I've found her."

He dreaded the words to come.

"Found who?" Mykhalo said already suspecting the answer.

"C'mon old friend." Bill said. "You know exactly who I mean. I've found the witch that will heal your shattered soul."

Mykhalo was silent for a long moment. He remembered wishing he hadn't trusted Bill with that one deep secret. He had felt betrayed. Why did he tell Bill he had a shattered soul and only a special witch could heal it and he had been searching for her for centuries?

The piano sang his betrayal.

Bill had no idea what it felt like to have a shattered soul. He was only trying to help.

"You're mad at me, I can feel it."

Bill was right; he was angry he had trusted him and that he persisted on this pointless quest.

Mykhalo's fingers hammered on the keys in a dramatic show of force and the piano's notes reflected what he felt.

"Bill, I'm no longer interested in finding or talking to any more witches." He said flatly.

"And why the hell not?" Bill countered.

"You know very well why not!" Mykhalo had tried to control his anger but it was beginning to bleed through into his words. "Because today's witches are useless, each and every one of them! I'm tired of looking for the right one. I don't think she exists. The prophecy was just a tease, a lie. I'm not talking to this or any other witch ever again."

There was a very long silence from the other end of the phone line.

"Then I guess I have my answer." Bill said pointedly.

"What answer? What was the question?" Mykhalo said.

He could sense Bill smiling even though he couldn't see it.

"How long it takes a vampire to give up. Three hundred years."

Mykhalo's eyes narrowed and he growled at Bill's words.

The memories finally ceased to torment him and his fingers stilled on the piano. The notes thrummed into silence. Mykhalo was completely alone.

One single bloody tear slowly ran down his face and spattered on a white piano key. He looked down at it. He watched the tear as it sat there, a shiny wet bubble of color until it went from fresh to dried and dark.

Mykhalo rose and turned his back on the piano.

He came around the side of the easy chair where Bill's lifeless body sat with his throat torn out and blood soaking through his clothes and dripping down to the carpet below.

Mykhalo placed a hand on Bill's shoulder.

"I will miss you dearly, my friend." He whispered softly.

# CHAPTER 1

My name is Susanne Joel Miller but my friends just call me "Zan," I run a bookstore called "Batty Belfry Books". Not some big chain bookstore with an attached coffee house where musicians come to play on weekends. Just a small-town bookstore in an old building aged enough to have its quirks.

"Batty Belfry Books" is crammed floor to ceiling with new books and old books. The antiques must be gingerly touched so they're in a room all to themselves. These books require a key and supervision if you're going to look at them, maybe even cotton gloves.

And then there is the unusual bunch of books. I do have a separate room dedicated to books of the "esoteric" nature. From time to time I have unique authors come in and give readings and book signings. These too are advertised in a way which would not upset the devoted, evangelical, church ladies up the street. So far, they treat me with polite, cheerful respect. I'm led to believe they don't have a clue as to what lurks in my closet.

Like my store with its odd collection of books, I can be a little unusual myself. I'm a witch. I tend to fly under the radar because it's good for business. It's fine by me. It's actually less shocking than they would have you believe. Most secrets are that way.

I live in a small town in Pennsylvania called Sleepy Pines. The police department consists of five officers, the fire-house is manned by eight people, and the large gas station is the biggest business in town. There is a now defunct railroad running through town complete with its own abandoned station house. Everyone talks about fixing it up and making a train museum, but no one has the funds. Some say it should be demolished, but there's no money for that either.

Sleepy Pines is surrounded by beautiful farmlands with rolling hills. Most of the populace is related to someone in the agricultural business. We have a community of Amish and most of the town businesses have hitching rails for them to tie up their horse and buggies. Nothing much happens in Sleepy Pines except for the farmers market on weekends and "Old Tractor Day" once a year in the spring. It's really too small for even my bookstore. Luckily, I have a very devoted clientele. Some of my business is supplemented by online sales which has made all the difference to keeping "the Belfry" open.

Did I mention nothing ever happens here?

The majority of the townspeople of Sleepy Pines think I'm a quiet, middle aged woman with a teenaged daughter and an odd attraction to bats.

Some have asked what happened to my daughter's father. I don't like to talk about him. His loss is still very painful to me even after all these years. I moved here when Bree was five. If they do ask, I just tell them he died overseas. It's close enough to the truth anyway. For a time, several of the women customers kept trying to set me up with their eligible bachelor friends. But when their attempts failed before they even started, they finally got the hint and let it slide.

Tuesday the 12th of January was a day just like any other day. I was sitting in the one La-Z-Boy chair I had squeezed into my small bookstore. But this day I was reading the local paper, the *Town Crier,* which serves many of the local rural towns, instead of a book.

I was reading the obituaries when I was brought up short by one. Bill Gibson had died, under strange circumstances, it said. No more information.

My heart sank and I gave a sad sigh. I had liked Bill.

Then my brain latched onto the words and I realized something didn't sound right. I wrinkled my brows and chewed on a lock of my long, black hair.

Bill Gibson was a dear, older gentleman, very well off and a frequent customer of my bookstore. He was one of the few

2

"mundanes" who actually knew the truth about me. He was a warm and caring man who didn't care about my past or my religious affiliation. He judged people by the way they lived their lives. He seemed to think I was a good, upstanding person. I was always grateful to him for that and told him so often. Both my daughter and I adored the old chap.

I frowned, as I thought harder on it. In fact, I didn't know a single person in Sleepy Pines who had a mean word to say about Mr. Gibson.

I read the words again "died under strange circumstances" and was unsettled by them.

The old sleigh bells hanging on the door jingled as someone entered and I looked up.

The grimace was immediately erased from my face.

"Ah, Tempest," I said with a motherly grin. "Done with school for the day?"

My daughter rolled her emerald eyes and glared back at me. Her black and blonde streaked hair flounced about her face as she shot a look back over her shoulder.

"Ma!" she whined. "Don't call me that!"

"Why not?" I teased for what must have been the umpteenth time. "I think Sabrina Tempest is a lovely name or I wouldn't have called you that."

"Bree is normal enough, thank you." she said as she dumped her heavy book bag on the counter with an added groan.

I cast a look at the book bag. It didn't look heavy enough for all the dramatics.

"Are they throwing calculus at you yet?" I said to stroke her teenage ego.

"Nah! Just everything else. You think you could tell the school I'm not planning on becoming a chemist, or a rocket scientist?"

I just grinned, gave her shoulders a squeeze, and tried to kiss the top of her head. She whined and wriggled away in disgust.

"Sorry, love. I had to do it, too!" I replied. "Now go in back and study or I'll throw the book at you."

3

An answering snort was her reply as she wearily slung the book bag over one shoulder and slunk dejectedly into the back of the store.

"Yeah, right! Which one?"

"How about the heaviest?" I said.

"I'm going, I'm going!" Bree said.

I smirked and turned back to my paper. But my thoughts were no longer on the printed words.

It was staggering to me even now how much Bree resembled her father. She was going to be taller than me someday, just like he was. She had the same oval shape to her face, the same wide eyes, the same way of laughing and walking even though he had died before she could have become aware of such things.

She resembled him most in his personality, always smiling and joking and resilient to any storm. Strong as an oak in high winds but flexible as a willow that was Bree and it was also her father. Only her perfectly rosebud mouth resembled mine.

Her hair was constantly changing colors, a detail which always made her easy to pick out in a crowd and spoke of her sense of rebellion she got from both parents. Luckily, her hair was the extent of her troublesome nature and having a young girl with purple or green or blue hair seemed to bother other adults more than myself. I loved her as fiercely as any mother can love a child.

But then my thoughts of such precious moments were jolted out of the past.

The sleigh bells jangled again as someone else entered the bookstore. I looked up but couldn't see the person clearly. The last dying rays of the setting sun flashed off the bells' brass and obscured him.

Something about the dark shape hidden by the flash of light made me shiver. I looked again but the person had disappeared behind a bookshelf. My inner sixth sense was screaming at me but I wasn't sure whether it was good or bad.

Cautiously, I put down the paper, stood up, and walked along behind the counter trying to look everywhere at once.

4

I saw a barely obscured, tall person wearing a dark fedora like the gangsters back in the roaring twenties used to wear and lean shoulders cloaked in some sort of overcoat.

He had his back to me.

"May I help you find something?" I asked.

"Just looking for your mystery section," was the reply.

The voice was unusual as well, deep and throaty, the words were slightly clipped off at the end as if English was not his first language. My brain scrambled to attach the dialect of a certain country to it. I prided myself on being able to match the accent with the country. But I needed to prod him to speak more to figure it out.

"The end of the row on the right. No, not your right, my right," I said.

I saw the hat sway from side to side and then move in the direction I had directed.

The warning was still shivering in my breast. I had to goad the stranger to speak more.

"Anything in particular in the mystery section? A certain author perhaps?" I said.

"Ah, Agatha Christie," the voice returned.

The hat was swaying from side to side.

"Top row, directly in the middle," I said.

"Ah yes," the thick voice returned.

The hat lifted slightly. I could catch a glimpse of his eyes between the brim of the hat and the top of the bookshelf. They seemed the palest shade of gray I had ever seen. The pupils moved from the books in front of him to lock on my own.

I swallowed with difficultly for I felt an icy fist had closed about my heart and had stopped it from beating. My inner voice was now screaming at me. It was warning me this person was not as he seemed to be, there was something sinister about him.

I had learned, through much experience, to trust my gut instinct implicitly.

I could only shiver.

"Hey, Ma," Bree's voice was right at my shoulder. She startled me out of my frozen state. "Can I listen to my new iPod while I study?"

It took a couple of breaths before I could trust my voice again. I hoped my daughter hadn't noticed the ghostly pallor of my skin.

"Of course," I said, just wanting to get her out of the room. "Just make sure you put your earplugs in so that you don't disturb the customers."

She started to leave.

"Aww man! Mr. Gibson died?" Bree suddenly said.

I jumped again. *What? She's still here?*

"Yes, I was surprised, too," I could only numbly return.

What was the matter with me?

"That sucks big time." she exclaimed.

"Sabrina!" I scolded. "Not in the shop!"

"Wha...? We have customers? Whoops! Sorry!" and she scooted for the back.

I closed my eyes and heaved a sigh of relief.

Then I remembered my suspicious client.

I straightened up and my eyes flashed back to the shelves.

He was gone.

My eyes did a wild search and found him all too easily.

He was slowly coming around the end of the bookshelf, watching me all the while, giving me plenty of time to take in his appearance.

My eyes immediately flashed to the gun which was hidden behind the counter in a small box. It was a 357 Smith and Wesson magnum my late husband had given me before his last tour of duty, the one tour he never returned from. He said he wanted me to be safe while he was gone. In all these years owning the bookstore, I had never used it.

I looked up again to find my customer's eyes still locked on me as if he knew exactly what I was thinking.

He was a tall man as I have said, at least six feet, probably more, thin but not too thin, with a ruddy complexion, with a finely chiseled face like a handsome medieval lord. He looked to be in his forties but

6

very well preserved at the same time, strong and fit as a twenty year old in spite of it. He wore a kind of long over-jacket like they would have worn in Edwardian England. It did not match his hat.

"Your daughter is rather…vivacious for her age, is she not?" the same accented, clipped voice said.

The voice was low enough to be persuasive, which immediately put me on edge, and he was talking about my daughter.

Just who was this guy anyway?

"They are always this way at that age, are they not? So confident, so assured of their own ability. But no wisdom to speak of. That comes later."

I could say nothing. I concentrated on breathing and feeling. I was, as carefully as I knew how, probing the energy of this stranger, trying my best to identify what exactly the threat was.

The conclusion was I was facing no normal human.

I put all my magical shields up, all the while struggling to be polite and professional.

He approached me slowly, keeping his voice low to distract me and lull me into a false sense of security. It felt like I was being stalked by a large, hungry lion. I did not hear the words he said. I just realized he was doing the same to me, probing, peering with his inner eye, and trying to discover what my difference was.

"Excuse me, sir," I said with a surprising surge of boldness. "If you're going to be discussing my daughter, don't you think I should know your name first?"

He stopped his stalking approach – much to my relief!

"Of course. How rude of me. Where are my manners?" he said as a small smile flashed across his face.

"My name is Mykhalo Von Ludwig and I am new in town," he stated, taking off his hat to be proper, revealing sandy blonde hair with just the barest hint of silver.

"Of course you are. I can hear it in the accent." I replied.

I had never heard of the name Mykhalo. It sounded like the English Makayla but with an "o" at the end.

7

I seemed to be controlling the conversation now, which gave me confidence.

"And that's not an American accent unless I really miss my guess. What country do you hail from, may I ask?"

He smiled again, seeming amused.

"Bavaria, Madame." he replied.

I caught him there!

"You mean Germany, don't you? Bavaria hasn't been a country for longer than you've been around. Unless you're an immortal."

I was only joking of course.

But then he really did smile, a wide smile which showed all of his white teeth.

It was at that second I knew what I faced, because of his teeth. They were too perfectly shaped for a man in his forties. The canines had no worn tips and they were an impossibly brilliant shade of white.

I knew at that second the handgun hidden behind the counter would do me no good.

I also felt the threat of imminent danger he was sending my way subside. I knew he had figured out my secret as well. He did not need to see the small, silver pentacle I discreetly hid under my clothes, swinging between my breasts, to know what I was.

"I see you are a 'daughter of the earth'," he said.

I tilted my head in wary admission of the fact. *So we were going to have that sort of conversation, eh?*

"Are you a 'child of the night'?" I asked.

He bowed slightly in acknowledgment of his truth.

"Madame's sight is quite clear."

It struck me then how completely ridiculous this exchange might seem to anyone else of the modern mundane world.

"Then you are truly from Bavaria," I murmured.

"Yes," was the reply.

"So… should I call you Count, or Duke or Lord Mykhalo?" I asked.

He smiled again, flashing those all too brilliant, white teeth.

"It is true my family was well off, but not that well off."

I considered my next words carefully before I faced him with such a direct question.

"Then what need do you have of my bookstore?" I asked. "And by the way we are not on the menu."

He chuckled.

"Madame, I am not hungry. Yet." he said. "But is it so unthinkable to you that one such as I might crave some mental stimulation? I really do like mysteries, especially those of Agatha Christie and Sir Arthur Conan Doyle."

*A vampire who liked mysteries, quite a concept.*

"Well, I can't fault your taste. But then again I would expect a vampire to have exquisite taste in most things."

There. I'd said the word aloud.

But he seemed fascinated by our oddly engaging conversation.

"I also like mysteries of the more intimate type. I was attracted to this bookstore because I felt there was a mystery inside it. I see I was correct. But your mystery, Madame, was all too easy for me to figure out."

It was my turn to smile. I refused to take my eyes off of him or turn my back on him and my shields were still up.

"Be that as it may, mind what I have said before," I insisted.

He bowed his head.

"I will," he replied. "For now."

This was not the exact answer I was looking for. But I could see it was the answer that would have to satisfy me for the time being.

"What brings you to Sleepy Pines, if may I ask?" I said, deciding to try a new turn on the conversation. "This isn't exactly the type of town I would expect to be on most vampires' tour list."

"You may ask. And you are wrong. Sleepy Pines is proving to be more interesting a stop on my itinerary than originally planned." Mykhalo responded as he cast an eye over my frame with more interest.

I chose to ignore his reaction. I raised my eyebrows, prodding him to answer my first question.

He gave a heavy sigh and returned his hat to his head as if he were preparing to leave.

"I am here at the behest of an old, dear friend," he finally offered.

At this, my eyebrows skyrocketed.

"What? There's another vampire in Sleepy Pines?" I asked, surprised.

He gave me a wry smile and cast his eyes sidelong in my direction.

"Not all of my friends are vampires."

"Oh!" I replied. I considered this for a moment. "Then, I'm sorry for how it sounded."

He sniffed.

"Apology accepted. You are probably relieved that a vampire convention is not happening just down the street from your quaint, little shop," Mykhalo said.

Now it was my turn to laugh as I shook my head.

"Somehow that just doesn't seem the vampire way to me. Too much competition."

He just smiled and nodded. He then tipped his hat politely to me and said in departure, "It was very nice meeting you. I enjoyed this conversation. We shall have to do this again sometime."

I could only nod and swallow carefully.

*I hope not.*

# Chapter 2

I hoped that was to be my first and last encounter with a vampire ever.

I was so wrong!

Two days later, I was running some errands around town. Trisha manned the store and supervised my daughter after she got off of school. I planned on getting home around eight in the evening.

One of my errands took me to the local shopping strip. There were the usual businesses at this place, a grocery store, several clothing outlets, a greeting card store and the ever famous, far too fancy, Starbuck's.

I had just put my bags away in my modest station wagon when the hair prickled on the back of my neck.

Someone was watching me.

I stood up straight and tall and cast my eyes about the parking lot. I was parked underneath a light and the vehicles next to me were all cars so it was easy for me to get a good look about. No one was near or approaching me. I glanced down at my reflection in my car's window. It was just after dusk so the lighting threw my appearance into dark, black and white contrast. My waist length black hair was blown about my face. *I should have braided it.* I didn't know it was going to be this windy tonight.

The shadows from the dim lighting made me look older and heavier than I really was. A mature woman in her late thirties looked back at me, a little heavier than I was when I was younger but still slender enough to be attractive. My hazel eyes were in shadow. My hair blew into my mouth and without thinking, I brushed it away. I had the same rosebud mouth as my daughter. Most of the time I thought she resembled her father, but looking at my reflection, I was struck by how much I looked like an older, more mature Bree. I smiled to myself. If she aged like me then she didn't have much to worry about as far as looks went.

But I still felt uneasy.

I wasn't the only person looking at me.

I cast my vision further.

The Starbuck's was close by. The night was warm for January so the patio chairs, tables, and umbrellas were still set up. A couple employees bustled around in the outside enclosure, wiping down tables, collecting trash and so on. There was only one customer and he was standing there looking at me.

It was Mykhalo.

He smiled when he caught my eye and beckoned to me.

I could have chosen to smile, wave back and drive away.

But I didn't.

I locked the car door and slowly made my way towards him not knowing what to expect. He bowed his head and smiled.

"I hoped we would meet again," he said with his typically accented voice.

I could only manage an uncomfortable smile. The silence between us was strange and heavy.

Finally, he removed his hat and said, "I so enjoyed our last conversation that I thought I might try another one, this time on more neutral ground. Do you have the time to sit and talk with me a bit?"

I looked back to the car uneasily, chewing my lip in indecision.

"Well, if it's not too long." I said.

I was not comfortable with the situation. In my shop, I was in my place of power. Here was "neutral ground" as he put it and I had no idea what to expect.

He motioned to a table behind him. Two cups of steaming coffee were already sitting there, a bare wisp of heat escaping from the plastic slit on the lids.

I looked at the coffee and I looked at him.

"You presume much," I told him. "What if I was a tea drinker?" There was a subtle shake of his head and the wind tousled his blonde locks.

"But you're not," he replied. "You like tea but you really, *really* like your coffee."

Here he closed his eyes and inhaled deeply through his nose. He paused one moment before opening his eyes and facing me again with the same subtle smile. "I can smell it in your blood."

A chill ran through me.

"I am also curious to see what your opinion is of this blend."

This confused me. I picked up the cup sniffed the enticing aroma deeply and took a small sip.

"This is Island Dream, isn't it?"

He nodded and I could tell he was pleased I had so quickly identified the brand.

"I've had this before and liked it very much. It was just a bit too pricey to take up permanent residence on my kitchen shelf."

His eyebrows hopped at this.

"I may have to remedy that, being as I am the main shareholder," he said. "I bought the company when it was very small and coffee drinking was a new practice in Europe. The investment has since proven to be a very lucrative one."

I cast my gaze on his cup as yet untouched, still sitting alone on the table.

"Vampires can drink coffee?" I said in a low voice so the workers couldn't hear.

He smiled and pulled my chair politely out for me.

"Of course I can drink things. It's the eating that gives me problems."

I automatically seated myself in the offered chair, highly aware I was turning my back on him. He then walked around and seated himself across from me and immediately busied himself with removing the plastic lid from the cardboard cup.

"You know, when I first meet a new friend, I like to play this game to get to know them. They ask a question about me and my life and then I, in turn, ask about them. You are the only modern day witch I've met that I find interesting enough to banter words with. Shall we play this game?"

I narrowed my eyes and considered his words carefully. I was seized with an insatiable curiosity about this dangerous character sitting across from me. How old was he? What historic events had he been witness to? What could I learn from someone who had actually been part of the events as they unfolded before his eyes? And he was offering to satisfy this curiosity.

The temptation was immense.

"What do I have to do to play this 'game'?" I said.

He smiled again.

"In order for me to digest this coffee, I need a few small drops of your blood to mix into it. That and the caffeine will fool my system into thinking I've fed and I will be more...ah...inclined to mind my manners. For a few hours at least."

"Uh – hunh."

"It is a good deal more respectful than biting your neck, especially without your permission."

He then sat there and waited for my response. And waited, and waited.

I was narrowly looking him in the eye for a long, pregnant moment. I was thinking hard.

Then an idea popped into my head, or actually a word: Balance. I acted on it.

"How many drops of blood do you need?"

He shrugged as if it was a small matter.

"Five should be sufficient for my needs," he replied.

"Hmm," I murmured, tapping my finger on the table as I considered.

"Tell you what," I finally said. "I'll give you five drops of my blood if you give me five drops of your own in my cup. Vampires do bleed, I take it?"

He rocked back in his chair, shocked. I was tickled at how well I had negotiated this. At least I was for the moment.

Finally he laughed, a real true laugh.

"Easily done," he agreed.

I watched him remove a small pin from his lapel which I hadn't noticed before. He then took a lighter out of his pocket and singed the end of it.

"Your hand please, Madame," he requested and I handed it over.

The hand which clasped mine was ice cold and the grip too strong to care about being gentle. The blow was quick and deft, the needle bit deep. I started and hissed in pain. He did not react to my pain but, of course, why would he? He suspended my finger over his cup and squeezed hard. I bit my lip and stomped my foot a little to deal with the sting. I watched as gradually a few, deep, red drops of my own blood swelled and dripped into his cup. He finally released my hand from his tight grip.

"By the pricking of our thumbs…" I whispered.

The wounded finger immediately went into my mouth and I sucked on it to ease the pain.

"Please don't do that in front of me," he said, averting his eyes.

*Ooops!*

I had forgotten with whom I dealt.

I quickly popped my finger out of my mouth and put it under the table, pressing another finger hard onto it to stop the bleeding.

He offered his hand and the pin was passed to me. I motioned for the lighter but he only gave me a ridiculous look and shook his head.

*Oh, right.*

A small smear of my own blood still shone on its brassy length. I struck him with the pin, hard in the forefinger. He never flinched. He just smiled at me and then suspended his finger over my cup calmly as if this was an everyday thing to him. The drops dripped steadily into my cup. I watched them flow and realized his blood dripped much faster than my own. I watched the drops spatter onto the dark, hot, liquid beneath and swirl as I stirred it into the coffee.

I raised my cup and my eyes to him and he mirrored my motion.

As the brim of the cup touched my lips, I stopped and locked eyes with the vampire sitting across the table from me. I paused for a long moment.

"Will this 'turn' me?" I asked.

His eyes twinkled across at me and the corners of his mouth turned up. He did not answer. He just upended the cup and drank the whole cup of coffee, black, with my blood as creamer, in one long draught. He then replaced the cup to the surface of the table and waited expectantly, his eyes daring me to drink.

My bluff had been called.

I was frozen for a moment. I finally took a deep, cleansing breath and swallowed a swig of coffee from my cup. I felt it travel down my throat, burning hot and hit my stomach. I swallowed hard again. It tasted like normal coffee, other from the fact I usually like my brew with creamer. But my stomach was telling me something new had been introduced and it wasn't sure what to do with it.

"No, you will not become a vampire because you drank my blood just now," he finally answered. "It takes more than that to turn a human. To 'turn' a mortal into a vampire requires the power and judgment of an elder vampire. I am too young."

He settled himself more comfortably into his chair as my mind raced to take proper advantage of this rare opportunity. A myriad of questions filled my mind and I wanted to ask them all at once. But I had to choose one to start with. I thought of the genesis of all the classic vampire stories most modern people knew and decided to run with it.

"What about Dracula? Is he real?" I asked.

"Of course he is!" Mykhalo answered with a teasing smile. "Any library will have that information."

I uttered a growl of frustration.

"Not that! Everyone knows that!" I muttered in exasperation. "I mean was he really a vampire?"

The Bavarian sitting across from me narrowed his eyes. He paused a bit before answering. This only made me squirm in suspense, which I could see he enjoyed.

"Having never met the man, I don't know." Mykhalo said.

I sat back in my chair, very disappointed.

"Well then, what did you think of Bram Stoker's rendition?" I continued, not wanting to give up on the subject.

He tilted his head to one side, amused.

"Dogged as a pit bull on this topic, aren't you?" he commented before relenting. "Bram Stoker took an obscure historical figure, already famous for his cruelty and sadism and embellished him with fictional folk tales of the region surrounding Transylvania. There is very little truth to the story. What I gleaned from reading the novel was Stoker was terrified of strong-minded, independent women. No big thing really. It was a common theme among the writers of the time. The ideal woman was depicted as frail and flighty with a weak constitution, whereas strong women were obviously creatures of deceit and corruption. No wonder Victorian males had a very hit or miss sex life! But to answer your question, Bram Stoker's 'Dracula' is definite fiction. It is a source of great amusement among others of my kind."

*Vampire humor must be very strange!*

"My turn for a question." he said. "How long have you been a practicing witch?"

I sighed and thought about it.

"Since I was twenty-one. I was not born into the Craft," I told him.

"I already knew that," he said and I raised an eyebrow.

"My turn!" I interrupted. "How old are you?"

He chuckled softly. "In human years or vampire?"

"Both!"

He sighed and I could see his mind reaching back over time.

"I was born in the year 1663 during the war of Leopold the First. I lived a normal, human life until the age of forty. And then a vampire elder found me and turned me. He thought I would prove useful."

*Vampires had elders!* This only sparked my curiosity more.

He paused for a long moment before continuing.

"Some people choose to become 'Nosferatu'. I did not. The change was forced upon me. I would have never chosen to exist like this."

He crossed his arms in front of him and with a frown and a sigh continued.

"Most of my kind like to think of themselves as immortal."

My eyebrows hopped a bit at this.

"And you don't?" I said. "But that's true isn't it? Aren't you an immortal?"

His frown deepened and his eyes glittered in frustration as his shook his head in denial.

"I certainly am not!" he clarified sternly. "I can be killed. So can any vampire. We do not die peacefully of old age. It is true there always seems to be some violence associated with our deaths. But we are not deathless beings. God is immortal. I'm something different. I prefer to think of it as having an indefinite lifespan."

I nodded in agreement as my thoughts spun.

"Now my turn," he said, changing the topic. "What tradition are you?"

I took another experimental sip of coffee. The flavor was starting to grow on me.

"I learned in a Dianic coven until they got too weird for me. Then I switched to solitary. I'm much happier this way."

He nodded as if in complete understanding.

I leaned forward, half afraid, half compelled to ask the next question.

"What's it like to be a...to be what you are?" I said in a voice barely above a whisper. I still had difficulty in saying the word *vampire* in public.

He smiled and did not answer me for a long moment.

Finally, he held out his hand to me.

"Please, take my hand," he said. "I promise not to harm you."

I started backwards as if stung. I tilted my head to the side, considering his request. I wasn't sure I wanted to...touch...him.

"Do vampires honor their promises?" I asked.

He smiled and shrugged.

"Not really," he admitted.

I held his glance for a long moment. He did the same to me.

"Just hold my hand. Nothing more," he coaxed.

His slender, white fingers awaited mine, poised and eternally patient.

I didn't want to take his hand. I knew I should not take his hand, knowing what he was. But, like a cat, my curiosity could not be denied and I acquiesced.

Slowly, I relented and slid my palm into his. His pale fingers wound about my own hand, like a python easing its grip on its prey, waiting for a breath to constrict its coils. The veins which branched across the back of his hand, stood out in faint blue contrast against his deathly white skin. His grasp was gentle but I could feel the inhuman strength which hid just below the surface.

Apprehension made me swallow with difficulty. My pulse was pounding in my throat. *I shouldn't have done that.* Why did I do that? I had a daughter to think about. Had he charmed me into obeying him?

My heart beat slow and loud in my ears as I wondered what he would do next.

I didn't have long to wait.

With my hand thus ensnared, he leaned forward until he almost came within my personal space. He stopped just short of it, sensing I did not want him there. I could not pull away. I was afraid. I felt helpless.

Our eyes locked.

"Now," he whispered in a tone as soft as an owl's feather." Tell me what you feel, Madame witch."

I could feel his cool breath on my skin as he spoke. I swallowed again and forced myself to obey him wondering why I was allowing such a thing. I steeled myself against a wave of emotions, memories which weren't mine, urges I shouldn't give in to, anything like that. I expected the kind of things Hollywood would love to expound upon.

But I received none of those things. Even my Wiccan senses had gone silent. There was just his pale hand holding mine which was flush and rosy with life.

His hand felt shockingly cold, too cold for any living thing.

"Your hand is cold," I said.

"Yes," he nodded.

His fingers unwound with terrible slowness from my own, releasing them. I snatched my hand back as if I wouldn't get another chance. Mykhalo barely reacted to this other than to give a sad smile which seemed full of regret.

"I am always this way, always cold," he told me. "Not just to your touch but inside as well. A vampire's blood temperature runs much lower than a mortal."

He withdrew his hand and leaned back in his chair. I sighed in relief at the increase in space between us. He seemed not to notice my reaction.

"As long as we stay out of the sun," he added. "The sun has the same effect on me as a bad allergic reaction. I will blister, even in the shade and act like I have the flu. I will never get warm. I have traveled to many hot areas of the world to test this theory and it has always been the same."

He turned his eyes away from me and toyed absent-mindedly with his disposable coffee cup.

"It has always been this way for me ever since I was turned. I have always been cold. And because of that I yearn for warm things; a warm drink, warm bodies..."

Here his eyes locked onto what small area of my throat was exposed. The glance was hungry and lustful. His lips parted and for just a second I caught a glimpse of his canines which were all too sharp for his age.

"Warm blood..." he added and licked his lips hungrily.

Yes, I really was sitting across the table from a predator. I shivered inside at the thought. I thought of my daughter Bree and what a creature like this might...could...would do to her. My heart blazed at the mere thought and my hands began to tremble.

20

He tore his eyes away and looked at the ground as if in shame.

"That, my dear, is one small detail of what it is to be me, the aggravating, eternal cold. Pray you never experience it as I have," Mykhalo told me.

The Bavarian sitting across from me shook off the serious tone and, with a smile, asked his next question.

"Do you cast curses and hexes?"

It was now my turn to smile.

"I haven't found anyone worth cursing – yet! It requires a lot of thought because if I were to curse someone then I would have to be all right with someone cursing me. We witches do have ethics, you know!" I said with a small snort. "Now me. Can you really turn yourself into a shower of bats, disappear, fly and all that?"

He tsked at me.

"That's several questions in one, Madame. But I will bend the rules for you. Vampires cannot turn themselves into bats. However, they can call a swarm of bats to disguise their departure, and the same goes for fog. Yes, we can climb walls and levitate to some degree. But Hollywood has made such a mockery of those things it's hardly worth doing anymore."

He tilted his head at me.

"Now my turn. Can you speak to the dead?"

I laughed out loud at this.

"That's not my talent! Unless you are including yourself. But I think that would classify as speaking to the undead…"

I suddenly stopped in mid-sentence considering my last word.

"What does that mean, *undead*?" I asked him. "Either you're dead or you're alive. How can you be undead? What is that exactly?"

He paused for a long moment. I heard him suck in his breath through his teeth and he drew back in his chair a little. His eyes glinted at me as if I had asked the question which must never be asked.

"What is it?" I asked. "Did I say something wrong?"

Mykhalo seemed to be considering his next words carefully.

"No, you said something right," he murmured quietly almost in a whisper.

Without bothering to explain this he took a deep sigh and then leant forward as if he was about to confide in me his deepest, darkest secret.

"When a person is transformed into a vampire, they die. Really die. That is why I'm so cold. But a vampire is not exactly dead. They exist somewhere between life and death."

I frowned trying to comprehend.

"You mean…like a ghost?" I asked.

"Not at all," he struggled to clarify. "Ghosts have souls."

I furrowed my brow.

"And you…don't have a soul?" I asked.

He held my eyes. His gaze looked sad and almost desperate.

"My soul is broken. Shattered."

This only served to perplex me even more. I did not know how to respond.

"Then…can it be…mended?" I asked.

His facial expression was confusing me more and more as this thread of conversation continued. He was staring deeply into my eyes as if they held the answer, not my words.

Finally, he sighed again as if I had disappointed him somehow. He spread his hands wide and shrugged without answering.

He did not know.

I was beginning to feel very uncomfortable so I decided to redirect the topic.

"So sunlight doesn't really kill you?"

This question seemed to irritate him.

"I will not sizzle into a pile of ashes in an instant like they show in the movies," he explained. "It will take a bit longer than that. But enough exposure to sunlight will kill me eventually. I can come out at dusk and dawn, especially in the wintertime because the sun's rays are weakest then. Eclipses also really run havoc with my system."

My eyes narrowed at this last bit of information.

"What sort of havoc?" I asked, almost in a whisper.

He tilted his head the other way now as he considered me. His expression was one of a mischievous child.

"Madame, do you really want to see me run amok?"

I felt a little shiver run down my spine.

He continued the questioning, his finger tracing lightly the pattern on the table's surface.

"Do you believe in God?" he asked.

I gave a big smile. *Ah, this question again!*

"I believe in balance and duality. Therefore, if there is a God then there must also be a Goddess. Yin and yang. I believe the power we call 'god' is the same no matter what name you give it; God, Jesus Christ, Yahweh, Allah, the Great Spirit, etc. It's all the same life-force. I've found this 'force' doesn't give a damn what name you call It by because It's bigger than that, just you recognize Its existence as reality. So, I guess you could say yes, I believe in God. In a rather unique way though."

I took another sip of coffee. The taste of his blood lingered on my tongue, harsh, metallic, and somehow compelling.

"So, how often do you need to uh – eat'?"

He grinned, showing his flashing teeth. His canines seemed a bit more pronounced than before.

"Not as often as you might think," he replied. "I can go for as much as two weeks without feeding. Being a vampire has a lot to do with control. Drinking this coffee is one way I have of controlling the urge to bite someone. I can drink things. I enjoy coffee and alcohol, especially beer. I just cannot stomach food. Caffeine is a great trickster to my system. And if I fool my system for too long, like I just did now, I start to lose control. To feed, really feed, I need to take my blood from the throat. I need to lose control and become the monster you've heard about. I also tend to look older when I haven't fed for a while."

"I'll make a note of that," I muttered into my adulterated coffee.

"So...do you always have to...kill...when you feed?"

"Not necessarily," he answered. "It's a common misconception. There are many types of bites one of my kind can inflict. But the age of the one doing the biting does make a difference."

"How so?" I asked.

He smiled at my curiosity.

"Well for one thing, there is a control issue to take into mind. A young vampire, newly turned, has very little control. Every time they bite a mortal, they have to kill. They just can't help themselves. They end up making many mistakes, such as feeding on a drug addict and getting a 'contact high' if you will or leaving an obvious trail of bodies behind them. The bloodlust in them is so strong. They have to learn how to say no. It takes many years of practice and many failures to accomplish this. Many vampires don't live past their first few years, especially if they have no experienced elder to guide them. It takes time to learn how to rein in their savage urges."

Mykhalo leaned forward and whispered to me in a sinister tone of voice.

"Now if I were to bite you, I could stop – if I chose to. It hasn't been very long since my last feeding. You might not even be turned."

I shivered and gulped down the spider of fear which was crawling up my throat.

He smiled and leaned back in his chair.

"But I wouldn't be very happy about it. I guess for you it would be like interrupting the act of lovemaking. It can be done but people tend to get rather...aggravated when something like that happens."

I forced myself to make a jest to alleviate the tension which was rising.

"Nice to know your kind suffers from bad timing, too," I said.

Mykhalo's teeth flashed at me from across the table and he winked.

He abruptly leaned forward and asked in a lowered voice, "So, do witches really have sex with the devil?"

I burst out laughing. I couldn't help myself. Even the Starbuck's workers looked up for a moment at the sudden shock of my mirth.

"Heavens no," I told him. "It's kinda hard to have relations with something you don't believe in! That wives' tale is so old..." I stopped suddenly, realizing he must have been around during the witch hysteria of Europe and the ever famous, in witch circles, 'Burning Times'.

"You were probably there," I said.

He leaned back in his chair, his disappointment obvious.

"Actually yes, I was. That's why I asked," he said.

"Sorry to disappoint you, then." I said to him.

"So, " I started. "Do crosses really work on repelling you and wooden stakes to the heart kill you? And is it true that vampires have to sleep in coffins and are repelled by garlic?"

At this, he threw back his head and laughed and my eyes were treated to another view of his ageless, white teeth.

"More inventions from Bram Stoker to heighten the suspense," he said, still smiling. "I don't eat food because my body cannot handle food of any kind. Therefore, I dislike garlic as I dislike food. But it means nothing to me. It will not repel me. Only a person's faith can do that.

"As to sleeping in a coffin surrounded by dirt," he paused and shook his head. "What a ridiculous notion! I sleep in a regular bed just like anyone else. The only difference is I sleep during the day and my bedchambers are usually rooms underground or ones which allow no sunlight in whatsoever. Coffins indeed! How absolutely ludicrous!"

He paused in his humor and thought about the rest of my question.

"Symbols of faith will give me pause to some degree. It depends on the strength of the belief of the one wearing it. A cross worn as a simple piece of jewelry by an atheist will have no effect whatsoever on me. Wooden stakes of the right type of tree I don't like much at all."

And he left it at that. Then his eyes got a new glint to them.

"So, what happened to Sabrina's father?" he asked abruptly.

I nearly choked on the coffee.

I stopped and glared at him over the lip of the cup.

"Was anything you just now told me, the truth?" I demanded.

He leaned back and smiled.

His only response was, "Touché' Madame."

* * *

Mykhalo watched as the witch called Zan got into her modest blue station wagon and drove away. His heart was heavy. He stood there long after she had left, lost in his thoughts. He finally sighed and walked around the corner of the Starbuck's to the employee parking lot.

Parked underneath a burned out street lamp was a stretch limo with black tinted windows. Mykhalo made his way to the vehicle without once looking right or left. The limo's back door opened as if commanded and Mykhalo slid at once into the richly upholstered confines and shut the door behind him.

The driver of the limo was a man of singular appearance. He was as wide as Mykhalo was thin but not from fat. The suit he wore sat awkwardly on the muscles beneath. He had thick brown hair tied back into a ponytail and wore black wraparound shades even at night. From his chin sprouted a bushy but carefully tended beard.

He was more than Mykhalo's chauffeur, he was the vampire's oldest living friend.

The big man swiveled about in the seat to look the Bavarian vampire in the eye from behind the safe confines of his shades.

"Somehow I thought you'd be more cheery than this," he told him.

The chauffeur spoke to him in German and Mykhalo responded in kind.

"She's not the one," Mykhalo said in a voice weighty with dashed hopes.

The big man's brows furrowed and he snorted in derision.

"I disagree," He retorted.

Mykhalo glared at him.

"How would you know?" he spat.

His friend sniffed.

"You always were too eager to give up."

Mykhalo made a sound like a growl.

"Bartal, I've been looking for the better part of three hundred years. You call that giving up easy?"

The man called Bartal laughed loud and short as he started the limo's engine.

"You're not the only one with 'special talents'," said Bartal. "You're just afraid to look deep and trust your intuition."

It was Mykhalo's turn to scoff.

"You've seen this witch?"

Bartal grunted in reply.

"Then tell me. What do you see in her?" he challenged.

Bartal looked right and then left and then carefully eased the limo out into traffic.

The big sedan accelerated with silky silence.

"She's the one," he said simply.

Mykhalo threw up his hands in frustration.

"What can you possibly see that I can't?"

Bartal chuckled softly smiling with one side of his face.

"You're a pup compared to me. Just trust me, she's the one."

Mykhalo glared at the back of his friend's head as if he could bore holes with his eyes.

"She doesn't know the spell," he said flatly. "She's never heard of a shattered soul."

Bartal shook his head.

"No modern witch knows the spell. It's been forgotten." They drove on in silence for a short while.

"That still doesn't mean she can't do it," he said shrugging his big shoulders.

Mykhalo shook his head and crossed his arms.

"You're impossible!"

Bartal heaved a great sigh as he pulled the limo to a smooth stop at a light. He turned about to face Mykhalo.

"Look. All I know is she knew you. The very first second she saw you she knew you were a vampire. Now how many modern day witches are able to do that?"

He turned his attention back to the road in front of him.

"Yes, the spell may be forgotten. But this Susanne Miller will find a way."

Mykhalo stared at Bartal, confusion wrinkling his forehead.

"Why are you so certain of this?"

Bartal only smiled and snickered almost privately to himself.

"Because she is Hope's bloodline. It's in her genes to help you. She's the only one who can. Trust me, Mykhalo."

## CHAPTER 3

The funeral for Mr. William Gibson was Saturday evening. The service was in the church with the internment in the graveyard adjacent to it. I was fussing because I had nothing black to wear. I ended up borrowing a black skirt which almost fit me from Bree. She had plenty of black clothing.

"Try to tone down the jewelry, Hon," I said. "And please keep your pentacles discreet."

I wasn't going to tell her *not* to wear them! But I was expecting a large turnout for this funeral with some of the older, less open-minded members of the community attending. I didn't want her to put salt in the wound of the relatives, who I barely knew.

"Already have!" she said. "See? My pinkies are bare!" and she waggled her bejeweled digits at me.

But then the smile faded from her face.

"Ma, I'm gonna hate this funeral," she said in a dreary tone.

"But I thought you Goths liked depressing things like this," I said, half already anticipating the response.

"That's all an act. This is real. And I'm not a Goth!" she said with some heat.

"I know, I know," I consoled, giving her shoulders a maternal squeeze. "You just like the clothes."

I gave a heavy sigh.

"Let's just muddle through this and get by as best we can."

She sniffed and said, "Like we always do."

The funeral was both like and unlike what I expected. The church was filled with older people. Bree and I were two of the few younger people there other than the relatives of Mr. Gibson.

I glanced uncomfortably around at all the prim church ladies sporting their tiny, golden crosses around their necks and squirmed. Every time I sat in a church pew it was glaringly obvious to me why I didn't belong there anymore and this wasn't my community. But I was there out of respect to dear Bill Gibson and so I toughed it out.

One thing I did not expect to find out was old Mr. Gibson was a Mason. The church was filled with older Masons wearing their little traditional aprons and lodge pins. Halfway through the ceremony they all lined up around the coffin and prayed for the soul of their departed brother. What I found most interesting was the prayer ended with the line, "So mote it be," a phrase witches also used. At the conclusion of their devotion, two senior Mason members came forward and laid evergreen boughs on top of the coffin. The symbolism of this simple gesture struck me and I found myself smiling in fondness for my dear, old friend.

Then the mourners all filed past the coffin in respectful silence. I took Bree's hand to reassure her and we lined up with the others and quietly shuffled to the front of the church.

Here my eyes met another surprise. The coffin was draped in an American flag. At the foot of the coffin was a triangular display case filled with ribbons and badges of merit. Bree wanted to know what the badges were for. I told her he must have served in World War II and, though I knew little about military honors, I told her the ones I recognized.

In the case were two purple hearts, a Croix de Guerra, a distinguished service cross, two bronze stars, and a silver star. There was a whole mess of brightly colored ribbons as well but I did not know what they meant.

It seemed Mr. Gibson had lived a great life defending his country long before I or my daughter were born. I wish I had had a chance to ask him about his war experience.

"He saw the elephant," was all I could say. This confused Bree mightily.

Then there was the ritual at the graveside. The balmy weather from the other day had disappeared with the arrival of a cold front and the air was windy and frigid, the ground frozen and hard as a rock. Bee and I stood arm in arm, squeezed together for warmth as our naked knees shivered and knocked.

Pantyhose were just not enough!

We prayed as respectfully as we knew how, the graveside ceremony would be kept short. Bree's eyes welled with tears at the minister's words and I hoped she wouldn't cry. I was worried her tears would freeze to her cheeks. Selfish of me I know. So I shut up these thoughts by saying my own prayer to the Goddess for safe passage for Bill's spirit to the Summerlands. Ah, for the warmth of summer!

The service ended and people gradually began to file away. Most fled to the foyer of the church to socialize a bit before dispersing. I accompanied them because I recognized Matt Yoder the chief of police of Sleepy Pines and I wanted a quiet word with him.

Matt was standing on the lower stairs to the balcony, shaking hands and saying goodbye to an older couple. I politely waited for them to leave and then managed to catch his eye.

"Susan! How wonderful of you to show!" he said and gave me a polite hug. "Is Bree here?"

"Of course! It was very important for her to come tonight."

"Good. I'm glad. Bill thought so highly of you and your daughter. He spoke of you often," Matt said.

"I'm flattered. But then, I know of no one who would say an unkind thing about Bill."

"Maybe some of his grandchildren who are only interested in what he left them," Matt grumbled. "But then I think they forgot what kind of person their grandfather was when they moved to the big city."

"Hmm," I said. I cast a quick look around to make sure no one was too close. "By the way, I meant to ask you something about Bill," I said in a more private tone.

He shrugged and smiled amiably. "Ask away."

"I was wondering if you knew what he died of? The paper's obituary was not much help."

Now it was Matt's turn to look about in a secretive manner. He motioned me upstairs a couple of steps and then stopped so I was uphill from him and he had the crowd to his back.

"I won't tell everyone but I'll tell you because I know how good you are with secrets," he said with a small wink.

He then scratched the side of his face uncomfortably and rubbed his nearly bald head.

"It seems Bill was killed by some sort wild animal. Now if this were out west, I'd say a cougar or a bear. But we have no cougars and a very few bears here and most of them are small and secretive. So I'm guessing it was a wild dog. Something along the lines of a Rottweiler or a St. Bernard."

You probably already know I was thinking no 'wild dog' had anything to do with Mr. Gibson's death!

He stepped closer and lowered his voice even more.

"His throat was completely torn out! That's why there was no open casket ceremony. There was no way for the mortician to hide it!"

He stepped back with another sigh.

"Law enforcement and animal control are trying to keep this as quiet as possible. We don't want panic to ensue if word got out there was a large, rabid dog roaming the area. But you will keep your eyes out for me won't you?"

I nodded although I already had my own suspicions as to the truth of the matter.

"Of course, Matt. Thank you for telling me. I won't spread it around."

We hugged again, exchanged pleasantries and departed.

I stepped outside, looked up at the sky, and frowned. It was almost sunset and a thick bank of clouds had rolled in. It smelled like snow.

"There you are, Zan!" said a warm voice at my elbow.

I turned around to see a large, older woman with long, gray hair and a brown cape behind me. The town knew her as Bethany Hess. But I called her "Sage".

She clasped me in a loving embrace, which I enjoyed for longer than was polite. But then again, her hugs were so warm and full of love few wanted to part from them.

"I'm so glad I tracked you down," she told me. "Look. Bree is feeling kinda lost after the church ceremony. I was going to take a few of us and go back to my place and have a candle ritual for Mr. Bill. Bree wants to go along. You're welcome to come, too."

I smiled a real smile and squeezed her glove-enshrouded hands.

"Sage Luv, you are a blessing from the Goddess!" I said. "Thank you so much for the kind offer. I think I just want to say goodbye to Mr. Gibson in private after everyone else leaves. But Bree is welcome to go along with you and the girls. I'll swing by and pick her up later if it's fine."

Sage chuckled.

"Why wouldn't it be? I'll have tea ready and waiting for you. I'll see you later then."

She hugged me again, kissed both my cheeks in the brisk winter air and left to round up the teenaged girls who always followed her in small bunches.

I took a deep breath of the cold air to cleanse my head and then made my way around the corner of the old church to where Mr. Gibson's final resting place lay.

But I stopped short once in sight of his grave and the newly turned mound of earth.

A familiar figure stood by the grave.

Mykhalo stood there, seeming untouched by the bitter cold. His dark trench coat ruffled lightly in the wind and his hat was off and held respectfully over his heart. The harsh winter wind set his sandy hair to dancing.

I remembered the tears shivering on my daughter's cheeks and my heart began to smolder with anger.

33

I pulled myself up and marched purposefully over to the Bavarian.

"You've got some nerve coming here!"

The steel gray eyes met my own with only the barest hint of surprise.

"I've always heard the criminal returns to the scene of the crime, but this takes the cake! How dare you come here?"

The hat was quickly replaced to his head and I thought I saw a snarl start to curl his lip. But I was too far gone to heed the warning.

"Do you want to destroy his final rest? Or did you not drink enough the first time?"

An inhuman sound issued from his lips which I can only describe as a feral growl and suddenly, his hand had lashed out and took hold of my elbow with a frightening grip. He spun on his heel and strode quickly in the direction of the nearest mausoleum and out of earshot of any of the funeral stragglers, dragging me helplessly along with him. I resisted and tried to stick my heels into the earth but the frozen ground was unforgiving and I stumbled. He just yanked me harshly back onto my feet and continued to haul me along behind him.

Surprised as I was by his instantaneous action, I was still too angry with him to realize what sort of true danger I was in by antagonizing a vampire. My mind was scrambling to wind up and let fire with a pretty hefty curse his way.

The mausoleum reached, he jerked me around the corner of it and slammed me up against the wall, pinning me by my arms. He glared directly into my eyes and it was then I saw what deadly thing lurked beneath.

And still I was too angry to be afraid.

"Let go of me, you monster!" I demanded, struggling and kicking.

"If you want to see a monster, I'll show you a true monster the likes you have never dreamed of!" he hissed to me in a lethal but soft tone. "Is that what you want?"

He leaned close and his canines flashed as he spoke.

"Why don't you go and finish your meal?" I said. "I wonder what a little formaldehyde would do to your system?"

He really did snarl then.

"Why do you care?" he said to me. I noticed his accent disappeared completely when he was angry. "He was just an old man. He was probably due to die any day. And I have to eat."

Somehow, I managed to shove him backwards, releasing his grip from my shoulders. But knowing his inhuman strength, he must have let me do it.

"The 'old man' was very dear to both me and my daughter," I said. "Why couldn't you have killed some dreg of society like a rapist or a murderer? Why did you have to kill someone everybody loved?"

He stepped back as if to keep himself from doing something he would soon regret. His hands kept clenching and releasing.

"He was not always some kind old man," he said in a stern tone of voice. "He was bold and young once, full of lofty ideals. The world was his oyster and he was going to take it and change it. What every young man wants to do before they get jaded. And then World War II happened."

This brought me up short.

"You knew him?" I said.

His eyes were shadowed but I could still feel the pain in them.

"So…this is how you treat your friends? You eventually kill them?" I said.

He only glared at me for a long moment before he turned away.

"Bill Gibson asked me to end his life," he said. "He had just been diagnosed with a terminal illness. He knew he would have a lingering end. He didn't want that. He wanted to go out fighting, like he had done in the war. He asked me to help him. So I did."

It took me a while to digest it.

"When did you first meet?" I said.

He turned back to me.

"I met him in the spring of 1945 in Germany. After we got to be friends, I shadowed his unit and kept him as safe as I could. He still got wounded several times. We've been friends ever since."

I mulled this over.

"And he knew…what you are?" I said.

At this, Mykhalo gave a broad smile.

"He always knew what I was. I was feeding when he first met me."

His smile disappeared suddenly.

"The other night you doubted whether anything I had told you was the truth. You have my word this story I just gave you, *is* the truth. Do with it what you like."

I stepped out from the growing shadow of the mausoleum thinking hard on everything which had just transpired.

At that moment, as I was lost in thought, the last dying rays of the setting sun peeked out of a break in the clouds and lit up the statue on the very top of the structure. It was in the granite likeness of an angel with wings outspread, eyes lifted reverently up to heaven, its alabaster hands folded in prayer. The rays of the setting sun fell on the sacred face of the angel and lit it up in orange fire.

"Mykhalo," I said never taking my gaze from the angel. "Do you believe in God?"

His eyes followed mine. He was silent for one long moment.

"I used to," he said softly. "But now it seems I am surrounded by devils. And I am the worst of the lot."

To this I had no reply.

## CHAPTER 4

The next weekend I was due to attend a Sci-Fi Fantasy convention as one of the dealers. I left the store in Trisha's capable hands. Bree and I packed up the bookmobile at "oh-God hundred" with every fantasy novel and sci-fi epic, paperback or hardcover, used or new and headed to the Holiday Inn in Port Jarvis.

Bree was going through an "Ultra-Violet" phase after seeing the movie. I had tried to convince her to just buy a wig. But she had insisted on dyeing her hair the same shade as the main character. I rolled my eyes, sighed and relented. *It could be worse!* She could be into drugs, stealing, hanging out with the wrong crowd or pregnant.

Instead, I just had to put up with a child with bright purple hair!

I observed this new change in attire as I piloted the van down the highway.

"You know, your hair will probably glow in the dark."

Her only response was, "Really? Cool! I bet it would look totally awesome under a black light, too!"

I rolled my eyes again.

"No nightclubs!" I insisted.

"Who, me?" She sounded petulant.

"I mean it, Bree!" I said in a sterner tone.

"Yeah, I know. I promise," she said with a reproachful sigh. "I was just trying to get a rise outta ya."

"It worked."

We drove on in silence. The traffic was light at this time of day. But the sky was ashen and looked like snow. Bree was gazing absently out of the window.

"Hey Ma," Bree finally said in a more pensive tone of voice. "When did you first know you were Wiccan?"

"You know this story dear," I said. "About twenty years ago, just before I met your father."

"But when did you *really* know?" she said. "I mean… like… inside. In your heart?"

I gave Bree a more sincere look.

It was a worthy question. It deserved a worthy answer.

I thought hard, reflecting back over the years.

"I guess at midsummer. Sage had invited me to a camp-out where there were a lot of Wiccans, Druids, heathens, and such. It was my first such camp-out. I remember wandering around and getting to know everybody during the day. Luckily, Sage was there to guide me away from any of the real weirdoes and there *were* a few of them. But later at night they had a drum circle. It was a warm night and people were dressed as lightly as possible. The moon was big and bright. The air was full of the sound of the drummers and the belly dancers and crackling fire. I wandered off to be by myself for a bit. I was looking up at the moon. She looked so close I felt I could just reach out and touch Her. She was so bright, you could have read a book by Her. And I remember feeling so awake and alive in that one moment in time. I felt connected to everything which had happened in the past and everything which was going to happen in the future. I felt I was finally where I needed to be."

I was silent for a long moment, reminiscing.

"I knew at that moment what I was looking for could not be contained within the solid walls of any church. It could only be attained outdoors where you could feel the wind on your face and the grass curling between your toes. Where one could feel the earth itself breathe and one could share in that breath. That was when I knew I was Wiccan in my heart and I did not need to wear a pentacle to tell me so."

Bree was quiet for a long time before she spoke.

"Mom, I'm not sure what faith I am," she said. "I mean, I know stealing is bad and so is murder and being good to your neighbor is not just a Christian thing, it makes good sense, and you should try to help people no matter what their faith. But all that is not a religion. They're just good, sensible ideals to live your life by. I'm not sure if I'm Wiccan and I *know* I'm not a Christian but what I am…I don't know."

I was quiet for a moment before I answered.

"And this bothers you?" I said.

"Well yeah! Shouldn't it?" she said. "I feel like I can't go on until I know what I am or what I believe."

I sighed.

"Look, I'm not going to force you to be Wiccan," I told her. "I don't need you to be part of my religion to approve or be proud of you. Religion should never be forced onto someone. That just breeds resentment. There's no deadline on this. But wait. Just wait. Things will happen. Look for the signs guiding your life. And then you'll know where you fit in on this little, blue marble."

I reached out and took her hand, squeezed it reassuringly. For once, she didn't shrink from my touch.

"Just know if you ever get confused about this or anything, please don't hesitate to talk it out with me. Who knows? Your abysmally, uncool mother might actually know something which might help you. Okay?"

She smiled and giggled but agreed.

"Thanks, Mom," she said.

"Anytime, poppet!" I said.

But deep inside I was worried, worried Mykhalo would find out my daughter did not believe.

If she did not believe in something, then she was prey to him.

* * *

The convention was busy that weekend. Business was steady at our booth and it kept my daughter and me hopping as we tried to keep up with the requests for books and different transactions. The stream of clientele finally started to abate a couple of hours before the dealer's room shut down.

At last, we both had a chance to breathe. I was able to take in the motley assortment of characters which always show up at these things. I chuckled at some of the costumed attendees assembled in the room. There were a few Star Wars Storm troopers, one a bit too wide to fit into his outfit, some Trekkies who seemed to be avoiding the troopers, a few Firefly browncoats and a couple of ladies in period garb. One of the ladies had a very realistic griffon puppet perched on her shoulders, which was drawing more than a few second looks, especially from the hotel staff.

"The masquerade ball must be winding up," Bree commented.

"Hmm," I said.

It was then I first noticed a familiar figure in a long trench coat and hat.

"Mykhalo?" I said loudly to the figure's back.

He spun a bit sharply as if not expecting to be recognized. His startling gray eyes met mine and he hesitated a bit before he smiled and approached my booth.

"I certainly never expected to find you here," I said to him when he got closer.

He smiled and ducked his head almost apologetically.

"Nor I you," he said. "But then, why wouldn't you be here? Another opportunity to sell books and this crowd does still read."

"Yes, they certainly do," I replied.

We stood there in awkward silence for a moment. Bree had her nose stuck in a book and barely noticed.

"Do you have time for a cup of coffee, Mrs. Miller?" he finally said.

I smiled in return and nodded. I told Bree to man the booth and she shrugged in her 'Yeah, whatever,' teenaged way.

He motioned me to the nearby restaurant and we went to the second level which looked down on the dealer's room. He chose a private table for two close to the window so I could keep an eye on my booth and, more importantly, my daughter.

"Would you like regular coffee?" I asked him after the waitress left. "Or the 'witch's brew' blend?"

His teeth flashed brightly at my attempt at humor and he chuckled softly.

"I'm rather partial to the 'witch's brew', if you are inclined to offer it."

We performed our odd little exchange of blood, completely unnoticed by any of the restaurant's patrons.

"By the way," I asked as he squeezed the drops of blood from my finger. "When was the last time you dined?"

He did not meet my eyes as he replied.

"Last night, or did you not read this morning's paper?"

"I did not," I said.

He smiled quietly.

"It seems some crazy daredevil tried to scale the cliff face at midnight at the edge of the highway. He was rather unsuccessful."

I knew the area he meant. There was a large hill which dropped off suddenly as if it had been cut or blasted into a high, steep granite face and the highway skirted the very base of it. PennDot had placed netting over the one side so loose shale wouldn't rain down onto the road far below and cause an accident.

"Indeed? Imagine that," I muttered uncomfortably into my cup. That had been more information than I really cared to know.

So I changed the subject.

"I never expected you to show up at a function like this," I told him. "Somehow I just don't see the Sci-Fi crowd as being the sort of circle a person of your persuasion would like to travel in."

He snorted.

"They definitely are not!" he said a little derisively. Then it seemed he caught himself as he looked at me. I must have flinched in emotion without meaning to show it.

41

"Then what are you here for?"

"Music," he replied. "I came to purchase some CDs. It's the best place to pick up music of a rather unusual flavor."

"You like Filk?" I said as, I'm sure, my eyebrows went skyward.

"I don't exactly like Filk, but I like music. I especially like folk and classical music. It reminds me of home," he said.

"Hmm," I mumbled into my coffee as I considered his words.

"I take it, since you're obviously the highly educated type, you can play some instruments as well?"

"Of course," was the answer as if I should have been able to guess.

"What kind, may I ask?"

He smiled, happy to comply.

"I can play the piano and organ. I prefer the harpsichord. I find it a more pure instrument. I can also play the flute and clarinet."

I feigned choking on my coffee.

"What? No violin?" I teased.

He guffawed at me.

"Just because I'm a vampire, you think I can play the violin, eh?" he said with a snort. "I can, but under great protest. I detest the thing!"

He tapped his long, white fingers on the tabletop.

"But I have learned some new instruments lately. I'm quite proud of my prowess with the acoustic guitar and the Native American flute. Such beautiful tones come from that woodwind."

I really was surprised at this.

"Native flute!" I said. "I would have never guessed! Did an Indian teach you?"

He laughed at this.

"It takes more to be Native American than being born of some Indian blood. You of all people should know that! And before you ask, no, I did not reward him by dining on him. He is another dear friend of mine."

He sipped from his cup, choosing to make the blood last this time.

"I also sing a bit. I'll have to serenade you sometime," he said.

42

I really did smile at this.

"I'd really like that." I told him. "I'm so jealous! I have no musical talent whatsoever. But Native American flute! I'm flabbergasted you know that!"

He chuckled. Obviously, this thread of conversation was good for his ego.

"Did you think I had just gotten off of the boat? I've been in America since the early sixties, my dear!"

"Oh!" I coughed. "Now that explains a lot!"

I drank another sip of my vampire-blood flavored coffee and looked down onto the strange people milling around the booths in the dealer's room below us. I noticed the dim image of myself reflected back from the window's glass. This brought a thought to mind. I cast my eyes just a little further across the surface of the glass looking for Mykhalo's reflection.

Just like in all the books, there was no reflection.

I glanced back towards the kitchen and the counter area of the restaurant. Along the top of the wall from end to end, was a large mirror facing the booths. Anyone sitting at the counter could see who was behind them sitting in a booth by looking in front of them into the mirror's polished surface.

Although our table was set with two coffee cups, I appeared to be sitting by myself.

Mykhalo must have observed the direction of my glance.

"Ah, so you've noticed," he said. "Yes, by the way, I also cast no reflection of any kind. Another thing the old stories got correct."

"Why is that?" I asked him.

He sighed as if my question aggravated him.

"I will tell you as it was explained to me several centuries ago when I was newly turned. When the first vampire was birthed, its very existence was an affront to God. And when the first vampire gazed onto a reflective surface, it shattered and along with it, his soul. From that day forward throughout history, no vampire has ever reflected in anything. This is the story I was told. Whether it is true or the creative

43

fabrication of an active imagination, I don't know. But no vampire has a reflection."

I was silent a moment as I digested this.

"None whatsoever?" I asked.

"No."

"Not even in a teakettle, or a car window or even a pool of water?" I persisted.

"No."

"How about photos or movies?" I said.

"Sorry, no. You can take a thousand stills or a million video movies of me and the best you will get is a blurred image which could be human shaped. Almost like ghost photography," he told me.

"Nada, eh?" I said.

"No reflection, whatsoever, at all, of any kind," he clarified.

He waited while I digested this new bit of news.

"Sounds like it's hell on the personal grooming front!"

He rolled his eyes but laughed.

"My dear, you have absolutely no idea how aggravating it is," he growled in frustration. "I have learned to feel what I look like and hope it's good enough. Do you know what it's like to not be able to fathom your own appearance?"

I had to admit, it was a thought which had never crossed my mind.

"That's a new one for me," I agreed.

I considered this a bit further.

"Then, how do you shave?"

He snorted derisively.

"I don't!" he replied. "I was never the bearded type anyway and since I had none when I was turned, I just stayed that way. Your appearance remains the same when you are turned."

"Sounds like a high price for eternal youth."

"It's a very high price for many of the assets which come with the existence, in my opinion at least," he replied.

I stirred the coffee and watched the brown liquid swirl as I considered all he had just related to me.

"So," I said, deciding to change the subject again. "What do you think of modern day witches?"

He snorted.

"Present company excluded, they're pathetic!" he said.

This hit me like a slap in the face.

"Excuse me," I said, allowing my insult to show in the tone. "Some of those people you call 'pathetic' are my friends."

He returned his silvery eyes to mine and faced my gaze steadily.

"I realize that. And most of your Wiccan friends, *most* not all, are pathetic. Really," he repeated his negative opinion to my face.

I was silent for a long moment while I digested this. I tried my best to control my rising anger. I tried to make sense of what he had just said.

"What makes my friends…'pathetic'…in your eyes?" I forced myself to ask him.

He tucked his chin in and smiled at my choice of words.

"You must understand, Mrs. Miller, the witches I grew up with and the witches of today are vastly different creatures. In my day as a youth, the local witch would think nothing of foretelling the future by cutting open the belly of a goat and reading its entrails as it expired, or drinking the blood of a bat, or mixing up love potions for sale or even casting a hex on a person for the right price. I mean, even witches back then had to earn a living."

He sighed and shook his head as he looked down on the people below.

"No, the witches of today have all become humaniacs, and are all too concerned with being politically correct. They live in their apartments and in their cities and visit nature on the weekends and picket against those who eat meat and think they are saving the earth that way. They have no idea what their ancestors went through. They've become squeamish and weak. They faint at the very trace of blood."

He was looking down on those gathered beneath us as if they were sheep and he was a wolf.

My daughter was in those ranks.

"Spoken like a true predator," was the only reply I could finally come up with.

He looked back at me in surprise. I saw a faint glimpse of the human he had once been, flicker in his eyes. And then it disappeared, swallowed by the hunger of the primal beast which lurked just beneath the surface.

To massage my own wounded ego, I decided to dare him.

"Okay, you played with me the first time we shared this drink," I challenged him. "Let me play with you. Look below us and pick out the witches below and tell me what you think of them."

He held my gaze for a moment. The corners of his mouth turned upwards for a second.

I knew he couldn't resist my challenge.

He turned his attention back to the crowd beneath him and pondered the assemblage.

"Those three teen girls there, see them? They're standing to the right of your booth."

I looked the way he was pointing and saw the girls he meant. It was obvious they were witches or Goths. Their outfits were dripping in pentacles, they were dressed all in black, and they had even dyed their hair. One girl was a blonde, the next a redhead; the last had a very fake shade of black. So typical, Hollywood-esque witch in appearance they were I nearly laughed out loud.

"They *think* they're witches. The one in the middle is really just trying to piss off her parents. The one to her left is just into doing something completely different from the crowd. The third is just doing it because she doesn't want to be left out *and* she likes the clothes. Give them six months and they'll all be into something totally different. Oh! And they probably also won't be speaking to each other."

I laughed.

"Probably because they will find out that two of them slept with the same boyfriend!" I said.

"Correct," he said. "It's all drama with them at that age."

"That was easy!" I told him. "Any witch with some maturity could pick those three out! Pick out a more difficult nut to crack."

"Oh you want more difficult, eh?" he said, concentrating. "Let's see. Ah! Now see that man there? The short, fat one with the wizard's outfit?" he directed.

I located the man he meant, dressed in blue with bad, homemade stitching, hovering on the steps at the exit.

"He thinks life has given him a bad rap so he's dabbling in witchcraft to get back at everyone. Six months from now, he'll be a Goth and playing with things he has no business dealing with. He'll probably end up attracting the attention of something he's not prepared to handle. And this bad something is going to reach out and have him for dinner. And by something bad, I don't necessarily mean myself."

I made a mental note of the guy and decided to keep a tighter watch on him, especially around Bree.

"Hmm. There goes a kitchen witch. Harmless to everyone, except herself. But hey, she's happy."

His sharp eyes darted about, searching for more prey.

"Ooooo! Now there's one! She's the real deal! Been around forever. There's a solid foundation in her schooling. She's got some real power within her. If she ever were to cast a hex on someone, I'd either start running or say your prayers!"

I leaned forward, looking for the woman he meant.

I picked her out easily and fought to keep my reaction from showing on my face.

Sage Hess had come up to my booth and was engrossed in deep conversation with my daughter.

I sat deep back into my chair and tried to hide my inward smile by draining the last dregs of coffee from my cup.

I cleared my throat noisily and changed the conversation again.

"So, what are the side effects of this 'witch's brew' coffee on a non-vampire?" I asked him.

He too leaned back and laced his hands together in front of him on the table with obvious relish.

"I was wondering when you'd come to that," he said.

47

"Well?" I insisted. "Are you going to tell me the truth or dance around the subject?"

He waggled his head from side to side.

"Maybe you'll have no side effects," he said. "But then, you *are* a witch and being such, your third eye is open. You'll probably have some very vivid dreams. They're harmless. But very amusing."

I slammed the empty cup down with a clatter on the saucer.

"Now you tell me!" I said. "Very amusing to me or you?"

Mykhalo smiled mischievously.

"Does it really matter?" he said.

# CHAPTER 5

The dealer's room closed around seven in the evening. Bree had decided to check out what class was going on in the esoteric room. So I roamed about in the con suite and tried to find out from the other attendees where the best eateries were in Port Jarvis. My plan was to pick up Bree and the two of us were to go out for a late dinner before the concert started at nine. But as I wandered about at the front desk, the weather outside caught my eye.

It had been snowing all day long. The snow already lay thick on the cars in the parking lot. I decided either to order take out or to investigate the hotel's restaurant. But it was nice to know the hotel held us hostage in such weather and I didn't have to go out and shovel the walk to the car.

I found out where the esoteric room was and read the list of scheduled events posted outside the door. It seemed my friend Sage was teaching a class on prayer beads and it was just finishing up. So, since the door was open, I decided to poke my head in and wait for Bree.

It was easy to spot her with her newly dyed, purple hair. She sat in the back, taking notes studiously. She took notes on everything, scholastic or not. No trees were being saved in her corner of the world!

Right away, my eyes were drawn to three recently familiar classmates sitting in front. The three teen witches Mykhalo had picked out were there. The red-haired one was fidgeting in her chair and looking very displeased. It seemed as if she were sitting on a tack and trying unsuccessfully to hide the fact.

"With a little practice," Sage was saying. "You will find having a set of prayer beads with you is an easy way to take advantage of a long trip to work or a bus ride to school to connect yourself with the Divine."

The redhead snorted in scorn like an impatient horse.

"Is there a problem, Miss?" Sage asked in her forever-patient voice.

"I'm a witch!" the red-hair declared proudly. "I didn't convert to Wicca to *pray*! If I had wanted to do that, I would have stayed a Christian like my lame parents! When are we going to learn to do spells?"

I saw my daughter bug out her eyes in horror. I fought to keep from laughing out loud but I finally had to hide my smile behind my hand. I curled my lips under to try to keep it from showing.

Sage caught my gaze and smiled in wise return. How could she stay so controlled so easily?

"My dear, you will find there are many ways to practice Wicca. And many different people, who aren't Christians, pray and use prayer beads. Buddhists use them and so do Islamic people. And prayer, in whatever form, is always a good thing."

"Well I am not Christian and I am certainly not doing something that people who killed so many are doing! I want to learn Wicca 101. Where's the Wicca? All I've learned is how to make is jewelry. Where's the magic in this?"

And with this, she stood up and, gesturing to her two friends, flounced past me and out of the room. The black haired girl followed instantly. The blonde girl glanced back and forth from her two friends to Sage apologetically.

"Ice? Aren't you coming?" barked the dark-haired over her shoulder.

The blonde girl slunk after them like a beaten dog.

"Sorry, Ma'am," she whispered quietly to Sage. "She's just on the rag."

And then she scuttled after them.

Bree looked after them and then back to Sage.

"I think next time you better scale your classes to the 'Hogwart's crowd," she said.

This seemed to release the tension and the whole room of remaining classmates dissolved in laughter.

Sage just smiled quietly and calmed the hilarity.

"Now, now. That's mean! We were all young and foolish once," she told us.

She motioned the class was over by gesturing to her watch and telling those assembled, "For those of you who aren't put off by a little prayer, we will be making our own prayer beads tomorrow in this room at eleven in the morning. I have some beads if you need supplies or you can purchase them from Gen who runs the "Mystic Toad Treasures" booth in the dealer's room. If you're interested, then take a supply list from me before you leave."

The session began to break up. I noticed the remainder of the class, including Bree, all wanted the supply list from Sage.

I went up to Sage to chat and collect my daughter.

"Well, that ended on a sour note," I said to her.

"What? Her?" said Sage. "Not at all! She's just as I said, very young and foolish and still figuring things out. She'll either turn around or not. It's her life and her decision."

Bree sucked her teeth and cradled her notebook to her chest.

"Still," she said. "Looks like a train wreck to me!"

Sage shrugged, not at all worried by the incident.

Bree fell in beside me.

"So who's your new boyfriend, Ma?" she said, quite out of the blue.

"Boyfriend?" I asked, startled. "What on earth, do you mean?"

She laughed and flung back her purple locks.

"C'mon! Don't pull that with me!" she teased, tapping me on the arm. "You think I didn't notice? The tall, mysterious man with an accent. A bit old but still handsome. When were you going to tell me?"

I felt my face grow hot.

"He's *not* my boyfriend!" I insisted.

51

"Un – hunh. Right. You just keep telling yourself that!" And she giggled, tickled she had gotten under my skin.

"No, you listen to me, Bree!" I said with sudden heat, grabbing her by the arm and jerking her about to face me. "That man is *not*, and never will be, my boyfriend! End of discussion!"

Bree's face had twisted up in indignant confusion.

"All right! Okay, I get it! Point made! What's gotten into you, Ma?" she muttered, cowed.

I continued to stalk onward, angry with myself for being so obvious to my own daughter.

"That man is dangerous! You are to stay away from him at all costs, do you hear me?"

There was a long disturbed silence from her.

"I hear you, Mom, but..." she said slowl, "if he's so dangerous, then what are you doing hanging out with him?"

I didn't have a quick enough answer for her response. And morbid fascination wasn't a reason a responsible parent should give to their child.

* * *

Our dinner was very unsettled. Bree kept giving me questioning looks and I kept avoiding her eyes.

We were supposed to attend the Clam Chowder concert later in the evening. But somehow things didn't go as planned.

Bree told me she wanted to go back to the room and watch TV instead of the concert. So I let her.

I tried to enjoy the concert. I sat at the back of the hall. I was surrounded by loud music and laughter and my mind was miles away.

What kind of parent was I? Here I was carrying on a friendship with a being who could easily kill my daughter or myself. I was courting disaster! Mykhalo was being so cordial and genuinely friendly – or so it seemed. He was a vampire! I should be scared of him. I should be running screaming from him. I should have nothing to do with him. I was the mother of a very attractive and bright, teenaged girl who was quickly putting two and two together. I knew all too well the effect which giving an ultimatum to a teen could produce. If I said not to go near this guy, she could run willfully towards him just to spite me. And I wasn't going to fool myself into believing, 'Oh, but she's a good girl and wouldn't do that!'

I couldn't stay at the concert anymore. I had to go and check on my daughter.

I left and went back to our room, half expecting her not to be there or have stuffed pillows down in the bed.

But Bree was there, wrapped up in blankets, sitting up and snoring in front of the flickering blue light of an old, black and white horror movie, I think it was *The Mummy* but I'm not sure.

I breathed a sigh of immense relief. I took the remote from her warm hand and turned off the television. I then bent over and smoothed the purple hair away from her face. She moaned and half woke up.

"Time for bed sweetheart," I told her and kissed her on the forehead.

She mumbled something inaudible in return and rolled over.

I made a move to tuck her in and stopped myself. I then bent over and brushed her hair away from her neck, checking both sides. Bree shivered and whined a little louder, "Ma, your hands are cold!"

Her neck was pearly white and clean just as it had always been. No classic bite marks anywhere to be seen.

I tucked her in with the thick blankets and inwardly berated myself for being so paranoid. I kissed her again.

I then sat down on my bed and gave a deep sigh of relief. I ran my tired hands through my hair. *I must really be going crazy!*

I decided right then and there it had to end. No more discussions with this strange man who was really a vampire. No more coffee flavored with the blood of the undead. No more amusing little discussions and courting death.

I had a daughter to look out for. I had Bree to protect. I couldn't keep doing this. It was stupid. Mykhalo was reeling me in, waiting until I became comfortable with his presence. This was not going to happen!

I curled into the hotel's warm blankets and starched sheets and said goodbye to Mykhalo and the strange conversations of the past few days in my mind.

It was all in the past now.

The important thing was my daughter was safe from him.

\* \* \*

Mykhalo was walking through the hallways of the hotel when he caught it, the faint scent of someone familiar. He stopped and paid more attention to the scent making sure of his suspicions.

Yes, there could be no mistaking it.

He took a deep breath to steady his emotions and then he pursued the smell. It led him out into the open lobby of the hotel. Before him was a sunken indoor garden with small tables and chairs set up for people to socialize. Although the area was bustling with activity and people, the tables were vacant except for one person.

A dark skinned, dark haired man sat at one of the tables, with a single wine glass in front of him.

Mykhalo was expected.

The man nodded to him.

He could have turned away. But Mykhalo knew he did not dare to ignore this man. He took another deep breath to steel himself against the conversation to come. And then he went at once to the table and seated himself across from the man.

"Michael," the man acknowledged in a soft low voice laced with a Spanish accent.

He winced in distaste at the mention of his English name but nodded in return.

"Hector," Mykhalo replied.

Their eyes scrutinized each other for one long silent moment, like warriors of equal strength sizing each other up before the beginning of a fight.

The man who sat across from Mykhalo was as dark as the Bavarian was light. His expertly styled locks were combed back from his high forehead, his eyebrows were dark and heavy and his facial features were finely chiseled. He possessed the handsome good looks of a male model except for his black eyes. They were dark pools glittering of infinity.

His eyes were definitely not human.

"Why are you here, Michael?" the man called Hector said.

He risked a smile.

"I could ask you much the same question."

The sheen in his eyes grew darker.

"Do not play word games with me," Hector told him. "You know I hold all your secrets."

Mykhalo tilted his head to the side.

"You began all my secrets."

Hector smiled in obvious relish of this fact. He slowly sipped his wine as he considered his next move.

"I could command you to tell me."

Mykhalo sniffed in wry humor at this.

"Oh you definitely could," he admitted. "But you won't. Not here and not now. Too many people about. You'd make a scene."

Hector bowed his head slightly.

"So tell me then."

Mykhalo smiled and did not speak for a long moment.

"No."

Hector sat back in his chair.

"'No' seems to be your favorite word with me."

Mykhalo raised his eyebrows but said nothing to this.

"Are you following me, Hector?" he finally said.

Hector smiled in return.

"I am always following you, Michael. I or one of my children."

The Bavarian sighed in return.

"Ah manipulation! It won't work with me, Hector."

But Hector shook his head. "It already has."

Mykhalo's expression hinted to the rejection of the idea.

"You know nothing of my motives." Hector caressed the edge of the wine glass.

"Except that you mean to kill me." Although his tone was soft, he almost laughed as he said this.

The Bavarian's face went dark. "It will happen," he insisted.

Hector sniffed and shook his head. "And yet I am still here. I have been here for so many centuries. You have had plenty of time. What's your problem?"

Mykhalo gave frustrated sigh.

"Don't you get tired of it, Hector? The constant killing, the half-life, the running from the sun? The spreading chaos and grief wherever you go?"

Hector leaned forward as if he was divulging some great secret. "Never!" he hissed. "Wait a few more years. Then everything changes. Then you will *love* this life I have bestowed upon you. And you will bathe in the blood of the innocent as I have done."

Mykhalo turned away.

"This is pointless! You have nothing to say. Nothing I have not heard a million times before." He made as if to leave.

Hector's words stopped him.

"You took my son from me," Hector said in a soft voice reeking of hate. "Now I will take your family from you!"

Mykhalo turned his head away eyes squeezed shut at the painful memories.

"You already have. Remember?"

The Spaniard gave a wry smile. "I remember. And I'm not talking about them."

There was a purposely-dramatic pause in his words which forced Mykhalo to turn and face him again.

"I know about Hope," he told him.

Mykhalo's eyes snapped open and his heart began to pound but very slowly. He did not dare to look at Hector.

"I know she had children," he said, his voice getting progressively softer. "And I know Hope's great granddaughter is here."

The last words he spoke in a whisper.

"And I will find her."

Mykhalo met Hector's gaze at last. The Spaniard was smiling vindictively as his eyes watched the emotions play across his face.

"Ah! There it is. I've frightened you again, haven't I?"

Mykhalo shot up and away from the table refusing to look at him anymore.

But Hector's mocking words chased after him.

"This is what happens when you tell me 'no'!"

## CHAPTER 6

I awoke to a strange sound in my room. It sounded like branches scratching on the windowpane except I knew there was no tree outside. I lifted my head off of the pillow and looked at the digital alarm clock by the bed.

It read two-thirty.

I got up and checked on Bree. She was still snoring comfortably, oblivious to everything. I then went to the window and peeped carefully through the curtains. Mykhalo's silver eyes peered back at me from the other side of the glass. I squeaked and jumped back, startled.

He chuckled and gestured an apology. He then motioned I was to come and join him outside.

I still have no idea why I did what I did.

I waved for him to wait a minute and I went and got my long overcoat to throw on over my sweats decorated in bats which served as pajamas. I then left my daughter sleeping soundly. I locked the hotel room after me and went outside to join him.

It was still snowing. I felt my slippered feet crunch through the snow but didn't feel the cold.

Mykhalo stood by the hotel's pool which was covered with tarp for the winter. The windows of the hotel rooms were all dark. His shadowy form was dusted in snow. But his eyes seemed to glow in the soft night.

"What's so important you had to wake me in the middle of the night?" I asked him.

He didn't seem to see me at first. And then he started as if just waking up.

"You're shivering," he said.

But I wasn't shivering. In fact I don't remember feeling cold at all.

"Come. I'll keep you warm," he said and held open his trench coat. It seemed black as a cave inside.

I suddenly became wary.

"No," I said and backed away a step.

He started to advance on me and stopped.

"Please. I just wanted to talk again. I so enjoy our little talks," he told me.

Something didn't quite sound right about this.

"It's a little late and cold for us to be talking," I told him in a strong tone of voice. "Why don't you come inside and we'll talk?"

It was his turn to hesitate and draw back. "But isn't it beautiful out here?" he said and lifted his head and arms up to catch the snow. "It reminds me of my home. The snow was so glorious there."

His accent seemed very sharp tonight.

"What do you want, Mykhalo?" I said firmly.

"Just to tell you more secrets of my kind. You seem so fascinated by them. And I'm so glad I finally have someone to confide in. It's been so long since I've been able to do that."

He began to approach me by circling slowly. I kept my eyes on him and faced him, turning to keep him in sight.

"This is a very strange function, this 'con'. It attracts some very strange people. People who think they know what it is to be a vampire," he was saying. Wary as I was, I was starting to be drawn in. "Do you not think it's strange there are so many works of fiction written about vampires? More than say, werewolves? What makes vampires so attractive to the literary public, I wonder?" he wound his words carefully.

"I guess it's the whole romantic appeal of them," I said.

"Ah, romance!" he said. "But you see this is even more perplexing to me. Because vampires are not at all romantic!"

The snow was seeping through my slippers and soaking my feet. I felt the wetness but still I did not feel the cold.

I should have been more wary. But I was beginning to feel a sleepy sort of fascination get the better of me.

"Not romantic?" I said. "Explain."

He tucked his chin in and faced me. His eyes flashed brightly in the dark hollows of his chiseled face.

"Gladly!" he said in a soft, tempting voice, laced with menace.

My instincts screamed a warning in my brain two seconds too late. He was suddenly behind me and close enough for his breath to ruffle my hair.

It was then my urge to flee left me. My inner voice was still screaming wildly for me to get away, but it was dimmer now in volume and I was unable to obey it. I could feel my will to fight begin to melt quickly, like the snow around my feet. I felt powerless to do anything but listen to his words. I knew he was playing with me like a cat with a mouse.

"You see, they're all written the same. The hapless woman melts at my look or my touch, just like you're melting right now." His breath fluttered against my ear.

He was close, too close, in my personal space close. And I could do nothing. I felt his hands grasp my shoulders gently at first but tighter so I wouldn't escape him. I felt his chest press up against my back. I didn't want him there! I wanted him to let go.

My limbs resolutely ignored me.

"The poor, hapless woman thinks this handsome, romantic vampire is not that at all. He's just misunderstood. Or worse, like you, they know he's evil, but they cannot resist the temptation. The urge to dance with the devil is so strong. I know you can feel it. Can't you feel it my dear? It's as real as the mist from your mouth."

I noticed though my breath condensed on the cold, snowy air, a white, ghostly plume of heat in the dark, his did not.

He was cheek to cheek with me now. I felt his cold hands travel up. I could feel his cold but not the snow's. His hands were at the base of my throat now tickling me their touch was so gentle.

"She thinks the vampire will take her about the waist and rain passionate kisses upon her hungry mouth. But he couldn't care less about kisses. She thinks he might make sweet love to her right then and there."

At this he pressed his body into my back. My heart fluttered wildly in my chest and again, my inner voice howled at me to get free.

But my body responded like that of a new corpse, limp and compliant to any prodding.

"But a vampire cares not about the act whether it be lovemaking or animal sex, it's all the same act and he couldn't be less interested in it."

I felt Mykhalo's lips brush against my neck and then he traced the side of my throat with a cold finger, right where the jugular vein runs up to supply the head with life giving blood. I could feel the pumping of my blood against the pressure of his fingertip.

"This is all a vampire cares about, this tiny spot of milk white perfection on the mortal's body," he whispered into my skin.

And still I could not react, except to lean my head to the side, baring the object of his desire to his full, hungry, attention.

"And then there are some who think the act of biting one on the neck is a pleasurable, nearly sexual experience. Make no mistake, my dear, it only brings pleasure to the vampire. All the human experiences is pain, pain like nothing they were expecting, pain like nothing they wanted. And by then it is already too late. The vampire will drink her dry and tear out her throat like the beast he truly is. So you see my dear, it is not a romantic experience at all... except to the vampire."

I tried desperately to call out in my mind for aide to any god, goddess, spirit, angel or whatever, to come and give me the strength to fight off this threat. I screamed for help in my heart while my traitorous body remained still and totally compliant to this predator hovering over me.

I heard him open his mouth less than an inch away from my throat. I felt him stroke the skin of my neck with his fangs teasingly, taunting me with the anticipation of when he would actually strike.

I closed my eyes and prayed desperately for help.

In my mind's eye, the image of the Lord of the Wild Hunt sprang suddenly, unbidden, to the surface. He was standing strong and powerful, knee deep in the snow, the antlers which sprang from his head cradled the full moon. His hounds were howling their hunting cry about him and the Lord's eyes were blazing red in fury.

There was a sudden flurry of movement about me and an inhuman sound like the scream of a dragon. Snow was tossed into my face and I was thrown roughly into the powder.

This jarred me back to my senses. I rolled away and looked up at my attacker.

I was in time to see Mykhalo's face melt into one of a stranger with brown skin, black eyes and hair tipped in snowflakes and sparkling, white fangs. He turned to his right and his face twisted into an infuriated scowl.

Something like a large, dark cape or a wing obliterated him from sight and then there was another enraged roar as two shapes went tumbling about in the snow.

Snow was kicked into my face again and I ducked away. Behind me I heard a sudden whooshing sound and an unexpected wind threatened to suck me backwards.

I cried out although what I said I do not now remember.

And then Mykhalo was back, stooping over me.

"Get away! Get away!" I screamed at him, flailing my arms and covering my eyes so I wouldn't be ensnared again.

"Hush, Zan! It's me! The *real* me! Get up! I've got to get you back inside."

"The *real* you?" I stammered, suddenly seized with the biting cold. "Then who was… ?"

"Another one," he said, pulling me quickly to my feet.

My legs felt frozen to the bone.

"Another vampire?" I said through chattering teeth.

"Yes," he said quickly.

He swept off his trench coat and flung it around me.

63

"Damn! You're colder than me!" he said and began to rub my limbs as he pulled me along after him. "I said you would have very vivid dreams. I didn't know you would actually sleepwalk!"

"Who was that? The other vampire?" I insisted, pulling back on him.

He tried to pull me along, which, having vampire strength, he was quite capable of doing. So I just plunked down in the snow.

"Mykhalo, *TELL ME*! Who was the other vampire?" I demanded, quaking with cold.

I could feel my fingers turning into icy claws.

"That was Hector," he said, relenting. "He's very old and very ruthless. I'm a gentle kitten compared to him! Please get inside before he comes back. Your daughter…"

My mind spun wildly.

Omigod, *BREE*!

This spurred me to run towards the hotel door.

"You will be safe inside. Too many people and bright lights. Quick now." He nearly shoved me towards the door.

He followed me inside the hotel. The heat from the inside of the building hit me like a wall. My legs were almost frozen to brittle twigs so he half-carried me down the hall to my room.

He stopped at my door's room and made as if to leave.

"Please stay," I said, touching him on the arm. I was still too shaken by the recent events to want to be alone.

He entered our room with a very uncomfortable look on his face.

I went and looked to make sure Bree was still there. She slumbered on.

"You're chilled to the bone. You need a hot shower to warm yourself up," he said to me softly so as not to wake her.

I gave him a good long stare before I finally complied and shut the door on him.

It was the quickest and hottest shower I think I've ever taken.

When I stepped out of the bathroom, wrapped in a towel, wreathed in hot steam, he was still standing just where I had left him.

Now thoroughly warmed up, I took a closer look at Bree. She still slumbered as if nothing had happened.

I returned to Mykhalo who was standing by the door. We just stared at each other, wordlessly for a moment.

"I didn't touch her," he said at last. "Bree, I mean. I didn't touch her."

"I know. I checked," I said.

I went into the bathroom and returned his trench coat to him.

"Why did you do that?" I said. "Why did you protect me? Am I your property now?"

"No," he answered.

"Then why?" I said again.

This time Mykhalo refused to answer me. I waited for a long moment and no answer was forthcoming.

"Mykhalo, do I need to fear you?" I said.

"Absolutely!" he said immediately. "I heard what Hector told you. And everything he said is exactly correct. It is not a romantic act at all."

"Hunh. You took your sweet time rescuing me then," I countered.

He hissed in irritation.

"That was because I am what I am," he said. "I had some difficulty overcoming the urge to join him. If he *had* drawn your blood, it would have been even more difficult."

"Then why did you protect me? I demand an answer."

He took a deep sigh and raised his eyes to me.

"Because I consider you my friend," he said as if he was genuinely trying to be truthful.

"Really? And vampires are allowed to have mortal friends?" I said in some scorn.

"No, they are not. I break the rules. So far, I have been successful," he told me.

I considered this for a moment. "Does Hector have friends?" I whispered.

"Don't speak of such things!" he snapped back in a hushed voice.

"I *WILL* speak of such things!" I hissed in some heat, raising my voice. "Because I have a daughter and I need to know this!"

Bree moaned and stirred in her sleep.

Mykhalo gave a frustrated sigh and glared angrily at me. "Hector doesn't have friends, he has minions. You would do well to steer clear of them," Mykhalo hissed.

"And now this Hector knows of me," I said.

"He was merely testing the waters," Mykhalo said in a vain attempt to reassure me.

It did not work.

"And now Hector knows of me," I repeated. "And he knows that I'm weak. Why was I not able to fight him off?"

Mykhalo shot me a look in the dark which was laced with dread.

"Hector is a very, very old vampire. Nearly ancient. The monster that is a primal vampire has now consumed whatever humanity there was in him. He exists to be cruel and cause pain and suffering on mortals."

"You seem to know him quite well," I said.

Mykhalo held my eyes for a long moment. Finally he leaned in close until he was inches from my face. I shuddered but quickly realized I was in full control of my reactions. So I faced him.

"Hector made me," Mykhalo hissed into my face.

He waited while I digested the information.

"No love lost between father and son, eh?" I was taunting him now and I knew it.

Mykhalo snarled.

"Why do you persist in aggravating me?" he growled. "Hector made me! He was *never* my father."

I considered the emotions playing across his face.

"You want to kill him, don't you?" I said. "Why? Other than the obvious."

"Other than the obvious," he repeated. "Then people like your daughter Bree and you will be safe."

He reached up and gently stroked the side of my face.

"You both are worth protecting and saving to me. I don't want our conversations to end. And I don't want to 'turn' either of you," he whispered almost tenderly.

I decided to test him then. I marched a step closer and while doing this, swept my long, wet, black, hair away from my neck exposing the object of his desire to his gaze.

I saw his eyes shift to my throat. His mouth and posture stiffened. His eyes glittered dangerously. He took a deep breath and stepping closer reached out with both hands for my head. I held myself rock steady. But he merely took my long, wet, locks and swept them back in front to hide my throat from his gaze.

"Please don't do that," he whispered, standing very close to me. He was still holding the ends of my hair. His hands were cool against my shower-heated skin.

I refused to retreat.

"What makes you so different, Mykhalo? Why didn't you attack me tonight?"

He sighed heavily and looked at his feet.

"I am very young," he told me. "My humanity is still quite active. It keeps me in check. Sometimes. But I am approaching the age where this is getting harder and harder. Soon, I will devolve into something without boundaries. Like Hector. I hope I die before that happens."

He then pulled back out of my space, which relieved me greatly.

"So you don't consider me pathetic?" I replied, a smile tugging at the corners of my mouth.

He smiled back.

"Never!" he chuckled.

He turned and strode to the door.

"I had better leave now," he said. "But I will be close by and keeping watch. You will be safe tonight. As long as you don't try to sleepwalk again!"

"Thank you, Mykhalo," I said to him but he was already out the door and I heard the lock snap shut.

I gave a tired sigh. I let the towel fall to the floor and changed into a new set of sweats. I then crawled into the same bed as my daughter and wrapped my arms protectively about her dreaming form.

I prayed for a dreamless rest of the night.

## CHAPTER 7

I had a lot to think about on the way home from the convention. I was so preoccupied I was surprised I didn't forget a box of books or even I had a daughter. But I seemed to remember everything and we were heading home.

Bree was playing with her new set of prayer beads. I could see she had to concentrate on keeping count so I did my best not to disturb her in her newfound ritual. She finally sighed and put down the beads.

"Done with your prayers?" I said.

"Yeah." She smiled at me. "It's harder than I thought to get started. But once I've said them a few times, it gets easier. I eventually get into the swing of it."

"There's a rhythm to doing a rosary. It's kinda musical in a way," I told her.

"Yeah, I know," she replied and fell silent.

"Are you saying a certain prayer or making it up?" I said.

"I'm just making it up for whatever the occasion is. It seems easier that way to me."

"Whatever helps you get in touch with the Divine," I said.

"Yeah. I'm hoping that this may help me find out where I belong. Just feeling things out like you said." She smiled at me. "See? I do listen to you sometimes!"

I chuckled along with her.

We were sitting at a light, an insufferably long one.

"May I see the rosary you made?" I asked.

"Sure." She handed it over.

I ran my fingers over the smooth, round, blue beads interspersed with smaller yellow rounds every few cycles. It had a warm, welcoming feel to it.

"Is the blue sodalite?" I said.

"No, lapis-lazuli," she said.

"Hmm. Expensive!" I said with raised eyebrows.

"Nah! I used the Christmas money I've been saving," she told me and she took it back as I handed it to her when the light changed.

"And the yellow beads, those are citrine aren't they?" I went on.

"Yup. I like the blue and yellow together," she said.

"Hmm. Very Egyptian if you ask me."

She shrugged.

"What were you praying for, if you don't mind my asking?"

"For Brittany," she said. "She's having some trouble lately."

This got a look of confusion from me. Brittany Kiem was Bree's "best friend forever". The two were thick as thieves in school, walking down the hallways arm in arm, giggling at the boys behind their backs.

"I hadn't heard that," I said to her. "What's up? Boy trouble?"

Bree snorted and rolled her eyes.

"I wish!" Bree said. "No, you remember how her grandma died last month?"

"Yes, we went to the funeral together," I said.

"Well, she's still hurting over it. She's pushed Brad away and just wants to stay in her room all day on her headphones."

Brad was Brittany's longtime boyfriend.

"She's not talking to anyone on the internet. Doesn't want to hang out anymore and when she does, she's a total downer on the party. She can't seem to shake the grief."

"Do her parents know?" I said.

"She says her parents are clueless!" Bree rolled her head at me.

"So says every teenager. And so say most adults of teens," I said.

"No, but her parents really *are* clueless!" Bree said and shook her head. "That whole family needs Dr. Phil or something."

I laughed at the way she put it in spite of the seriousness of the situation.

"When we get back, I'll talk to the school counselors on Monday, see if we can do something to help her."

Bree bugged her eyes at me.

"Oooh boy! Mom's gonna meddle!" she said.

"Well, in this case, it may be called for. We'll see. Until then you keep trying to draw her out and keep her reacting to others. And doing your prayer beads for her wouldn't hurt either," I added with a smile.

"Sure, Ma. Will do," she replied with a grin.

\* \* \*

It was so easy for me to forget the events of the weekend after we got home. I just settled into my normal routine as if nothing had ever happened. Bree went to school and told me about her teenage issues every day. I bitched at her to study more and get good grades. I ran the bookstore. Everything seemed normal. Mykhalo was strangely absent from my life for a few weeks and I was half grateful for the absence.

But I also wondered why.

Then Valentine's Day came and brought with it a strange gift, but not from Mykhalo.

Matt Yoder came into the bookstore the next day around noon with two other men around his age. I noticed his friends wore tiny, Masonic brass pins on the lapels of their winter overcoats.

"Hello Matt!" I said with a smile when he walked in. "I haven't seen you for a while. What you been up to? Caught that big dog yet?"

"No, not yet." he said with a return smile.

Then he looked secretively around the store.

"You have any customers besides us?" he said quietly.

I shrugged, confused but not worried.

"No Matt," I said. I then flashed him a sultry look but just in jest. "It's just you and me here. What did you have in mind?"

"Lord! Don't tell my wife you just did that!" He laughed back.

He then nodded to the other two men and they left.

"Look. Bill Gibson made the lodge brothers privy to some information concerning you about six months ago. He had something he wanted you specifically to have and he didn't want to put it in his will. He was afraid his children would start squabbling over it and cause trouble for you. So he gave it to us for safekeeping and told us to give it to you about a month after his death so, hopefully, they would have forgotten about it."

This really did perplex me.

"What sort of...thing?" I said.

My eyebrows must have gone sky high when I saw Matt's two friends come hobbling in the front door, hefting a large trunk between them.

"We're not exactly sure. He said it was for no one's eyes but yours. So we never opened it," Matt said. "I'm pretty sure it's just a bunch of Bill's war trophies. He knew that if he willed them to his children, they probably would end up being sold on E-bay and he found the idea infuriating. He knew if he gave these things to you, you would keep them and treasure them for the rest of your life. I'm sure that's what he wanted."

The trunk was huge! And looked very heavy.

The two men plopped it down with a grunt in front of me.

"Where do you want it?" one panted.

I sucked my teeth and bit my lip, considering.

"Well, it can't stay here if there's anything valuable in it. Hmm. Better take it to the antique room. This way," I said to them and proceeded to lead them down the narrow hallway to the back.

"Please tell me we don't have to walk up or down any flights of stairs with this thing!" one complained. "It feels like it's loaded with bricks!"

"No, just the last door on the right," I led them. "It's the place where I keep all the rarest books because it has the lock from hell on the door."

I was very proud of this room. It was large or was until I had it packed to the gills with old tomes and oddities. It had a thick, oaken door which looked like it belonged on a castle with a huge, iron lock which required an old skeleton key to open.

I led them down the hallway and teased the lock open. They hobbled into the room huffing and puffing with their load and dropped it in the first empty space they came to.

"It will be fine just there. I'll deal with it later. Thank you," I told them.

They nodded politely to me and left.

Matt hung back a bit.

"Here's the key that will open it. Don't lose it! There isn't a spare!" he said.

He handed over an old, silver army chain with Bill Gibson's dog tags on them and one single, solitary key.

"By the way, Bill also told the brothers at the lodge to watch out for you. If you're ever in any trouble, Susan, any at all, please don't hesitate to call us. I mean it," he said to me, taking both my hands in his.

I thanked him profusely for this and walked him to the door. I then flipped over the "Closed" sign and locked the door behind them.

I checked every room in the building even the basement and the attic to make sure I was totally and completely alone in the bookstore. Then I went into the antique room and locked the door behind me.

There! It was just the mysterious chest and myself.

I stared at it for a long moment. It was a drab, olive green army chest. There was a bit of dust on the edges but otherwise it looked secure.

I knelt on the floor in front of it and ran my hands reverently over it, imagining the places it had seen. I couldn't ask Bill Gibson what he had done in the war or what he had seen. But maybe the things inside this chest would give me the slightest hint of what he had gone through, a snapshot in time.

I looked at the key on its chain in my hand. I read Bill Gibson's full name on the tags.

All I had to do was unlock this chest and it would tell me his story.

And I couldn't do it.

I put the key on the chain around my neck, the same one with the pentacle and slipped it under my clothes. I then left the room making sure to lock it securely before I left.

Why couldn't I open it?

# CHAPTER 8

Mykhalo visited me in my dream that night but not in the way you might think.

I was swept from my bed and taken far away by the dream to another time and place. When I next opened my eyes, I seemed to be an invisible watcher seated on the shoulder of a young soldier.

Bits of information seemed to filter into my brain automatically. I knew it was during World War II. It was mid-March, 1945. The war was almost over. We were in Austria. The group of soldiers was lightly armed, expecting little resistance. My soldier was an American and a sergeant. He had been seriously wounded in action and decorated for it. Maybe that's why he walked with a pronounced limp. He had been reassigned to a sort of a clean-up detail but of what sort, I did not know.

I also knew my soldier was Bill Gibson.

I gazed around eagerly at the foreign landscape. It seemed so unusual to see it in color. I was used to the black and white stills in history books and documentary shows on TV. Things were still drab colored because it was barely spring and the buds hadn't started to sprout. Most of the landscape was brown and yellow with every now and then a flash of red from a Nazi flag trampled into the mud.

Bill and his unit were standing on the muddy street of a small town. I could hear the natives speaking German around him interposed with the clearness of the American words, which I understood.

I wasn't really listening to the words the men spoke. I was still looking around at the town and taking in all the details. There was some rubble from a few buildings which had been burned out. Things were not as neat and tidy as the modern tour pamphlets showed. War had devastated the whole country.

A local farmer walked by leading his horse and cart. Both the horse and the farmer had gaunt features, ravaged by the current events. But I could not take my eyes off the horse. It was golden with a thick, white mane which covered the animal's eyes and a thick white tail sweeping behind. It was the most colorful thing, other than the deposed Nazi flag in the mud, on the whole street.

The group of American soldiers moved out, led by a local survivor. I somehow knew Bill spoke German so he was acting as interpreter of the group. The Austrian was taking them to the nearby salt mines.

The soldiers were searching for something. But what?

After a walk of about a mile through rugged but blasted countryside, they came to the salt mines. The soldiers checked their weapons and their flashlights briefly and then entered.

Bill told them to fan out and each take a separate tunnel. He also instructed them not to get lost or separated from their partner. Bill went with the local man.

Each tunnel had a set of rails for running the carts of salt back up to the surface. The tunnel Bill took was dark and close and seemed to be running steadily downward. Their progress was slow and cautious. The Austrian led Bill to a huge chamber with a few large wooden crates inside. They checked the crates only to find them broken open and empty.

The Austrian muttered an apology and Bill seemed to understand he was saying something about looters.

He shrugged and motioned him to lead him onward. The Austrian seemed uncomfortable about going any further down this passageway. Bill was immediately suspicious and questioned him. What I understood from Bill's thought process was the man said it was 'haunted'.

Bill set his lip and insisted. The Austrian obeyed but his hollow face flinched in the flashlight's beam.

This tunnel seemed to get wider and roomier as they went on. Bill kept their progress slow as he fanned the light everywhere, trying to see if anything was hiding in the shadows. Finally the walls fell away as they came to another large chamber.

The Austrian stopped and said in a voice which trembled with nervousness, "See? Nothing. We go back now."

"Wait a minute!" Bill growled and grabbed the man by the shoulder.

He fanned the light's beam about the room to find it was full of very large wooden crates.

Suddenly, there was a scraping sound from the far end of the large room.

The Austrian shrieked and twisting free from Bill's grasp, fled up the tunnel. The sound of his madly pounding feet echoed back to his ears. And then an eerie silence enveloped the room.

Bill cursed after him.

The scraping sound came again followed by a long hiss as if from an angry cobra which had been disturbed.

Bill grumbled and drew his Colt 1911 pistol, advanced cautiously into the room, and fanned his beam around every corner of every crate he came to.

There was definitely something in the room. He could hear heavy breathing.

He hobbled onward, wits aware, eyes searching every black corner.

Bill turned the corner around one crate and stopped with a choked cry of shock, dropping the flashlight. The light's shivering beam fell full on what had startled him.

A dead Nazi soldier lay in front of him, his throat torn out, and his windpipe hissing uselessly. Over the soldier hovered his killer.

The murderer slowly straightened up. It was a tall man with sandy blonde hair dressed in a Nazi uniform.

But it was the long fangs on this person, dripping in blood which had riveted Bill to his spot.

I recognized the person immediately even if Bill did not.

It was Mykhalo.

Bill raised his handgun and took aim. But his hand shook with fear. In all his days of fighting the war, he had never encountered something like this.

The creature standing before him smiled scornfully.

"That will prove ineffective," he told him slowly, in perfect German.

Bill refused to listen and unloaded an entire magazine into Mykhalo whose smile only increased. The bullets tore holes in the Nazi uniform and gun smoke filled the room.

"See? What did I tell you?" he said.

Then Mykhalo's smile vanished. His face became hard and cold. He began to advance on Bill in a threatening manner.

Bill's hands were shaking so badly he knew he would never be able to reload. So he pulled his knife. The dim light of the flashlight glinted along the dagger's blade.

Mykhalo only laughed.

"Now that might tickle!" he said to him, chuckling.

"Stay away from me!" Bill ordered.

This was the moment the flashlight chose to stop working. The light went out throwing them both into total darkness.

But the expected attack did not come.

Finally, Bill heard the vampire's voice come again from right in front of him.

"Why are you speaking peasant German?"

It was then I realized, through my mental link with Bill he had unintentionally spoken in Pennsylvania Dutch not modern German.

"I have not heard such words in over a hundred years," the creature in front of him continued speaking into the dark. "And your accent is so strange. Where are you from?"

Bill was barely able to stammer out, "A-a-a-mer-i-i-ca."

"Ah! That explains it." was the reply in the dark. "Then you are not a Nazi?"

"No," he managed to force out.

"Hmm. That is good. Very good," the voice intoned back in very clipped, heavily accented English this time. "Then I will not hurt you. Besides, I have fed very well for one night."

The flashlight's beam suddenly clicked on again, held in the creature's hand. He politely handed it over

"I detest Nazis with a passion!" he said.

Bill was slowly starting to get control of himself.

"But…you're wearing…" he stuttered.

"How else was I to get close enough to them without arousing suspicion?" he said to Bill. "But I am forgetting my manners. I am Mykhalo von Ludwig of Bavaria. And you are?"

Bill's jaw just flapped a few times before he was able to manage words.

"Bill. William Gibson. From Pennsylvania."

Mykhalo smiled in a much less dangerous, more welcoming way.

"Ah! That explains the peasant German. The Amish," Mykhalo said. "Now, I am very eager to help the Allies. What are you looking for?"

"You want to help?" Bill said. "But why?"

"As I have said before, I detest Nazis," Mykhalo patiently told him. "And the Hitler regime. They have made a mockery of proper Bavarian ideals. Anything I can do to frustrate them will give me intense pleasure."

It took a minute for Bill to digest this information. His hands had finally stopped quaking in terror.

His eyes were drawn back to the new corpse on the ground behind them.

"Are there any more of those guys hiding out in these salt mines?" he said, suddenly concerned about the rest of his unit.

Mykhalo smiled, revealing his bloodstained fangs again.

"There *were*," he replied with some humor. "As I have also said before, I have fed well this night. The tunnels are now safe for your men."

"Good," Bill said with a relieved sigh.

"Now just *what* exactly were your men looking for?" Mykhalo said again.

He turned his back politely on Bill as he wiped his face off on a white handkerchief in his breast pocket as if it would make this American better able to deal with him if he didn't have the blood from his last victim on his face.

"I'm a Sergeant in the Monument's Group," Bill told him. "We are searching for art treasures stolen by the Third Reich."

"Ah. And what will you do with these art treasures?" replied Mykhalo.

"Why, return them to their proper museums so the public can appreciate them again," Bill said.

"All the public or just the Americans?" Mykhalo asked, pointedly.

"We do not loot art treasures," Bill said with some heat.

Mykhalo nodded, considering for a moment.

"Then I will gladly help you search for them," he said. "I know of many places they were hidden. In fact, I was 'haunting' this chamber to protect them from the Nazis. Would you like to see them?"

I felt Bill's heart skip a beat. He obviously had a great love for fine art.

"That's what is in these crates?" he asked eagerly.

"Yes. Hitler disapproved. They proved to be too modern for his taste. I think he was going to burn them," Mykhalo told him.

I felt Bill's heart skip another beat in horror at this bit of news.

"But I also know of a castle nearby with a good deal more of his special favorites hidden in the dungeons. You had better call your men and get some large trucks."

The expression on Bill's face looked like a kid who had suddenly been dropped in a candy store. I could see him wrestling with the notion of whether to tear all the crates open so he could gaze at them himself or call his men for the proper lighting to appreciate them better.

"I had better leave before your men get here. The bullet holes in my uniform would raise too much suspicion, thank you very much for

80

that! Now I shall have to find another tall Nazi with no blood on his threads to strip!"

Mykhalo turned as if to leave.

"We shall be in touch, you and I. Look for me in the shadows, Bill Gibson."

Mykhalo saluted him. Bill returned the honor. The vampire then melted into the darkness of the salt mines.

I awoke from the dream feeling torn in two. On the one hand, I was glad I finally knew a little about Bill Gibson's experiences during the war.

But on the other hand, I had looked into the eyes of Mykhalo the vampire.

It reminded me too much of the night with Hector before I knew it wasn't my friend I was talking to. It reminded me I did have an ongoing acquaintance with a predator.

How could this possibly be all right with my beliefs?

* * *

The weekend after the delivery of the chest, I attended an unplugged music night at the local coffee house.

Again, Bree had something else to do so she was off with her friends. I was supposed to meet Sage there.

This coffee house hosted an open mic night every Saturday and the local talent would show up and ply their art. Some were quite good. Some were downright awful, I mean, don't tell Simon Cowell awful! So how good the show was depended on who showed up and how long they were allowed to work the mic. They were only allowed two songs per artist and then they had to hand it over to the next guy. So you usually were assured a mix of really good, to halfway decent, to bad music. One never knew. This is what made it so popular. It was different each night.

This particular night the talent ended up being good to almost great. There were a couple sour-noted performers at the beginning.

Sage and I winced through their performances. But after this, the talent got steadily better.

We sipped our gourmet coffee with lots of whipped cream and sprinkles and chatted quietly through the performances.

The last performer got up to play. I recognized the artist.

It was Mykhalo.

He looked quite different. Gone was the Armani suit and the tie. He was casually dressed in a plain white shirt, left open at the neck and tan slacks. He carried an ornate acoustic guitar with him which had pieces of mother of pearl set into the frets. He held the guitar lovingly as he settled himself onto the stool and strummed a few chords experimentally

"Well, here's somebody new," I mentioned to get Sage's eyes off me.

Mykhalo's eyes met mine. He smiled quietly in my direction and winked at me.

"Do you know this musician?" Sage asked as if she had discovered my secret.

I hastily gulped my coffee.

"I've seen him around town a bit. He's come into the store a couple of times," I replied.

I tried to sound casual as I said this. But I felt I was failing miserably.

We turned our attention back to the mysterious singer who had chosen not to introduce himself to the crowd. He was saying this song was one of his favorites.

He then turned his attention to the guitar and began to pull the first few notes from the instrument. His fingers scratched along the strings and then his strokes became more certain of what they had to do. The guitar had a rich, pure tone to it.

From the first few chords, the song immediately began to draw us into its magic.

Mykhalo's fingers flew over the strings and his arm confidently strummed the notes loudly as they rose in pitch. I was surprised at his command of the instrument and the ease with which he pulled the notes from the guitar. Although he had told me he was musically inclined, somehow I had trouble believing it until now.

But he was good, very good.

Mykhalo began to sing. His voice was deep and rich. Something I didn't expect. He hung back a bit from the microphone, probably because he didn't need it. His words carried to every corner of the room. The words were clear and melodious like a bard of old. Both the words and the tune drew the listener in, weaving a spell about them. He sung a melancholy ballad which sounded much like a filk song one would hear at a convention. It told the story of a ship which carried a deadly cargo from the new world to the old. It was obvious to me two of the ship's passengers were vampires even though the word was never spoken in the song. There was just a ghost of a suggestion as to their true nature.

The sound of the guitar's voice echoed in the suddenly quiet room. It seemed as if the very walls of the building were listening in rapt attention to the gloomy song. Everyone seemed captured by the story. The song itself was vampiric in a sinister way.

And then Mykhalo's voice and the notes dropped suddenly in volume making the listener lean forward to hear the words as the song wound down. The ballad was approaching its inevitable end.

Mykhalo's arm stilled. The last strains of the song hummed, vibrating into stillness and silence at last in the frozen attention of the room.

There was a long pause. I had forgotten to breathe. So had much of the audience. There was an almost audible gasp and people began to breathe again and finally to applaud. The spell was broken.

He bowed politely to the applause.

"Well, that was a dreary ballad!" Sage spoke up at last.

"Oh, I don't know. I kinda liked it," I said.

"That's 'cause you have a thing for the Spanish guitar. You always have," Sage said. "Well, on that cheery note, I'm leaving."

"What? The night's still young."

I pouted like a child.

Sage laughed and patted my cheek maternally.

"The night may be young but I am not!" she said gathering up her purse and her heavy shawl. She hugged me and made to leave but turned around and came back as if she had suddenly remembered something.

"Oh! By the way," she said. "Stay away from that man! He's trouble!"

She gestured to Mykhalo before leaving.

I looked back.

"Don't I know it," I muttered quietly to myself under my breath.

I took a deep drink of the last sip of coffee in my cup. When I lowered the cup, Mykhalo was sitting across from me.

"So what do you think of my musical skills?" he said, still smiling.

"Hmmph!" I snorted. "You should be on American Idol."

Mykhalo threw back his head and laughed loudly.

"Not going to happen!" he replied. "Besides, I'm not American."

We grinned across at each other, then fell into an uncomfortable silence.

"So, you do know the woman from the convention," he said as if to break the ice.

"She's one of my oldest and dearest friends," I said. Then, as an afterthought, I added, "She says I should stay away from you."

At this, the corners of his mouth turned up.

"She is a very wise woman. I knew that when I first saw her," he told me.

We lapsed into another silence. He absently stroked a few chords on his guitar. I recognized the strains as a few of the unmistakable notes from "Classical Gas".

"Careful!" I cautioned him. "You're dating yourself with that!"

He chuckled softly.

"No, I'm dating *you* with this song," he corrected easily. "*This* dates me."

And he immediately began to strum a series of notes which sounded like they belonged on a piano. I recognized the melody as one which belonged to one of the great composers of the seventeenth century.

"Isn't that Beethoven?" I said.

Mykhalo smiled quietly.

"Johann Sebastian Bach actually," he informed me, his accent becoming rather thick.

"Did you know him?" I said.

"Who do you think taught me how to play piano and harpsichord?" he replied.

"You're joking!" I laughed back.

His smile only deepened and, glancing up at me, he winked.

I could not tell if he was teasing me or whether he really meant it. And I also got the distinct feeling that was the way he wished to keep it.

I considered him quietly for a moment. I remembered the dream from the night before.

"So," I said slowly, drawing him in. "You hate Nazis, eh?"

His fingers tripped into silence on the guitar strings. He turned his head sideways and narrowed his eyes.

"Have you been sleepwalking again?" he asked.

"No, just dreaming," I said.

"Ah."

He gave a grim sigh and stood the guitar up on his lap, embracing the instrument easily with his arms. I sensed I had spoiled his urge to play.

"Yes, I hate Nazis. Always have. The Third Reich took away my people's glory and replaced it with a shame which will take centuries to erase. My beloved Bavaria is a much more diminished place than what I remember."

I nodded considering.

"What about skinheads?" I said.

"Same thing only more foolish and loud," he replied, sternly. "Why all this curiosity about World War II things?"

"A chest was delivered to me from Bill Gibson. I think it has his war souvenirs in it," I told him.

His naturally pale face seemed to drain of color. He swallowed carefully.

"Have you taken a look inside?" he said.

"Not yet. I couldn't bring myself to unlock it and I don't know why."

This seemed an obvious relief to him.

"Right after receiving the chest, I had a dream about the night you met Bill Gibson," I said to him. "You helped him retrieve the art treasures the Nazis looted from Europe."

"Yes, one of my more shining moments during the war," he said almost bashfully.

I nodded again thinking.

"So, is this how it's going to be? Everything you don't want to tell me, I dream about?"

"Perhaps. Dreams are fickle. You can't always trust them," he said.

He toyed absently with his guitar strap turning his eyes away from me.

I looked at him narrowly as long as he faced away. I wondered about his mysterious past. What must it have been like living in a country where so much cataclysmic history of the world had taken place?

Then he looked up and I immediately dropped my eyes to my now empty coffee cup.

"Have you lived in Germany all your life?" I said.

"I have traveled the world extensively but Bavaria is my home. I will always return there," he replied.

He seemed to sense this question was just a prelude to the topic I was really trying to broach.

"What about during the second World War?" I said, narrowing my focus.

"I was home," he answered.

His tone of voice altered from casual to more serious. He already seemed to sense what I was focusing on.

"So...what about Hitler? Did you actually get to meet him at any time?" I said breathlessly.

"Yes, him I did meet. Briefly though," was his terse reply.

The humor had fled from his face. It seemed the memory was not a pleasant one.

Dare I take this discussion one step further?

"And? What was your impression of him?" I persisted.

He sighed. I could see he didn't want to revisit that particular time in his life.

"There is no brief answer to that, my dear," he said, trying to evade me.

"You met Hitler!" I said, eager to learn his personal impression of the man history had dubbed so notorious. "This is important!"

He heaved another heavy sigh and frowned. But he gave in to my wishes. "I did not like his speeches or his message. I have never been one to catch the disease of prejudice. I have carefully avoided it all my life. I was shocked many of my human, mortal, countrymen were being swayed by his vicious words. I thought such a puny, little man could not have such big an impact. But as time went by, I saw… this was not the case. So I decided to meet the man to find out for myself what exactly he was made of."

He paused and looked away, lost in thought for a moment.

"Being a political figure it was, of course, expected for him to meet the common man to perpetuate his standing with the masses. It was an easy enough thing for me to arrange as I had enough powerful friends who were willing to work this out for me. Having an abnormal life span can garner you friends in high places if you learn how to work the system. I had mastered that talent long ago.

"He would make countless public appearances and shake the hands of many people. I decided to be in one of these lineups. Just one look in his eyes, one touch of his palm and I would have my answers, I was certain of it. My vampire instincts tend to give me more details on an individual at first glance than a mortal's."

Here he lapsed into silence and his gray eyes became shadowed and dark.

"And?" I prodded him back to the present.

He turned his eyes back to me. They were clear and glittered with a warning light.

"I could smell his blood before he even entered the room."

Mykhalo's voice was soft as a cat's purr.

"He was blood to be wasted," he murmured softly, as if not seeing me.

"Excuse me?" I said, not understanding.

He stirred and glancing up at me, smiled apologetically.

"We have this saying among vampires, 'He or she is blood to be wasted.' It means something is wrong with their blood and a vampire would be a fool to dine on them. Either they have some disease or are under the effects of some drug which would run havoc with our system. In any case, Adolf had both red flags that I could tell immediately. Then...when he shook hands with me..."

His voice trailed off as he searched for the correct words in English to convey precisely what he meant.

"The light in his eyes was so...intense with black ambition. He would do what he wanted, whether the world was willing or no. He was so puffed up with his own ego. He was right in his mind and woe to those who questioned his ideals. No, this puny, little despot was a very dangerous man. I was filled with dread for my country when I looked into his eyes. I immediately felt sorry for his relatives. He truly had brought shame to his family with his plans for world domination. I had no idea how prophetic my thoughts, at that time, were. I had no idea the world could be dominated by just one man. But here he was, smiling up at me and shaking my hand. He gave me chills."

Hitler had made a vampire's blood go cold with fear. I felt my own arm prickle with dread.

"Then...if you knew all this...why didn't you..."

"Stop him?" Mykhalo finished for me. "Don't think I didn't want to! Don't think I didn't try! But men in power are heavily guarded. It is not as easy as you might think to assassinate a world leader, even for a vampire. If I could have simply waved my hand to make him disappear from all time and space, believe me, I would have. I hated what he did to my country."

I was silent a moment, considering.

"Maybe..." I mused quietly. "If you could have waved your hand in such a way...you wouldn't be a vampire?"

He turned his eyes to me. For a long moment, he just held my gaze.

"Exactly," he said. "Although doing away with Hitler would have been a kinder act to the world. My desire to be human is a little selfish when compared to that."

I held his eyes but bowed my head to him.

The space between us was filled with a heavy silence. I realized he had been witness to so much horror. I had often wondered at the drastic change World War II had left on most people. How different was this change when it related to an undead surrounded by death and yet unable to die?

It was a chilling thought.

I tried to shake the ominous thoughts from my mind. But instead my mind automatically went to a threat much more relevant to my own life in the here and now.

I thought of Hector. And then I thought of my daughter.

My eyes met his. Somehow, I sensed his thoughts had grasped onto the same idea.

"Have you been keeping watch over me? Is that why I haven't seen you in so long?" I said.

"My! Now who is acting possessive?" he teased, again trying to way lay my words.

"Please, Mykhalo. I must know. Am I in any danger here?" I said.

His smile vanished and he became serious once more.

"So far, not I'm aware of," he said. "Hector knows of you but it seems he does not know where you live. That is a very good thing."

"Is he interested in harming me?" I asked nervously.

Mykhalo growled and crossed his arms across his chest, not pleased with where this discussion was headed.

"Hector is interested in harming me. Therefore, if I am interested in you, then you are in danger because he will use you to inflict pain and suffering on me. *That* is the real danger," he told me frankly.

I swallowed carefully.

"Does he know I have a daughter?" I said and a flurry of apprehension began to grow in my chest.

"As to that knowledge, I am not sure he even knows she exists and *if* that is true, it is a very good thing indeed," he told me.

I forced myself to sigh the worry out.

The man across the table from me cocked his head to the side like a confused dog.

"Why are you still so concerned about your daughter and me?"

"But I never spoke..." I stammered.

He frowned and his gray eyes glittered at me from across the table.

"You didn't need to! Your body language tells me plainly enough you are afraid of me threatening your daughter. And if I missed your body language...well, I have drunk enough of your blood to have dreams of my own," he said.

My head jerked up at this. I started to feel like my privacy had been violated but, with an effort, I pushed it down. There were other more important matters to discuss.

"I know you believe you should break off this friendship," he said to me. "And given what you are and what I am, that is a most wise decision. However! Hector has now entered the game. And when it comes to him, I am the best suited person to protect you from him. I don't want to tell you anything about him because the less you know the better for both you and your daughter. But, other than the obvious, why are you so worried about your daughter and I?"

I stared long and hard into his gray eyes.

Could I trust him? Of course not!

I decided to tell him anyway.

"Bree is undecided in her faith," I told him.

"What?" he said, not comprehending.

I gave a frustrated sigh.

"She doesn't know what religion she is! As long as she doesn't have a faith, she is vulnerable to any vampire," I told him.

"Ah! So that's what's got your Mommy senses all in an uproar!" he chuckled. "Don't worry about that one!" he laughed. "She's as safe as she can be."

"But didn't you hear me? She's…" I stammered.

"Wiccan." Mykhalo interjected. "Just like her proud Momma. She just doesn't know it yet. But she's definitely Wiccan."

"How do you know that if I don't even know?" I fumed. "And I'm her own mother?"

Mykhalo just laughed again at me.

"Just trust me on this one will you?" he assured me. "Her power is bubbling over the sides of her cup. Which is not surprising, given her age and being new to this puberty thing. Lucky you, though, she's got ten times more sense than most girls her age do. She's a cat and will always land on her feet no matter how many times you drop her."

He gave me time to digest this.

"I don't understand," I finally managed to force out.

"Neither do I. I just know it's there in her," he replied.

"If that's true," I said slowly, puzzling this out "Then what about Hector?"

Mykhalo sucked his teeth and whistled.

"Now there's the real question. I don't have the answer. Time will tell."

# CHAPTER 9

My sleep was troubled that night. It was almost as if I was afraid to dream, afraid to let go of the day. But dream I finally did. It was far from comforting.

I dreamed it was a normal morning like any other. I was bustling around the kitchen, making breakfast for Bree, trying to rouse myself to wakefulness. Bree was seated at the table working on a research paper while she finished her toast and downed her milk.

I sighed groggily and turning around to face my daughter at the table, leaned against the counter, hunched over my coffee. Bree was scribbling notes onto her notebook while drinking the last swallows of milk from her glass. Her glass emptied, she returned her full attention to the book and paper in front of her.

I was oddly fascinated by the empty milk glass. The white film still clung to the inside. For some reason my gaze was drawn in until I almost felt like I was reaching a meditative state from just staring at the glass.

The glass suddenly twitched and began to fill from the bottom to the top with deep red blood.

I watched in stunned silence as it filled itself and began to flow over onto my daughter's homework.

Bree started backwards but only for a moment. She then seemed to fall under the same spell as I, unable to tear her eyes from the glass magically overflowing with blood.

She reached out and took the glass in both hands and drained it sloppily as if she was dehydrated. She slammed the glass back down onto the table and watched impatiently, as it filled and again drained it, hungrily of its blood. Again and again, it filled and she drained it each and every time.

Suddenly she seemed to come back to herself. She turned her eyes to look at me.

I gasped in horror and dropped my coffee cup. I barely heard it shatter, barely felt the hot liquid splash my legs and bare feet, barely felt or heard any of it.

The white of Bree's eyes had turned red.

"Mom," she said in the very scared voice of a child. "What's happening to me?"

I had no idea how to answer her.

I stepped towards her, arms outstretched to gather in my daughter, my poor child with the bloodstained lips and teeth of something she shouldn't be.

There was a whooshing sound and a roar and she was suddenly jerked backwards away from me as the whole house wall disintegrated behind her and was sucked away as if from a wind tunnel. I heard her screaming for me. I screamed back in return.

There was a loud, deep feline sounding roar which laughed mockingly at us both.

I kept screaming for my daughter.

But Bree was gone.

I awoke with a jerk and sat up. I was bathed in sweat and my heart was pounding like a wild, caged bird in my chest.

It was just a dream, a dream which had left me with a feeling of impending dread.

\* \* \*

I surprised my daughter the next day by picking her up at school. Usually she just rode the bus to the street where I had my bookshop and then would ride home with me when I locked up the Belfry.

94

But I had this strange feeling of wanting to know where she was at all times after the nightmare.

"Well, this is unexpected," she said as she climbed up into the bookmobile.

Once again, she had changed her hair color. This week it was a strawberry blonde. The purple still peeped through a bit because her girlfriends hadn't done as good a job as normal.

I caught a glimpse of her books as she spilled them haphazardly onto the console between us.

"Ah! You're studying Shakespeare now eh?" I said. "Romeo and Juliet."

"Yeah. We started it this week," she muttered, fumbling in her backpack and grumbling about where her iPod had gone.

"I hated Shakespeare when I was your age. I just couldn't get it," I told her. "What do you think about it?"

She shrugged as if she didn't care.

"'S okay I guess. Like anything else they tell us to read," she replied.

"Do you *get* Romeo and Juliet?" I said.

"Oh sure! That was easy!" she said and waved it off like it was no big deal. "Boy meets girl and they both fall in love. But their families are against it. Typical! Boy and girl get tangled into situations beyond their control. Predictable. Girl is tricked into 'killing' herself. Boy doesn't get the message and *really* kills himself. Ooops! That wasn't supposed to happen. Girl wakes up and sees him dead and then *really* kills herself. Both families feel real bad about the whole situation. End of story."

I wrinkled my brows in confusion.

"How long have you been studying this?" I said.

"A week," she said. "They assigned us the book yesterday. I read it cover to cover last night."

I snickered and shook my head.

"That's my little Bookworm!" I said with maternal pride.

She grinned in return.

"There's just one thing I don't get," Bree went on. "I mean, I get Romeo and Juliet is this huge, tragic love story. I get that it is very popular and very romantic. But…well…does anyone else get the fact both Romeo and Juliet were just so messed up?"

I laughed out loud at the way she put it.

Bree frowned.

"You're making fun of me again!" she pouted.

"No, I am not!" I said, still chuckling. "I'm just so tickled at your interpretation. And as a bit of advice, maybe you better not tell Mrs. Yoe your literature teacher, quite the way you told me. She doesn't strike me as someone with any grasp of humor!"

I chuckled again and shook my head in mirth.

"Now please explain to me why you think Romeo and Juliet were 'messed up'?" I asked much more politely.

Bree frowned and rearranged herself in the van's seat.

"Well, it's just that I feel…well…to kill yourself because you lost a friend or even a lover is just so wrong!" she said.

I smiled and that would have been enough for some parents. But I kept prodding her.

"And why? Why is it so wrong?" I asked, still grinning.

"Because!" she said, bugging her eyes out at me as though the answer was as plain as the nose on her face. "It's *stupid*! Life is a gift! And to choose your own end is just a terribly callous and selfish thing to do especially if it's because someone you loved just died. I mean is that what *they* would have wanted for you? If yes, then that person is a very bad friend and you're better off without them. But that's just my two cents worth."

I looked at my daughter fiddling with her iPod and thought I had the most brilliant child on the face of this earth! I couldn't have been more proud of her.

We were stopped at a traffic light so I reached over, without warning and gathered her in and forcibly showered hugs and kisses on her head. She whined and struggled.

"Your two cents is worth a lot more to me, my brainiac little kitten," I cooed lovingly at her.

"Yuck! Ma! Leggo!" Bree wailed and tore free.

The car behind me honked its horn.

"See! You're pissing people off!" Bree complained as she straightened her ruffled locks.

"Yes, but they don't count," I said as I resumed piloting the van. "They don't have you for a daughter."

I heard Bree mumble something about hoping nobody from school witnessed the pathetic display of maternal affection. She grumbled more but I didn't hear the details.

"So is Brittany enjoying Shakespeare too?" I said, trying to change the subject a bit.

There was silence from her.

"Oh great!" she said at last with a heavy sigh. "You just *had* to bring her up!"

"What's wrong?" I asked as my mommy's teenage drama radar went off.

Bree just shook her head and rolled her eyes.

"Speaking of stupid things, Brittany is acting stupid," she grumbled. "We aren't speaking anymore."

I sighed in return.

"What happened?" I said and my voice took on a sterner tone.

"It's not me, it's her, Mom," Bree went on.

"Well, isn't she talking to the school counselor?" I said.

"No!" Bree replied petulantly. "She's supposed to, but she stopped going! She says the school shrink doesn't know what he's talking about. So she stopped going. So, I told her parents. Well, Brittany didn't quite like that idea!" Here Bree's head began to waggle in scornful imitation of her friend. "She says when I tattled on her, she got in worse trouble with her parents and that was some strange way for a 'best friend forever' to act. So she's not talking to me anymore."

"Hmm." I mumbled. "Sounds like Brittany's parents need the counseling as much as she does."

Bree nodded in the over-expressive way of adolescents and spread her arms.

"I agree but how is that going to sound coming from me?" she said. She sighed again and rubbed her face wearily. "This mess is just getting worse and worse. It's a train wreck winding up to happen and nothing I try to do makes it any better. And I can't look away and I can't stop it. Ugh! What do I do now?"

I sighed and taking my daughter's hand, gave her a reassuring squeeze.

"Just keep doing your prayer beads each and every day," was all I could tell her to make her feel better. "It's in the Goddess's hands now."

She looked at me and sneered grimly.

"Which goddess?"

# CHAPTER 10

Life went on as usual for the next few days. With an effort, I concealed my heightened sense of worry about my daughter and forced myself to let Bree ride the bus home.

She spoke no more of her friend Brittany. This bothered me greatly but I had no idea how to broach the subject. So I just let it be.

I should have known that would be exactly the wrong thing to do.

Friday afternoon was a slow day at the bookstore. I spent most of the day looking for things to do and yet not wanting to do them. The desired customers seemed nonexistent.

It was almost time for Bree to show up when I decided to take a bathroom trip just to brush my hair. I was brushing my hair in front of the mirror like I had done a million times before. As my hand swept the long tresses from back to front, my fingers entangled with the chains around my neck and brought the pendants to the outside of my shirt quite by accident. The flash of my silver pentacle caught my eye first. I stopped the brushing motion and watched its reflection as it swung back and forth in the mirror.

The key to the trunk swung with it.

I seized the key and gazed at it for a long time as it lay nestled on my palm's skin.

Was it now time to discover what secrets the old army trunk held?

I looked at the clock. It read two-thirty. Bree wouldn't come into the store for at least forty-five minutes. I had the time to kill.

I went back out into the store and flipped the open sign over and locked the door knowing my daughter had a key to get in.

I then pulled the giant, skeleton key from my pocket and made my way to the antique book room. The door swung back with a groan of complaint. I pushed it back to almost closed.

The trunk sat on the floor where the masons had left it, awaiting me. I knelt before it and ran my hands over its surface. It seemed warm and familiar to my touch.

The small trunk key slipped easily into the lock and turned with a soft clicking sound. I took a deep breath and raised the heavy lid.

Just as I had thought, the trunk was filled with old souvenirs from the Second World War.

I let out my breath in a relieved sigh.

I reached my hands inside and began to pull out objects one by one.

At first glance, there were four thin books. A quick perusal told me these were Bill's war journals. I put them aside to read later. There were five larger, long books underneath. Upon closer inspection I found these to be photo albums. They mostly had old black and white photos with the white, jagged edges of old pictures of different places his campaigns had taken him in Europe.

The last album was in color, a rare thing for the time. I flashed across a picture of his unit posing in front of a local pony trap. I recognized another golden pony hooked to the cart not unlike the one in my dream. The mountains in the background looked like Austria. There were more books underneath the albums but these were official art tomes with large photos on laminated pages of different, well known works of art. Some of these books were in German and French. All of the art novels had small pieces of paper stuffed between the pages with lots of notes scribbled on them. I realized these must be the books Bill referred to while searching for the lost works of art. I quickly checked the copyright dates at the beginning and they just ascertained my suspicions.

Under the books was a neatly folded and pressed dress uniform. Under that, his field uniform and two pistols in their respective holsters. I checked and yes, both pistols were not loaded. Beneath them was an edition of *Mein Kampf* in mint condition, a common U.S. G.I. souvenir. There were also two very ugly unloaded pistols which I recognized as being of German make.

I removed all these things and found only one other thing lying alone on the bottom of the chest.

It was something long, wrapped very carefully in a strip of cloth. I picked it up slowly. It felt from its weight to be made of metal. Slowly I unwound the package. The thought of a grenade briefly flashed through my mind but I quickly dismissed it for it was the wrong size and length. I expected it to be a bayonet end for a rifle.

I couldn't have been more wrong!

When it was finally unwound, I found I was holding a long, canvas bayonet sheath around a much smaller knife the length of my lower arm. Bright metallic color flashed from the hilt and turning it over, I gasped and almost dropped it.

The hilt was alabaster wrapped in gold plate and definitely not German made.

I slowly unsnapped the top and slid the knife out of its sheath to properly admire it.

It was a dagger with an old hilt and a newer blade. The blade seemed new and had strange letters I could not read, etched deep into its surface. The hilt was the most amazing artifact I had ever handled. It was gold and white with intricate designs encircling it from one end to the other. My immediate first thought was I should be wearing gloves to handle this like they did in a museum. On closer inspection, I discovered there was no cross guard to the hilt but it was fashioned in an ornate, lotus style cup into which the blade's tang was inserted. The pommel had a scarab of deep blue lapis lazuli set into the end. The designs between were of obvious Egyptian style.

I imagined this must be a rendition of Art Deco work which was popular around the twenties. I thought that because it seemed more probable. I mean I couldn't actually be holding a real ancient Egyptian dagger or even the hilt of one... right?

"Well! You're a pretty thing! What stories could you tell, I wonder?" I murmured reverently to the silence of the dagger I held.

It was then the emanations of the dagger struck me. I could literally sense the blade humming and vibrating in my hand with magical power. This was no ordinary weapon! A buzzing purr began to whisper in my brain. I suddenly felt something old had opened its eyes and was regarding me with strange, alien emotions.

Fear gripped my heart. Without knowing why, I quickly slammed it back into its sheath and rewound it in its cloth with shaking hands. I replaced it into the trunk and hurriedly put everything back in on top of it and slammed the lid shut.

The unwelcome buzzing in my head began to subside a little. I could breathe once more.

I sighed in relief and slumped wearily over the lid.

What was I scared of?

I took another deep breath.

What had touched me?

# CHAPTER 11

The hand which had actually touched the hilt of the dagger felt strange the rest of that day, almost like it was numb. I scratched it, spread lotion on it, and slapped it against my thigh to stop the buzzing, all to no avail.

I had touched something ancient and it had touched me. I knew this with my heart not my brain. I was not prepared for this dagger. It was more than I could handle right now, I knew that deep in my gut. And yet I could not shake its effect on me.

What was worse, I knew some strange presence about it was now aware of me and I was terrified. I knew nothing about this weapon and what's more, I was afraid to show it to anyone who could tell me for fear of them falling under the same spell as myself.

Why had Bill left such a thing to me? Was he immune to its effects? Was it just because as Mykhalo had said, my third eye was open that I noticed such things? And what on earth did he expect me to do with it? I obviously couldn't hang it on my wall like a war trophy. This could well prove disastrous!

The dagger nagged and preoccupied me all evening. I began to dread the night. I was sure I would have some horrible dream about it.

Before Bree went to bed, I asked if I could borrow her prayer beads. She seemed surprised at the request, but then, why wouldn't she? Doing a rosary was her spiritual ritual, not mine. But she shrugged and said sure. She asked no more but her green eyes spoke volumes of questions.

I offered her no explanation as of yet but made sure to thank her.

I did my normal preparing for bed chores and then slipped under the comforting blankets, holding the rosary in one hand. I turned out the light and lying there in the dark, took a deep cleansing breath and began.

"Goddess, banish all negative thoughts from my sleep," I said slowly and quietly began to repeat this over and over into the darkness.

The smooth, round beads slipped reassuringly through my fingers one at a time.

Sleep finally took my prayerful form.

I did not get my wish. I did dream and it was far from normal.

When next I opened my eyes, I was no longer in my bed but sitting on a man's shoulder like the dream before. This man was dressed strangely, in a long, velvet blue jacket with ruffles of a white undershirt sticking out of his collar and sleeves. There were bright, brass buttons lining the front of his jacket and his long blonde hair was tied back in a ponytail with a black ribbon tied in a bow. Almost as an afterthought I noticed the man upon whose shoulder I was perched was swaying slightly. I realized we were sitting in a horse drawn carriage and it was swaying as it traveled along the road.

With a sudden shock I realized the shoulder I was sitting on was Mykhalo's!

So this was his world and his time. I immediately began to take everything in, the ornately brocaded gold fabric lining the inside of the coach, the pattern of the clothes on the white curtains hanging on the window obscuring the landscape outside, the person sitting across from him in the coach.

This person gave me a sudden pause. He commanded one's gaze and respect. He was dressed similarly but in deep purple velvet and a few more ruffles at the throat. He clutched a crystal-topped, expertly carved cane. He had a stern face which was decidedly not handsome. His double chin seemed to blend in with his ruffles, his head was balding and not in an attractive way, he was getting thick around the middle with age, straining his bright buttons and his eyes were gray and completely without sympathy.

The eyes looked familiar somehow.

Just then, like before, I began to sense details that Mykhalo, I'm sure, already knew. I knew it was the year 1708 and Mykhalo was forty years old. I knew this person sitting across from him was Baron Garibold Von Ludwig, Mykhalo's father. I knew he was ruthless to his staff and many people hated him. I knew Mykhalo was always trying hard to please him and Garibold was always disappointed in his son no matter what he did. And I knew pleasing his father was very important because Mykhalo was the eldest son of seven children. Much was riding on his shoulders.

I also knew or sensed the senior Ludwig doubted his estate would be better off with Mykhalo running things so every situation was now a test of his fitness – a test he was usually doomed to fail.

This was just another test.

"Do you know what it is I do for the Holy Church, my son?" Garibold asked.

Some dim sense told me they were speaking German to each other and because I was keyed into Mykhalo's mind, I could understand the language.

I felt Mykhalo trying hard not to show any emotion.

"I know the church officials call you the 'guard dog of Holy Rome'," he responded as dispassionately as possible.

The only response to this was a sneer of scorn.

"And why do you suppose that is?" he demanded.

I felt a slight intake of Mykhalo's breath.

"I'm sure that I do not know sir," he said as honestly as possible.

The Baron snorted like a giant, bloated pig.

"Forty years and you do not know your father's job! Oh, you'll make a fine leader when you take over!"

He guffawed derisively.

I felt the barb prick Mykhalo's heart. I also felt him toss it onto the pile of other barbs this man had thrown his way through the years. The pile was mountainous.

My heart ached for this young, handsome man who had been swallowed up by time.

"They call me the guard dog of Rome because that is what I do, protect the faith from any religious threats," he told Mykhalo and then he leaned closer as if to impart his son with secret information. "Not just human threats."

Mykhalo's eyes narrowed, his interest now truly piqued.

"What threats are there, other than human? I don't understand."

"Things such as the damned, threats you dare not speak of after dark. Vampires, werewolves, demons and witches," he told him.

Mykhalo's mouth twitched upwards against his will.

"Father I do not believe in such things. And I am shocked that an intelligent, educated man as yourself would," he replied.

I felt he knew he was taking a risk speaking to his father in such a way but he also deemed it was a necessary risk.

Garibold just sat back on his cushioned seat and regarded his son with a wry smile.

"You can speak in such a way because I have done my job well. Someday soon I hope all people can say that such creatures are fantasies and the subjects of an over active imagination or stories you tell to frighten young children."

He nodded in satisfaction.

"No matter what you believe now. You will change your mind soon," Garibold told him.

Mykhalo was really confused.

"And how are you going to change my mind on this matter, sir?" he said.

Baron Garibold Von Ludwig just smiled ominously at his son.

"Because you are going to take over for me," he told him. "I cannot do this forever. Already time is catching up to me. You are the most physically fit and bright of my sons and, since your marriage to Esmeralda has, for many years, proved fruitless, we must, of course, find another purpose for you."

If it had been possible for me, I would have fallen off of Mykhalo's shoulder in shock. He had been *married?* But then I stopped myself. Of course he must have been married! He was of noble blood. If he had shown no interest in any lady, then one of appropriate breeding and station would have been provided for him. What he felt about it would make no difference. It was just the way things were done in those days.

When the name, Esmeralda, was mentioned to him, I felt no pang of any sort of emotion from Mykhalo's heart. It was plain to me from his reaction that the union was not to his liking.

Mykhalo doubted everything his father had just said. He still didn't believe such creatures were real, in fact he believed his father had fallen off his rocker! But he wasn't about to invite more verbal abuse by telling him so. With an effort he tried to conceal it from showing on his face.

From Garibold's next words, he must have failed.

"I see your doubt. That is of no consequence to me. You will do this willing or no. But you will need the proper training and tools."

"So is that where we are headed now? To school me in this?" he inquired as politely as he could.

"No," Garibold said. "I have commissioned a local witch to create a magical weapon which will kill any damned creature no matter what. We are going to pick it up."

Mykhalo's eyes narrowed even more.

"But I thought you just said that witches were enemies of the church," he said slowly, hoping not to incur his father's wrath.

"They are!" Garibold insisted. "But they have their uses. And be assured God's damnation will still find them sooner rather than later. But it is silly not to take advantage of such talents before their final, spiritual purification."

Mykhalo was still confused.

I was not! I wanted nothing more than to be out of the dream by this point! This Garibold man was not to be trusted or even dealt with in my mind.

But the dream continued to sweep me along helplessly in its undertow.

Mykhalo cast a look out of the curtained window behind him. I saw as he did so, a few large wagons and armed, mounted soldiers

107

accompanying them along their way on the rough dirt track they called a road.

"What are the wagons and soldiers for then?" he asked his father.

The Baron smiled. I found it to be a cruel smile of one who anticipates bad things with an unholy relish.

"Payment," he told him. "You will soon understand everything my son. It is time you started following in my footsteps."

I picked up the definite feeling from Mykhalo he wanted to do nothing of the sort. But there was also the accompanying jaded emotion the argument had happened long ago and was not worth rehashing. Mykhalo had learned to just nod and go along with whatever his father said.

And he prayed his father would come to a quick end so he could be free of his constant judgment and ridicule.

The carriage followed a sharp turn in the road and came to an abrupt halt. A dog barked outside and the sound of chickens came to their ears.

The elder Ludwig stepped out of the carriage and Mykhalo dutifully followed his father without a word.

They were standing in front of a modest cottage and barn. Chickens scratched in the yard and roosters announced their arrival. The house's dog bristled and came up to them, growling threateningly. The Baron waved his crystal-handled cane and the dog cowered and slunk away baying at them.

There were crates and wooden boxes arranged haphazardly around the yard. Mykhalo noticed most of the boxes were crammed with old books and dusty scrolls. It looked as if the occupants were making ready to move somewhere else.

"Agnes!" Garibold bellowed to the house. "I've come for my commission!"

From somewhere inside, a door slammed.

"I heard ya! I'm coming!" barked a female voice in reply.

A middle-aged woman appeared on the porch of the house. She was thick but not overly so, in her shape. Red curls tumbled about her shoulders and hung in front of her eyes and her white face was peppered with freckles. She was dressed in a simple, countrywoman's attire: white blouse, dark green skirt and a very smudged and dirty apron. And she was barefoot.

She sauntered out to meet them, wiping the blood from a newly beheaded chicken from her hands on her apron.

"Ye got the payment?" she demanded tartly.

"You have the dagger?" Garibold countered.

They glared at each other for a long moment. Mykhalo had the distinct feeling she liked his father no more than Garibold liked her kind.

"Come and see," she said, beckoning to them. "Husband's putting the final touches on it right now."

She walked away from them and it was then I noticed two things about the curious woman. She walked with a decided, hip-rolling limp and she was so tiny the top curls of her head barely reached Mykhalo's chest.

She led them to the barn, which seemed to be more of a workman's shop than an actual building for housing livestock. There were iron implements and newly forged iron tools scattered about outside. The crooked wooden door screeched as she opened it and went inside.

"Seb!" she shouted. "They's here for it!"

"I know. I heard their horses," an answering voice replied.

She led them around the dusty, cobwebbed corner of a stall to a where her husband sat at a table lit by a lantern and strewn with engraving tools. He was a bent, thin man with a smudgy face, a bushy mustache, and three-day's growth of beard. A pair of tiny spectacles perched on the very end of his thin nose.

He was polishing the handle of the dagger I had just touched earlier in the day for the first time.

In my dream, my hand burned and itched.

The gold inlay flashed brightly against the white alabaster. The steel of the blade shone in bright contrast to the colorful hilt.

Sebastian, the master engraver, handed the dagger over to the Baron for his inspection.

109

"I had the hilt in a trunk of old cast offs. It looked bad when I started but cleaned up pretty. I just fitted a new blade to it," he told the nobleman.

Garibold grunted as he turned the knife over in his big hands.

"What's this engraving say?" he asked.

"Writing I had from one of my old, Italian scrolls. It's Coptic, I believe," the woman informed him. "Since the hilt's Egyptian, words had ta be Coptic not Latin, begging your lordship's pardon."

Garibold turned to her and frowned.

"You put words you can't even read onto the blade?" he asked in an irritated voice.

The witch scowled back at him.

"I kin read better than whats I talk!" she spat back. "Me gots the gist of it well enuf, Sir! It says something about withering all evil it touches. Stuff gets lost in translation but that came through loud 'n clear. Besides, it were the words it wanted on its metal. Make no mistake. Them words and the spell I slapped on it oughtta sizzle any damned thing it touches, be it werewolf, ghoul, vampire, or even demon from Hell itself. Trust Agnes! She know how to be-spell things!"

Garibold grunted.

"Me husband *is* a master engraver. This is the way things hasta be done. I don't tell ya how ta run your holdings and you don't tell me how to do me magic or me husband how ta engrave," Agnes added.

"Awfully gaudy looking, don't you think?" he put in doubtfully.

The look on the witch's face told Mykhalo she thought the Baron was awfully gaudy looking as well.

I snickered in complete sympathy.

Now it was the master engraver's turn to scowl.

"That were the hilt it wanted, Sir," he retorted with some heat. "I don't tell the energy what it's to look like."

Mykhalo intervened by touching his father on the shoulder.

"Why don't you look at it in the sunlight, father? It's so dark in here..." he suggested.

Garibold nodded with another grunt.

Mykhalo exchanged glances with the master engraver and his witch wife. Seb shrugged and turned away. Agnes just stared at Mykhalo for a long moment as if she had just seen him for the first time and finally graced him with a broad smile, revealing three gray teeth and two gaps missing teeth. She nodded at him in approval.

"Your boy's smart! You should listen to him more," she said poking the lord in his side.

Mykhalo's face blanched white at this indiscretion. But his sire, with a scowl, chose to overlook it.

So all four of them trooped out to the patch of sunlight before the master's carriage. Once there, Baron Ludwig scrutinized the blade again as the sun's light flashed and sparkled along every inch of the magical dagger.

The farm dog quietly slunk into the background again.

"Is good enough, Sir?" Seb said in trepidation.

"Yes, very good. I am pleased," Garibold finally said to everyone's surprise.

Had the dagger's spell started to work on him?

"Good!" said Agnes smiling again. "Now about the payment, Sir…"

"Yes, what about it?" Garibold said impassively as he shoved the dagger into the sheath provided for it.

"Well, Sir," stammered Seb trying to be very polite. "You promised to pay us in gold and move us someplace where the witch hunters will never bother my wife and me."

"Did I?" Garibold replied, very quietly and a tone of malicious enjoyment began to slide into his voice.

I hung my head, suspecting what was to come. 'Can we stop the movie now before it gets ugly?' I wanted to say, but I knew no one would listen. I had a sick feeling in the pit of my stomach.

"I don't remember making any such promise," the Baron said quietly. "However I do remember promising the Holy Father in Rome to purify any witch I came across."

Seb's face quickly drained of all color. Agnes had begun to back away at the beginning of this exchange. Her face was hard, her blue eyes wide. She looked like a cornered cat.

"Agnes! Get out of here! Run!" Seb suddenly shouted to her and he lunged at the Baron.

Their dog began to bark wildly.

Agnes didn't wait to be told twice. She turned and ran like a scared jackrabbit. Her stride showed no sign of its previous limp.

Mykhalo had been standing a little behind his father. When Seb lunged, he stepped back and I felt a wild hope spring to the surface this might actually be his chance to get free from his father.

Garibold swore an oath as he felt Seb's wiry arms wrap around his fat frame and pin his arms helplessly to his sides.

The Baron then shouted for his soldiers.

In spite of his large size, the Baron proved to be quite flexible. Quick as a cat, he twisted in Seb's grasp and managed to get one arm free. He switched his cane to his free hand and began to club Seb with it.

The dog growled and lunged at the two, ignoring Mykhalo.

Now Seb was an engraver, he was no fighter. Bad though the angle was for attack, the onslaught of Garibold's cane was too much for him and he crumpled. This only gave Garibold the opportunity to do his worst on the man hunched at his feet. His large arm rose and fell on the master engraver, raining heavy blow after blow on the man huddled in a ball in the dirt.

There was the loud report of a nearby musket and the dog fell, thrashing and whining piteously into the dust. Chickens scattered, complaining loudly.

Garibold's arm paused its beating when his soldiers came near. He pointed with his bloodied cane to the surrounding forest.

"Get the witch! She ran into the woods! Shoot her!" he barked.

They fled from their master's wrath, one struggling to reload his musket as he ran.

The Baron raised his arm for more blows but paused.

The master engraver curled in a heap on the ground, had started to laugh.

He spat out a great mouthful of blood and began to speak.

"I curse you Baron Garibold Von Ludwig!" he was saying. "As you beat me with your cane, so shall I beat you with my words. I curse you and all the Ludwigs! All your sons will die horrible deaths, as will your daughters. Only one of your seed will live. His soul will be splintered. His life will be torment and longer than any life has a right to be. He will hold all your deaths in his own bloody hands. Hunger will be his only master and god. Blood will be the only legacy you have sired. I curse you! I curse you! I curse you!"

There was an explosion and a large cloud of gunpowder filled the air. A soldier had come up to his lord and silenced the engraver's mad ravings.

Mykhalo was chilled by the poor man's words. With an effort, he pushed it aside and took a musket from another soldier, declaring to his father he would join in the hunt for the witch. He just wanted to get away from the area before his father realized he had been slow to assist him, too slow.

Watching the scene, helpless as I was on his shoulder, I felt sick to my stomach.

He bolted for the woods. Once inside the sheltering trees, he paused and took a brief look back. His father was ordering the rest of his men to pack up the couple's possessions into the noble's wagons. The engraver's body was being carried into the house. Several more soldiers were preparing to torch the building.

Mykhalo didn't wait to see more. He fled deeper into the woods. His only thought was to find the witch and ferret her away to safety. It wasn't because he had any feelings for her, he didn't. He just wanted to save her from his father's righteous venom. He had already seen enough blood this day he didn't agree with and had been helpless to prevent. He didn't want to see anymore. He didn't want to think about what had just happened.

He didn't want to remember the man's curse.

He could hear his father's men crashing around in the brush ahead of him, shouting every now and then to one another. He hoped Agnes could hear them too. He hoped she knew these woods well enough to stay hidden from them.

But suddenly there was the report of three guns. His blood turned to ice. Hope died then in his heart.

He marched slowly towards the area he had heard the guns. The acrid smoke from their black powder muskets drifted back to his nose. Presently he saw their uniforms materialize out of the mist and greenery in front of him. They were laughing and joking as if they had just shot a prized buck.

"We got her!" one told him jubilantly. "The witch has been sent to Hell."

Mykhalo pasted on his impassionate look, the one he had learned so well from his father and replied. "I'll just go and check to make sure she's dead. You know what terrible shots you are."

They shrugged, laughing as if it was nothing.

They faded into the vegetation behind him.

Mykhalo marched onward grimly determined.

Soon after, he found her body. She was splayed out on the forest floor; blood smeared over her face and down her front so thick it was difficult to figure out where the killing shot was.

Mykhalo sank to his knees in front of her. He cupped his head in his hands and prayed in desperation. He wished fervently this day had never happened, it was all just a bad dream. Well, for me it *was* just a bad dream; for him it was a reality. So much of his past, I now understood.

Mykhalo was jerked abruptly back to his senses by a hand suddenly grabbing his arm. He looked over and rocked back on his heels in shock.

The witch was alive although she certainly wasn't well.

"No, I'm not dead yet, pretty one," she was saying to him. "I soon will be. But I can't die until I say something. Until I puts to rights what is wrong."

She motioned for patience while she caught her breath. Her blood-spattered bosom heaved as she struggled to force her lungs to work.

"I seen what happened back there," she told him, jerking her thumb back the way they had come. "I seen your da beat my man and I seen my man curse your family and I seen them kill my man. Bad day to be you, eh?"

She ginned wryly and then coughed and gasped. She took three deep, rasping breaths before she went on.

"I also looked in your eyes and then into your heart before all hell broke loose. Youse got a good heart. Like your pretty mother. Youse good person. Too good to be saddled with so evil a curse. I can't take it off of you; I've no time left for that. But I kin alter it somewhat. Give me your hand, lordling. I *try* to fix this."

He was too stunned to do anything but obey her. He cupped her small, dirty hands in his strong ones. Her hand shuddered. He could feel the life starting to leave her.

"You will die someday. And your death will not be sad but a joyful wedding for the splintered halves of your soul. You will find peace. Look for two witches. They are the beginning and the end. Your catalyst. Watch for the two witches. Guard that dagger!"

She opened her mouth as if to say more. But her last breath rushed out and with it, her spirit. He found himself holding the hand of a new corpse.

He sighed. The sigh nearly turned into a sob. He bowed his head and made some pathetic attempt to say last rights over her.

I suddenly was being pulled away as the picture disappeared into the mist of my dream.

The next thing I saw were both my hands holding the dagger I had found in the bottom of Bill Gibson's chest, the dagger that had started its journey in so horrible a fashion. I felt the presence which accompanied it but it no longer seemed threatening. It still felt incredibly ancient.

I felt rather than heard words coming from it and understood the emanations.

'I am your guardian servant. Fear me not.'

* * *

The hunger had been growing inside Mykhalo for several nights. He knew what he should have done. He should have left Sleepy Pines for a larger town like Harrisburg or even York. But his fascination with Zan had distracted him from his normal routine and now he cursed the situation he found himself trapped in.

He had to feed.

He could avoid it no longer. He did not have time to travel to Harrisburg. The hunger he was enslaved to had come upon him too suddenly. He knew before the sun dawned he would have to find someone in Sleepy Pines to kill.

He cursed himself. This had happened before. He knew the consequences. He thought he had learned from his past mistakes. How was it possible he allowed himself to get into the same position again? Small country towns were not good places for a vampire. One person dying under mysterious circumstances would attract a lot of attention, more than in a big city. If Mykhalo was in a big city, he would have days to target a victim who would be easily overlooked; a twisted husband who beat his wife too much, an alcoholic, a person prone to violent tendencies who would probably kill several innocent people on a whim. If he was really desperate, he might even go for an addict although the blood from such a person was distasteful and he would have to hide for several nights until the contact high wore off.

But he no longer had the luxury of time. He had to find someone soon. Already he could feel the blood rage building within him. It took all his strength to fight it back, to not kill the first person he met.

Bartal could have helped him, of course. But he did not want him involved in this.

Better for him to know nothing whatsoever of what was to come. He did not want his friend to be responsible for cleaning up his mess.

116

Mykhalo took himself to the far side of town the minute he awoke for the night. He wanted to be as far away from Zan and her daughter as possible. He wandered aimlessly. His feet took him to a small copse of trees between two dormant cornfields. He was out in the middle of nowhere.

He shrank up against the nearest tree feeling weak and shaky. He needed blood desperately. He doubled over in his battle within himself. He always felt sick when he denied himself blood, sick and eerily human in all the wrong ways.

Maybe, he told himself, just maybe if he could fight it off all night, he would call Bartal to come and help him. He knew if he made it to dawn without harming anyone, he would be too weak to get himself back to the safety of darkness. If he could just fight off his demon side that long, there might be hope.

The winter night air was very cold. It started to snow.

And then he heard the footsteps coming towards him.

The bloodlust within him soared. He tried to fight it but the craving tossed him aside as if he was a dead leaf.

He stood up and looked in the direction of the footsteps. Dimly, Mykhalo hoped it was a deer or some other forest creature.

But the hunger laughed at him. All his normal senses sharpened. It was a human who approached him. He could smell the blood pumping in their veins and practically hear the heart valves opening and closing.

His mouth watered and his teeth grew. His hunting senses took over.

The faint scent of perfume came to his nostrils. A woman then. His senses reached further. He could almost hear her thoughts.

Her emotions were in turmoil. Nothing was working out. Despair had overtaken her. He could smell her salty tears raining down her face. She was young and did not know how to cope with all her problems. She was walking blindly through the dark woods, not paying attention to where she was going or even caring where she ended up.

Mykhalo crept closer, stalking her like a hunting cat.

117

She had left in a hurry. Her hair was disheveled. She had only grabbed a light hoodie, not enough of a coat to warm her against the chill night air. But she didn't care about that. She didn't care about anything anymore. Life was pain.

She wanted to die.

Mykhalo was mere steps behind her. He drank in the essence of her scent and all it carried one more time. He stopped following her.

Just once his inner voice screamed at his demon. He couldn't do this. She was just a child, an adolescent. If he killed her, there would be a huge public outcry. Everyone would notice a missing teenager. He had to choose someone else.

But his demon hunger was beyond caring about the wisdom of his choices in dining.

His hunger spoke.

"If you truly want to die…"

The girl jumped with a fearful squawk and spun about.

Their eyes locked his ice white to her frightened blue. Eyes meeting eyes was all he needed to ensnare her.

"Then come here," he told her.

It was a command not a request. He held out his hand to her.

Her eyes never left his face. She was mesmerized at his glance. Free will left her and she did as he bid.

She placed her small warm hand in his cold grasp and allowed him to pull her close. She removed her hood to reveal her neck to him. Mykhalo's eyes drank in the sight of her. She was a beautiful child on the verge of womanhood, play acting at being an adult with no idea of what it truly entailed. Such a pretty little thing she was, all milk and honey, innocence and fascination. His thumb stroked her neck marveling at the smoothness of her warm skin. She tilted her head to the side surrendering her flesh to him. Her neck was before him, pulsing with life giving blood. He watched the skin as it stretched tight over the veins of her jugular. Just once more his inner voice screamed to let her go and run away.

And then he buried his fangs to the hilt in her throat.

The spell upon her was broken. He felt her scream through his teeth. She began to flail at him with her fists. He only squeezed her closer to him, crushing her in his deadly embrace. It was always the same with his victims especially the suicidal ones. They *thought* they wanted death. And then the intensity of the pain it brought caught them off guard and they fought in panicked desperation. Only then did they realize they never really wanted death to begin with.

But by then it was already too late.

Her blood flooded into his mouth and down his throat and he drank hungrily. It was delicious, fresh, young and pure. She kicked and scratched him but he did not feel it. He continued to drink until her feeble attempts to fight him off became weaker and weaker. It took only a few scant minutes before she at last went limp in his arms.

He tore his mouth away and flung himself away from her. On his back on the forest floor, he scrambled up against the nearest tree. He gasped as the world spun about him so fast it made him dizzy.

But this time there was no piano to save him.

He closed his eyes against the rush of emotions and feelings. He felt all powerful and hated it. The cost had been too high.

Things finally slowed and he was able to process the world around him. A thought occurred to him.

Maybe he hadn't killed her.

He bolted to her side. The snow had gotten heavier while he had recovered and blanketed the ground about them. He quickly checked her vitals, hoping against hope.

But he was wrong. He had completely drained her. Her open eyes were going misty and the snow was not melting from her exposed skin.

Mykhalo crumpled in grief. It had happened again. What number was it this time? He had lost track. The demon hunger had left him but so had the young girl's life. And it was all his fault.

He stroked her hair gently. He wondered about her family, her parents, did she have brothers and sisters?

Two great bloody tears ran down his face. There was no possible way he could apologize for this, none at all. He hated himself.

Mykhalo sighed and then took three deep breaths. He had to disguise the killing somehow. Sleepy Pines was too small a town to have to deal with the slander of vampire killings. What he did next disgusted him. But it had to be done.

He ripped her throat out. He had done the same thing to Bill Gibson at his death.

Better the inhabitants of Sleepy Pines think there was a mad dog on the loose than a vampire in their midst.

Mykhalo then washed the blood off his face and hands in the new fallen snow. He looked at the dead girl's body and bending low, kissed her once on the forehead.

"I'm so sorry," he told her. "You deserved better than this. Please forgive me somehow. I'm sure your parents won't."

He stroked her hair and with a sigh, rose to his feet.

He looked up at the falling snow. The flakes were getting bigger and the snow was falling faster. In an hour all signs of the attack would be obliterated by the snowfall.

As Mykhalo strode away he pulled out his cell phone. He needed to make two calls, one to Bartal and the other to the local police. He wasn't about to let his victim lie there for months while everyone searched and worried and waited.

He heard Bartal pick up on the other end. Speaking in German he gave his code phrase for when this kind of thing happened.

"I've been to Hell again."

## CHAPTER 12

I was very preoccupied at work the next day. Luckily, the day was pretty busy so I could keep my mind focused on my job.

Then two o' clock rolled around and the clients just stopped walking in the door. I sighed in relief. Finally! I had a spare moment to myself to decompress a bit.

I brewed a cup of tea, curled myself up in the recliner and stared out the window at the freezing rain while I sipped my brew. Quite unbidden, a Bible verse popped into my head. Exodus 22:18 "Thou shalt not suffer a witch to live."

I frowned and shook my head. How could King James have made such a historical blunder! But then I corrected myself in the very next thought. King James had a political agenda he had worked into his translation of the bible. He wanted all witches exterminated from his kingdom and through an incorrect translation of one word, he had shaped the future lives of many people for centuries to come. All because of one word his crew of approved priestly scholars got wrong, the Hebrew "chaspah" which they translated erroneously to mean "witch".

Of course it had been a very easy mistake to make. Aramaic was closest to the original lingo which had been spoken by Jesus and his disciples, is an obscure tongue which is rarely known or read in most Christian circles. This coupled with the fact the words of the original bible went from Aramaic to Hebrew to Greek to Latin and finally to English. I guess chances were something was bound to be 'lost in translation'.

But "chaspah" meant murderer not witch.

I shook my head and sighed in sympathy. Because of that, many people who weren't witches were accused and killed. At the time, the definition was pretty vague. A witch could have been the midwife down the street, the local herbalist trying to help cure people with potions which either did or did not work, or the old lady you didn't like. But the neighbors coveted her property, so they screamed "Witch!" got their pitchforks and torches, and then they had her land. Maybe there was a trial, maybe not.

The hatred against witches started in Germany. The publication of the "Malleus Maleficarum" or the "Witches Hammer" on Gutenberg's new printing press started the hysteria and then it spread to England and the New World. The "Burning Times" had come and no one was safe from accusation.

*"So, do witches really have sex with the devil?"* Mykhalo had asked me.

*"You were probably there,"* I had said.

*"Actually yes, I was. That's why I asked."*

I sighed and frowned again. Had we come very far from then to now? It was true it was no longer legal to burn witches at the stake. But people still tormented known Wiccans mercilessly. They were accused of Satanism, which was absurd, and animal sacrifice and sexual deviancy and more horrible things which never had any place in our religion. Wiccans still felt ostracized and excluded because of it. To some, the torment was too great and they chose to end it. Tempest Smith was an adolescent Wiccan who chose to live her faith openly and as a result was bullied until she committed suicide. I gave Bree the middle name of Tempest in her honor.

So much pain and suffering because of people who refused to see the truth in our faith. We are first and foremost people who choose to worship differently. No more.

I found myself thinking of the dagger and poor Agnes and her husband. I found myself thankful I lived in the modern day and there were no more legally sanctioned witch hunters! I also felt so thankful I did not live my faith openly. Too often witches who did made themselves targets for those who refused to believe in the goodness of their faith. I found myself musing the gossip which was so rampant and taken as fact far back in medieval Europe was still alive and well in the here and now on a completely different continent. No matter how many times we tried to educate people on who we are as a people, fear and suspicion still won out. I suppose people needed a master of all the things which go bump in the night, when really they should be looking within their own closets and bedrooms.

I percolated on such ideas every time I had a free minute. I suddenly realized how scattered and jumbled my energy was and it would do no one any good especially myself.

Then, for no particular reason, I thought of my daughter. I shuddered without knowing why. There certainly was no chill in the air for me to react to. But I felt chilled to the bone.

I looked at the clock. Two-thirty on the nose.

The door to the bookshop abruptly sprang open and with a rude clanging of the bells, Bree burst in. Her face was flushed and streaked with tears and her eyes were puffy and red.

"Bree! What on earth...." I said in surprise.

"She's dead, Mom! Brittany's dead!" she burst out and rushed into my arms.

Trisha, my coworker, followed her and tried to fill me in.

"They called an assembly at school but pulled my Chrissie and Bree out and sent them to the principal's office to tell them," she said as I clung to my sobbing daughter.

A million questions suddenly flooded my mind.

"The police questioned them and then called me," she continued. "Since I was just down the street, I volunteered to drop off Bree on my way home. The whole school is in a tizzy about it."

"Why didn't you call me?" I demanded.

"Because I had two bawling girls on my hands, that's why!" she said. "It was a little hard to get in a word edgewise, so I just stopped by here on the way home."

"How?" I said. "How did she do it?"

Bree just shook her head and tried to catch her breath.

"I don't know!" she said. "No one would tell me anything other than the cops. They found her…b-b-body. Ma! She's a body now! She's gone!"

I didn't know what to say so I just gathered her into my arms and held her tight.

"Why, Ma? Why did she do such a stupid, stupid thing? Why didn't she talk to me? I tried to help her! It's not right!"

Bree could only wail her indignation to the world.

I let her wail. What else could I have done? My mind was spinning. I felt like I had done something wrong. We all had seen the signs. We all had tried to help her. We should have tried harder. Bree was so correct. It just wasn't right.

Trisha excused herself and left to take care of her own distraught daughter.

Bree finally detangled herself from me and crawled sobbing into the recliner. I closed up the shop early and locked the door. I gave her a box of tissues and wound her up in the afghan blanket Sage had crocheted for us years ago. I asked what she wanted me to do to make her feel better. She just wanted to be held and comforted. I crawled into the chair with her and curled my body around my daughter and just let her sob her heart out. I have no idea how long it was, but it was dark outside by the time we came back to the present. It matched the way we felt inside.

I asked Bree if she would feel better with some chamomile tea. She sniffed, hiccupped, and nodded, but then said she would prefer peppermint. I kissed her on the top of her head and went into the back kitchen to brew it.

While there, I flipped open my cell phone and made a call to Matt Yoder at the police department.

"Hello, Matt?" I said when I heard his voice pick up.

"Oh," said the very flat sounding voice. "It's you. I expected you to call. I guess you heard the news. How is Bree taking it?"

I lowered my voice even more and turned to face the door in case she popped around the corner.

"Not well," I said.

"Yeah, well that's to be expected," he said with a heavy sigh. "It wasn't the nicest way for me to end my shift either. Some days I hate my job!"

I frowned, understanding Matt was a close friend of the Keims, Brittany's family. I choked back the tears and tried to get a business-like hold on my emotions.

"I was wondering how it happened?" I said in a very quiet voice as I monitored the teapot.

"Wow! You don't waste any time getting to the meat of it do you?" he said.

"Matt, please. I have to know," I prodded. "It seems no one's talking."

He gave another heavy sigh.

"Now, Suz. You know I'm not at liberty to discuss the details while it's still under investigation!"

He sounded indignant.

I snorted in return and stomped a foot like an impatient horse.

"And you know that I'm not a reporter! I keep my secrets! Even Bill Gibson knew that," I said.

There was a grumble from the other end.

"Look. I'll make it easy on you," I suggested. "I'll mention a way people normally commit suicide and you just say yes or no. Or you could just hang up on me right now."

More perturbed grumbling from the other end of the line.

"Did she hang herself?" I said with a deep swallow.

"No."

"Was there a gun involved?" I went on soberly. Knowing Brittany it was highly unlikely since she was afraid of guns.

"No."

"Drugs?" I ticked off. I sincerely doubted this one but maybe she had hidden something from the adults.

"No."

"Gassed herself in a car?" I suggested.

"She doesn't have a driver's license!" he said.

"Hmph! Never stopped me!" I said. "Drowned herself in the quarry?"

"It's a bit cold, Suz!" he growled.

"Jumped off a building or a rock ledge?"

"*NO*! Okay look! I'll give you a hint which will probably shut you up for good!" he snarled back in frustration. "We still haven't caught that wolf dog, or St. Bernard thing yet. Satisfied?"

I nearly dropped the phone.

"Susan? Are you there?" he said.

"Yes, I am," I replied numbly. "I'm satisfied. I'm sorry to have bothered you. Please give my heartfelt sympathy to the family if you see them tonight."

I ended the call without waiting for his answer.

I hung my head and struggled to choke back the tears. My grief was quickly morphing into anger. I could feel a type of rage swelling up from deep within me I have never felt before. All I could do was focus on one thought.

Mykhalo had killed Brittany, my daughter's best friend.

Half of me argued with myself.

Why was I so shocked? I knew what he was, what he was capable of. That's why my conscience kept telling me to stay away from him. Why had I refused to listen? What was this hold he had over me? He wasn't my pet vampire! He never should have been my friend to begin with. He was an undead creature and a predator. Why didn't I expect this to happen? Why didn't I see this coming? He had killed Bill. Now he had killed a teenaged girl. What excuse could he possibly have for this?

My thoughts raced. I had to do something. I *could* do something this time. I had the dagger. Another thought stopped me.

Not in front of Bree. She had to go somewhere safe first.

Sage, I thought.

I quickly dialed her number and breathed a sigh of relief when I actually got her on the other line and not her answering machine. I asked her to come over immediately and told her it was an emergency.

She was at the bookstore in minutes.

126

I unlocked the main door and let her in.

"Zan, is this about Brit...?" she began.

I stopped her with a quick motion.

"Yes, it is." I whispered. "I need you to take Bree and do your warm, fuzzy thing, magic on her. There's something I need to take care of."

Sage gave me a withering look.

"Your place is with your daughter right now!" she hissed in a scolding tone. "She needs you!"

"This *is* about my daughter!" I insisted. "This is about me protecting her from any more grief. I can't explain it any more than that right now. Just please take her and keep her safe. I'll do what I should have done a long time ago."

Sage gave me a penetrating look.

"I don't understand any of this," she said. "I'll do what you ask, but your reason had better be a damned good one."

"It's the most honorable one a mother can have for her daughter," I told her resolutely.

I let Sage go and roused Bree. I gathered up her coat and put her tea in cardboard cup to drink on the way. When I came back into the room, steaming cup in my hand, they were both looking at me with conflicting expressions.

Sage went to warm up her car but gave me another disapproving look as she left.

Bree was...well, I could tell from the look on her face she was beginning to figure things out in spite of her sudden grief. She hesitated and then grabbed my arm.

"Ma, does this have something to do with that foreign friend of yours?" she hissed in a secretive tone.

I shot a look to see if Sage was outside yet.

"Maybe..." I said. "I'm going to make things right."

Bree nodded and was quiet a moment.

"Be careful, will ya?" she told me.

I gave her a tight hug.

"Of course, my little bookworm. Now go with Auntie Sage and say nothing about this!"

"She'll still suspect something," Bree muttered.

I gave a grim laugh.

"Oh, she already suspects something! That's an elder for you!" I told her knowingly.

She nodded and gave me a stern look as if she might not see me again. She then left the shop.

I took a deep breath.

"My dear little girl, you suspect far too much," I whispered to myself.

## CHAPTER 13

I busied myself by turning down the lights in the shop and closing the blinds on the display window. I made sure the front door was closed but unlocked. I turned on the one, dim reading light by the recliner.

I then went to the trunk in the back room. I flung open the lid and began digging items out and spilling them carelessly on the floor. The dagger glittered up at me from beneath the two old pistols. I shoved them rudely aside. Pistols were of no use to me in this instance anyway. I snatched up the dagger and freed it from its rough sheath. I rushed out of the room barely remembering to shut and lock the door.

I arranged myself on the recliner, placed the dagger on my lap, and covered it with the afghan which had so recently warmed my grief-stricken daughter.

I took a deep cleansing breath to still my thoughts and remind myself what I was here for. That done I focused my thoughts and my energies.

Mentally I shouted out into the ether of space, 'Mykhalo, come here, *NOW*! We need to talk.'

To normal people this may have sounded ridiculous. But then Mykhalo was not normal. He was already dead and he was already keyed into my mind, thanks to our shared blood drinks. I knew he would respond to my summoning.

I closed my eyes and concentrated on feeling his energy. I felt him clearly. I felt him receive my mental demand and respond. I felt him leave wherever he was and approach. I felt him cross the darkened town and the city's streets. I felt him draw near my bookstore.

And I felt him enter without ringing the doorbells.

"That's quite close enough," I said to the air in front of me.

I opened my eyes and looked right back into his face, sliced with deep shadows from the darkened room. He stood on the other side of the counter about five feet away from me.

"That was quite an impressive display," he said slowly.

His eyes traveled over my form as if he was looking at me with another sense I did not possess.

"You are shining," he said softly. "You have never showed me any example of your power... until now."

His words were cautious, wary. He could feel the strength of my emotions. He picked his words with care.

I needed him to disobey my first command, to come closer to the chair. He slowly did so, creeping like a stalking cat hunting a prey which could hunt him. His motions were smooth and graceful. He approached me because I willed him to do so. I was controlling the situation, not him.

He came within two steps of the chair and stopped, looking down on me.

It was then I chose to make my move.

In one smooth motion like a cat, I came off of the chair. I swept the blanket off my lap and snatching up the dagger with my other hand, hurled myself at him until it was held a few threatening inches from below his chin.

"Give me one good reason why I shouldn't slit your throat for what you've done!" I fumed at him.

Our eyes locked his silver to my hazel. There was a long breathless moment where neither of us spoke.

With extreme care, he cleared his throat.

"Well for one thing, you can't kill me that way," he stated. "You will slit my windpipe and make me very unhappy until I heal, but you won't kill me."

He carefully and gently took hold of my hand, brought it to the side, and tilted the blade up until the tip was pointing to the section of his neck just under his ear and angled the hilt downward.

"There," he instructed dispassionately. "Cut in and down. There you will cut either the carotid artery or the jugular and I will bleed out very quickly just like a normal human. It is a very merciful if messy death."

We regarded each other silently for a moment.

"Or you could stab me anywhere in the chest and the dagger will do what it was made to do. It all depends on how much satisfaction you want to gain from my death. You are in your place of power."

His low voice lapsed into silence.

The air between us buzzed with electricity.

"Well?" he said. "Here's your chance. What are you waiting for?"

"I guess I expected you to fight back," I stammered out at last.

The corners of his mouth twitched up briefly.

"I will not. If you want to kill me, then I will not resist you. But if you are going to do it, do it now and be done with it," he said, his tone grim and serious.

As he said this, he took a step forward into the blade. I saw the dagger's edge press into his white neck and the skin bulge around it.

"I will not blame you for what you have done," he told me.

I saw my hand began to shake. I tried to harden my resolve, to remember what he had just done to my daughter's friend, what he *could* do to Bree or myself, how everyone in this town would be safer with him truly dead. I tried to call on the power of the dagger. But it suddenly seemed to be a knife just like any other knife. The magical presence within it wouldn't respond when I called it.

I crumpled like a coward onto the recliner, still clutching the dagger, completely frustrated with my lack of willpower.

*What was the matter with me?*

Mykhalo heaved a long disappointed sigh. But he did not attack me or take the dagger away. In fact, he never moved from the spot next to my chair.

131

"I guess you heard about the girl," he said presently.

"She was my daughter's best friend," I told him.

"Oh," was the answer. "Then I am truly sorry."

"Sorry?" I said. "Oh no! Sorry doesn't cut it this time! Why Mykhalo? Why did you have to kill a teenage girl? What could possibly make that right?"

"Nothing," he said.

"Then why did you do it?" I said. The tears were beginning to flow again.

He sighed and crouched down beside me, linking his fingers together. He tried his best to explain what I could not understand.

"I killed her because she was already dead inside. She called me to her. The despair in her heart was so great she hungered for death. And I was close by and heard her. I hadn't fed for a good while. I was unable to resist the call."

A memory flashed through my mind of Brittany young and laughing.

"But how could you kill her?" I said. "She wore a gold cross at all times."

Mykhalo snickered.

"She may have worn it every day of her life but it made no difference," he said. "She did not believe in the faith it represented. It was just a pretty piece of jewelry to her, no more. As such, it could never protect her from me."

I hung my head in my hands and the tears began to flow again.

"What do you want of me?" I sobbed.

His hand touched me briefly on the shoulder and then pulled away, confused at what to do or say to console me.

"Just your friendship and nothing more. If I can safely manage it," he said into the dark.

I dashed the tears from my face.

"And what do you want for yourself?" I said.

"Your life," he said.

I looked at him quickly in the shadows and my expression must have told him he had made a mistake.

"I mean...I want a life like yours," he clarified.

I wrinkled my brows, even more confused.

"You want to be a woman who owns a bookstore?" I said, knowing it was wrong.

"No!" he chuckled briefly. He sighed, frowned, and scratched his head in aggravation at the best way to describe it.

"My life is linear," he explained. "Your life is circular. In my life, the world changes all around me but I stay the same. The only thing that changes for me is the area I inhabit and the next person I feed on. In your life, everything changes around you and you are constantly changing with it. *That* is what I want."

He stood up.

"I know you believe in reincarnation. I don't. But I'd like the chance to find out for myself if it is really true," he said.

He began to pace the floor behind the counter, explaining as he walked.

"What I really want is to live a normal, human life. I want to grow and change. I want to fall in love and marry that one special woman, not one of a certain station which is chosen for me. I want to have a child with this woman and get baby spit on me. Yes, even that! And to watch them learn to walk and talk and learn to express complicated issues and get married and have children of their own. I want to fight with the people closest to me, and make up, and have relationships which grow deeper with time. I want to get gray hair, and wrinkles, and arthritis, and get bent and stiff, and need a walker to get around one day. I want to *LIVE* not just exist."

He paced back to stand in front of me. His face was shadowed but I could still see his eyes.

"But that will never happen for me the way I am right now. So I want the next best thing. I want to die," he said.

I thought about these words as I regarded him standing there before me.

"I can't kill you Mykhalo," I said into the dark.

"I know that now," he replied.

He was silent for a very long time.

Finally he spoke, nearly whispering his words.

"What I am most afraid of is hurting those closest to me who do not share my curse. I know by being their friend, I expose them to risks they would normally never have to face. I could kill them, or a close friend of theirs in a weak or hungry moment. I have always dreaded that possibility. I am a vampire. Which means in order for me to live, people around me must die. This is just a scientific fact of being what I am."

He turned to look me in the eye.

"And now what I feared most has happened yet again. I have hurt another friend. I never intended to do that. I truly regret it. And there's nothing I can do to take it back or lessen the hurt in your heart. It is right you should want to kill me. I wish I could kill myself. But the vampire spirit in me assures that will never happen. Vampires don't commit suicide. It is impossible for them."

He turned away.

"I am totally without salvation from God or you or anyone. All I can do is continue this sham existence of mine and hope someday a vampire hunter will find me and judge me worthy of death."

He gave a tired sigh into the dark.

"I miss the splintered halves of my soul," he said in a voice filled with regret.

"The side of you that has a conscience still seems to be intact," I said to him.

He gave a quick grimace of self-loathing.

"That was left for my own torment. It might be easier for me if it too was gone," he said.

He was quiet for another moment.

He made a move as if to leave and looked back at me. His eyes fell on the dagger held loosely in my right hand.

"I see Bill left you the dagger," he said in a voice a bit louder. "Please don't ever misplace it. Don't think that because you were unable to use it, it is useless to you. It is a powerful weapon against my kind. It has killed many Nosferatu before I saw that it found its way to Bill. Keep it close to you at all times. It will do a much better job protecting you than I can. Please don't forget what I have said, Zan Miller."

And then he was gone from my presence and my store, again without ringing a single bell.

## CHAPTER 14

The next few days passed slowly. There was another funeral to prepare for. Counselors were called in to school to help the other children deal with their emotions over Brittany's "suicide". Bree's normally perky and jovial nature changed. She became grimmer in her manner and her ways. I was concerned for her but the school counselors told me her grieving process was progressing normally.

Why didn't I believe them?

This funeral was much harder for us to endure than Bill's. Bree had written something to read at the ceremony, but was so overcome with emotion she was unable to do so. I tried to take over for her and could barely keep my composure as I read her words. When had my daughter become such a poignant writer?

The funeral over, we tried to reassume normal life. It was very difficult. Bree spent the next few weekends home, looking through old photo albums or just staring aimlessly out the window.

My heart ached for her.

I finally couldn't take it anymore. I charged Sage with the job of taking her out of the house one Saturday with the express intention to do something fun with her and get her to laugh. Sage told me she'd take her to the mall and maybe a movie. I gave my approval but only if the movie was a comedy.

"Just keep her from buying anything black, will ya?" I chided as they left the house.

I closed the door on them and sighed in relief. I finally had our little house all to myself! I intended to make the best use of it.

I started a roaring fire in the fireplace, turned the lights down inside the house, lit a few candles and set the coffee pot on to brew. I meant to spend the whole night getting wrapped up in a good book. I was going to be a total lazy slug and love it!

But I had barely gotten a few pages into the book I was reading when there was a knock at my door. Grumbling, I threw down the book and dragged myself out of the warm, comfy couch to answer it.

Mykhalo stood on the porch.

"Oh!" was all I could say in surprise. "So…you know where I live."

He smiled in return.

"I have always known. I just felt no need to bother you at home," was his reply. "I have something rather important to discuss with you."

"I see," was my answer even though I did not see. "Okay, do you want to come in?"

He seemed uncomfortable by the prospect of being invited inside.

"Aren't you worried that I might…" he began.

"Yes, but then again, the heater repairman could kill me as well after I invited him in to do his job. So really, what's the difference? At least if you hurt me, you'd be man enough to feel regret."

He thought about it and at last, shrugged.

"You make a very good point," and he stepped inside.

"I was just making a cup of coffee. Would you care for some?" I offered politely as I took his coat.

"As long as it's not virginal, if that's to be permitted," he suggested almost shyly.

I gave him an amused look.

"Are you developing a taste for witch's blood?" I said.

He shrugged as if it didn't matter.

"And you are surprised by this?" he said.

I sighed and shook my head.

"I'll get the matches. The kitchen is this way," I led him.

We did our little blood ritual in front of the kitchen sink and the window overlooking the back porch and yard.

"People are going to think I'm a diabetic!" I commented as he squeezed my finger over his own cup.

"I do believe I am not the only one who is developing a taste for odd things," he commented.

I shrugged and tried to make a joke out of it.

"Bavarian honey!" I teased.

He chuckled without looking at me.

"So this is your house," he commented as we left the kitchen and I guided him to the living room.

"Yes, this is home for me," I said, plopping back down on the couch.

He was looking around at the obvious Wiccan flourishes, the horseshoe above the door, the star wreath woven of grapevine, and the bookshelf groaning under the weight of too many books with esoteric titles.

He seemed to immediately target on my altar to the Green Man in the corner.

"This is your…shrine?" he asked.

"Yes, in a manner of speaking," I replied. "I worship the face of god as Cerrunos or the Green Man."

He turned to regard me in confusion.

"'The face of god'?" he repeated, not comprehending.

"Yes." I explained further. "Wiccans see the Divine in all things. Some worship a god and a goddess, some find they can better relate to a version of god in one of any number of pagan pantheons and pick a patron deity like I myself have done."

He gazed around the room further and shook his head.

"In my time you would be tortured to death in any number of ways for even entertaining such ideas," he said.

"I don't live in the shadows at home," I replied boldly.

"Don't you worry about going to hell?" he said.

I sighed and prepared myself for another, long winded explanation.

"It might surprise you to know the ancient Celts never believed in hell. If you were a bad person, you were simply doomed to repeat the lessons of life in other incarnations until you finally got it right. Hell is a Christian invention the Roman priests used to strike fear into the pagan people's hearts to force them to convert," I said.

He sipped from his cup and nodded.

"That certainly sounds like Rome. Their religious officials were always pretty inflexible. Even with Vatican II, nothing's changed much," he muttered.

He looked around at the furniture.

"You have no pets."

It was a comment which could have been a question.

"No, Athena died back in November and I thought it best to wait a bit before getting another pet," I said.

"And Athena was a..." he led on.

"A dog. She was a pit bull we rescued. Sweet as could be. She was old and got cancer," I said.

He sighed in relief.

"I'm sorry to say this but I am glad. Animals don't like me much," he said almost apologetically. "Cats hiss and run away and dogs either attack me or run, too. It's a shame because I loved dogs and horses at one time. My family used to breed Black Forest horses."

I cocked my head in pleasant curiosity.

"I've never heard of that breed but then, I don't know much about horses. Bree always wanted to learn to ride but I never earned enough at the bookstore to afford to do it right and horses can be an expensive proposition."

He smiled in comprehension.

"Horses have always been expensive throughout history," he said. "I'm not surprised you've never heard of the breed. They're virtually unknown outside Germany. I still own a small number of quality animals from my family's bloodline."

I smiled at this.

"How often do you get to see these horses?" I said.

"Never," was the reply. "Horses panic around me. So I don't go anywhere near them. The breeding program is just me being sentimental, really. Every month I send off a check to the trainer and

140

the family who cares for them and every summer, they send me pictures of all the carriage shows my horses are in. They do quite well. But I can never get near them for even the most sensible one will go berserk."

He sighed wistfully.

"I guess they're my tie with the past."

He fell silent then.

"I know a pagan couple who have their own small breeding farm," I said, trying to cheer him up. "Ravenwing and Red. They're good people. They worship Epona."

"Epona…" he whispered. "Now there's a name I haven't heard in two centuries."

The conversation lapsed into silence broken only by the snaps and pops from the fireplace. I rose quietly and stirred the coals of the fire which was dying down.

The tranquility of the moment was broken by the abrupt sound of shattering pottery.

I jumped and straightened with a shock, still holding the poker for the coals. My eyes immediately went to Mykhalo's hands. No, he still had hold of his cup, although the brew was sloshing over the sides. He was not reacting to heat of the liquid. The sound apparently had startled him as well. But he was looking towards the kitchen.

It was then I noticed I had forgotten to bring my cup of coffee into the living room with me. It was still sitting on the edge of the sink in the kitchen.

Mykhalo met my gaze and there was a strange look in his eyes.

"Bree has come home early," was all he said.

A frightening thought suddenly leapt to the forefront of my brain.

Had she drunk out of my cup, the cup with Mykhalo's vampire blood in it?

"*SABRINA!*" I heard myself crying out loud.

I bolted to the kitchen.

Bree lay sprawled on the kitchen floor surrounded by bits of broken coffee cup. I noticed with a sickening feeling in the pit of my stomach, there was very little coffee remaining to be spilled.

141

Mykhalo crouched by her side and put his fingers to her neck.

"She still breathes. She's just unconscious," he reassured quickly.

"She drank the whole cup," I whispered numbly.

He nodded and ran his fingers through his hair.

"She must have heard us talking," he said.

My heart was pounding in my ears.

"I knew she was onto us. I could see she was figuring things out, bit by bit," I told him.

My mind was racing.

"I need to call 911," I said and made an attempt to go for my cell phone.

"*NO!*" Mykhalo exclaimed and grabbed my arm to stop me. "*DON'T DO THAT!*"

The tone of his voice brought me up short. He had never raised his voice to me and even more rarely had he touched me.

"She needs medical assistance. I need to call the paramedics," I insisted.

"If you do that, you'll be sorry," he warned.

He got onto his knees and slid around to her head. Gently he lifted her torso up, cradling her head carefully. Bree flopped around in his arms like a rag doll. He pried up her eyelids one at a time and checked both pupils. He was careful and tender in touching her.

I felt a tightness begin in my chest and throat. I felt utterly helpless. Here was this undead creature in my kitchen telling me *not* to summon the authorities?

"What will drinking your blood do to her?" I gasped.

"It won't kill her nor will it turn her," he reassured. "But it *is* doing something strange to her. Where is her bedroom?"

"Upstairs," I said.

He motioned with his head for me to lead him there. Bending low over her body, he scooped her up and cradling her head against his shoulder rose to his feet in one smooth motion.

I bit my lip and led the way up our short flight of stairs to her bedroom.

I held the door open to her room for him and then hurried to pull back the blankets. He set her down lightly in the bed and tucked her in as tenderly as if she was his own daughter. He stroked her hair and the side of her face.

"We still need to do something," I said, chewing my lip in worry.

"Zan, listen to me. If you call the paramedics, they will put her in the hospital and given what has happened the past few days, probably shoot her full of all sorts of antidepressant drugs. That is the *last* thing she needs right now."

He felt her cheeks and rubbed her hands.

"Apparently, vampire blood affects witches differently, especially adolescent ones," he said. "It appears by drinking my blood, even that small of an amount, she has opened a doorway."

My breath caught and I swallowed with difficulty

"What sort of doorway?" I asked. My chest felt tight, like when you get caught doing something wrong as a child.

"I'm not exactly sure," he said. "This is *your* area of expertise. Stay close by. Keep her warm. When she awakens, she may have questions only you can answer."

He stroked her strawberry blonde hair.

"She *will* awaken, Zan. You can be sure of that. She's a strong girl just like her mother."

He was saying this just to stroke my ego. But it did help.

He stood up to leave.

"Please try not to worry," he said and touched my shoulder briefly.

And then he was gone.

I barely cared that he had left. I could only stare at my daughter's pale face and stroke her hair. I held her hand and rubbed her arm.

Why had she eavesdropped on our conversation? Why had she drunk from my cup? What was she thinking?

She wasn't thinking, I told myself; she was only being a spontaneous teen.

I wished I knew where her mind was.

Somehow, still holding her hand, I fell asleep and dreamed.

143

## CHAPTER 15

In the dream, I was far away from Sleepy Pines, Pennsylvania. I wasn't even in the United States. I was standing on the top of a sand dune looking out across an endless desert. The air was hot and dry.

An African lioness stood next to me regarding me with bottomless, golden eyes. I had the distinct feeling she was no normal lion.

The lioness turned her face away. She pricked her ears and gave a soft growl of anticipation. I followed her gaze and nearly fell to my knees in surprise.

Ancient Egypt stretched out before me, not old and weathered by the sands of time, but young, new and pristine.

And before the buildings, monoliths and pillars of a great city of ancient Egypt, a battle raged. Warrior fought against warrior, king against king. Their struggle raised a great dust cloud into the bright sunshine and sweat glistened on the soldiers' straining bodies.

The lioness next to me growled in eagerness and began to move down the dune towards the pitched battle. I watched her and glorified in the beauty of her body in motion, the way her shoulder blades rose and fell smoothly under the tawny skin, the way her weight barely sank into the desert sand, the way the pale freckles of her belly undulated against her powerful ribcage. She began to trot lightly, as if she were landing on clouds and then to gallop, her great legs churning, her tail wafting in the wind for balance. But her head was held level and her eyes focused intently on the object of her desire. I recognized the light of a predator on the hunt in those eyes.

Her speed increased as she approached the battle. I noticed she was close enough for the soldiers to see her. Each man as he saw the large lioness bearing down upon them suddenly forgot the battle. They screamed, threw down their weapons, and fled. Some threw down their weapons and fell to their knees, their arms raised to implore and beg.

The great lioness treated them all the same. She tore into each soldier she caught up to, whether they were fleeing her or begging for her forgiveness. She cared not for their prayers. She just attacked, killed and moved on, staining the sand red with their blood, rending the air with their screams of agony. She killed, bathed in their blood, and moved on. No matter how many fled her, none made it to the city in time. One by one, she terminated each life before her. She cared not for which side was winning. She destroyed soldiers on both sides, from poor, farmer soldier, to the lofty, ruling king. She cared not for what they were fighting about. It was not important to her. The only passion she had was for killing.

I followed, unable to interfere and afraid to try and stop her. For I understood I followed no real flesh and blood lioness. I watched her kill and kill and kill until her face and body up to the shoulders was drenched and dripping in human blood, her bright eyes pools of gold swimming in a sea of splashing red.

Then she stopped killing. She turned and looked at me. I took a step back, fearful I would be next. But the light of the predator was gone from those tawny eyes.

She wanted me to pay attention.

She turned away from me and entered the great arched doorway of the golden city before her. I followed her silently. Into the city, she led me and down the main thoroughfare. There were statues everywhere but only of one particular deity, one of a female goddess with a lioness' head. She had many guises. In some statues, she carried two long, leaf bladed short swords, others she was decorated with scorpions or with a crown of dual cobras. In every statue, she was garbed in blood red attire.

We moved onward and deeper into the city and the many-pillared buildings grew closer. Every pillar, every wall, was covered in

146

frescoes and raised murals all depicting stories of the lioness-headed goddess. And each piece of artwork, even the statues, was brightly painted in colors which glowed. I had never known the statues were originally colored. I had always seen pictures in the historical books and they were the color of the eroded rock they were fashioned from. Then I thought what four thousand years must have done to such colors made from natural products. Of course, the paint had worn off! I glanced away from the statues for one moment and back to the creature leading me and noticed she was changing. She was growing smaller and younger.

We passed under the roof of a great temple with murals on the walls, their colors still bright and new as if they had just been painted yesterday.

The lioness by this time had dwindled to a very small and cute cub. She was still covered in blood, although now it was cracked and dried, her eyes were still quite fierce. She looked back at me once as if to make sure I was following and paying attention. She came to the foot of a seated goddess and mewing as if to its mother, jumped up into the marble statue's lap. She turned around a couple times and then curled up to take a nap, rolling onto her back like a cat does when they're completely at ease with their surroundings. I could hear a deep rolling purr of satisfaction rumbling outward from the cub. Her bloated belly was spattered with immature, tawny spots and bloodstains. She purred loudly and went to sleep.

I stepped closer and it was now I raised my eyes to the face of the statue which held the sleeping lioness cub. I gasped and staggered to my knees in shock.

The face of the painted marble statue was my own!

* * *

I awoke with a start from the dream. The digital clock at her nightstand read midnight.

I looked into my daughter's face. She was sleeping peacefully now. I stroked her hair and smiled at her. And then I straightened up and gathered myself. If I was going to do this, midnight was the best time.

"Bree, wake up honey," I said in a loving tone.

Almost immediately, her eyes popped open as if she was awaiting the call. She smiled back at me but it was not Bree who smiled.

Her normally green eyes were purple.

"You are not my daughter," I said slowly, in a level voice.

"No."

The voice was definitely not Bree's voice. It was accented and clipped.

"Who am I speaking to?" I inquired, careful to use a respectful tone.

The thickly accented voice replied at once.

"I am a handmaiden of the goddess Hathor," she said.

"Yes," I said. "And why are you here?"

Bree's face smiled back in a pleasant way.

"I am here to supply balance. You and your daughter will need me and the aide of my Lady in the time to come," the strange voice coming from my daughter's lips told me.

"Is there anyone else in there?" I said, feeling a little tremor of fear go up my spine.

Bree's smile deepened.

"Oh yes, young mother!" was the reply. "Your daughter has been chosen by Sekhmet."

My thoughts whirled, trying to mentally access the name.

"Chosen? For what purpose?" I said.

"Soon you will march into a nest of vipers. Sekhmet has chosen your daughter. She will protect you and 'Bree'. Your daughter will be Sekhmet's avenging hand. I am here to keep Her from losing control with Her destructive urges. I am here to supply balance."

I nodded, understanding only a bit better than before.

"Please, let me talk to Sekhmet," I said.

148

The smile vanished from Bree's face.

"Are you sure you want to do that?" was the question.

"If my daughter has been chosen, then I must meet her new goddess. Please give me that," I said.

"As you wish," was the answer.

Bree's eyes closed and she relaxed back into the pillows.

She suddenly sat up straight and tall in bed and lifted her chin proudly. Her eyes opened to regard me.

Her eyes were blood red.

"Greetings, little mother," came a different voice. It was the deepest female voice I have ever heard and rumbled as if she was purring.

"Greetings, Sekhmet," I said and bowed my head.

I then lifted my eyes to hers and we regarded each other silently for a moment.

"You named your daughter Tempest," the goddess' voice finally said. "How appropriate."

She smiled and purred deeply.

"Excuse my ignorance, Great Lady," I began. "Aren't you a form of Bast?"

She laughed and I heard the echo of a lion's roar in the voice.

"Never!" she chuckled. "My sister is off dancing and loving men. I have better things to do!"

She cocked her head and regarded me with curiosity.

"Why have you endangered your life and that of your daughter's with this...male?" she demanded.

I didn't understand at first, and very respectfully told her so.

"Why are you consorting with a predator?" she asked again and this time her voice growled.

I hung my head. I somehow suspected that begging her forgiveness would only enrage her.

"Like the blood of battle fascinates you, he fascinates me," I said quietly.

There was a rumbling purr from the bed. Or was it a growl? I kept my eyes respectfully cast downward.

149

"You must kill him," she told me.

I bit my lip.

"I am unable to do so, Lady," I said.

"Why not?"

I chewed on my lip.

"One, and most important, I am weak. Two, Wiccan law forbids me to. 'Do as thou wilt and it harm none.' Three, he has a conscience," I said, keeping my eyes down.

There was a wordless rumbling growl.

"Hmm. Laws, conscience and weakness. This is why you need our interference?" the strange voice coming from my daughter's lips purred back at me. "I chose to manifest because of the problem of blood. Vampires think they rule in this regard. They are sadly mistaken! They think they are timeless. They don't know the meaning of the word! They think they are all powerful. They are pathetic! What they *really* need is to be taught a lesson. And your daughter will assist me in this."

I risked a glance upward and saw her red eyes blaze. So I quickly cast them down again.

"Your weak 'fascination' has attracted the wrong kind of attention" Sekhmet's voice snarled at me in a scolding tone. "Because of your leniency, others of his kind, without much control or conscience, are flocking to this little town in droves. You are a magnet to them! You are endangering more than your daughter here. The vampire problem must be dealt with, whether you are willing or no. I will help you in this if you allow me. If not, you will be trampled under my claws."

I felt my skin prickle and my heart pound in fear at these words.

'Oh, *shit*!' I thought to myself but dared not to speak it.

"My Lady, I don't understand," I said in a frightened whisper.

Sekhmet's voice chuckled back at me.

"Soon you will," I was told. "You and your daughter are now under my protection. Do not interfere with my plans and all will go well for you and I will help you deal with this 'weakness' issue. Pay attention to the signs to come. I will be watching over you."

The strange voice then chuckled again as if quite amused.

"Tempest."

Bree fell back into the covers.

Almost fearfully, I stroked my daughter's arm. It was hot and dry to the touch.

She stirred and moaned briefly as if she was having a bad dream. I came closer and stroked her forehead. Her eyes opened and looked into mine with their own familiar green color.

"Ma?" she said. "What happened? I was having the strangest dream."

"Did you dream about African lions?" I whispered.

Bree's eyes bugged out in amazement at me.

"Yeah! How'd you know?" she said.

I smiled and stroked her face lovingly.

"Shhh, my little bookworm. It's late. Go back to sleep. We'll discuss your dreams in the morning," I cooed back to her, kissing her forehead.

"But I might forget them!" she fussed.

I snorted.

"Trust me, my dear, you won't forget *this* dream! Now go back to sleep. I'll stay beside you all night long. I'm not leaving," I reassured her.

# CHAPTER 16

I slept late into the next day. When I finally awoke, I found myself in Bree's bed alone but wrapped up in her blankets. I yawned stretched and looked at her alarm clock.

It read ten of two.

I sat bolt upright as the events of the night before came flooding back into my mind. I flung off the covers and left the bed and Bree's room. As I made my way down the stairs of our small house, I wondered whom I would meet downstairs, my daughter, or something else in my daughter's skin.

The delicious aroma of cooking meat drifted by my nose and my stomach yowled impatiently.

Bree was bustling around the kitchen. I quietly seated myself at the table and waited for her to notice. She turned around, saw me, and nearly dropped her plate of food. I jumped nearly as high when I saw what her preferred food choice was on her plate.

As a mother of a modern teenage girl, I was prepared for her to experiment in all sorts of strange but current things, odd fashion choices, weird diets, exercises and such. I had even learned to tolerate her brief foray into trying out vegan and vegetarian diets. But nothing had prepared me for this.

"You'll make a terrible Jew with that diet, my dear," I said with a raised eyebrow. "Don't you know that you are boiling the calf in the mother's milk?"

A steaming red slice of steak, still mooing it was so rare, lay on her plate and the glass of milk she also held was steaming as well.

She stammered a weak excuse.

"I had a craving," was all she could come up with. "I was famished."

I snickered at her.

"It seems being host to a couple Egyptian goddesses has some rather weird side effects," I said.

Bree said nothing but sat down at the table and dove into the steak with her knife and fork as if the thing was going to walk away. I got the distinct impression that if I had grabbed the plate, she would have snarled possessively at me. She attacked the glass of warm milk with the same gusto, polishing off half a glass in nearly one voracious swallow. I found this just as unusual. You see Bree had always hated milk. From the time she was weaned, she had wanted nothing more to do with the liquid. I had to force her to drink one glass a day, usually with her breakfast. I had never seen a girl who preferred soda with her hot, fresh, chocolate chip cookies.

"Slow down, Hon," I cautioned her. "You'll get sick if you eat that fast. Don't worry. I'll make my own."

I got up and started rummaging around in the fridge for something to eat. I wasn't exactly in the mood for steak!

I decided on a simple chicken sandwich and started picking out the ingredients.

"I thought boys made cravings," I said in a jesting tone. "They're also quite bad for the waistline."

Bree just shrugged.

"You'd know better than me," she said with some salt in her tone. "But what do vampire boyfriends do to you?"

I nearly slammed down the butter knife.

"For the last time, he's *NOT* my boyfriend!" I growled. "We just talk."

"Uh hunh," Bree said in a very unconvinced sounding tone.

"No, *really*! That's all we do is talk," I insisted.

"You care for him," she said in a teasing tone.

"Well…yes. But I care for a lot of people. That doesn't mean they're my lovers!" I said. "I cared for Bill Gibson."

154

Bree wrinkled her nose at this.

"Ewww! Gross! Don't even suggest that, Mom!" she said.

One corner of my mouth turned up at this.

"There! See? A woman can have a friendship with a guy and not get romantically involved," I said, jabbing the butter knife at her.

"Yeah, but your, what's his name…Mykhalo, is a bit too handsome to be just a friend. And a *vampire* to boot!"

"He's just a friend!" I repeated.

I began to slather mayo on the bread with a vengeance, growling in frustration as I worked the knife.

"You mean you never had a 'date'?" she said.

"Never!"

"He's never held your hand?" Bree said.

"No!"

I decided I would leave the whole bit about him holding my hand to milk a few drops of blood out of me wasn't quite the same thing as 'holding my hand'.

"Or touched you tenderly?"

Bree was persistent!

"Not like that," I said. I guess piercing my finger with a lapel pin didn't quite count as 'tender'!

"Or kissed you?"

I took Bree's now empty glass and glared at her. I wished the glass had been disposable so I could throw it at her smug, little, adolescent face.

"Vampires aren't interested in kissing. More warm milk, Kitten?" I said pointedly.

"Yes, please," she replied and then added "Just nice long, white necks, eh?"

"Whatever! I guess so" I said, starting to get exasperated by her incessant inquiries.

"So! Has he ever ogled your neck, Ma?" Bree went on.

"Sabrina! That's quite enough, young miss! Shut up and eat your bloody cow!" I snapped.

I took my sandwich to the table and seated myself across from her. I regarded her quietly for the first few bites of my meal. She avoided my gaze.

"So...how long have you known that my...'friend'...is a vampire?" I said.

She had slowed down in her attack of the meat on her plate and she now chewed carefully as she considered the answer.

"Since the night in the hotel room," she answered.

I raised my eyebrows.

"How much did you hear?" I said.

"Pretty much all of it," Bree replied. She took a swallow from her glass.

I tapped my fingers on the table considering.

"Did you know the coffee you drank last night had a special 'creamer'?" I said.

Bree snickered.

"You mean your 'Bavarian honey'? Yes, I knew."

"You little sneak!" I exclaimed, only half joking.

But Bree only rolled her eyes.

"I'll never drink coffee again!" she moaned. "What a hangover!"

"That'll teach you to spy on me!" I growled.

I smiled and became thoughtful.

"I talked to Sekhmet last night," I said, seriously.

"I know. I was there," was her reply. "Well...in a manner of speaking...I guess."

I scrutinized her face.

"So how do you feel about being host to two deities?" I said.

Bree frowned and stopped eating to give the answer her full attention.

"Very strange!" she said. "I guess I feel both flattered and scared. Do you have any idea who Sekhmet is?"

By this time, I had recalled everything I had read on the lioness-headed goddess which I could not remember the night before.

"Yes, she's the goddess of war and revenge, death and destruction," I said. "Her priests had over seven hundred statues of her in one temple and used to pray to a different one each morning and night to keep her anger appeased. She nearly killed the entire population of the world, the legend goes, until Hathor tricked her into drinking beer stained with pomegranate juice, which she thought was blood and got her drunk."

"Yeah, I know. I looked that up on the 'net this morning! Why couldn't I have impressed a more cuddly form of god?" she said rolling her eyes.

I frowned.

"Because this is what our situation warranted. And this is the deity who can best deal with it. And that is also why you have Hathor inside to keep Sekhmet's destruction on a tight rein," I said.

I sighed heavily. This was my entire fault.

"I'm sorry to have dragged you into this," I said honestly.

Bree's attitude suddenly changed.

"No, Ma," she said and grabbed my hand with both of hers. "I'm glad to be included. I can finally pay you back for being my mother. I'd be going nuts just sitting around waiting for you to come back to me."

"Bree," I cautioned her gravely. "We're going to war. This could get us both killed."

She met my eyes. I saw in my daughter a power I had never before noticed. For the first time I actually saw a hint of her soldier father in her.

"I know, and I'm ready," she replied seriously.

I shook my head.

"You have no idea what you're suggesting!" I said. "This is going to be a whole lot worse than you could ever imagine."

Bree nodded with a grimace.

"Yeah, that's sorta the way war turns out to be from what I've been told," she said. "It changes everybody and this will probably change me. And you know what I say? Bring it on!"

But she was just a child to me and more importantly, *my* child!

I gave her a long, narrow look. I then got up and left the table and the room. I went into my bedroom and got the Egyptian dagger with the Coptic inscription etched on the blade.

Coming back into the kitchen, I cast the dagger on the table in front of her.

"You think you can handle war?" I said sternly. "Fine! Can you handle this?"

Bree just stared for a long time at the dagger, her food forgotten. I sat down across from her and watched her closely.

Slowly, she put down her silverware and reached out for the dagger with trembling hands.

"I've had dreams of a dagger like this since I was six. I never knew it was for real!" she said.

I saw her take it in both hands and draw it closer to her. I saw her eyes begin to spin and change color.

The back door suddenly banged shut making me jump nearly out of my skin.

"Zan! I need to talk to you!" Sage declared as she marched into the kitchen.

She froze when she saw Bree holding the knife.

Bree never reacted. She was still holding the dagger and the pupils of her eyes were still spinning. They seemed to be turning red.

"Lord and Lady!" Sage breathed in a stunned whisper. "What on earth is going on here and who is *that*? And what are they doing in Bree's body?"

"Shhh, Sage dear." I cautioned in a low but serious voice. "You should be more respectful when speaking to a goddess."

"A what…?" Sage started but the words froze on her lips.

Bree had raised her blood red eyes to regard the new person in my kitchen. The air in the room was electric and hot like the wind which blows over the desert.

Sage gasped and covered her mouth with her hands.

"Greetings, Burning Sage," came Sekhmet's accented feline voice from Bree's lips. "I am glad you are here. You three have much to discuss and prepare for."

Then Bree shut her eyes and bowed her head. We all felt the presence of the goddess leave the room.

Sage was still staring at Bree as if she had never seen her before, as if she had turned into a coiled cobra on the kitchen table. She wrapped her hand knitted shawl a little tighter around her as if it would protect her.

"No one has called me 'Burning Sage' since my elder, Black Hawk, gave me that name. It was just 'Sage' plain and simple," she said in a tremulous voice.

"Coffee or tea, my dear?" I asked calmly, getting up from the table and going to the sink. "As the Lady said, we have much to discuss."

"Tea. Green tea with plenty of honey as usual," she said almost as an afterthought.

She was still staring at Bree. I could see the wheels turning in her head. She sat numbly down at the table.

Bree had come back to her own body. She blinked at Sage, smiled and said, "Ma always said it was rude to stare at anybody."

Sage looked at me. There was a strange mix of fear and gravity on her face.

"You two have been holding out on me," she said at last, breaking her silence. "I think I deserve an explanation. In fact you *promised* me one several days ago!"

I gave a heavy sigh.

But before I could say anything, Bree decided to break the ice, rather dramatically too as it turned out.

"Mom is dating a vampire!" she burst out, giddy with the news.

"Sabrina Tempest Miller!" I scolded.

Bree looked crestfallen. She slid a chastised look toward Sage.

"Well, it's true!" she muttered into her glass of milk.

Sage noticed the rare steak on her plate. Her brows wrinkled. She looked at the glass Bree was draining and her frown increased in girth.

She looked back at me.

"Why is Bree suddenly on an all animal diet?" she said. "And you expect me to believe that there are *VAMPIRES*? C'mon! We were all amused with 'Buffy' but let's be serious!"

I sighed again and growled to myself. I pinched the skin between my eyes in exasperation.

"Sage, you remember the singer at the coffee house? The one you told me to stay away from?" I said.

Sage blinked, not comprehending at first. Then her eyes flew wide.

"The man who sung that strange song with the Spanish guitar?"

"Hmm. The same one. *He's* the vampire," I said.

I handed her the cup of tea but she barely noticed it.

"So...that's what a vampire looks like?" she said.

"Hey! He fits the profile" Bree interrupted in a jesting way. "Good looking, a foreigner, well-educated an obvious appreciation for the arts..."

"Bree, this is no laughing matter," I sternly warned her.

"I know! But that's just the way I wrap my mind around it," she said.

Sage was still sitting there, digesting everything.

"Sage?" I asked. "Do you believe us?"

She made a hissing sound as she sucked her teeth.

"I don't want to!" she said slowly, considering. "But it fits in with everything I've been seeing when I scry. It's impossible! And yet, everything makes sense now."

I exchanged uncomfortable looks with my daughter and sat down next to her.

Sage's eyes latched onto the dagger.

"May I hold it for one moment?" she asked politely.

Bree looked at me as if I had just told her to donate her favorite toy to a charity. I nodded sternly.

Reluctantly, she pushed her new prize across the table to Sage.

Reverently, Sage picked up the dagger and I saw her eyes become distant. I knew Sage had some power to see where objects had been and whom they were associated with. I thought this would prove most interesting.

"This blade has the blood of many strange creatures on it," she said in a soft voice.

Bree leaned forward eagerly.

"What sort of…strange creatures?" she said.

Sage was still falling deeper into the images in her mind and barely heard her.

"Creatures that look like us but are not. Nosferatu, lycanthropes, unquiet spirits, damned forever by the cultures they came from. No god or goddess accepts these beings. They belong in the grave but reject it. Their power is black, evil, and old. They live among us and feed off of us. Predators of the human race."

Sage suddenly dropped the knife with a sound of disgust. She gave it a horrified look. She got to her feet and going to my sink, feverishly washed her hands under the tap.

"That blade has a lot of yuck on it!" she said. "I never want to touch it again!"

Bree snatched it up and cradled it protectively to her heart like a teddy bear.

Sage considered her reaction as she dried her hands on a nearby towel.

"Okay. *Now* I believe you! I saw where the blade has been. It has been to ugly places and done ugly things. But it was all to protect humanity. Now I believe you both."

She sighed and gave Bree a narrow look.

"And its power sings to one person at a time. Zan is not that person. *You* are, Bree. I wish it were Zan. She has more experience and sense than you can possibly possess at this time in your life."

"My daughter is not alone in this, Sage," I said. "Her body plays host to two Egyptian goddesses right now."

She raised her eyebrows.

"Oh really? Which two?"

"Hathor and Sekhmet."

Sage rolled her eyes and tossed her hands helplessly in the air.

161

"Destruction and creation. Beautiful! Well, all I can say is you better watch yourself, Missy! You have the power within you to tear down a mountain or rebuild it, right now. Make sure you know where the 'on' and 'off' switch is!"

"Sage is right," I counseled my daughter. "The dagger is yours but please, please, *please* don't forget her words! This does *not* make you all powerful."

"I know that," Bree replied and her tone became quiet and distant. "I am not all powerful. But Sekhmet and Hathor are."

I sat down at the table and put my head in my hands.

"It's happening all over again," I moaned.

I felt Sage put a hand on my shoulder and rub reassuringly.

"What's happening all over again?" Bree said.

"I promised myself, when your father died, to never love another warrior again. I never expected the warrior to be my own daughter. Here we go again! And again I'm afraid of losing someone I love."

"She's under the protection of two very ancient and powerful goddesses," Sage reassured. "I seriously doubt you have much to worry about there, my dear."

I kept my mouth shut but my thoughts spun.

"She didn't mean me, Sage," Bree said.

I glared at my daughter and begged her with my eyes not to go on.

"She meant her vampire friend. Mykhalo. Isn't that his name?"

I bit my lip hard.

"Yes, that's his name," I said.

"The man I warned you about? This man I now find out is a vampire? He's your...friend?"

I nodded glumly.

"How could you let this happen, Zan? Don't you know how dangerous he is? He could be getting close to you to lull you into a false sense of security before he goes for the jugular. And this time I mean *literally*!"

"Yes, Ma, I'd like to know why, too," Bree said to me in a voice more serious than I had ever heard her use. "What did you tell yourself to make it all right?"

"Nothing!" I spat out. "I know what he is, what he's capable of! I know he's dangerous! We just kept bumping into each other and we kept having these talks…"

"Un hunh!" grunted Sage. "He's reeled you in, like a trout on a line!"

"No!" I nearly shouted at them.

I whimpered and shook my head in exasperation.

"He has a conscience. He feels regret for what he's done," I said.

"Predator!" Sage scolded.

"Then why did he save my life?" I countered. "Why did he beg me to kill him? Why hasn't he threatened my life in all the chances he's been given to cause me harm in secluded areas? *Why*?"

"Why are vampires getting ready to converge on this little town?" Bree stated.

"They are?" Sage inquired.

Bree nodded and sucked her teeth.

"Oh yeah! Sleepy Pines is about to have a nice, big, vampire convention because Mom's carrying on with this 'Mykhalo' character!"

"He breaks the cardinal rules," I said.

"So that's the battle I've been seeing when I scry!" said Sage.

"What battle?" Bree and I asked at the same time.

Sage just looked at us as if the light bulb had just gone off in her head.

"Every night, when I do my candle magic, I see the same vision. I see a battle raging in the middle of Sleepy Pines' main street. It happens at night. The church is burning and everyone is screaming. Things that look like people but are not are attacking the town, people I know and love. And then the whole scene goes red."

I exchanged worried looks with my daughter. Sage's description gave us both chills.

163

"The only thing I was able to figure out about my vision was why everything goes red. That was easy if you consult any calendar with the moon phases on it. Four days from now, we will experience a lunar eclipse. The moon will go red. The dream happens that night."

"We need to prepare," Bree insisted. "We need some sort of plan."

Sage nodded.

"I'll contact the area covensteads and the local elders. The Indian tribes I am friendly with have known something big was on the horizon. They've been rumbling about it for months. I'll also contact the few Buddhists I know."

I took a deep swallow of soda and winced as the fizz burned my nostrils.

"I think it would be a very good idea to notify the warrior's guild of the local druidic groves as well. Maybe not all of them, but those warriors we trust, those who have actually seen real fire-fights overseas and have lost comrades," I added.

Sage nodded her agreement.

"But...do we need to tell them everything?" Bree asked. "I'm sorry but if you tell most people, even our kind, this town is about to be overrun by vampires, they'll look at you like you've got six heads!"

I nodded.

"And the other half will go crazy and show up with every weapon they've stashed and hoarded for years! Especially the ones who can't fight but *think* they can!"

"Good point, Kitten," Sage laughed. "But no, we need not tell them *everything*. Just to gather and raise energy that night."

"Some we can trust with the full story. Bran, the Blood Raven will take it seriously and prepare well for it. So will Black Hawk, although he may not be able to help us the way he wants as he is on his deathbed," I said.

"Black Hawk has been waiting for this," Sage told us. "If he does die in the next few days, it will probably be because he could help us better from beyond."

Sage fell into a brief silence as she considered.

"I think your suggestion of Bran is a very good one," she went on. "He has seen actual war in Baghdad. We could probably trust him with everything, and I do mean everything pertinent to this issue. You should have him move in here and act as bodyguard for you and Bree."

"Do I really need a bodyguard?" Bree said.

Sage gave her one of her wise old looks.

"You should conserve your energy and that of your goddesses for the battle to come," she counseled strictly. "Bran will guard you both whenever Bree is not at school and your mother is not running the bookstore. It's probably a good bet unfriendly eyes are watching us close and they are getting familiar with our daily and nightly routines and those we know. A bodyguard with a strong spiritual awareness could be a very good thing to have around right now."

"All right. I agree," I replied.

Sage got up to leave. She had a lot to accomplish. She got to the door and turned around.

"One more thing," she said. "We need to do an emergency ritual for you two."

Bree gave her a quizzical look.

"But the moon isn't full," she said. "The timing for a ritual is all wrong. We're losing energy right now."

"Never mind that!" Sage warned. "By the time the moon is full, it *will* be too late! There are ways to do this and have it work. We need to surround you both with protection and power for the upcoming fight. We also need to make and bless talismans for you both which will connect you to each other and sing to each other when you are apart. I have a sneaky feeling you will need such talismans. We should do this ritual as soon as possible, never mind what phase the moon is in! Think about it and get back to me a.s.a.p. on it. I'm going to contact Bran first so he should be turning up soon. I'll get to all the others as fast as I can. Be careful you two!"

She shook her finger at us.

"Blessed be, Burning Sage," I said as she left.

"B.B. to you, too," she called back over her shoulder.

And then she was gone from our house.

Bree and I looked wordlessly at each other for a long moment. I took a deep, cleansing breath.

I quietly got up and started clearing the dishes.

"I guess I know what we're doing today!" I told her. "Bree,, get the sweet-grass. I'm going to smudge the hell out of this place!"

* * *

The next few days were busy. Sage and I contacted everyone in the magical community we knew of and told them to make ready for battle.

I contacted the elder druids I trusted and apprised them of the situation. The druids followed the spirituality of pre-Christian Ireland. Whereas Wiccans typically believed in five sacred elements, the druids believed in three. *Where do you think the Christians got their idea of a Holy Trinity?* The few druids I knew were elders and had military experience. They took my words to heart and galvanized their warrior guild to prepare for spiritual battle. Wards were hung on the doorways to protect those who lived inside from intrusion. Prayers for strength and protection were made to the ancestors.

Sage had connections to the local Native Americans and the very secretive Pow-Wow practitioners. They followed a form of Germanic Christianity. Colorful hex signs of protection were made and hung on the doorways of their houses. Prayers were offered for strength and protection.

There were several Wiccan covensteads in the area and even more solitary witches like myself who I had to contact. They all were eager to take part. But it was painstaking calling them all because there were so many. Many times, I had heard the saying, "Getting Wiccans to agree on anything is like herding cats." Well, this is not exactly true. But they are all individuals and all have individual ways of worshipping and drawing power so it was very complicated getting them all on the same page.

I let Bran deal with getting those of Norse persuasion together. Theirs was a small but very strong group and each one seemed to have family members in law enforcement, the military, or community militia. Together they were a force to be reckoned with and I definitely wanted them included in the 'war preparations', so to say. Even if they did look like a bunch of aging bikers!

Soon our small town was buzzing with magical people, most of which lived their faith secretly. They looked, acted, and dressed like normal people but magic sang in their blood and their souls. I could feel it as I walked down the streets of Sleepy Pines. Every now and then, a person I barely knew or maybe even one I didn't would slide me a quiet wink and a nod and I knew who they were.

The storm was coming.

And certain people knew and were gathering their magic close to them, preparing. It was like thunder carried through the ground, not heard but felt through the soles of your feet.

We were ready. I could feel it like the electricity in the air before the lightning. I could feel the magic in the people around me.

And it felt delicious.

* * *

Mykhalo's cell phone jangled its familiar classical tune and without looking, he pulled it out of the breast pocket of his suit and answered. But at the sound of the voice on the other end, he cursed inwardly.

He should have looked to see who was calling. He should have ignored the ring-tone altogether.

"Hello, Michael." Hector said.

"How did you get this number?" he asked in German.

He could practically see the Spaniard smiling in triumph as he replied.

"Did you really think your cell was safe from me?" Hector replied. "It only takes me twenty-four hours to discover your new

167

number. You probably even have the ring-tone set to something by Bach. You are so predictable, my friend."

Mykhalo sighed in frustration.

"What do you want, Hector?" he growled.

There was a pregnant pause. And then Hector began to sing softly, "Are You Lonesome Tonight?" with certain words changed.

"Are you hungry tonight...?" Hector let the words trail off into space. He chuckled softly. "Why do you always avoid my dinner invitations?"

Mykhalo refused to answer.

"You have a young lady friend...I believe you call her Zan. And she has a very pretty little daughter everyone calls Bree, so fresh and innocent. How are they doing?"

Mykhalo's heart began to pound very slowly and loudly in his chest.

"Have you touched them?" he asked when he could finally trust his voice.

Again came the soft sinister chuckle from the other end of the line.

"No, not yet." Hector said. "But I do plan on it. They seem so...delicious."

There was another long pause.

"Oh my. I've upset you again. I can hear it in your breath."

Hector seemed to enjoy switching from Spanish to German every other sentence.

The language didn't matter. He knew Mykhalo spoke each fluently.

"Leave them alone," Mykhalo pleaded softly.

This time Hector really did laugh.

"Begging for their lives? Now that is rich!" Then his taunting voice grew even softer.

"Don't you get it, Michael? I *have* left them alone. Now it's time to pay up."

Mykhalo had to take three deep breaths before he could trust his voice.

"What do you mean exactly by 'pay up'?"

Hector sighed in obvious relish of the words to come.

"I told you at the convention I knew about Hope. I have always known about her from the time you spared her as a babe. You did not save her life then. I *allowed* her to live. It amused me to no end watching you invent this pretend family. I found it somewhat pathetic your rejection of what you truly are, of your *real* family, the Nosferatu.

"But I found your behavior with this child truly amusing. Even your choice of name for her was laughable. Hope. As if the name could protect her from me. So I allowed her to live and mature, to marry and have children. She did so because I wished it to happen.

"But there was always a price to pay for my leniency."

Mykhalo had started to pace back and forth like a caged lion. His hand on the phone was trembling.

"What price, Hector?" he said in a louder more demanding voice.

The Spaniard sniffed in derision.

"Did you not think it odd no one in Hope's family lived long enough to die of old age?'

Mykhalo felt his already cold blood turn to ice.

"If you insist in making a fool of yourself with this imaginary family you've created then I will exact a price. No member of Hope's bloodline lives long enough to hold their grandchildren. They can grow and mature and fall in love and have children. But they will never touch a grandchild."

Sudden realization dawned on the Bavarian.

"Zan's husband and parents! They died within two weeks of each other."

Hector laughed in triumph on the other end.

"Yes! Did you really think the car wreck was an accident? My lovely children took care of her parents. And I paid her husband a private visit while he was defending his country. But you already knew that part being as you were there."

Mykhalo had to sit down to process the revelation.

"Zan nearly died of grief during that time. How dare you?"

169

He sensed satisfaction from the Spaniard.

"She was pregnant. It was time to pay the piper."

Mykhalo was too stunned for words for a long moment.

"Why are you telling me this?" he finally managed to get out.

"Because you asked me," Hector replied as if the answer was obvious. "And to tell you the time of reckoning has come again. Only this time I've decided not to be so lax with Zan and her daughter. I don't feel like waiting anymore."

Mykhalo's mind was racing to try to figure out some way to stop Hector.

"You've pursued me for centuries, Hector. If I offer myself up, will you spare Zan and her daughter?"

It was time for Hector to be surprised.

"Well now. Isn't this an intriguing turn of events? You willingly offer up your undead life to save two mortals who would never live as long as yourself. I wasn't expecting that scenario."

Mykhalo didn't want to hear him prattle on. He just wanted an answer that would keep Zan and Bree safe.

But Hector chose to prolong the suspense.

"Maybe I'll just repeat history and feed them to you. How hungry are you Mykhalo? I know it's been a while."

Mykhalo had to shut his eyes against the painful memories.

"Don't do that to me again. Please."

Hector laughed even louder.

"Twice in one conversation I've made you beg my mercy. This really is my lucky night!"

Mykhalo wanted to scream, to cry, to strangle Hector with his own bare hands.

"Just tell me," he demanded. "A trade, my life for theirs. Is it acceptable?"

Hector sighed and paused just to torment him.

"No promises. Meet with me," he said at last. "Come alone and unarmed and we'll discuss certain…possibilities. Agreed?"

Mykhalo squeezed his eyes shut and swallowed with difficulty.

"Agreed."

## CHAPTER 17

Monday was a normal day at work just like any other day. Bran had moved into our house. He was chaperoning Bree back and forth to school and me to and from to the bookstore. I must say I appreciated his company although Bree did get some looks from her classmates when he showed up to pick her up from school. I can't say I blamed them though.

Bran did have a rather unusual, even threatening appearance!

He stood well over six feet and was as burly as a body builder although his muscles weren't as well defined. He wore his shocking red hair tied back in a ponytail and he was covered in tribal tattoos. He was the type of person normal people would cross to the other side of the street to avoid. To look at him, no one would guess the jovial nature which lived within.

Bran was a wonderfully funny guy. But he also knew how to handle himself in a dangerous situation.

Rik and Bran had been in the same platoon and had been in the same tour of duty when my husband fell. I had always suspected Bran knew certain details about Rik's death but was unable to disclose such details to even me. I saw this in his body language, the sad looks he slid me when he thought I wasn't looking, the hurriedly cut off sentences, the awkward silences between us. Bran had introduced me to Rik and they had joined the service and gone through basic training together. And then they were shipped off to the Middle East.

Bran came back, Rik did not.

Bran stayed close to me all through the years since Rik's death. I think he felt obligated to Rik's memory to watch over us and keep us safe.

But the important thing was I trusted him implicitly with Bree and my own safety.

Monday was a normal day at work for me. Bree had a function after school and Bran decided to pick her up around seven. So this left just Trisha and me manning the shop.

It was awfully busy for a Monday night. The customers finally slowed down around six-thirty.

This was about the time Mykhalo showed up.

"Hello there," I said casually in front of Trisha. "Did you finish that last Agatha Christie novel?"

Mykhalo immediately picked up on my deception.

"Yes, and I was wondering if you had any more of her works, especially in an older publication," he replied before lowering his voice to a more secretive tone. "I need to speak to you alone."

I winked the eye Trisha couldn't see to him.

"I think I have an old compilation of her works in the antique room if you'd like to have a look," I suggested.

"Yes, I would be most interested in something like that," he said.

His voice had a sense of urgency to it.

I called out to Trisha I was taking a customer to the back room. She acknowledged this with a wave and said she would cover the store's front for me.

I beckoned Mykhalo to follow me and took him to the antique room.

Once inside I turned to him.

"Okay. What's up?"

"Where's Bree?" he said. Mykhalo almost looked nervous.

"With my friend Bran who is acting as her bodyguard," I said. "She's safe. I just got a call from her on my cell phone."

He seemed to breathe a sigh of relief.

"How is she?" he said urgently. "The last time I saw her…"

172

"She's fine," I reassured. "You were right. She did have questions only I could answer. And she is a very strong, young woman."

An inquisitive light came into his eyes at this.

"Now. What is going on?" I repeated more insistently.

"You may be in danger here," he said, stepping closer to me. "There are certain…unsavory individuals…flooding into this town."

"Mykhalo, I'm aware of this," I said to him in my most serious tone of voice.

The inquisitive look increased in surprise and he furrowed his brows in confusion.

"I will not be able to protect you for the next few days," he said.

"I know," I said. "We're expecting a lunar eclipse. I remember what you said happens to you during an eclipse. That's why Bran is acting as our bodyguard. We're safe."

The look turned to one of complete bewilderment and I just had to laugh.

"Mykhalo, you're not the only one with power!" I said.

He scratched his head, not expecting this reaction.

"Well, be that as it may…you need to do something. Like magic or whatever it is you do…" he began.

I laughed again.

"Like make a protective talisman for my daughter and myself? We'll do that tonight when we get home," I said, still chuckling.

"This is no laughing matter!" he replied with some heat.

The smile vanished from my face.

"Oh, I'm well aware of that, Mykhalo, my friend!" I said. "We've been rather busy preparing for the vampire convention."

He stepped closer still.

"You are being watched," he whispered.

I nodded.

"I know," I said. "I still have a few tricks up my sleeve. And worrying about this will help no one!"

He seemed to be looking helplessly around the room. His eyes suddenly latched onto the old army trunk.

"Is that the chest Bill left to you?" he said.

"Yes it is," I said. "Would you like to take a look inside?"

He nodded.

I went over to the trunk, unlocked it, and opened the heavy lid.

Mykhalo immediately began pulling out objects with only a cursory look at what they were. The trunk still seemed to interest him when it was empty and everything inside was piled outside it. He peered closely at the empty inside and then looked at the bottom of the trunk on the outside.

"This trunk has a false bottom," he said. "It's much more shallow inside than out."

With renewed interest, I began to inspect it more closely.

I pulled out my pocketknife and began to dig and pry at the inside edges of the trunk's floor.

This proved to further startle Mykhalo.

"Do you always carry a pocketknife on your person?" he said.

"Uh – hmm," I muttered back, absorbed in my chore. "They're very useful."

I flashed a wink at him.

"Thought you knew me, eh?" I said.

To this, he did not respond.

With a grunt and a small cry of triumph, the false floor suddenly sprang upwards into my hands.

"There we go!" I said, quite pleased with myself. "Now let's find out why Bill thought it was necessary to hide something in the false bottom."

We both peered eagerly inside.

My eyes went wide with surprise.

I was staring at the back of a small, but obviously very old, framed picture.

Wild possibilities sprang to my imagination. Was this some old, long lost work of art which had been looted during World War II? Was it an unknown Rembrandt, or Van Gogh? Why had Bill ferreted this one picture away? Was it so dear to him he just couldn't part with it?

The desire within me to know the answers to these questions was intense.

I carefully reached in and picked up the painting. Once again, I thought I should be wearing gloves to handle this artifact. It looked and felt very old. It even smelled ancient.

I lifted it out of the trunk and carefully spun it over so the artwork was exposed to our eyes.

Almost immediately, when Mykhalo saw it, he uttered something which sounded like German profanity, which shocked me. I saw nothing whatsoever to swear about.

The little painting was a portrait of a woman, nothing more.

She was seated with her hands folded in front of her. A signet ring with a black stone flashed from one hand. Her skin was milk white and flawless; her eyes were a warm shade of honey brown. Her raven black hair was piled high upon her head. She was not smiling. The whole appearance of her face was one of unspeakable beauty and charisma. I felt drawn in by those magical, brown eyes.

She was dressed in the high fashion of the 1500's. Her gown had puffed and slash sleeves. She wore a high-backed, lace collar which met at the square neckline of her velvet bodice. She was dressed in red velvet and her bodice was black brocade. Strings of pearls were draped across her bosom and a red cross glittered and flashed on her breast.

"What's the matter?" I said. "What's there about a woman's portrait from long ago, to swear about?"

"Bill kept it!" Mykhalo exclaimed. "He *never* should have kept it! I told him to get rid of it!"

"Why?" I asked. "Did he steal it? She's beautiful! Who is she?"

Mykhalo was grumbling something truly evil sounding in German.

"What's the matter?" I inquired more insistently. "And *who is she*?"

He scowled at me angrily.

"She's the Countess Elizabeth Bathory," he told me. "And you should burn that portrait immediately, like Bill should have done when I told him sixty years ago!"

175

I was horrified!

"Burn it? *Why?*" I exclaimed. "It's so old it must be valuable! She's so beautiful."

Mykhalo's eyes flashed silver fire at my incredible ignorance.

"She was a horrible, sadistic woman!" he informed me. "Her ghost dwells in that picture. Destroy it or she will make your life a living hell from beyond the grave!"

He suddenly snatched the picture from me.

"Here! I'll do it just to make sure it gets done this time!" he growled.

But I snatched it back from him possessively.

"No, I can destroy it myself if it must be done," I assured him.

He snarled again and his face went dark.

"Just make sure that you do," he insisted. "That picture has caused more harm than you could possibly imagine!"

I quickly put the portrait back in the trunk, along with the false floor and all the other objects and locked it securely.

"I'll take care of it in the ritual tonight. It probably should be buried in a graveyard to lock the spirit in," I reassured him.

Mykhalo paused and then nodded.

"Make sure that you don't forget," he said.

"I won't. I promise." I told him and I really meant it.

I rose to my feet and motioning him before me, ushered him out of the antique room.

We re-entered the storefront. Trisha was up on a ladder going through some books on the top shelf. She couldn't hear us if I spoke low.

"Maybe you should prepare yourself tonight, too," I suggested to Mykhalo.

He looked at me in surprise.

"How do you expect me to do that?" he said.

I shrugged.

"Well, you could always pray."

He gave me a jaded look.

176

"If I didn't know any better, I'd think you were trying to convert me, like a Christian," he scoffed.

I snickered in return.

"I never try to convert anybody!" I assured him. "But really. What could it hurt? My experience has told me prayer is always good, even if it's not a Christian prayer."

He snorted and then said something which truly surprised me.

"For your sake, I will consider it."

Something outside the Belfry's front window suddenly attracted his attention and he stiffened.

"Who is that man with your daughter?" he said.

I followed his gaze.

Bran had just pulled up in his big, black, construction truck and was opening the door for Bree.

"That's Bran, her – *our* bodyguard," I told him.

"Ah. One of your Wiccan friends, eh?" he said.

"Well, he's of Norse persuasion but you get the point, near enough," I said.

Mykhalo was looking at Bran with great interest. I noticed Bran looked much taller than my vampire friend did.

"He's a vampire slayer. Did you know that?" Mykhalo whispered.

I stepped closer and lowered my voice even more.

"Have you met him before?" I said.

He ignored this question.

"I can see the blood of the undead on his hands."

I looked from Mykhalo to Bran and back. Bran hadn't noticed us yet. His attention was focused quietly on the city street around them.

"Then maybe you should leave through the back door," I suggested.

"Why?" he whispered in reply. "I do not fear death. I welcome it. Seeing him guarding you both gives me hope."

He sighed and put his hat back on, pulling it down low to hide his eyes.

"Maybe my prayers have been answered before they've even begun," he mused then turned and, tipping his hat politely to me, left my bookstore.

I watched him turn left down the street without another glance at Bran escorting my daughter. I saw Bran's eyes suddenly latch on this departing figure and I noticed him freeze in mid step, grabbing Bree by the arm and halting her.

Bran's green eyes then turned and met mine on the other side on the shop window.

I did not smile but I nodded and mouthed wordlessly, "Yes, that's him."

* * *

"Mykhalo, we need to talk." Bartal began.

He spoke in German.

Mykhalo had just stirred from his daily sleep. The sun's rays still glimmered dimly on the horizon. He was shrugging himself into his customary starched white shirt.

"Did something happen while I slept?" he asked.

"No. Same mess coming. Different night."

"We need to focus on preparations for the eclipse…" Mykhalo started.

Bartal grabbed his arm.

"Blood brother, we really need to talk. Now!"

This stopped Mykhalo. Bartal only called him 'blood brother' when the topic was serious and extremely private. He faced him and their eyes met, his ice gray to Bartal's black.

The skin around his dark eyes was creased with concern.

Bartal was rarely worried about anything. All the perilous situations the two of them had encountered all their lives, he always kept his cool. It had to be something serious to get Bartal worried.

"I want to be with you when you go to face Hector," he said simply.

Mykhalo shook his head.

"Not possible. He said to come alone. Besides I need someone of your experience to run damage control when the storm clouds break over this little town. The majority of these people have no idea what they're up against. You do."

Bartal took hold of his other arm.

"Mykhalo, *listen to me*! I have a very bad feeling about this."

Mykhalo listened.

"What sort of bad feeling?"

Bartal took a deep breath.

"You will get your darkest wish in the next few days."

Mykhalo said nothing for a long moment.

"Which one? That Hector will die or I will?" he tone was joking but his expression was not.

Bartal only held his eyes and did not reply.

Mykhalo turned away from him. The emotion in his friend's face was too raw for him.

"We've been through situations where I could have died before," Mykhalo said softly.

"This is different. I'm certain of it."

Mykhalo did not know what to say. "If it happens...I want to be there with you fighting at your side. I want to be able to say goodbye and all those things a friend is supposed to say before I don't get another chance."

Mykhalo felt a stab of pain in his heart. He fought to master a myriad of emotions which threatened to break free. He fumbled for the right words.

"I understand. Really I do. But your place is in the town, not at my side. Besides you've been at my side most of my long life. You know my feelings toward you. I will always feel what you cannot say. If I die it will just be easier for me to sense it."

He turned about and put his hands on his friend's shoulders and squeezed them reassuringly. Bartal bowed his head and his breath caught in his big chest.

"Spoken words are not always necessary. I will still hear the words in your heart even if..." Mykhalo could not finish the sentence.

Bartal raised his head to look him in the eye. His face was lined in confusion.

"What's happened to you, blood brother? You've never spoken like this."

Mykhalo turned away. He picked up his business blazer and busied himself with pulling it on. He did not look at his friend.

"I remember all the times you visited your family's graves. You stood outside the cemetery gates because you weren't permitted to walk on sacred ground. You just stood there silent and thoughtful. You never spoke a word or brought any token of affection.

"You said it was because the dead could not hear you so what's the point?"

Bartal shook his head.

"What you said just now does not sound like the Mykhalo I have always known. What has happened to you?"

Mykhalo smiled to himself and his friend saw it.

"What has that witch been doing to you?" he said.

It was a good question. What had Zan been doing to him?

He sighed and shook his head in acknowledgement of the fact.

"Let's just say my friendship with her has changed my perspective on things, things I thought I was certain of all my life. Now I'm not so sure. And it's all her fault. I tried to keep this relationship casual. But I don't think it's casual anymore."

Sudden realization broke over Bartal's face.

"You love her!" he said grinning broadly.

The pleasant look vanished from Mykhalo's face.

"Shut up!" he growled. "That must never happen!"

"And why the hell not? What's wrong with loving her?"

Mykhalo's face was quickly growing dark as a storm cloud.

"Because it's dangerous for her, that's why! The passion might bring on the hunger."

But Bartal disagreed.

"And then again it might not."

180

"Stop it, Bartholomew!" Mykhalo spouted. "Whether I love Zan or not is beside the point. She must never know. I will not kill another friend!"

The big man only scoffed.

"*You* stop it! Zan is like no other woman you've ever run across. She's strong. She can handle it. Quit being a martyr! Take a chance. You might even like it."

Mykhalo glared at his friend. But Bartal was not put off and faced him.

"And if you're gonna take a chance on this witch, you better grab that happiness soon. Your time is very short. Mark my words."

Mykhalo took a deep breath.

"I have enough regrets."

Bartal marched up to Mykhalo and faced him like it was a dare.

"This isn't one of them."

# CHAPTER 18

Sage had spent all day cleaning and smudging the sacred space in her basement. Even though we were not planning on doing the ritual at my place I had smudged my house, too. I felt better knowing both houses had their respective energies properly cleansed. Therefore both our environments would be strong and inviting to all positive energies we might need in the days to come. It is like inviting good ghosts instead of malicious ones into your home.

Sage knew I felt better doing a ritual outside, surrounded by nature but in this particular case, I completely understood working our magic surrounded by the safety of her basement walls. We needed a safer area to do the spell in, one which had not only secure spiritual doors but solid doors in the real world as well.

But given her age and the fact she lived alone, Sage needed help with some of the cleansing. She wanted certain pieces of furniture moved out of the basement. So Bran and I assisted her with this while Bree buzzed about her house and gathered supplies we would need or she thought we would need. Bree's constant fault with spells was always amassing too many supplies just in case we needed them!

Bran and I were wrestling a large chest that Sage had been meaning to donate once she got some help moving it up the narrow steps of her basement. Once up the stairs, we twisted around a corner and deposited it with much huffing and puffing into her living room, somewhat out of the way.

Bree sped past us on her way to the basement, laden with an armload of candles. She was humming to her iPod and tossing her hair in time with the beat. Her hair had recently changed color, yet again, to a bright shade of blood red. Somehow though, I thought this shade would last longer than any of the others. She had also taken to dressing in bright red. I had started to call my daughter 'the stop sign' or 'the reverse Goth.' She merely stuck her tongue out at me and continued bouncing along in her life.

Bran and I just shook our heads and kept toiling along.

"So Bran," I puffed in a low voice. "When were you going to tell me you're a vampire slayer?"

He gave me a sharp look and held my eyes for a long moment.

"What little birdie told you that?" he muttered back in an equally low tone.

"No little birdie but maybe a little bat," I said to him with a slow smile.

"Hmm," he hummed. "Wouldn't be a little *Bavarian* bat, now would it?"

I chuckled.

"I didn't start out to be a vampire slayer," he informed in a rather evasive way. "You remember my opinion of 'Buffy'?"

I snickered.

"It disgusted you!" I said.

He nodded and removing his knit cap, wiped his steaming brow.

"Let's just say I ran into some things I wasn't prepared for in Baghdad," he said. "I was completely expecting to get shot at, lose my buddies, get wounded, hell. Maybe not even come home. But I wasn't expecting *that*!"

He then knelt down in front of me and pulled a short knife out of the top of each of his heavy hiking boots and handed them to me for my inspection.

They were simple knives, fashioned from one solid piece instead of a hilt attached to a blade. There were no fancy carving on the hilts and they were obviously homemade but very well done.

But my eyes noticed the knives were black and not fashioned from metal at all.

"Ebony?" I asked.

He made an affirmative sound.

"I will never be caught unprepared again!"

I handed the knives back to him and he wordlessly replaced them in his boots.

"It must be very hard to find wooden stakes in the desert," I commented.

He grunted and nodded.

"Almost as precious as water there. Especially where I was deployed."

He would say no more and I knew better than to press him for more details.

We went about our work in silence until Sage interrupted us.

She gave us a meaningful look and said, "Now."

She caught Bree's arm as she skipped past with one hand and with the other yanked her iPod earplugs.

"It's time," she said solemnly.

Bree's unuttered protest died on her lips and the grimmer one I had become familiar with after Brittany's death came over her face.

We three filed down the darkened stairs. Bran nodded to us and closed the door. He was not to be part of the ritual. He was to guard the doors from any unseen forces who would try to cause us harm or interrupt the flow of energy.

I gasped when I got to the foot of the stairs. Bree had lined every nook and cranny with candles. Their soft light flickered and danced on the walls of the basement filling the room with a warm, inviting glow. Only candles lit the room.

I glared at Sage with a look which admonished her for giving in to Bree's whims.

Bree was standing between us and noticed.

"What?" she said. "I like candles."

Sage sighed.

"I decided that tonight it would do no harm," she confessed.

"Yeah, unless the fire marshal shows up!" I growled.

Sage chuckled and shrugged deeper into her shawl.

"I temporarily disconnected the fire alarms. I'll plug them back in when we're done."

I shook my head helplessly and let it slide.

There were candles of each corresponding color on every one of the five quarters of the room set in a star formation, green, white, red, I noticed the major candles, the ones on the quarters, had yet to be lit. There was also a bundle of candles in the center of the circle near the altar and a blue duffel bag which I recognized as Sage's beading bag.

Sage lit the smudge stick, blowing reverently on it to encourage the dried herb to catch. Once this was done, she smudged us both and then passed the smoking stick to me to smudge and cleanse her before beginning the rite and entering the circle.

We then took up our corresponding places around the circle. We each took a deep, cleansing breath. As I prepared my spirit, I looked around the room. I thought how fitting it was we three should be doing this ritual.

Maid, mother and crone, we were here.

We did the opening ritual and conjured the quarters, welcoming in the essence of the five elements: fire, air, water, earth and spirit. The corresponding candles were lit.

That done, Sage stepped to the center and recited solemnly with Bree and myself repeating each line after her.

Power of Sacred Fire
Hear our desire
Power of Sacred Air
Harken to our prayer
Power of Sacred Earth
Show us our worth
Power of Sacred Waves
Come to our aide
Spirits of the Past
Help us to stand fast

Sage then motioned to us the come to the low altar in the center. We each knelt around it in the shape of a triangle. Sage pulled the beading bag closer and, opening it, lifted out tray after tray of multi-colored, semiprecious beads and opened them for us. She handed Bree and myself a measured cord and a tiny, corked jewelry bottle.

"Make your talismans," she instructed. "The bottle is the focal point. We fill it last of all. But feel free to use any of my beads which call to you at this particular moment. Consider well what beads you will use to surround it."

Bree and I looked at each other and began to rummage around.

Sage closed her eyes and began to chant something in another language as we sorted and decided and created our necklaces.

I was drawn to the beads which were labeled 'mother of pearl'. Odd, I thought, because I don't consider myself to be a pearl sort of lady. But this was the vibe I got and we were in a sacred circle surrounded by flickering candles and the spirits of ancestors and energies of elements. So I went with it. I chose nothing but mother of pearl beads to surround my bottle.

I noticed Bree had gravitated to green beads which were labeled 'bloodstone'. I smiled and thought it extremely appropriate. I felt Sekhmet would highly approve of her choice.

We worked silently, absorbed in our task. Sage's chanting surrounded us with the feeling of love and protection.

We both finished our necklaces at about the same time and held them out to Sage. We knew better than to interrupt her chanting.

But she seemed to sense we were done. She opened her eyes and her chanting subsided into humming. She picked up a pair of scissors and motioned for me to lean close to her.

I obeyed without question.

Sage leaned over, still humming and lovingly stroked my hair with her free hand. As she came to the ends of the lock of hair, she brought forward the scissors and snipped off a small bit. She put down the scissors and took my necklace from me, twisting the lock of my hair into a tiny, black rope, inserted it into the bottle and corked it securely. She returned the talisman to me and nodded.

187

I knew this meant I was to hold the necklace and concentrate all of my thoughts and energy into what I had just created.

Then she repeated this motion with Bree still humming the tune of her chant. Sage returned her talisman to her and motioned for her to meditate as well over it.

We were silent as we did this. Sage's humming ceased. For a space of time, there was only the sound of our breathing and the flicker of the candles about us.

Sage then gestured that I was to hand Bree my necklace and she was to mimic my motion at the same time. She stopped us before our creations left our hands. We froze there, my hand with my pearl necklace offered and my daughter's hand covering mine. Bree mirrored my action in reverse.

Sage's right hand was holding my arm and her left hand held Bree's. She instructed us to repeat the charm as she spoke it line by line.

Lock of mine, lock of thine,
Warrior's stone, Mother's milk,
Strength of goddess, touch of silk,
Parent to child, daughter to mother,
Protection to both, envelop and cover,

A shell so strong, no evil can crack,
Fight it! Repel it! Send it back!
None shall sunder, none shall bite,
For the Lord and Lady aide in the fight,
Sacred light and sacred power,
Uplift us both in the deadly hour,
Evil shall flee, evil shall run,
And be burned into dust by the sacred sun,
As we will it, so mote it be!

Sage withdrew her hands and gestured that we should exchange talismans. So I took her bloodstone necklace and Bree took my mother of pearl.

Sage nodded again and we donned our fresh, new, talismans, pulsing with powerful protection.

The bloodstone felt warm under my hands and on my skin. I looked at my daughter as she caressed the pearls on her neck and my black hair glistened back at me from its new home in the bottle.

We smiled wordlessly at each other. I knew she felt as I did, safe and protected inside this circle. I knew I would carry the feeling of safety in the days to come.

"Goddess bless these two in the battle to come when the moon bleeds red," Sage murmured into the quietness of the room. "Protect them, bless them and keep them safe from all harm. Give strength to their arms, power to their words, confidence to their spirits and victory to their cause."

Sage gave a great sigh and with a creak and groan, rose to her feet. We followed suit. Quietly, we closed the circle in the reverse order than we opened it. The directional candles were pinched out, the elements politely dismissed.

When we had finished, Sage clapped her hands three times.

On the third time, I literally felt the energy *pop*!

The sacred space was once more just a basement. The spirit of divinity had left us human again.

We hugged each other laughing and then filed up the stairs to relieve Bran from his guardian post.

Sage fired up the coffee pot.

It wasn't until much later I remembered. I did not keep my promise to Mykhalo.

I had completely forgotten about the portrait!

* * *

189

The next day was just another day at work. I did go through my chores with a heightened sense of clarity. That night was the first night of the full moon. The next night was the lunar eclipse.

I did notice a lot of the local esoteric community I was acquainted with was stopping by. Mostly just to check in on me and make sure I was all right. I really wasn't too worried about things though simply because it was daylight.

I should have known better!

An hour before sunset, customers of any type dried up completely. I assumed all my pagan friends were home gathering energy. I talked to Bree who had stayed late at the school library to do some research for a paper which was due the next Monday. She said Bran was already there and helping her study. She told me she and Bran would show up around eight in the evening when I closed the shop. We planned on all three of us going out for a late dinner.

I felt safe having just talked to her. I told Trisha to go on home around seven-thirty.

At ten of eight, I saw the familiar black truck pull up and park alongside the curb across the street. I started to turn off the lights and lock the inside doors. The weather forecast for the night had been for uncommonly low temperatures for mid-March, so I had worn my cape to work, which I usually reserved for outside rituals in winter. It was deep green and made out of heavy wool, with a cavernous hood and armhole slits in the side. It was the warmest thing I owned and I hated being cold. So I donned that, put the hood up and going outside locked the front door to the shop. I then turned around to face the street and stopped in shock.

The black vehicle wasn't Bran's truck but a different one which just looked very similar.

This was an instant red flag!

"Mrs. Miller?" said a strangely deep, yet nasal voice right at my shoulder.

I nearly jumped out of my skin in fright.

"Yes?" I said in a tremulous voice before I remembered responding to my own name might *not* be a good thing right now.

A tall, black man stood next to me. He looked to have the physique of a body builder. He was dressed in a modern, leather trench coat which fell to his knees. He was bald and his eyes were strange. They seemed a shade lighter than his skin.

He smiled in response to my voice. His teeth were very white.

He raised one hand as if to wave at me. But the gesture had nothing to do with a greeting.

I don't remember him grabbing me, or hitting me with any hard object.

I just remember a sharp pain at my temple which came from inside my head.

Everything around me suddenly went black.

## CHAPTER 19

I remember dreaming.

I was walking through the woods in early spring. It was midnight and the sky was clear and the moon full and the woodland splashed with night shadows. I seemed to know where I was going. Large wolves flanked me on either side, trotting easily beside me. When they looked at me, their eyes glowed red.

I knew these were no normal wolves.

The trees gave way to an open clearing. In the exact center of the clearing was a stone rimmed well. In front of the well stood a person with their back to me. The person turned about to face me and smiled in welcome.

It was the Lord of the Wild Hunt.

I could not see many details of him because the moon was over his shoulder, throwing his body into shadow. But I knew the powerful silhouette and I recognized the antlers branching from his head, even though the antlers were small and their edges were softened with spring velvet.

I stepped closer to him. He smelled of freshly tilled earth and mown grass. He welcomed me in joy as a father to his daughter. I felt safe there. His wide, brown hands grasped my shoulders and he who rarely spoke words spoke into the silence of my mind.

'Zan, if we stood in front of a raging bonfire and I told you to walk into it, would you?' he asked me.

I was confused.

"Why would you ask me to harm myself, Lord?" I said.

I sensed amusement from him.

'If I told you the fire would not burn you, that I would protect you from all harm, would you take that leap of faith?' he said in his rumbling voice.

I gazed up into the shadow of his horned head.

"If you assured me of your sacred protection, then of course, Lord. I would do as you ask," I said.

I sensed satisfaction from his comforting presence.

'Sometimes child, the fire cannot be avoided but needs to be faced. It needs to be walked through. You will need to have that faith in the Divine to get you through this trial. Now turn about, Daughter of Wood and Stone.'

I obeyed without question.

I felt his broad, sun tanned hands on my shoulders.

'Now Daughter, walk into the fire's heart. Walk into it and know I am here by your side, protecting you and guarding you from all harm. Have faith.'

There was now a fire in front of me. I could see its leaping, crackling flames towering high above me and feel the heat on my face. I could smell the cinders as they were blown about. The heat from the flames made my eyes water and sting.

I took a deep breath and swallowed hard. I clenched my hands into fists at my side.

I stepped into the dream's fire.

* * *

The next thing I remembered was the bright swirling colors of the expensive Persian rug I was splayed face down upon.

I was someplace else, someplace strange and alien. The smell of old wood and antiques told me this. I also sensed the room was full of people...dangerous people.

There was a hiss above me, like the sound of an enraged female cobra puffing itself up to look more threatening.

194

"Just one, tiny, little nip," a female voice purred seductively over me.

There came a sudden growl, a screech, and a crashing of furniture.

"Master said no! Not this one!" the oddly deep, yet nasal voice of the black man I had just recently encountered, blasted at the female voice.

The hiss came again from across the room, angrier but more subdued and chastising.

"I don't like when Master plays with his food before dining!" the woman's voice hissed back. "What are we? Cats?"

The black man was standing next to me. I could see his army boots.

"This one is important," the man retorted. "The Master has some special plan for her. Feed at will on the town. But leave this one to him. Those are his orders."

"I'm hungry!" pouted the woman's voice. "And she's here now. And she's warm and pulsing with delicious blood! Can't you smell it?"

"Control yourself, Giselle," the man barked back. "Or the master will dine on you!"

Another voice, male this time, spoke up from the other direction.

"She is awake. And listening."

I could no longer feign helplessness.

I rolled over on my back to face them.

I was in what looked like a library, the kind they have in old English manor houses. The room was decorated in wood paneling and lots of antique furniture and mounted heads of wild game.

And on every chair or couch there was seated or perched a human. Cancel that. They couldn't be human. Each one was too perfect. Every woman was fastidiously coiffed and dressed in clothes befitting a Parisian model, every man of chiseled countenance and handsome to look upon. I hated them immediately for it and wondered if this was the norm. Did every vampire have to be a specimen of

195

human perfection in his or her prime? I wondered if there were any fat, ugly, or old vampires.

For vampires they were, each and every one. If I weren't a witch, it would have been obvious. But being a witch only made it clearer to me. I could feel the malice issuing out from them in dark waves and see the soulless light in their eyes. Unlike Mykhalo, I could not see any conscience in their faces. Their moral compass was gone.

And they could have cared less about it.

They were all leering at me as if I was naked.

Why did I suddenly feel like a roasted pig on a plate with an apple in its mouth?

My inner voice was screaming at me to get out of there as fast as possible. My eyes told me this would not have been possible. So I just lay there and looked at them looking at me, while my heart was pounding a staccato beat like gunfire in my breast.

The woman vampire who had been cast across the room was observing me with great interest now she had brushed off the splinters. She was creeping closer to me, behaving like a cat stalking a bird that was suddenly suspicious. I realized whatever fear I felt was feeding their hunger, especially hers.

She must have been a very young vampire.

I locked eyes with hers, took a deep breath, and forced myself to smile.

"I wonder..." I said quietly to her. "Since you cast no reflection of any kind, how do you do your hair?"

She stopped and her eyes flew wide in shock.

She snarled in return and began to mutter, "Why, you impudent little...!"

The black man stepped in between us and shoved her back away from me.

A man behind me laughed and commented in a voice with an obvious British accent, "Cheeky little piece of meat, isn't she?"

I swallowed my terror and shot him what I hoped was an icy look.

There was a sudden unspoken ripple in the assemblage and all the vampires backed away from me.

Someone was coming. My heart began to dance to a new fearful beat.

The door opened and their ranks parted.

I stood up quickly and brushed off my cape.

When I looked up again, a different vampire was standing in front of me.

He had dark eyes and hair. He was impeccably dressed and smelled of expensive cologne. His skin seemed heavily tanned and he was clean-shaven. In spite of his obvious handsome looks, he had heavy brows, which made him look very menacing. He looked like Spanish nobility or an unmasked Zorro. And his appearance came with a feeling of allure, almost palpable in sensation. I could have felt his power from across a room, but he was right in front of me. He was standing close enough to have shaken hands with me.

I did not want him to touch me.

My inner voice had faded completely away by this time.

He smiled the way a serpent would have smiled to a cornered rabbit.

"I am..." he began to say.

"Hector," I finished for him. "I know. We've met."

He looked somewhat different without the snow frosting. His curly black hair was sternly brushed back and gelled like a male model.

His lips parted in an even greater smile. It was chilling how bright his teeth were.

"Ah, you remember me!" he said. "I'm flattered. But please allow me to introduce myself properly. I am Don Hector Salamanca."

So I was right. He *was* Spanish nobility.

He bowed with much flourish.

I once again forced myself to swallow my fear.

"Charmed, I think," I said. "Somehow I expected you to be taller."

He cocked his head to the side with only the slightest hint of a scowl.

"Charles is right. You *are* quite a 'cheeky piece of meat,' as he puts it. Ah, you will be an amusing one to play with!"

I tried to stand taller. I was hoping that looking down on him would give me the personal strength I needed to face him. It would have been much easier to do this if I was wearing heels.

Hector began to circle me, as he had the night at the hotel where he had taken on the guise of Mykhalo, enjoying the feeling of having cornered his prey.

"I don't plan on playing your game, Hector," I said. "You already dabbled with me once. I didn't enjoy it then and I won't enjoy it now."

He smiled at me and stepped closer, already sensing my extreme aversion to his proximity.

"No one enjoys me dabbling with them, my dear," he spoke in a low voice as if he was confiding some great secret to me. "But do you really think I care about their enjoyment?"

The thought of what he might do to me sent my heart racing for the hills.

He casually walked past me to a bar by the wall where he poured himself a drink of what seemed to be red wine. With his eyebrows suggestively cocked, he offered me a glass. I shook my head in denial.

"She will not drink," he said to the group gathered. "She does not wish her senses to be dulled so soon. Clever. But it will not help her."

He slowly wound his way back to me, holding the glass under his nose as if he was enjoying its delicate bouquet.

"I daresay by the time you leave here, my dear, we will get you to drink something!" he suggested slyly, with one eyebrow upturned.

An amused chuckle circulated quietly through the room.

I raised my chin defiantly.

"You may try," I dared him. "But you will not be successful."

He chuckled again. My pluck was only entertaining him.

He sipped the wine slowly, savoring every drop. He stepped closer to me, close enough to be in my space, close enough to bother me and he knew it. He looked deep into my eyes as if trying to guess what I would do next.

His free hand suddenly lashed out and clutched my throat tightly.

I gasped in surprise.

The other vampires in the room leaned forward eagerly as if the feeding was about to commence. Part of me prepared myself for this to be it.

Hector smiled maliciously at me and loosened his grip. His thumb gently stroked the curve of my neck where the jugular was. I could feel his long nails on his other fingers bite into my skin. My skin prickled and crawled in revulsion at his touch.

"Such lovely skin you have, so perfect and white," he whispered quietly to me as if I were his lover. "Shall I tell my children what lovely, pure skin you have, how deliciously smooth it is right here on your throat? Shall I share you with them or keep you all to myself? You choose this for me."

His hand drifted deeper down my throat, probing underneath my polo shirt where it was not welcome. And once again, as before, I could do nothing to stop him.

I hated his touch.

His fingers found the cord on one of my necklaces. His curiosity got the better of him. I felt him loop his finger around it and slowly drag it out into full view enjoying the suspense of the discovery.

It was the leather cord from which my silver pentacle swung.

He held it in his hand and looked at it for one long moment, his attention interrupted.

"You think this will protect you here?" he whispered, almost passionately into my ear. His breath tickled my skin.

His lip curled in disgust. He let the pentacle swing, glittering and then falling into full view of the rest of those gathered.

"She fancies herself a witch," he told them. Again, the amused chuckle rippled among them.

Anger began to boil in my heart and I felt my face grow hot. I never appreciated being mocked for any reason.

He turned to face me.

"I am not afraid of witches," he told me boldly. "Maybe if you were a witch from yesteryear that might give me pause, but not now. Not today. The witches of today have lost their teeth. They have no power when compared to my kind."

I tilted my head and smiled back at him.

"I beg to disagree," I replied. "We still know how to fight. And yes, we still *do* have our teeth."

Hector laughed even louder at this.

"Perhaps you mean your gifted daughter and you how do you say 'bodyguard'?" his accent seemed to get very thick here.

The smile vanished from my face.

"Ah! Now I have your full attention," he said with a wide grin.

He waved a hand to his cohorts.

"Baptiste. Sal," he called.

Immediately the black vampire and another equally imposing individual stepped to his side.

"Find the girl and her warrior-guardian. Kill him. Bring me the girl untouched. Go now!"

The two other vampires gave me a look of sadistic joy and happily left to do their lord's bidding.

A flurry of maternal worry fluttered briefly in my heart. I tried to tell myself my daughter had the least to fear from this group. But still the fear was there. So I fought to master it.

I forced myself to laugh in his face.

"Go ahead!" I dared him. "My daughter has a little surprise for you I don't think you're going to like very much."

At this, he spun on me.

"No!" he spouted in sudden anger which made everyone in the room step back. "It is *you* that will be surprised!"

He fought to take a deep breath and control his emotions.

"No, my dear," he said and his voice was soft and sadistic once again. "This night will be full of surprises for you. You have much to discover."

He turned to the nearest person and said.

"It is time for her to meet Michael. Please go get him for me."

Five vampires silently left the room, sliding me sly looks and smiles as they did so.

Hector went to the desk, seated himself behind it, and propped his booted feet up onto the tabletop.

"Have you ever been to Transylvania, my dear?" he asked, out of the blue.

I was confused as to where he was going with this line of conversation.

"Never, although I hear it's an interesting place to visit," I said.

Hector sighed as if disappointed.

"A pity. You really should have seen more of the world at your age. Now you will never get the chance," he teased. "Never mind. Back to Transylvania. It is a beautiful place filled with beautiful people. Why even the simple farmers are brilliant. Do you know why that is?"

I shook my head.

"I'm sure I don't know."

He leaned across the table and told me in a very intense tone of voice.

"It is because of us! Because Transylvania has a healthy population of hungry vampires, the people are so beautiful and brilliant."

He leaned back in the chair with a sigh.

"You teach your children the human being is just another animal. Well if that is true then there must be a predator to keep the animals' numbers in check. That's how it works for every other species on this planet. But no. Although you teach it, you don't live it. You act as if you're above all the other animals, wasting and using up this planet."

"What's your point, Hector? Get to it!" I demanded impatiently as if I had somewhere important to be.

"You believe in balance?" he said quietly. "Well I believe this world needs more vampires to keep the balance. There are too many wasted lives out there. Weak people who should have never made it past childhood, foolish people who have squandered the gift of life they've been given, and just plain stupid people. We Nosferatu weed out the wheat from the chaff so to speak. And believe you me, this country has got a lot of chaff!"

He swiveled his chair about as he spoke.

"I just spent an entire month in 'Nuevo' Jersey looking for you before I realized I had been sent on a wild goose chase. Let me tell you, that state has mostly chaff in it! It could use a good cleansing by a group of hungry vampires. It's a blood buffet!"

I was unimpressed by his words.

"It seems you kidnapped me only to spout off your opinions at someone," I taunted him. "I seem to have fulfilled that purpose, so can I go home now? I have this important thing called a life to get back to."

Terrified as I was, I was starting to tire of all this infernal chest beating.

Hector smiled at me mockingly.

"Oh I'm far from being done with you," he told me. "And don't you want to see your surprise? Why here he comes now."

The door burst open and the five vampires returned, dragging in another very unwilling person who was fighting them every step of the way. His arms were shackled tightly behind his back.

They deposited him with a grunt of effort in front of me and he fell to his knees and stayed there.

He was shirtless and barefoot and the nice dress slacks he wore looked like they had seen better days. His silver hair hung messily in a long swath in front of his face hiding his features.

He had been beaten recently. His back was crisscrossed with red welts and purple bruises. I was amazed their prisoner could be abused so severely without drawing blood.

I supposed they were saving the good part for last.

"I believe you are already well acquainted with Michael here," Hector said with obvious relish. "Michael, say hello to Susan Miller."

At this, the kneeling man flung back his head and stared into my eyes.

"Zan?"

It was Mykhalo!

Before I thought about controlling my emotions, I had fallen to the floor in front of him. I reached for him in sympathy but he drew back.

"What are you doing here?" I hissed at him in concern.

"I could ask you much the same question," he said.

"It was not by choice," I told him.

He grunted in reply.

"Likewise," he returned and gave those surrounding us a venomous look.

There was a snort of scorn from behind me.

"Why, Michael. She cares for you! How touching," Hector's voice said.

I slowly rose to my feet. Anger had replaced fear. I had nothing prepared to say just yet, I was so angry, so I wasted my breath on a foolish question.

"Why do you call him Michael?"

Hector chuckled at my ignorance.

"Because that is his name!" he replied. "Well, Mykhalo is Ukrainian for Michael and his mother was Ukrainian. But three hundred years ago, when he was born, the Ukraine was a possession of Poland. He hates being called Michael, so I jerk his chain with it every chance I get."

Hector stepped closer to us and began to wave his finger at me in a scolding manner.

"You have been a very foolish mortal, Mrs. Miller," he admonished me. "Carrying on a friendship with one of the undead? Do you know how dangerous he is to you?"

"I know he's dangerous," I replied. "I have known from the first day I laid eyes on him."

Hector gave me a derisive look over his shoulder.

"And yet you chose to ignore the danger and get close to him. What did you think? You were special? That he was your witch's pet, a vampire familiar?"

He suddenly stepped very close to me and declared angrily in my ear, "He is an animal! A predator! We all are! Michael is no different than any of those gathered in this room. He is no different than myself! You took a great risk with your life, Mrs. Miller."

I refused to look at him and set my jaw angrily.

"I see," he whispered. "You do not believe me. You have not seen his animal side. It is hard to believe in what you haven't seen or experienced, isn't it?"

He walked back to his desk and seated himself comfortably again as if this was going to take a while.

"I think Mrs. Miller needs a history lesson, don't you?" he asked the other vampires gathered. "Now listen carefully. There will be a test on this later."

He gave a deep sigh and interlaced his fingers in front of him.

"Michael never told you what happened to the other members of his family, now did he?" Hector asked, narrowing his eyes slyly at me.

I looked at Mykhalo. He avoided my gaze. He only glared at Hector and cast his eyes downward. He refused to speak.

Hector chuckled with barely restrained glee, so eager was he to tell me.

"He killed them!" he said. "He murdered each and every one of them, from his despicable father to his beloved sister, to his wife whom he didn't love but nevertheless wished no harm. He feasted on each and every one of them! Now what do you think of your 'dear friend'?"

My jaw dropped in horror. I tried several times to say something but no words would come out. There had to be some mistake, some reason. No! What reason could there be to kill your entire family?

I looked back to Mykhalo. His head was still down, his beautiful, silver touched hair swept over his eyes. He refused to look at me.

"Ah! Now you're shocked!" Hector laughed. "He's not as harmless as he seemed before, is he? Granted, he was ordered to kill each one of his family by my lovely Elizabeth. But then young vampires are so barely in control of their urges, aren't they Giselle?"

The dark haired woman from earlier merely curled her lip and scowled at his remark.

My mind had seized onto a familiar name.

"Elizabeth? Who was she?" I was finally able to stutter out.

Gee, could Hector's scoffing smile get any wider?

"I'm so glad you asked about her!" he said. "Elizabeth was a very special vampire lady, at least she was to me. Countess Elizabeth Bathory, from what is now called Slovakia. But when I met her, it was called Hungary. Times change, wars come and go, and borders change with the years."

He sighed almost wistfully at the memories.

"She was married when I met her but that was no matter. Her husband was extremely permissive with his young bride. I have never met a woman so gifted for cruelty and sadism. She was perfection itself! Beautiful, complex, mesmerizing, and amazingly talented in the art of pain and torture. She taught me many new tricks. I adored her, I worshipped the ground she walked on."

Mykhalo suddenly straightened his back and looked Hector boldly in the eye.

"I killed her, too," he said abruptly, almost proudly, one corner of his mouth upturned in a wry smile.

Hector shot to his feet and came around the corner of the table so fast it was frightening. His fist slammed into Mykhalo's face, knocking him backwards.

The Bavarian only shook off the blow and smiled back at him.

This reaction only seemed to further enrage Hector and he grew quiet once more.

"I still remember some of the tricks my darling Elizabeth taught me," he growled at Mykhalo. "Maybe I should try them on your little, human friend here and let you watch?"

The smile vanished from Mykhalo's face and his eyes glittered a warning.

"Hector, I promise you one day I will tear open your throat!" he told him in a deadly whisper.

Hector only laughed at this.

"You've had nearly three hundred years to do so," Hector sneered back at him. "I doubt it will happen."

Mykhalo snorted back at him. "I still have time."

205

Hector nodded.

"Yes, all we have is time."

"Why do you insist on tormenting him so?" I demanded.

Hector returned his attention to me.

"Haven't you been paying attention? This is what I do. It's how I while the centuries away."

"No," I said and getting bolder, I took a step closer to him. "This is different. You get special pleasure from torturing Mykhalo. Is it just because he killed your love or is it more than that?"

Hector snarled at me, revealing his canines.

"Just killing Elizabeth was enough to make me hunt him to the ends of the earth! But you are right, my dear. It is more, much more than that."

I remembered the conversation Mykhalo and I had the night in the hotel room.

"He breaks the rules. That's it, isn't it?" I said.

Hector snickered at me, somewhat impressed.

"Your witch friend here is very shrewd, Michael. She has keen sight," Hector said with an affirming grunt. He seated himself and downed the rest of the wine in his glass with one greedy gulp as if preparing himself.

"You are correct, Mrs. Miller. Michael here breaks the rules. He grapples to hang onto his humanity and his conscience, which is ridiculous for a vampire! He insists on having human friends, which is very foolish for them! Perhaps he hopes one will bestow eventual salvation on him? Preposterous! And he is a kin-slayer both of mortals and his own undead kind. Shall I go on? I'm sure I can add more to the list but for now, those will suffice."

He sighed again.

"Michael started out as my greatest hope. A powerful avenging hammer with which to beat Rome. He has turned into my greatest disappointment and must therefore be punished for all eternity. We tried to teach him the laws of the Nosferatu. He refused the teaching and killed his teacher, something I never thought could happen with so young and inexperienced an undead."

*His teacher?* "Elizabeth?" I suggested and Hector nodded.

"I will not make the same mistake again," he told me. "This time when I beat him, you will be the club!"

He strode up to Mykhalo and dragged him to his feet by his hair. Mykhalo towered over Hector and glared icy daggers at him.

It was then I noticed the one bit of jewelry he wore. I had never seen it before because he must have always worn it under his expensive suit. A simple black cord sat around his neck, and from it hung an iridescent, glass bottle filled with something dark.

In one smooth move, Hector yanked it off his neck, cast it to the floor, and stomped on the bottle, shattering it.

"Your home is far away from you, Michael," he whispered gently to him. "Deal with it! If you can!"

He motioned to the others in the room.

Again, the five vampires came forward and picking him up by the arms wrestled him from the room.

A tall, blonde vampire woman with eyes of blue ice came up to me and pointed for me to follow.

I did so meekly.

We were led down a dark hallway and up a flight of stairs and finally ushered into a large room with curtains completely covering the wall at one end. It almost looked like a small, private theater except there were no chairs. There was an observation balcony above the stairs we had entered through. The floor was wood paneling with strange dark stains and smears on the floor next to the walls.

There were chains and shackles on the walls at either side.

"This is my favorite room in the house," Hector declared proudly to us. "The former owner, like me, enjoyed his 'torture theatre' as he called it. I saw no reason to change the decor."

He made a gesture and Mykhalo was immediately shackled to the wall.

Two other vampires went up and drew the curtain with the help of a pull cord on either side. The curtains were pulled back to reveal a monstrous window looking out onto the night sky.

"Here you will spend the night and the next day," Hector told us. "Of course Michael will be none too happy when dawn comes. But you will be able to help him with that Mrs. Miller. If he gets too much sun, all you have to do is give him a few drops of your blood. That will help. But be cautious. He may want more than a few drops after he gets started. Now I hope you will excuse me. We all have a dinner date we seem to be rather tardy for. Have a good evening!"

There were chuckles all around as the group of vampires departed and locked the great doors after them.

I was free but Mykhalo was chained to the wall.

We were alone in the great room together.

I allowed my tough exterior to collapse. I crumpled onto the floor in a heap and gave in to all the pent up emotions I had been restraining.

I just sat there shaking like a leaf, too exhausted by my emotions to cry.

## CHAPTER 20

I was dark inside for quite some time. Mykhalo made not a sound, nor spoke any word to me. It was as if I was alone in the cavernous room, my whimpers echoing from the great oaken walls.

I finally managed, with a great effort, to pull myself together and dash the tears away from my face. I stood up and paced the vast room, wrapping the cloak tighter about myself.

"This is all my fault," Mykhalo finally spoke up. "I am truly sorry to have dragged you into this."

I turned and regarded him for some time. He remained where he was and made no attempt to fight the chains which bound him. He did not look at me.

I gave a great sigh and broke my silence at last.

"What he said about what you did to your family…" I started in a voice flat and devoid of emotion. "Hector lied. Didn't he?"

Mykhalo did not move or raise his head.

"No," he replied simply.

But this was a question which did not deserve a simple answer.

"Look! The little I know about your sire tells me he delights in using any bit of personal information for pain. So he *had* to have lied about that, right?"

Again, I was rewarded with the same flat, simple answer.

"No, he did not lie about that part."

I felt shock, horror, a million different emotions at the admission and none of them were good.

"How could you kill you own family?" I said in utter disbelief.

He snorted wryly.

"Do you have any idea how many times I asked myself the same thing?" he spoke to the floor.

"Answer my question!" I demanded in a voice with some heat.

He paused.

"It is a long story," he said.

I sniffed scornfully.

"We seem to have plenty of time for talking," I told him as I seated myself on the cold, hard, wooden floor.

He heaved a heavy sigh and sat back against the wall. His eyes were shadowed and dark.

"It is not a story for delicate ears," he insisted evasively.

"My ears are not as delicate as you think!" I insisted. "And quit avoiding the issue!"

He sighed again. I sensed retelling this story would hurt him more than the beating he had just received.

But for some reason, I no longer cared about his feelings.

I saw his eyes shift to mine and hold them for a long moment. His eyes suddenly looked very old and tired.

He finally relented and nodded.

"You dreamed about the dagger Bill left you?" he began.

I nodded in response.

"Well, after the witch died, my father put it to good use. Three months after he took possession of it, strange things began to happen around my family's household."

"What sort of strange things?" I asked, intrigued in spite of myself.

A small smile flickered briefly across his face and then died.

"Things I know now were a sign that our family was being watched by unfriendly inhuman eyes. Apparently, my father had killed a very important undead and it was like stirring up ah, how do you say, a hornet's hive?"

"Hornet's nest, but I get your point," I corrected quickly and dropped it so he could continue.

He nodded.

"Yes, that. We suddenly seemed to be the center of attention for a very old group of vampires. That was the first time I was kidnapped by Hector. It was the winter of 1708 and I was forty years old. I should have died then."

He swallowed with difficulty and hung his head.

"I wish I had."

"Was that when Hector 'turned' you?" I prodded.

His shadowed, gray eyes flickered up to meet mine again and I saw the inner fire of a very old hatred spinning there.

He nodded wordlessly.

After a few breathless moments, he was able to continue.

"Hector had me kidnapped and locked in a bedchamber. Later that evening, he came to me and attacked me. He continually came to me every night after that for a month and fed on me. My humanity died then."

He stared down at his shackled hands.

"He threw me into one of his dungeons and left me to adjust to my new reality. As I have said, it was the middle of winter and he stripped me nearly naked before throwing me into my cell. I have never known such blistering cold as those first few nights. Then I realized that for some strange reason I was not dying of exposure. It was definitely cold enough for a normal person to have frozen to death but I did not. I did not know I was already dead. A vampire's blood is impervious to cold.

"He came to retrieve me the third night and I was nearly mad with hunger and barely in control of myself. He demanded to know where my father had hidden the dagger which caused his undead fellows so much grief. When I refused to tell him, he had his servants usher in Esmeralda, my wife."

Here his face twisted into a mask of grief and pain. With an effort, he erased it and continued.

"I never really loved her. It was an arranged marriage. But we had settled into an agreeable, comfortable friendship and neither of us wished the other any harm. Hector slashed her shoulder in front of me

211

and, me being new to what was going on in my body, and having no control to speak of, I," his voice fractured into silence in the darkness.

"You killed her," I finished for him.

He nodded.

"When he saw how grief-stricken I was at what I had done Hector just laughed. And again, I was thrown in the dungeon for three days and nights until once more I was nearly rabid with vampire induced starvation. Then he again had me dragged into his presence and put the same question to me. When I refused once more, another family member was produced and slashed in front of me and once again, I behaved exactly the same. This continued until each one of my family members was dead by my own hands."

He closed his eyes and balled his fists as if to keep the sight of his memories far away. After a moment, he tossed his head, took a deep breath, and continued.

"You will find many people named Ludwig today of German descent. But they are all very distant relations of mine. I exterminated all those from my immediate family. And I have to live with that knowledge."

He took a deep sigh and was quiet for a long time.

"After the murder of my last, closest kin, Hector passed my tutelage over to his lover, Elizabeth."

Here he paused and looked up at me through the mess of his long blonde locks.

"You asked me one time if Dracula was really a vampire. Count Vlad Dracul never was. But Countess Elizabeth Bathory was born with a vampiric nature. She just needed Hector to make the transformation complete. She was the true vampire that history forgot."

Mykhalo took a long breath and paused. Then he continued.

"I was starved as before, but this time, I was beaten and slashed as well while other vampires licked my wounds, until I nearly fainted from blood loss. Then they tossed me into the dungeon cell again and this time, presented me with a living baby to feed on. I forced myself not to harm the child and during the night, I actually managed to attract the attention of a passing monk through the bars of my cell window. I told him my sad tale but not the fact I was a new vampire. I begged him to take the baby and raise her in safety, far away from the castle I was imprisoned in. He agreed and promised to pray for me."

Mykhalo suddenly fell quiet and a sad smile flickered across his face.

"The priest asked me what the child's name was. I told him to call her 'Hope'."

His eyes seemed to become glassy and wet at the memory.

"They continued to beat me and starve me. The next night they presented me with another baby to feed on, I again tried to flag down the passing monk. But my tormentors had been watching and killed him in front of my eyes. They took the baby and told me refusing to dine on the child would do me no good. Then they fell on the baby in front of me and killed him."

Mykhalo's face had become shadowed and blank by this time.

"I think I gave up soon after. They continued to beat me and offer me victims on which to feed and I obeyed without question, despising myself and everything around me."

His voice was low and devoid of emotion.

"Then came the night I had a chance. They thought they had broken me so they took off the restraints in front of Elizabeth and left me to her whims. I waited until she came very close and then I allowed myself to lose complete control. I pounced on her so quickly she didn't have time to react and tore her throat out! I then killed everyone else in the room, her handmaidens and closest advisers in the dark arts, everyone. I painted the walls with their blood and escaped. I fled as fast as I was able, through the deep snowdrifts and hid in a cave when morning came."

He sighed and inclining his head backwards, rolled it helplessly against the wall behind him.

"It took me years to figure out what I could and couldn't do, more years to gain control over my hunger, and many decades avoiding Hector at all costs because I was too inexperienced to challenge him.

"I also tried carefully to have mortal friends without harming them. Sometimes I was successful. Sometimes I wasn't. The guilt over what I have done has always followed me and nearly consumed me many times. A normal human accumulates enough regret in a regular lifetime. I seem to have triple the amount to deal with."

His voice fell silent. I pondered his words for a long while before I trusted myself to speak.

"What happened to the baby?" I asked.

His face seemed to brighten a little.

"I managed to track her down and guarded her life from a distance. She was just called Hope with no last name at all and was raised in a church orphanage. She lived a good life. She grew to adulthood without any harm, fell in love, and married a man with the surname of Bayer who was very well off, and they proceeded to have six children. I have followed her descendants ever since and tried to guard their lives whenever able. Hope's great, great grandchildren live in the Netherlands, London, Brazil, and Seattle. I look over them as if they are my children, the only children a being like me is able to have. They have restored hope within myself that I am still capable of doing good things. If not for them, I think I would have succumbed to the darkness in my heart long ago."

I was silent for a while, digesting all this information. It didn't justify what Mykhalo had done to his family. But at least now, I understood a little better what the situation of the time had been. And I understood a lot better what sort of mental mayhem Hector was capable of and might throw my way.

My eyes fell on the thin, pink, welt which was forming around Mykhalo's throat.

"What was in the glass bottle around your neck?" I asked in a softer voice.

He looked up at me through his blonde hair.

"Earth from under the cornerstone of the house I was born in," he answered.

The answer barely surprised me at all. It made perfect sense.

"No vampires do not *have* to sleep in coffins surrounded by earth of their mortal homeland," he explained. "But keeping some sort of talisman on my person with earth from home helps. Most Nosferatu have some sort of jewelry on them like that. Hector has a ring with a crystal bead filled with earth from Salamanca, Spain on his left hand. Look at any vampire if you have a chance and you will see some sort of earthy talisman on them they never remove."

I nodded in comprehension.

"And what will be the effect on you now it is gone?" I said.

Another wry smile flickered across his face.

"Things that weaken a vampire will have more effect on me," he replied. "You shall see when the sun rises."

He nodded to the great window at the far end of the room. I looked out the window. The night sky seemed peaceful and serene, filled with the blazing, white light from the full moon and the sparkle of stars around it.

"Will the sunlight kill you?" I asked, quietly.

He snorted in derision.

"You mean, will I burn away to dust and ashes at the first rays of dawn like in the movies?" he snickered again. "No. But I will not like it either. If I get enough sunlight over the next few days, I will sicken to the point of death. I will burn slowly from the inside out, kind of like what your microwaves do to a potato only a bit less dramatically than that – for the watcher at least."

His eyes slipped to my throat and then he turned his face away as if he had stared too long at my breasts in a lecherous manner.

"Of course, Hector was correct about one thing. Biting you will help me to deal with the sunlight and give me some strength to resist it. But I may also, as he said, be unable to stop once started. Nor will you be able to stop me. You see, Hector has distracted my meals as of late and I was not able to feed well before now. I am extremely dangerous to you, Zan. I would not recommend coming any closer. Please believe me in this."

I swallowed with difficulty and wrapped my cloak a little tighter, trying to hide my neck.

He smiled briefly at my attempt and nodded, understanding the motion.

"Where is Bree?" he asked suddenly.

"Safe," I responded.

"Are you sure?" he prodded.

No, I wasn't sure! I was terribly worried about my daughter; where was she, how was she doing, what was she doing. The fact I was missing would instantly worry her, especially knowing what could have happened to me.

"Yes," I lied to him.

I refused to tell Mykhalo any more. I was afraid whatever I told him, Hector might pry out of him. Now I understood Mykhalo's reluctance from before to tell me anything about his hated sire.

Personal knowledge was dangerous if Hector acquired it.

I caressed the glass talisman around my own neck and prayed to the goddess she was safe.

I stood up and, approaching the great windows, inspected them.

I wondered if I could break the glass.

I took my fist and pounded experimentally on the surface. It made a dull thump and bowed slightly under my blow.

I frowned and sucked my teeth in frustration.

Industrial strength Plexiglas! Unbreakable.

I uttered a curse and leaned into it.

I looked outward and down. This only added to my frustration. There was no walkway outside the window, not even a ledge to perch on. And the window was situated on the top floor and very high off the ground. Mykhalo probably could have scaled the wall outside. But I never would be able, even if I wasn't afraid of heights!

I growled in aggravation. I looked out of the window at the surrounding moonlit scenery.

*Where the hell are we?*

I could see nothing for miles around but forests and rolling Pennsylvania hills with great slate rock shelves jutting raggedly out of the soil. Above the treetops to the right, I could see a glow, which told me there was some sort of civilization over in that direction. But there

216

was no other sign of human habitation anywhere within view of the great window.

I tried to remember but I could not think of any place near Sleepy Pines which had an old, English-style manor house with a honking, big window on one side like this. I tried to think of parks or hunting preserves or big, privately owned properties, where one could hide a house like this.

I came up with nothing.

"Forget it," Mykhalo said to me. "The best way to escape is to wait for the vampires to come back tomorrow at dusk."

"Why do I not find that very reassuring?" I said.

I investigated the front of the room near the entrance. The doors were large and reinforced with heavy wrought iron. They looked ready to withstand a siege let alone my puny fists banging on the inside. The great doors were shut and seemed locked from the outside. No escape there!

I peered into every corner of the balcony both from the underside and the topside after scaling the stairs. There was nothing I could have used for a weapon. The room was quite unadorned and bare except for the ominous looking shackles attached to the walls on either side.

"What I don't get is if this is a 'torture theater' as Hector seems to so fondly put it, where are the tools of torment? Shouldn't there be racks or chains throughout the room or at least a single iron maiden?"

Mykhalo sniffed in scorn.

"I don't think Hector has owned this property very long," he informed me. "The house is definitely to his taste but he likes the bustle of the city more. Although the seclusion of this place would certainly appeal to him as a place of secret amusement. I don't quite think he's had the time to decorate as he would like. I have seen his torture chambers before and they are usually not this bare!"

He pondered something briefly and continued in a softer tone.

"The iron maiden was Elizabeth's favorite contraption. But she used it particularly with the young ladies before she drained them of their blood to bathe in. She seemed to think by taking blood baths, she would gain everlasting beauty and youth."

217

My stomach flip-flopped to this bit of news.

"Lovely gal!" I muttered, curling my lip in disgust. "Hector has unusual taste in women. Elizabeth and Hector must have been a perfect pair! I'm glad I don't have to deal with her as well."

Mykhalo was silent for a moment, lost in memories.

"She was the more vicious of the two," he commented softly. "Elizabeth was more into physical torment. Hector specializes in psychological torture."

A thought blinked abruptly into my mind.

"Does he still desire the dagger?" I asked.

His blonde hair swayed as he nodded.

"More than ever," Mykhalo said. "I have kept it out of his reach for many years. Bill was a very good custodian. Please tell me the dagger is safe as well."

"It is," I replied and I would give no further details.

Mykhalo looked at me and nodded, intimately understanding why. There was no need for further explanation between us.

I pondered the events of the night.

"Why did they try to get you to kill every third day when you were first turned?" I asked.

Mykhalo sighed heavily.

"Have you forgotten all the vampire lore I have told you?" he scolded but gently. "Remember one of our very first discussions, I told you a vampire's existence is all about control?"

I nodded.

"Well, when a human first undergoes the change to undead, their control is at an all-time low. They need to feed frequently and they always hang on the edge of losing it and becoming a destroyer of everything in their path whether they hunger or not. As time goes by, they learn their limits and how far they can push the rules a Nosferatu must adhere to. Hector is so old, he could probably go two months without feeding. He has that sort of control. But he enjoys the violence of the act too much and indulges himself weekly. Every now and then, he allows himself the luxury of total loss of control and runs amok for several nights in a row. This is one of those special times."

"Just how old is Hector? Do you know?" I asked.

Mykhalo sniffed in derision.

"Oh I know his age and that's why I step carefully around him," he told me and then raised his head and met my gaze. "Hector's human life began around the time of El Cid in Spain. He is close to one thousand years old."

A chill ran up my spine.

"Don't the authorities get suspicious when they find a body count after one of his 'parties'?" I asked.

Mykhalo's head swayed limply as he shrugged.

"He's seen so much humanity come and go he no longer cares. But he has managed to carefully disguise his destruction by cleverly coinciding them with disastrous events of the world. Hurricane Katrina was one of his parties. I'm sure he's spent a great deal of time in Iraq. Kosovo was another. He's spent many years in the Congo when people were being butchered in masses. No one checked to see exactly what every bloated body had died from. And should I even mention the Black Plague of Europe? There were bodies everywhere and the political system had dissolved in many areas because the officials had all died. Perfect playground for a vampire to run amok!"

He shook his head in aggravation.

"Every time I hear many people have died in a certain region in the world, I immediately assume it was Hector and his cronies, having another blood party. I usually discover I was correct. Him or one of the vampires he has schooled. I have gotten rather familiar with his calling card over the years."

Mykhalo tried to stand. His muscles flexed as he experimentally tugged at his bonds. They rattled and clanked but held fast. Then he threw all of his force against the shackles. The result was he was whip-lashed, painfully back to the wall and then to the floor.

"What are you trying to do? Escape?" I asked.

He was still grimacing in agony from the chains.

"No," he hissed through his teeth. "It is plain to me now Hector expected you to approach me and that I would try to attack you."

Here Mykhalo smiled.

"He miscalculated your intelligence."

I returned his smile. We just held each other's eyes for a long moment until it began to get uncomfortable.

"Dawn will be here soon," he said. "Get what sleep you can. I obviously cannot get to you to harm you."

I looked at the full moon through the window. It had advanced across the night sky a little as we had talked.

I walked over to the wall opposite from him and, facing Mykhalo, curled myself into a ball within my cape.

My eyes met his before I closed them. I saw the look he had fixed me with and the emotion which shone forth was clear and plain as a fresh, raw wound.

More than anything Mykhalo wanted to protect me.

Instead, he was the greatest threat to my safety right now.

# CHAPTER 21

The rattling of chains awoke me with a start.

Mykhalo was standing up and straining wildly against his chains like a newly captured mustang. His naked torso was sliced with orange light.

Dawn had come.

I shook off the soreness which had come from sleeping on a hard, cold floor and springing to my feet, ran to him without thinking.

"Stay away!" he nearly roared at me. His eyes locked with my own and I gasped in horror.

The pupils had gone white!

"Mykhalo!" I exclaimed. "Your eyes!"

He growled in frustration as he sagged against the chains.

"Yes, the eyes, and the teeth!" he snarled. "The only two things Hollywood got crystal clear about my kind!"

He stood up and strained against the chains as the orange light faded to lighter more brilliant shades of the sun's rays. He fell back panting and shivering as if feverishly cold. It was obvious he was in severe pain and there was nothing I could do to help him.

Or was there?

I faced the morning sun as it tipped over the horizon, thinking hard. I slipped off my pentacle with a prayer and a blessing. As the sun harmed and drained Mykhalo, I did my best to draw strength from its warming rays. My lips murmured a silent chant.

I then spun on my heel and strode up to him coming well within the danger zone. In a quick move, I draped my pentacle around his neck and jumped back as he lunged towards me, like some feral animal.

Mykhalo paused suddenly as his blazing eyes fell on the silver pentacle swinging from his own neck.

"What have you done?" he asked in utter confusion. "This can't help me. I don't believe!"

I smiled slowly at him.

"In what?" I challenged. "Wicca or me?"

He took a step backwards, his thoughts spinning wildly.

"To you, my pentacle is not a symbol of faith because you don't believe in Wicca. But! Do you believe in *me*?" I put to him.

His wild eyes blinked and their color became a bit more normal.

"Wear my pentacle not as a symbol of your faith, because it isn't," I explained. "Wear my pentacle as a symbol of our friendship and believe in *that*! Let your faith in *that* protect you."

His jaw flapped uselessly for a few moments as he struggled to put into words the myriad of emotions he felt.

His eyes met my own again and this time they seemed to be wet and glistening.

I smiled knowingly at him and strode up to the great window.

"What are you going to do?" he gasped out.

"Hush," I crooned. "And let the witch do what she does best."

I took three deep breaths as I gathered my strength. I spread my arms wide to welcome the sun's first rays.

As I had drawn down the moon many times before, this time, I drew down the sun. I raised my face to the sun and prayed with all my heart and soul. I prayed to Ra, to Apollo, to Lugh, and more. I prayed to the image of the sun in the hearts of many goddesses from every culture, from Hathor to Brigid, from Ishtar to Sekhmet. I felt its forgiving, life giving presence in every folktale and myth passed down from one family member to another from time past memory. I prayed for warmth and strength, for health and vitality, for healing and growth. I felt the power of the sun flow into me and take up residence in every pore of my being. I felt it from my toes to my fingertips to the roots of my hair. I felt it blaze inside every chakra point and swirl like

222

a firestorm in my belly, warm and comforting. I felt my body glow in vitality and life.

I wrapped my arms close to my heart, embracing the healing power of the sun, welcoming its very essence in my life. My cloak was suddenly far too warm for my body. I held it close to my heart like a dear child, returned from a long absence. I welcomed the reappearance of the sun from the cold, dark days of winter.

I held the warmth and then I released my hold over it and sent it back to its source. As the power of the sun left me of its own accord, I clapped my hands once, twice, thrice. I felt my form become blanketed in shadow after the last clap. I opened my eyes.

The sky was dark with clouds. No sign of the sun could be seen. It was still light enough to tell it was day but the sun had hidden his face.

I smiled and bowed gratefully for the blessing given.

I turned my back to the window and strode across the room to where Mykhalo cowered, shivering and sick with exposure on the floor.

In one smooth motion, I swept off my cloak and wrapped his quaking form in its voluminous depths. He stopped shivering almost immediately. He made no attempt to harm me.

He sighed in relief.

"How…what did you do? How did you get the clouds to form just then?" he asked in a weak voice.

I just smiled peacefully.

"Shhh," I consoled. "Time for you to sleep. I will stand guard against the sun's rays."

"But how…" he murmured as sleep claimed him.

"Mykhalo," I said gently. "I like you very much. But I'll not tell you *all* my secrets!"

\* \* \*

The great oak doors suddenly banged open and Hector strode into the 'torture theater' followed by his undead entourage.

I stood and faced him boldly. I still was feeling the after effects of the sun's blessing. I felt strong and able to handle whatever the elder vampire threw at me.

This witch no longer felt helpless!

He looked me over critically and seemed disappointed.

"So you survived your first night here," he said.

It was a statement, not a question.

"Yes," I replied haughtily. "Although the state of comfort you provide your guests leaves a lot to be desired!"

His eyes narrowed and he sneered at my reply.

"Fiery to the last, eh?" he muttered softly.

He turned his attention to Mykhalo who rose with a clatter of chains. He started to say something but then his eyes fell on the pentacle swinging from his neck.

He laughed.

"So she converted you!" he chuckled.

"Not exactly," Mykhalo replied.

He slid a sly look my way and I smiled back.

Hector's eyes went from Mykhalo to me and back, trying to puzzle it out. He finally set his jaw and, striding purposefully up to the shackled vampire, took hold of the pentacle as if to rip it off of his neck like before.

But then the Spanish vampire uttered a shriek of surprise and pain and jumped back, cradling his wounded hand.

His palm was smoking. The smell of burnt skin rose pungently into the air.

I laughed out loud. I couldn't help it.

But then the smoking quickly dissipated and I watched the blackened skin with the raw, red pentacle design burnt into it, heal and knit before my very eyes into healthy, untouched skin once more.

Hector's eyes fastened on me and the look which came from within was dark and threatened only pain.

He forced himself to smile.

"So you think you can hurt me, eh?" he hissed. "This is nothing! Nothing compared to the pain I can inflict on you!"

He gestured to one of those behind him. Giselle approached and handed Hector something wrapped in a red cloth. He unwound the cloth to reveal a small picture frame I instantly recognized.

"I believe you remember this portrait, Michael," he said as he displayed the artwork to him.

Mykhalo suddenly shot to the end of his chains with a vicious sounding, German curse.

"You said you would destroy it!" he shouted at me. "You promised!"

I *had* promised! I had really, really, truly meant to dispose of it.

"I…I…forgot," was all I could stammer out in an apologetic tone of voice. "I'm sorry."

Mykhalo nearly roared at me like some enraged beast. I shuddered and stepping back, hung my head, wishing I were anywhere else right now.

Hector chuckled and then 'tsked' at me in amusement, waggling a scolding finger.

"Don't be so angry at poor Mrs. Miller," he reassured Mykhalo in his own mocking way. "It wasn't *really* her fault. Do you remember the day when you killed my beloved Elizabeth? Come on, I know you do! This picture was on the wall. Her eyes fastened on the eyes of her portrait and, as she died, she sent her spirit to reside within this picture."

He sighed wistfully and turning away, stroked the painted face lovingly.

"My dear Elizabeth," he crooned lovingly. "She was more lovely than even my memory had made her all these years since. This is all I have to remember her by."

His eyes then turned to me. The adoration in Hector's eyes morphed into malice.

"Her spirit takes care of this portrait. No one can destroy it no matter how much they want to. She sees that something happens and the picture survives. That's why you forgot all about it, Mrs. Miller. She wanted you to forget. So you did."

He turned to face me.

"We are together again at last," he said. "Now we shall see which is more powerful, the spirit of my dear departed Elizabeth or you."

A shiver ran down my spine.

Hector observed my reaction with some relish and then cocked his head to the side and began a new verbal tactic.

"You know I was really expecting there to be a certain dagger in the chest," Hector went on. "But my children found nothing. I have been searching for it for quite some time. I wonder if you would know where it might possibly be?"

I shrugged.

"Maybe you should try at a knife and sword show," I suggested, dryly. "I only deal in books."

There was a pause from him and then he sneered.

"Maybe your daughter has it?" he suggested.

I met his eyes. With a supreme effort, I concealed my fear for my child. My vision scanned the throng of his undead cohorts behind him. Turning my gaze back to the Nosferatu standing before me, I smiled calmly.

"Whatever happened to Baptiste and Sal?" I asked abruptly. "Did they have other plans or were they unexpectedly…delayed? Maybe permanently so?"

The malicious smile vanished from Hector's face. He glared at me with a look so full of hatred I actually was forced to take a step back.

Silently he passed the portrait to another vampire.

Suddenly he rushed forward and grabbed me by my throat, slamming me with frightening force up against the wall.

A small squeak of fright ripped out of me.

I could hear Mykhalo shouting and straining against his chains but the words were not clear. All I could focus on was Hector's face too close to mine and his bright, white canines which were uncomfortably close to my cheek.

I struggled helplessly. My hands clutched his cold arms and tried, to no avail, to pry them off. When this proved ineffective, I spat on him.

He snarled and slapped my face hard, spinning my head to the side and knocking my skull against the wall behind me. Mykhalo was now screaming at Hector in German.

I did not need any translation to know that the words he was speaking were not exactly polite!

Hector gestured behind him with one hand. Two other vampires immediately came forward and began to shackle me to the wall.

"I'm done bantering words with you!" he hissed in my ear. "My only regret is Elizabeth is dead. I would have enjoyed watching her work her pain magic on you before she bathed in your blood. But then maybe we can do that with your daughter."

I could feel the bruise on my cheek beginning to swell and throb, interfering with the vision from my right eye.

No man had ever struck me before. I never would have tolerated such a thing from anyone.

He stepped back and released my throat. He wiped my spittle off his face with a pristine, white handkerchief. Then a medieval looking dagger suddenly appeared in his grasp.

"*NO!*" Mykhalo screamed, suspecting what was to come.

But Hector didn't stab me. He used the dagger to cut the neckline of my shirt with the bookstore's logo on it, one of my favorites I might add. Slowly, almost romantically, he spread my torn shirt apart to reveal the full length of my neck. Then he stroked the skin of my throat almost lovingly.

"Such beautiful skin," he murmured, stepping closer to me. "Still white from winter and untouched by the summer sun. What lovely clothes blood wears."

He stepped even closer and I wriggled as far from him as the chains allowed, which wasn't very far. He bent his head close to mine and tickled his lips along the side of my neck, teasing.

"I smell your fear," he whispered to me. "How enticing a scent it is! So delicious!"

227

I felt my stomach lurch. My heart was pounding a tango in my throat and I'm sure he knew it.

He chuckled softly so that only I could hear and stepped back.

There was a sudden motion from his arm and pain lanced downward from my shoulder. I gasped in shock.

Hector had slashed my skin wide open from my shoulder to the top of my breast.

He chuckled as I hissed.

"Don't worry," he taunted. "It isn't deep. It doesn't need to be. Your friend, Michael, apparently needs some encouragement, maybe even some force-feeding. This should do the trick nicely."

Once again, he stepped closer and this time, licked the stream of blood that was running down and staining my shirt. A look of sheer ecstasy filled his face but with an effort, he controlled it. The pupils of his eyes were swirling, changing color from black to something lighter and more sinister looking, if it was possible.

"I had forgotten how delicious a witch's blood is," he told me, smiling. "It's a shame I can't share you with Michael."

He turned to face Mykhalo and gestured once. The Bavarian vampire collapsed as if struck unconscious.

Hector turned back to me and wiped my wound with his fingers. He then approached Mykhalo and wiped my blood across his lips while two other vampires freed him from his bonds. He turned back to me with a grin of satisfaction as he licked the remainder of my blood from his fingers.

His eyes had gone white and his teeth had grown.

He motioned the other vampires to leave and then turning to me, bowed deep.

"Enjoy the eclipse, Mrs. Miller," he told me.

And then he too left.

I heard the sound of the massive lock being turned.

I was alone. Mykhalo was unaware of anything as of yet.

But he was free and I was bleeding profusely from my shoulder wound.

It was going to be an interesting night.

# CHAPTER 22

I prayed as I waited and watched the full moon advance across the night sky. I watched the first blush of red stain its pure, white face.

It was then Mykhalo began to revive.

I shivered in dread.

'Here it comes,' I thought to myself. 'Lord and Lady protect me!'

I took a deep breath and squirmed a little within my bonds. The cut on my shoulder stung horribly and the dried blood cracked and began to weep anew.

Mykhalo's eyes opened and locked onto my own.

They were as white as the moon.

I did not recognize the spirit that swam within them.

"Mykhalo," I said slowly, carefully. "Think. You really don't want to do this."

He snarled and began to rise to a crouch.

"No, I don't," he agreed. His voice was very deep and strange. He licked my blood from his lips.

He bared his teeth hungrily. His canines flashed as he did so. They were much longer now.

"What do I have to do to help you control your hunger?" I asked.

He hissed like an enraged cobra. He suddenly looked much stronger and bigger than I had ever seen him.

"Keep talking," he said. "Keep distracting me from my purpose."

I swallowed with difficulty and tried to keep from shivering.

"H…How many friends have you…'dined' on?" I stammered fearfully.

He smiled maliciously and then, with an effort, erased it.

"The answer would not comfort you," was his reply.

He was climbing to his feet slowly now, like a stalking predator with cornered prey, enjoying the experience of prolonging the hunt.

He began to approach me in a threatening manner.

My mind spun wildly.

"You still wear my pentacle," I stated abruptly.

He paused in his approach.

"Yes," he replied, his tone prodding me to go on.

"It burned Hector," I told him. "What will it do to you if you attack me?"

He truly did stop now and engage his mind.

"Do you still believe in our friendship? Even now in this state?" I asked.

He paused and licked his bloodstained lips.

"Yes," he replied and then, out of the blue, he added. "I wish I had some coffee."

This answer so surprised me I laughed in spite of myself.

"I really enjoyed our discussions over coffee," he said with a sad smile.

In spite of how fast my heart was pounding, I chuckled.

"I did too," I told him, an unexpected smile trembling on my lips. "I've developed quite a taste for 'Bavarian honey'."

Then the sinister side of Mykhalo returned.

"It's a shame it won't ever happen again!" he muttered.

He was suddenly right on top of me. His palms slapped the wall behind me as he struggled to push himself away and master his hunger.

I cried out in terror. A word was ripped from my lips, a word I didn't understand or know I was thinking about.

The second I uttered the word, Mykhalo fell to the floor with a cry of pain.

The pentacle had turned red hot! I smelled his skin singe and burn.

But almost immediately, the talisman faded from angry red to cool silver and black again.

I heaved a sigh of relief.

"There's a ward on the pentacle," I told him, breathlessly. "Try to hurt me and it will burn you."

He grasped it as if to remove it and cried out again in agony.

I smiled. I was relieved at my escape but sad it had hurt him.

"You cannot remove it either," I told him. "It will force you to play nice."

A sound came from him that sounded like a sob of frustration.

"I'm so hungry."

A little of my fear left me.

"What would happen if you drained another vampire?" I suggested.

"It would help a little," he panted without looking at me. "Vampires do bleed. But their blood is a different consistency. Me killing a vampire is like you living on fast food. It's not very satisfying."

"Then we just have to delay things until they come back," I said with a little hope.

"They will not come back in time to save you!" Mykhalo growled.

And again, he was back on his feet, his arms trapping my head like before, towering over me.

I gasped and my heart began to beat in fear again. I had really never noticed how threatening a tall person could be, let alone a tall vampire! His blazing white eyes seemed to be burrowing into my very soul; his teeth were so white and so close.

My pentacle on his chest was warming up again.

He took a deep breath, trying to control himself.

"I never really wanted to hurt you. You must believe me in this," he said.

His hand stroked the side of my head tenderly. I shivered at what might happen but did not resist his touch.

"I wanted so much more for you, for us," he said softly. "Things could have been so much different if I wasn't...*this*."

I squeezed my eyes shut for one breathless moment and opening them again, realized they were glassy and wet.

"No, they would have been no different," I replied. "Because if you weren't a vampire, we never would have met."

I took a deep breath and tried to gulp down my fear.

He bent his head to the side and licked my bloody shoulder. He sighed.

"Hector was right. A witch's blood is so delicious, especially without the coffee."

His face was so close to mine. His white teeth were stained red from my blood.

The pentacle was glowing hot but hanging so it did not touch his skin.

"Maybe you could turn me," I suggested in a scared whisper. It was stupid, I know, but anything to not be killed.

"Don't be ridiculous!" he spat, scornfully. "My life is no life at all! Why would you want that for yourself?"

His head bent to the side and his cold lips found the gash on my shoulder. I shuddered in revulsion although I knew he was fighting it too, fighting the urge to bite me, fighting to save what little he could of his quickly fading humanity. The thumb of his opposite hand stroked my unbruised cheek gently and I could feel his hand tremble with the effort of restraining himself from what his vampire instinct really wanted him to do. I shuddered and fought to keep the tears from falling. My eyes looked up to the window.

The moon had gone red and a little bite was missing out of the left corner.

Then I felt Mykhalo's hands stop shaking. His arm wound me closer to him like a lover, pressing our bodies together. His hold on me became frighteningly tight and forceful.

'No!' I thought helplessly to myself.

232

He had given in!

Two fat tears rolled down my cheeks.

I smelled again the scent of burning flesh from the pentacle. But Mykhalo was beyond caring or feeling any pain.

I felt the tips of his canines scrape my skin and travel up my collarbone towards my throat, bringing goose bumps to the surface as they went.

And then I heard it!

"Mykhalo!" I hissed in a loud whisper. "Stop! Stop! Listen! They're coming back!"

I felt him sheath his canines with a growl of frustration. He clutched me closer for one instant before abruptly releasing me. I gasped and nearly fell in surprise but the chains biting into my wrists held me up.

We could both hear the tramp of many feet by now. And then came the clatter of the massive lock as it was turned. The doors were swung open and five vampires came hurtling into the room as if they had been fired from a cannon, eyes glowing and teeth bared.

Mykhalo uttered a growl of welcome and spun to meet them in violent eagerness. He clutched the nearest one to his chest and tore his throat out with a triumphant roar. I turned my head to avoid the splash of blood as it flew my way. But two more were on him almost as fast. He whirled and caught the one by the throat and snapped it like a twig. He dropped the lifeless body and it fell into a crumpled mass of flesh and clothing at his feet. The other barely had a chance as he knocked it into the wall and fell on him like a starving lion. Once he had latched onto the fallen vampire's throat, he stayed there, feeding on his blood in a voracious manner. It took six vampires to wrest him off his victim and slam him into the opposite wall.

Then Hector strode into the hall smiling.

# CHAPTER 23

Hector stepped over his fallen family members with barely a glance.

"Polishing the floors again, I see," he said, dryly. "It has always amazed me to observe how much better you are at killing your own kind than the countless mortal victims this world has provided us with."

Mykhalo struggled against those holding him and shouted something rather rude in Spanish at Hector.

It needed no translation.

Hector merely sniffed in derision and replied in kind, in German. It also required no translation.

Hector turned his smiling face to me.

"So sorry to interrupt you both at this most opportune of moments," he began smugly. "But we seem to have a guest. Just look who came knocking on our door this most auspicious night."

He gestured behind him.

Two vampires came forward dragging a small person with them and flung this person at my feet.

It was a teenage girl dressed in red, with dyed, red hair.

"*Bree*!" I screamed.

My daughter sprang to her feet and rushed into my arms, clinging so tight I could barely breathe.

"Did they hurt you?" I hissed in her ear. "Did they search you?"

"No and no," she said still clutching me like a newly returned teddy bear. "But they weren't nice either!"

She burrowed her head into my neck as if for comfort. But it was really so she could whisper in my ear.

"Oh Ma! I'm so scared and confused!" she said. "Once I found out where they had taken you, I convinced Bran to let me go in alone. I thought the first vampire I ran into would make *Her* show up. But She hasn't! And here we are in a whole nest of the suckers and She's still not here! I've called and called to Her and nothing! Now what do I do?"

I stroked her blazing red hair as well as I was able within the shackles and shushed her worry.

"Hush dear," I consoled. "Mama has a plan."

I didn't really. I just had a ghost of an idea, not an actual *plan*. But acting on it meant I was going to have to hurt my daughter's feelings.

As she whispered these things in my ear, I noticed the other vampires filing up the stairs to the balcony. Gads! There were a lot of the, as my daughter so succinctly put it, 'suckers' this time! Their numbers seemed to have swelled. And from the way they were acting, I guessed we were going to be the show of the evening.

Bree pulled back and it was then she noticed my swollen cheek and my slashed and bloodied shoulder.

"Did Mykhalo do this to you?" she hissed.

"No," I told her. "Hector did it to goad Mykhalo to attack me. Mykhalo hasn't hurt me yet."

Bree turned her now blazing green eyes onto the Spanish vampire.

"What did you do to my mother?" she demanded.

She rushed at the still smiling Hector.

He waited until she came close enough and then the smile vanished and he slapped her with the same force he had used on me. It felled her like a stone.

She glared hatefully up at him from the floor, shielding her wounded cheek.

I gave a cry of parental fury and lunged against my chains.

"Don't you touch my daughter again you monster or I'll…" I screamed at him.

"You'll what?" Hector laughed. "You can do nothing! Nothing at all. I am the master of this ceremony tonight. By the time this night is through I'll have you both screaming at my command."

He stepped forward and glared down upon my daughter.

"My only regret is that Elizabeth is not here to join in the celebration. Your daughter is just the kind of victim she would have most enjoyed tormenting. Young, beautiful and, of course, the most important part, virginal! She was convinced the blood from virgins was the best quality to bathe in. It is a shame she's not a blueblood. That was just the recipe which was most effective for her."

I sniffed derisively.

"Beggars can't be choosers, my Lord" I sneered back at him, venomously.

Hector glared at me.

"Indeed," he said softly. "The longer I live the more I realize most of the nobility of this world is now of my kind. A pity in some ways. We shall have to re-invent nobility it seems."

He walked around Bree who was crouching on the ground and trying her best to glare back at him fiercely. He considered her quietly for a moment.

"The spawn is much like the parent," he mused, as if to himself. "Fiery to the last. At least your blood breeds true!"

He turned his attention to me once again.

"Make no mistake, Mrs. Miller, this is to be your last night alive," he assured me. "Whether by Michael or myself or one of my children, it makes no difference. You will die tonight. The only detail you need worry yourself with is that your daughter will perish before your eyes."

He crouched down and, gently this time, took my daughter's chin in his hand and forced her to look up into his eyes. I saw the moon's red light flash off a gold ring on the first finger of his left hand, the hand he held my daughter's chin in. A dark mottled crystal bead glinted there.

"Now my dear," he said in a soft, patient voice. "Tell me where you hid the dagger. If you do not, I will have Michael feast on your mother before your very eyes and you wouldn't want that to happen now would you?"

The other vampires chuckled eagerly.

Bree's eyes met mine in desperation, pleading for help.

I frowned and gave a frustrated sigh.

I would have to do it. I would have to hurt my daughter.

I bit my lip.

"Bree honey, listen to me," I began gently. "Brittany never committed suicide."

Bree's eyes went wide and she tore her chin out of Hector's grip.

"What are you saying?" she said.

Hector's eyes narrowed, wondering what my game was.

"Then...if she didn't kill herself..." she stammered. "What happened...?"

My eyes switched to Mykhalo.

She followed them.

Mykhalo stopped struggling against those who were restraining him. His eyes locked on my own, pleading with me not to tell.

I saw his head shake a denial back at me and his lips mouth the words, 'Not again.'

Bree's eyes turned back to my own and I saw a horrible realization suddenly take root there.

She knew! Bree now knew what had really happened to her troubled best friend.

She began to shake her head in denial and her face began to twist in anguish.

"What are you doing?" Mykhalo exclaimed at me. "You're hurting her! How can this help?"

I sank back against the wall, smiling grimly.

"Just watch and wait," I directed.

Hector was looking from me to Mykhalo to Bree, again trying to puzzle through what had just happened.

He began to smile.

238

"Michael? Is this true?" he inquired. "Did you actually kill this poor girl's best friend?"

At the word 'kill' Bree cringed.

Hector laughed and clapped his hands in sadistic glee.

"So you *do* remember the lessons Elizabeth and I taught you! You *can* still rip a mortal's heart out!"

My eyes were fastened on my daughter. She was still shaking her head back and forth, trying to deny the truth she had just figured out. She had curled herself into a ball and was beginning to rock maniacally.

I felt a stab of pain in my heart for what I had just done. But I was also fervently praying for Sekhmet to show herself.

"Awakener, please awaken. Awakener, please awaken," I mumbled beneath my breath.

My eyes flashed Mykhalo a warning.

"After all this time, Michael! You can still surprise me! You are still true to your kind!" Hector was saying.

Mykhalo caught the warning look from me and pulled back against the wall, trying to position one of the vampires between himself and Bree. He didn't understand yet. He just obeyed without question.

There was an abrupt rumble that shook the room without warning, like an earthquake.

Pennsylvania does not get earthquakes.

Everyone in the room became still, aware something strange had just happened.

My eyes were wide and fastened on Mykhalo. My lips squeezed into a tight, firm line. I could only see one of his eyes but the look he gave me was almost one of fear.

The vampires were looking about warily. Hector had fallen silent. He had risen to his feet and was backing away from Bree although he didn't understand why.

I looked up to the full moon. It had gone black with a ring of blood red.

I turned my eyes back to my daughter, crouched on the floor.

She had stopped rocking. She was just sitting there, perfectly still. She was so still; I could barely tell she was breathing.

"Bree, honey?" I whispered to her.

Bree raised her eyes to mine.

They were as red as the bloody moon!

Her lips parted in a smile and her voice purred at me, full and deep.

"Nicely done, little mother!" Sekhmet told me in a soft tone.

She had only whispered to me but the tone of her voice rumbled and throbbed through the wooden paneling of the room like tumbling boulders. The air was immediately heavy and thick. It felt hot as the desert and I had trouble breathing.

The shackles suddenly came loose and fell clattering from around my wrists.

I fell to my knees and pressed my forehead to the floor. Words began to come tumbling, unbidden from my lips. I chanted without knowing what it was I was chanting at first. Then I realized I was chanting the many sacred names of Sekhmet.

"O Flaming One, come forth!" I babbled without control. "Oh Mother of the Dead, Lady of the Tomb, Destroyer by Fire, O Lady of the Bloodbath, the One who holds back the Darkness, O Warrior Goddess, O Devouring One, O Sekhmet of the Knives, O Burner of Evildoers, O Beloved Sekhmet! O One Before whom Evil Trembles, O Lady of the Flaming Mane, O Keeper of the Light of Life and Death, O Lady of the Sacred Flame, She who is the Flame within Darkness, O Lady of the Silent Roar, O Terrible One, come forth and protect us!"

The words finally stopped bubbling from my lips and there was absolute silence.

I peeked up from where I lay upon the wooden floor.

Bree's form was no more. Where she had once crouched there now stood the towering form of the goddess Sekhmet in all her red-maned glory.

She glowed in power and was wreathed in flames. Her tawny dappled skin burned like the sands of the desert. Her red mane was beautifully braided and hung to just below her shoulders, she was

240

dressed in red and her eyes glowed crimson like the eclipsed moon above us.

She turned to the shocked vampires restraining Mykhalo and gestured briefly. They shrieked and burned to ashes before my very eyes.

Mykhalo fell to the floor, covering his face in horror.

Sekhmet snarled and the room echoed with the timbre of her voice.

"I will deal with you later!" she promised and passed over him, leaving him unharmed. She turned her back on us.

I scrambled my way over to Mykhalo. He lay shuddering on the floor, his hunger completely forgotten for the time being, staring at her back as if he had seen a demon.

"W...who...w...w...what is that?" he could only gasp out.

I smiled and curled myself around his quaking form.

"That, my dear friend, is a face of God. An avenging face," I informed him. "Be careful what you say to Her. She could kill you with a thought!"

I could feel Mykhalo tremble and quake with fear within my arms.

"You knew this was going to happen!" he ventured a whisper.

"Yes," I replied calmly.

There was a strange peace and stillness within my breast, as if someone had turned down the volume on the rest of the world and just left us unable to hear what was going on around us. My fear had been completely erased. Even if I died in the moments to come, I was not worried.

"What do we do now?" he hissed.

I snickered.

"Try to stay out of Her way," I whispered back, smiling. "It's Her show now."

Sekhmet strode towards the vampires slowly. There wasn't an ounce of hesitation from her. She moved like a lioness prolonging a well-enjoyed hunt.

"So long have you Nosferatu existed in scorn of the rules of Death!" she was saying.

Her deep voice thrummed about the confines of the room and vibrated through the floorboards as she spoke.

"Your kind has the audacity to flaunt your power as if you are ageless and timeless," she told them and the ridicule in her voice was unmistakable.

"Well! Now look into the eyes of one who truly *is* ageless and timeless and know what fear once felt like."

Hector was backing frantically away from her slow advance. His eyes were wide and I could see him struggle against the fear which sought to master him.

"Who are you?" he managed to croak out.

Sekhmet smiled, purring.

"Were you not paying attention when the little mother announced me?" she scolded. "I am the Light that you run from, the Dawn that you fear, the Fire of Judgment that burns all of your kind, the Dungeon that you thought you escaped. And I have come to collect you back to the Eternal Sleep you have always evaded. Come! Accept my welcoming embrace and it will not be so painful an experience!"

Mykhalo started to rise to his feet.

I clutched his arm and pulled him back.

"No!" I hissed. "She did not mean you! She said She would deal with you later!"

I dragged him down to the floor beside me again.

"She has something special planned for the others," I spoke into his ear. "That is why She has appeared here, this night. Just wait and watch."

He hesitantly obeyed.

Sekhmet's feline eyes scanned the throng before her.

"No one is brave enough to accept my offer?" she asked. She smiled with a soft chuckle. "Just as I suspected."

She brought both hands up before her. There was a thickening of the heavy air in the room and the space above her hands began to sparkle. Then the dagger my daughter bore materialized out of the sparkling mist, hovering in the space above them.

The dagger flashed and glowed as if it was newly forged, its Coptic etching stood out clearly for all to see.

"You desire this knife, wrought of mortal hands and will?" she spoke to the gathered vampires.

Hector leaned forward eagerly then stopped himself.

Sekhmet smiled and her red eyes glowed with an unspoken promise.

"I put this challenge to you. If you desire this object so highly then, by all means, come forward and take it from me. If you can lay hands upon it, then I will go away and trouble you no more."

She smiled seductively at the vampires before her.

## CHAPTER 24

Hector turned and gestured quickly to one of his children, a vampire woman with straight brown hair and deep brown eyes.

She obeyed immediately. But the closer she came to the goddess, the more hesitant her footsteps became.

She drew within a few steps of the deity standing before her and looked up into her face. But Sekhmet's eyes were down, looking at the dagger suspended in the air above her hands, still as a carved marble statue.

Timidly, she reached forward for it.

Suddenly she shrieked and dissolved into a pile of ash before the goddess's bare feet.

Sekhmet's eyelids lifted and the dagger was suddenly clasped within her hand and shone like golden fire.

"I am Sekhmet of the Knives," she spoke in a soft but lethal tone. "And I thirst for battle blood!"

She surged forward with a lion-like roar, flames crackling about her form. Vampires screamed and shrieked and scattered like quails before her deadly advance.

The room was thrown into chaos.

Just as quickly as the vampires were startled, they swiftly recovered and swarmed the goddess.

I was not too worried. I knew she could have burned them all to a crisp with a glance if she wanted to. She had toned down her power for this fight.

The lioness was simply toying with her prey.

Mykhalo and I ducked as a twisted smoking wreckage of what had once been one of Hector's children flew past our heads.

I laughed. Somehow I was feeding off the joy of the goddess. This was just like a good bar fight to her!

A wooden crash came to our ears.

I looked up to see another hapless undead had been thrown into the balcony and had shattered the railings there. My eyes fastened on the splintered boards and a thought suddenly occurred to me.

Wooden stakes!

Without considering my actions further, I sprinted for the balcony.

Mykhalo shouted a warning to me.

I probably should have listened. Getting to the balcony meant I would have to run past Sekhmet and charge through the heat of battle to get there.

It was not the smartest thing to do!

I had only made it halfway there when a flying form banged into me and we both skidded across the floor together in a tangled mess of arms and legs.

We pitched up against the far wall and stopped. I prayed the form was already dead. But as I stirred and tried to push free I found out I was wrong.

Longs claws clutched me and an angry voice hissed in my ear.

"'Who does your hair?' Indeed!" Giselle's voice said scornfully. "Maybe yours needs some help!"

I rolled desperately onto my back and tried to push her off. But she was much stronger than I expected for a young undead. Giselle easily pinned my wrists to the floor and her long fanged face lunged into my vision.

A cry of surprise was forced from my lungs.

And then Giselle shrieked nearly in my ear as she was forcibly wrenched off me.

I rolled clear before coming to a crouch to see what had happened.

Mykhalo had her clasped tightly to his chest. His face was buried in her neck. Giselle was jerking and thrashing like a helpless puppet on a string. And then her arms just quivered and stopped moving, frozen in time, bent like a cold, dead spider.

I backed away, shuddering, into the wall, unable to do anything but watch him feed on her and drain every last drop from her form. Her skin sucked in close to her tendons and bones, her muscles lost definition. She was reduced to a collection of bones over which her skin was tightly stretched.

Mykhalo finally tore his mouth away from her with a gasp. He let her lifeless husk roll carelessly off his arms and flop in a twisted mass on the floor. He panted for a few moments before coming back to himself. He turned to look at me.

His pupils were white as Giselle's dead skin and her blood stained his mouth and neck.

I swallowed with difficulty and shuddered in dread.

"Better now?" I managed to force out in a quavering voice.

He dragged my cape across his bloodied mouth.

"Some," he replied. "I never wanted you to see me feed."

He was right. It wasn't like in the movies. It was horrible!

I glanced back toward the balcony. The fighting around it had cleared somewhat. I again tried to bolt for it with Mykhalo covering my passage.

This time I safely made it up the stairs to the balcony.

There was the body of one undead impaled on the railings. I tried to twist off another broken railing but finally had to resort to kicking the posts to get two wooden stakes of different sizes to use as my weapons.

Mykhalo shouted a warning to me and I sprang back and ducked.

The fighting had once again gotten too close.

I tried to hide behind the railing and take stock of my surroundings. The back of the balcony was piled with corpses. The place smelled of blood and fire. Sekhmet was fighting ten undead at one time and having absolutely no trouble whatsoever. The problem was avoiding those undead who had been knocked into the wall and

247

were picking themselves back up again to rejoin the fight. I had attracted the attention of two while trying to acquire stakes and Mykhalo was busy with them.

"Get downstairs to the doors!" he shouted at me.

I obeyed him without question and fled down the stairs, trying my best to step quickly around any scattered bodies in case they weren't quite dead. The air was hot and full of the sound of mayhem.

I made it safely to the doors and propping my back against them, spun to face the room full of fighting figures. I glanced wildly about at the bodies cast haphazardly at my feet and ascertained they were all, thankfully, dead.

"Mykhalo!" I shouted out.

I couldn't see him. I could only assume he was still fighting on the balcony above me.

I thought I heard him shout back to me but I couldn't be sure it was him or what he said.

Then the door behind me gave way and I toppled through it with a squawk.

Someone immediately clutched me by my arm and jerked me through into the hallway beyond before finally wrenching me to my feet.

I hoped it was my rescuers.

But when I turned to look, I found Hector's face gazing back at me.

# CHAPTER 25

I noticed the hand which had fastened on my arm was the hand with the gold ring. I immediately smacked the gem hard with one of the wooden stakes and heard it shatter with a satisfying crunch.

Hector growled in fury and suddenly both of his hands were on my throat.

"No, little miss!" he snarled at me. He was no longer smiling. "I'm not letting you talk anymore! You're far more trouble than a useless modern witch is supposed to be! Maybe I won't drink you dry. Maybe I'll just strangle the life from your precious neck. It would certainly make me happy right now. Maybe I should have done that to begin with!"

His fingers began to tighten.

I gasped and tried to call out to Mykhalo. But no sound came out.

I tried to stab Hector with one of the stakes but my hands betrayed me. Against my will, my fingers opened and they fell clattering to the floor.

"What have you been playing at, little mortal?" he was saying. "How did you call forth a demon from beyond to deal with us? Didn't you know that wouldn't make us very happy?"

I wanted to tell him Sekhmet was no demon but an ancient goddess but my voice was having trouble doing its job. In fact my windpipe was having a lot of trouble too.

I gasped, coughing for air and flailed with my arms. Hector was slowly pushing me to my knees.

"Yes, that's it," he was saying. "Grovel on your knees before me. That's where little mortals like you belong! You think you've beaten me? You haven't! I'll escape this. And then I will kill every person you find dearest to you, starting with your daughter! You haven't won this fight, Mrs. Miller."

His face was beginning to fade from my vision.

I coaxed my thoughts to pray and once again, words I was not aware I knew, formed silently in my mind.

"O Great One of Healing, O Lady of the Waters of Life, Lady of the Purifying Flame, Lady of Radiance, O She Who is the Precious Flame of Hope, hear me and come to my aide!"

Some dim part of my brain registered the nearly forgotten fact not only was Sekhmet a goddess of death, war, and destruction but a deity of healing and patron to the Egyptian physicians.

My world was growing very dark.

Then there was a sudden boom and a crash followed by a blazing white light almost brighter than the sun.

The result of this was Hector's offending hands were suddenly torn free from my neck.

I coughed and gasped painfully. My eyes vaguely saw the two massive doors to the torture theater go flying, blasted off their hinges as if by some great explosion.

Hector had been knocked away by the blast. I was crumpled helplessly on the floor.

I numbly thought I saw the face of a great African lioness lean over me in concern. She was wreathed in golden light. I felt warm fingertips touch my bruised throat gently and all pain was erased.

I could breathe again.

When next I opened my eyes, Mykhalo had me in his arms. He cradled me and I saw worry etch his handsome features. His eyes were their normal gray shade again.

I stirred and tried to sit up.

Sekhmet was still there. She stood between Hector and I. Hector was plastered up against the wall like a movie poster and Sekhmet's gesturing finger kept him there. She was growling something angrily at him.

I took another deep breath and tried to focus on her words.

"I could burn you away into the sands of the desert now if I so wished!" she was saying to him. "But I believe someone else would like that honor!"

She stepped back and turning to look at me, smiled encouragingly.

I took another deep breath and slowly climbed to my feet.

My eyes grew hard as I glared at Hector, pinned helplessly to the wall. He struggled but it did him no good.

I strode up to him until I was inches away from his face.

"So we modern witches are useless, eh?" I told him. "Then why do you tremble so at what my daughter conjured up? You are wrong Hector. My kind still *does* have their teeth."

I turned to the goddess. I did not need to say anything. She simply knew and tossed the Coptic dagger to me. I caught it as if it was second nature.

I turned back to Hector and without pausing, slashed him from his shoulder to the top of his chest.

"Don't worry," I reassured him, mockingly. "It isn't deep."

I then turned to Mykhalo.

"You promised not too long ago to tear his throat out," I said angrily. My eyes turned back to Hector.

"Do it!" I commanded and turning my back on the Spanish vampire, I let the dagger fall clattering to the floor.

Mykhalo approached Hector. I chose not to watch. But I heard what he told him.

"This ends here tonight," he said. "You will murder no one else nor torture any more of my friends. Oh, by the way my name is not Michael. It's Mykhalo!"

These last words he spoke with a roar of vengeance.

Hector screamed in terror.

I simply knelt in front of Sekhmet and waited for it to be over.

The sounds from behind me were horrible. I heard Hector choking and thrashing. I heard Mykhalo growling in eagerness as he fed hungrily on his sire's essence. I heard the sickening thump of his body as it hit the floor.

And then I heard silence.

Presently Mykhalo joined me kneeling at my side, eyes cast downward.

"I will accept whatever judgment this 'face of God' decides is best," he spoke quietly to her.

I rose to my feet and stepped back. This was between him and the goddess, not me.

Sekhmet approached Mykhalo.

"So this is the catalyst that began all this trouble," she purred thoughtfully.

Mykhalo kept his eyes down.

"Look at me, Nosferatu!" she demanded in a terrible voice.

Mykhalo shuddered but obeyed.

She pushed her lioness face in close to his and stared deeply into his eyes. I could sense Mykhalo struggling not to tremble.

"Having drunk your sire dry, do you now still thirst for blood?" she asked him.

Mykhalo swallowed carefully before choosing to speak.

"I am what I have always been for three centuries," he replied honestly. "I will always thirst for blood."

She nodded, purring.

She turned her red eyes to me.

"Honest and brave. Surprising for a Nosferatu," she said and she began to circle him as she spoke, considering. "This one actually has the wisdom to fear and respect me, unheard of in his kind. I understand better your dilemma, little mother."

She came around to stand in before him again and, bending over, cupped her hands in front of her. We both watched as her cupped hands magically began to fill with what looked like blood.

"Drink from this sacred chalice if you wish to acquire your dreams. But be cautious. When I say to stop, you *must stop* or be consumed by the flames of my judgment."

I stepped to Mykhalo's side and whispered in his ear. "This is a test. Do exactly as She instructs. Refusing would not be wise."

I saw him shudder again in dread as I stepped back.

"Little mother, you will not be permitted to touch him to help," Sekhmet told me.

I bowed my head and stepped back even more.

"Now, little dead man," Sekhmet told Mykhalo. "Drink from my Waters of Life."

Mykhalo hesitantly clasped her cupped hands and began to drink the blood which filled her palms. I saw his Adam's apple bob as he swallowed. I saw a predatory light come into his eyes and he desperately grasped the goddess's cupped hands and began to drink with a more voracious thirst. He drank for a long while, getting more agitated and hungry as time passed.

Sekhmet's eyes looked up at me mockingly. Mykhalo continued to drink in a desperate, wild manner, as if he could never get enough.

"That's enough, now. Stop!" she commanded.

I saw Mykhalo's brows knit as he tried to pull his lips back. I felt the vampire instinct was refusing.

I saw his left hand quietly clasp my pentacle and squeeze it hard.

He tore his lips away with a gasp and coughed.

Sekhmet straightened. She seemed disappointed. She glanced angrily at me. I gave her an apologetic look and shrugged. I hadn't 'touched' Mykhalo in any way.

"Very well then," she told him. "You have won your deepest desires. Your time is now short. Use what is left to you wisely. You shall not burn at the end."

She began to fade and dwindle in size. Her form finally gave way to the small frame of my daughter hiding underneath.

Bree collapsed silently to the floor and lay quite still.

I ran to her side and crouching down, gently stroked her fake, red hair away from her face. I felt her breath on my fingertips and sighed in relief. Mykhalo knelt down beside me.

"Are you all right?" I asked without looking at him.

"Yes," he reassured me. "I no longer hunger. Strange."

He scooped up Bree and I picked up the Coptic dagger and we cautiously began to make our way down the hallway.

"Are you still a Nos…a vampire?" I asked in a hushed tone. Somehow, me saying the word Nosferatu seemed just too ridiculous!

"I think so," he said. "I don't feel any different other than I have no insatiable thirst for blood anymore. What was the stuff She made me drink?"

We turned right down another hallway.

"Sacred blood," I responded.

"Yes, but that's just it," he said to me. "The sacred blood of what?"

I shrugged.

"*That* I don't think we're supposed to know," I said back to him.

# CHAPTER 26

We came to a long stairway and just as we set foot on the first of the steps, Bree began to move. She squirmed and moaned.

"Put me down!" she groaned. "I'm not a Chihuahua! My legs still work."

Mykhalo nearly dropped her in his surprise.

"Bree, honey?" I said, cradling her head. "It's okay now. The bad guys are all gone."

She wriggled out of my embrace and staggered to her feet.

"No, they're not!" she insisted. "There's a small band of suckers guarding the front doors. Bran is clearing the way right now but he needs help."

She tried the stairs but her knees buckled and she clutched wildly for the banister. I rushed to catch her.

"How do you know that?" I demanded.

She sniffed and gave me the 'my mother is so clueless!' look.

"C'mon, Ma! I was away but not unconscious!" Bree told me rolling her eyes at me. "I saw what happened back there and what's happening up ahead before she gave my body back."

"Pardon me, but you seem a little weak in the legs," Mykhalo added.

"Don't worry!" she reassured, waving it off as if it was nothing. "She said it would pass quickly. It's just a 'host hangover'. And by the way, nice work back there! Maybe my Mom was right about you!"

Mykhalo and I exchanged unsure looks.

"I guess this means you're still on a meat diet?" I muttered, not meaning for her to hear me.

"You betcha!" she replied. "Man! Do I have a hankering for some 'bloody cow' right now!"

The return of her teenage wit comforted me somewhat.

"Quiet!" scolded Mykhalo. "Did you hear that?"

We all stilled and listened.

The sound of shouting and combat came to our ears.

"Hurry!" urged Bree. "Bran needs us now!"

We each took Bree by the hand and rushed down the flight of stairs.

We hit the landing and Mykhalo pointed to the right.

Bran was spinning, dancing in a deadly arc, ebony daggers leading and keeping five vampires at bay at one time.

Mykhalo snarled and rushed to join in.

One undead saw him and flew eagerly to meet him, teeth bared and eyes blazing. Mykhalo picked him up without a thought and raised him high overhead, shaking him in his fury. The vampire thrashed and screamed wildly. And then Mykhalo tore him in half.

Bree and I jumped back out of the way as the pieces fell to either side.

"My Lord! What was in that blood?" I gasped.

"You don't want to know!" Bree told me.

Another vampire saw Bree crouching down by the stairs and flew shrieking at her. I shouted a warning.

It was unnecessary. Bree screeched and slashed in one quick moment. She then had to duck as the attacking vampire exploded into ash right above her.

Bree just stared at her hand as if it belonged to someone else.

"How in the Hell did I do that?" she muttered.

"Just keep doing it but watch your language next time!" I scolded.

Bran had used the distraction to jump on the back of another vampire. As the big man bore it to the ground, he slashed its neck with both knives. The vampire melted with a scream.

Mykhalo had the other two immobilized in both hands against the wall. One he had pinned, the other's throat he was tearing out.

"Here let me help you with those two, friend," Bran said.

He strode up and stabbed the pinned vampire with both knives. Not caring to watch it disintegrate, Bran turned to us.

"You two okay?" he asked.

Neither one of us could trust our voices yet so we just blinked at him and nodded.

Bran turned to face Mykhalo as he finished with the last undead and cast its husk aside.

"Bran, the Blood Raven, or so I've been told?" Mykhalo asked, wiping the blood from his face.

Bran nodded with a smile and extended a blood soaked hand for the German vampire to shake.

"We've met though," Bran said, as his smile increased. "Don't you remember Baghdad?"

"I remember," Mykhalo said, smiling back. "You had a few less tattoos then."

Bran laughed, barely panting from the exertion of the fight.

"I'd like to swap war stories more but I think we better get the ladies home and you underground. The dawn is coming soon."

"Yes, that would be most wise," Mykhalo agreed.

Bran ushered us out of the manor house.

Outside we found the night air tinged with nearby smoke. The free wind ruffled our hair and we breathed deep its gentle blessing. The sky was already starting to lighten.

I saw figures, many dark, shadowed figures, marching toward us over the immaculately tended lawns. I clutched Bree closer to me as I peered through the dim light to see who they were.

"Zan!" I heard a familiar voice call.

"Sage? Is that you?" I called back.

"Yes!" came the reply and the old woman sprinted up to me.

But ten feet away, she pulled up short.

"You…haven't been bitten have you?" she asked in concern.

"No. You?"

"No."

We rushed into each other arms and clung tight. Words immediately began to pour from my lips.

"What happened in Sleepy Pines? Is the town all right? How many families were attacked? Anyone hurt?"

"Hush, Zan dear, hush," she consoled stroking my hair in a motherly way. "Things aren't as bad as you would expect. A lot of fires were set and buildings burned. Only a few were attacked. We had our people scattered in just about every household and there were wards on every doorsill. Even the church ministers pitched in and helped us in their own way. We were ready! It was exciting but we were ready! You can relax now."

I looked at the people coming up to join us. I could tell by their dress they were all of the esoteric community, the people the rest of the world had branded as weirdoes and freaks. Their ritual clothes all seemed a bit battered by now.

I felt surrounded by family.

Bree came up behind me and rubbed my back, reassuringly.

"The bad guys are all gone now, Mom," she said with a chuckle. "All except for him."

She jabbed a thumb Mykhalo's way.

I separated myself from their embraces.

I slowly went over to Mykhalo and stood looking up at him in the fading dark.

"He's no bad guy," I insisted loudly. "You'll never be that to me."

And I wrapped my arms around him and held him tight.

He hesitated only a moment.

And then his arms returned my embrace.

# CHAPTER 27

The campfire's flames crackled and popped, sparks rising high into the spring night air. The tongues of flames perfectly framed the bright moon who sat above us with just a slice missing from one side.

We were gathered around this campfire, a motley assortment of people in strange clothes and robes depending on the nationality of their faith. Some wore deep hooded dark robes and others barely enough to stay decent in front of the children. I wore my deep green cloak even though it was a little too warm for it this night. It still had the stain from where Mykhalo had wiped Giselle's blood from his mouth. Somehow, I just couldn't bring myself to wash it.

The campfire's popping hushed the laughter of the youngest children running in the field behind us, playing with their flashlights while the grown-ups worshipped.

Sage stepped to the forefront and all eyes turned to her. She was dressed in silver robes and adorned with Native American talismans.

She held out her arms to the flames and lifting up her chin, began to speak in a loud voice so all could hear.

"We gather here tonight, many people of many faiths, to pay tribute to the blessed deliverance from the danger of this past lunar eclipse. We say thanks to the spirit of Divinity within us all, by whatever name we choose call it. We say thanks to the Great Spirit, to God the Almighty, to the Lord and Lady, the Green Man, and Sekhmet and many more besides. Thank you for standing with us. Thank you for bestowing the strength to defend our families, our friends, and our homes. Thank you for the grace of sparing our lives and driving our enemies far from us and those we love. And thank you especially for touching our lives each and every day, not just in times of trial but times of peace as well. We are most grateful for your protection and attention. May we continue to prove worthy of such Divine protection and love for the rest of our lives."

She bent over and picked up from the ground an abalone shell bowl and cast its dusty contents into the flames. There was a hiss and a roar from the fire and the flames momentarily turned purple with sparkles as they leapt higher into the air. As the flames fell back to their original height, Sage stepped back into the crowd. One by one, each of those gathered came forward and cast something into the fire, sometimes it was powder, sometimes it was alcohol, for some tobacco and for others it was more personal, the significance of which was only known to that person and to the divine.

I stepped forward silently and cast a handful of coffee grounds into the flames. It seemed fitting somehow for me.

When everyone had finished, Sage again stepped forward and closed the circle. She turned to those gathered and released us to celebrate life.

There were eager shouts and howls of excitement. Drums seemed to magically appear and some women threw off their robes to reveal belly-dancing outfits underneath dripping with coins and flashing ornaments. Three people had brought pennywhistles and their clear tunes rose with the dancing flames into the air.

The buffet tent was opened and soon there were knots of people gathered, conversing over plates of steaming food. Mike the Mead Maker had shown up with plenty of different varieties of homemade mead. Mead maids seemed to materialize out of thin air and the mead was distributed in many different glasses from cardboard cups to tankards and ornately etched drinking horns.

Laughter and campfire smoke twined together in the warm night air and the ground vibrated from the throb of the drums and belly dancers' feet. Spelldreamer had arrived. I could tell because his fire-dancing apprentices were spinning their art in front of the fire. I noticed he had brought his fire swords and was regaling the kids by first spinning the fiery blades and then swallowing them while they were still burning.

My eyes scanned for Bree. I found her easily enough. She was dressed in a filmy red gown, bedecked with coins and jewels. She had recently picked up belly dancing. She wasn't very good but was learning quickly from Cheznian our dancing expert. Cheznian looked as Irish as they come with her pale skin, freckled face and hair which hung in tight, red golden ringlets. But when the belly dancers came out, she would habitually put them all to shame.

Cheznian had positioned herself in front of Bran and his djembe drum. The faster his hands pounded, the faster she danced. It was a game they would frequently play at these functions. He drummed and she would dance and they would each strive to throw the other off tempo. She smiled seductively at him and I could see him struggle to concentrate on his drumbeats. I saw Bree behind her, trying her best to mimic Cheznian's swaying hips and easily undulating spine. Her wide smile never wavered. Bree was actually keeping up rather well, well enough to distract the other men gathered.

I wound my way closer, ever the protective mother.

Cheznian suddenly tossed back her red curls and fell to her knees in front of Bran giving him a nice view of her cleavage. Bran's drumbeats suddenly faltered.

There was a shout of laughter from all gathered and Cheznian rippled back to her feet, grinning from freckled ear to ear her smile of triumph. Bran just shook his head and relinquished his drum to the next person, muttering something about needing a drink. I saw her approach Bree and she began to give her student more pointers. I left them to ripple and sway together to a new beat.

I followed Bran to the mead tent and we both chatted as we poured ourselves some of Mike's excellent home brew.

I noticed Bran look into the woods to the side and stiffen abruptly.

"What is it?" I asked.

"We are being watched," Bran replied.

I tried to control my heart from its wild fluttering.

"By who?" I demanded.

Bran just as suddenly relaxed.

"By the only vampire who doesn't worry me," he replied.

I glanced into the woods but saw nothing. I turned my eyes back to Bran.

"You knew Mykhalo from before?" I asked.

He nodded and turned his back to me as he sipped his mead from his very long and ornate drinking horn.

But I would not be put off. I circled around again so I could stare up into his emerald green eyes.

"How?" I persisted. "You said you were in the Gulf War together. Tell me."

Bran didn't meet my eyes. He seemed to be looking everywhere but at my face.

"Bran, *look at me!*" I demanded.

He sighed heavily and obeyed.

"Tell me how!" I said.

Bran sighed again. His green eyes glittered at me in the dim lantern light of the tent. His tattoos peeking out of the neckline of his shirt seemed like claws.

"Tell me," I insisted in a resolute whisper.

Bran looked at his feet and then into my eyes.

"Rik didn't die in a roadside bombing," he told me slowly.

I was confused. Why was he now talking about my dead husband?

"I asked about Mykhalo," I said slowly. "Why are you now talking about Rik? Are you trying to distract me?"

"The two events are related," Bran told me before lapsing once more into an aggravating silence.

"Then you shall tell me here and now!" I ordered.

Bran motioned me to a couple of stumps where we could sit and talk more privately.

"The government lied to you," he began in a low voice. "Rik never died in a roadside bombing. There was a bomb that took out all but three of our unit. But we escaped it Rik, Jason and I. We fled to the first shelter we could find which turned out to be a wrecked house with a large underground basement. We pried up the trapdoor and dropped down below because we knew that pursuit was not far behind. There were only three of us. We knew we could be taken out all too easily. After we found out the building had a basement, we discovered it also had a tunnel for smuggling things back and forth. So we took that way."

He rubbed his eyes and then grasped the drinking horn with both hands. I noticed they were trembling slightly.

"Rik was in the lead. So he ran into the vampire first," he said.

I gasped.

"Not…Mykhalo?" I asked.

Bran smiled and shook his head once.

"No, not Mykhalo. From all you've told me the past few days I believe it was Hector. I mistook him for someone from the Mid-East with his complexion. He fell on Rik so fast we couldn't react in time to save him. He died quickly. I'm not even sure he knew what hit him. Jason did. Jason saw…we both saw…the teeth. Jason's bullets went wild. Hector killed him in spite of getting hit. Then Hector turned on me."

Bran dragged a sleeve across his brow which had started to bead with sweat.

"I unloaded everything I had into him and he just laughed like it was nothing. Then he tried to attack me. That's when Mykhalo stepped in. He pulled Hector off of me and knocked him into the wall. Then he splashed something on his face. It must have been holy water because Hector screamed like I have never heard any human scream before. He ran off immediately and left me alone."

Bran gave a long sigh.

"Mykhalo never harmed me. He checked to see I wasn't wounded and then showed me the way out of the tunnels. We waited until dark and then he escorted me back to my base."

Bran turned his green eyes back to me.

"He shadowed my unit the rest of my stay and made sure I was warned if there was any trouble up ahead. I would have died several

263

times if it hadn't been for Mykhalo. And yet, I still wish it had been me who had died and not Rik. He had a wife and baby girl back home to support. I didn't have much of a family.'

I looked out to the rest of the encampment celebrating and socializing around the fire.

"We are your family now," I told him and gently took hold of his hand.

"I know," he whispered softly into the dark. "And I thank the Lord and Lady for that every day."

He laid a big hand on top of mine and squeezed in response.

"You know I still wake up some nights in a cold sweat, hearing that scream echo over and over in my dreams."

I patted his hand reassuringly.

"I hope the nightmares will end soon," I told him.

He smiled back to me in the flickering light of a tiki torch.

"I'm kinda hoping what we did the other night would stop them," he replied. "You know I can't shake the feeling both Mykhalo and Hector were running from something and bumped into each other unexpectedly that night."

He shrugged as if it wasn't important.

Then his eyes shifted to the darkness of the trees. He was silent a moment, lost deep in thought.

"You need to go to him. He's waiting."

I got up and dropped a grateful kiss on his forehead.

I turned away from the campfire and all the noisy revelers and made my way into the woods. My thoughts were swirling. It had been so long since I had thought about Rik, my late husband. I had been under the influence of so many mixed emotions at the time. I had to suffer the deaths of both my parents and my husband within mere weeks of one another. I had just put my parents' remains in the ground when they sent back Rik's body to bury. And yet I had never seen him. Bran had counseled me not to look. I was so upset and not thinking straight, so I just went along with his advice.

I felt like I had lost my entire family in the space of a month. The last words I had with my parents were angry. We had been fighting

264

about my choice in religion. They told me I would burn in the fires of hell. I had said some stupid thing about hell being warmer than the alternative.

And then they were gone. In an instant I had no way to apologize to them for my harsh words, no way to smooth things over and say the things a child is supposed to say to a dearly loved parent on their deathbed. My last words to them were words of anger and hate. I so wanted to say I was sorry.

But they were gone forever.

In times like these most people would have run to their beloved mate. I barely had a chance. Erik was far away. I couldn't just pick up the phone the minute it happened and tell him. I had to wait. When I did tell him, I just skimmed over the event. I never gave him the details of how I really felt. It was a bad time to talk to him. He couldn't stay on the phone long. There was gunfire in the background.

Then he was gone too.

I had no one to talk to about anything I was feeling.

My family was dead. I had to figure out some way to go on without the most important people in my life.

I had almost immediately packed away every sign of Rik, every picture, every gift he had ever given me, his clothes, even the engagement and wedding ring. They all had gone into several trunks and been placed in the attic. Bree, thankfully, had been too young to notice. The shock of it all had made her come early. I remember the darkness I lived in for the next few years. I had been very antisocial. I took to wearing black and staying home on weekends and pretty much stopped having a life.

Bree had saved me then. Even as a baby, she had been the only person who could coax me to smile again and to stay with the world to some degree. The pain subsided gradually and I stopped wearing my grief on my sleeve. But I had refused to date or show any sign of getting in a loving relationship with any man although there were certainly many offers. Bran had even offered once. I refused them all. I had promised myself never to fall in love with another soldier or any person with a warrior like spirit.

And then Bree had become like her father, the hero, and the soldier.

And then Mykhalo had somehow drawn me into his world, resulting in me feeling something for this poor, tormented vampire. Was it love? If it was, I didn't want to admit it to myself.

Somehow, the fact that Rik might have known Mykhalo, however briefly, was a reflection in the mirror I just didn't want to face. Not yet. Not now.

Yet here I was walking through the woods at night to confront him about this!

I had to pick my way carefully because the ground was uneven and strewn with raspberry vines and Multi-flora rose thorns. I felt something tug on my cape which didn't feel like forest underbrush.

I turned slowly to see Mykhalo standing behind me. His gray eyes glittered at me in the dark and the moonlight glanced off his quiet smile.

"I thought I would find you here," I told him.

I held out my German tankard to him.

"Sorry it's not beer," I said with a smile.

He smiled in return and I felt his cold fingers wrap around my own as he removed it from my grasp.

"Would you like some witch's honey to go with it?" I asked as I watched him raise it to his lips.

The tankard stopped at his mouth.

"No, I am still not 'hungry'," he replied, his words echoing into the depths of the tankard.

He took a long swallow and passed it back to me with an approving grunt.

"Very nice blend, even if it isn't beer," he commented.

I smiled in reply and took a long sip myself and felt the mead travel down my throat bringing with it pleasant warmth.

"I see Bree is herself again," Mykhalo said as he observed the people gathered around the fire. "I am glad to see her as just another adolescent. She can go back to her normal, mortal life."

My eyes narrowed.

266

"And what about my life?" I asked.

He turned his eyes back to me and considered me for a time. And then he stepped closer, close enough to whisper into my ear.

"You too should return to your normal life. But I would like to beg the honor of one night with you in private. We have much to discuss," he murmured softly.

I couldn't look at him. I was afraid he'd see the emotions in my eyes. I stared downward at the reflection of the moon in the tankard before me.

"Things like how my husband died?" I pointedly told him.

The pleasant expression was wiped from Mykhalo's face and he stepped back.

"He told you!" he said in shock. "He promised never to tell you."

I raised my chin in defiance.

"I pried it out of him." I cocked my head to the side and it was now my turn to consider him.

"Why?" I said. "Why did you make him promise not to tell me the truth of my husband's death?"

He refused to answer.

I stepped closer to him. Into his eyes suddenly came a hunted look at my move.

"What were you and Hector doing in the Gulf? What were you running from?" I asked, meeting his eyes with a demanding glare of my own.

He took the tankard from my hands and drained it in one, bold, swallow. He then stepped so close he was inches away from my face.

"Come to my house tomorrow evening and I will answer all your questions then," he whispered to me.

I turned my face to look him in the eye. He was so close I could feel his breath on my skin.

"You have a house in Sleepy Pines?" I asked, somewhat angry at this revelation. "I never knew."

"Yes, I own a place on the outskirts of town, in the country. Bill helped me find it a couple of years ago," he replied. "If you come tomorrow night, I will clear up all murky details of my life."

His eyes peered deep into my own, as if asking himself whether I could be trusted. He raised a hand up to my face and stroked my hair gently. His hand came to a stop on my cheek, his thumb caressing my skin tenderly. He stepped closer almost touching my forehead with his.

"I promise," he told me.

The moonlight glittered on his eyes and his teeth.

And then he was gone.

# CHAPTER 28

Mykhalo's house in Sleepy Pines was just the kind of house I expected a vampire to live in. It was at the end of a long lane, lined with ancient, spreading pin oaks in a secluded spot out in the country. It was a large white Victorian style mansion, the kind you don't own without servants or maids to keep it clean. Its lawns were well manicured and looked as if the grass had never stopped growing all winter. The landscaping was beautiful and there was a riot of spring color from the flowerbeds out front. Beyond the circular parking area, just in front of the house were two old weeping cherry trees framing the walk up to the front door. The wind gently rustled their cascading branches, scattering pink petals along the walk. The flowers were so bright on these trees they seemed to glow in the dark of the fading sunset. I had to stop for just a moment to admire them they were so beautiful.

I quietly got out of my car and walked up the petal-strewn steps to the front door. I felt uncomfortable here all alone. The setting was a bit ostentatious for my tastes. I expected to be mistaken for the hired help or someone applying for the position, not an honored guest. Maybe I shouldn't have worn blue jeans.

I expected there to be a security guard with angry looking Dobermans patrolling the premises or at least a gardener to greet me. But I saw no other people.

I straightened my simple jacket and knocked on the door. I expected a maid or a butler at least to answer. But nothing happened. There was no response. And yet I knew there had to be someone in the house because I could hear Native American music. There was an Indian flute in the background.

I waited patiently listening to the faint tunes of the flute coming to my ears. But no one answered the door. I called "Hello?" quite loudly and still no answer or interruption of the flute.

I frowned. I felt like I was invading the homeowner's privacy even though I had been invited. It was just so eerily absent of people. Retreating down the steps, I made my way around the house to the backyard if you could call it that. It was really too big to be a backyard. It too was as neatly cared for as the front. There was a stone walkway covered by a trellis which could barely be seen through the thick tangle of rose vine climbing over it. It was still a bit early for roses to bloom but their buds were forming and I could already smell them.

In the backyard was a large Koi pond overhung with weeping cherry and willow trees with the first light green blush of spring leaves caressing the almost mirror like reflection of the still waters. The haunting sound of the Indian flute grew clearer. The grass was scattered with wrought iron furniture painted white and placed in certain areas to let the viewer fully appreciate the beauty of the grounds. Beds of tulips and daffodils grew near the lawn furniture.

I turned my back on the yard to take in the house. It seemed bigger in back than the front. It had two porches, one on the second floor and one on ground level which seemed to wrap itself entirely around the house. As I took in the detail of the architecture, I mused how southern it seemed, as if from the Civil War era. It seemed just the kind of house a ghost would enjoy haunting. Maybe the flute music was from the local spirit.

My eyes traveled down the three floors of the mansion and took in the smaller details of the expansive porch.

It was then I saw Mykhalo. He was sitting on the white steps of the porch playing an Indian flute. He was dressed all in white and so he seemed, at first, to blend into the house, which is why I hadn't noticed him before. He was dressed a bit more casually than I had ever seen him, no tie and his starched, pressed shirt was unbuttoned at the neck.

He smiled at me and stopped playing the woodwind.

"So you're a chameleon as well!" I said to him as I approached.

He smiled and bowed his head.

"That can be a useful trait to have in my profession," he replied.

"And just what is that?" I asked. "Your profession, that is?"

He rose to his feet.

"Depends on what time period you catch me in. The past one hundred years, it seems to have been investor," Mykhalo told me.

"What was your profession when you were human?" I said.

He snorted and rolled his eyes.

"To be whatever my father told me to be. I had no choice," he grimly admitted.

"And if you had a choice?"

He looked at me and his smile deepened.

"Nothing that would have made much of a profit, I can assure you," he said.

I smiled in return.

"Tell me anyway. I'm curious," I persisted.

Mykhalo slid me a sly look.

"Your curiosity is insatiable, my dear. Hasn't it gotten you in enough trouble with me lately?"

I laughed in response.

"And once again, you're being evasive. Needlessly, this time."

He sighed and leaned against one of the posts holding up the porch. He looked down at the Indian flute he held in his hands and lovingly stroked its smoothly polished wood.

"I always dreamed of being a musician of some sort. But I was born at a time when musical prodigies were everywhere in Germany. I was a little outclassed."

His eyes then turned to survey the landscaping behind the house.

"I also wanted to be a gardener. Spring is my favorite time of year because the flowers are so brilliant. All my properties have tons

271

of flowers, especially bulbs and roses. That was something my father never would have approved of."

He crossed his arms in front of himself and gazed out towards the Koi pond.

"I also used to have childhood dreams of having a stable of thirty horses with flaxen manes and tails and a manor house filled with Great Danes of every color. But then Hector made me a Nosferatu and there went that dream! Suddenly the animals I loved the most ran in fear from me or attacked me. That's one of the things I miss the most about being human: being able to interact and bond with animals. Life became cold and colorless for me after that."

I had nothing to say which would have cheered him up so I chose to change the topic.

"So you're an investor. That's how you can afford such a beautiful estate?" I asked.

"Well, having an indefinite lifespan certainly does have its perks," he told me. "You know that whatever financial ruin the world you live in is going through, you can wait it out. And, if your observation skills are very keen, you quickly learn to notice trends and make wise investments. My coffee plantations in the Caribbean have been very good to my wallet, you might say. I bought this house with the profits. But this is only one of my houses."

I looked around me, and tried not to think of the daily cost of such a property, and then tried not to multiply that several times over!

"I own about ten estates in America," he replied casually as if we were talking trivial things. "I own many more abroad, all specifically set up for my needs."

I nodded.

"Meaning basements with no windows, I assume," I said.

He snickered pleasantly.

"Yes, very deep basements!" he replied.

"Any castles?" I inquired.

He laughed easily.

"Just a small one in Bavaria. The heating bills are astronomical in the winter!" he chuckled.

"Any secret passages hidden in bookcases?" I teased.

"That property has many secrets," he said stepping closer to me. "Maybe you'll get to investigate it someday."

I looked up into his eyes and fought not to be drawn in. My eyes slipped to his collarbone where something flashed there.

It was a small, round, glass bead on a simple black string filled with something dark pillowed on the white skin of his neck.

"Earth from Bavaria?" I asked in a soft voice.

"Yes," he replied in an equally soft tone. "As a vampire, you learn to keep many spare earthly talismans, just in case."

I nodded in understanding.

"But are you still a vampire?" I asked.

The smile vanished and he looked at his feet as if he was ashamed.

"Yes, I am," he said sadly. "I tried to get a suntan the other day. It didn't work. I am still a vampire."

"And the bloodlust? What of that?" I asked.

He sighed in frustration and ran a hand through his golden locks.

"I'm still not hungry." I could tell this confused him.

I raised my chin and swept back my hair, exposing my throat to him.

"And what effect does this have on you?" I asked him pointedly.

He looked for a long time at my neck. He raised his hand to my shoulder and stroked my bare skin with his cold fingers. I shivered at his touch. Finally, his eyes shifted to mine.

"I'm more interested in a point higher up," he said, evasively.

I suddenly stepped backwards up the stairs, away from him.

"Stop it!" I told him.

His smile shivered and faded in confusion.

"Stop what?" he said innocently. He advanced a couple of steps towards me.

I retreated higher again this time and reached the top step of the porch.

"Stop trying to vamp me! It won't work!" I insisted.

I was starting to get a little irritated and a bit scared.

"Is that what you think I'm doing?" he asked as he advanced the last few steps towards me.

I backed away again.

"Aren't you?" I demanded. "As a vampire, can't you seduce anyone you wish with your voice and get them to do anything you want? Aren't you doing that now with me?"

The look which came over his face was abruptly one of irritation and maybe even insult. He took three quick steps toward me and stopped. He paused momentarily before continuing.

"My dear, I have *never* tried that with you! I have always striven to be honest especially with all that we have recently gone through together," he said.

The porch was wide but the wall behind me was near.

"And how do I know that to be true?" I said.

"After all this time, you are still suspicious of me? Zan! I'm hurt!" he said softly enough to be persuasive.

This only served to make me more suspicious.

"Yeah, I bet you are!" I scoffed.

Mykhalo looked me full in the face and his eyes began to glitter dangerously. He bent over slowly, almost gracefully and laid the Indian woodwind carefully down on a nearby chair. I saw the last rays of the setting sun flash and fade abruptly over his shoulder before he straightened up.

"My dear Zan, you know not what you say," he began slowly. "If I wanted to really 'vamp' you as you so delicately put it, do you really think I would waste this much time talking to you? If I wanted you for myself, I wouldn't speak of it. I'd just take you here. *NOW*!"

In a rush and with a roar, he was on top of me before I could move. I lifted my foot to step back and I was suddenly being hurtled backwards at frightening speed to slam up against the wall. The air left my lungs in a sudden, frightened gasp and my arms were pinned in his crushing grip. My heart began to pound in terror and my mind was screaming at me in anger, why did I insist on poking the sleeping dragon? His eyes were blazing at me and starting to change color.

"Is this how you truly want me to treat you?" he demanded of me.

His eyes had gone white and his teeth had grown. No, he definitely *was* still a vampire I told myself.

His face lunged forward and to the side. I felt his fangs press hard into me and then stop just short of piercing the skin. He held himself like that for a long, breathless moment, the tips of his fangs pressing painful indentations into my skin.

Shuddering uncontrollably, I forced myself to swallow and take a trembling breath.

"Is this how you treat all your friends eventually?" I finally had the boldness to say.

I felt him growl through his teeth in frustration. The hands on my arms twitched in their indecision.

He then abruptly flung me to the side and turning away from me, stalked to the bottom of the porch stairs where he stopped. I quaked in fear where I had landed, unsure of what to do next. My right hand began to massage the painful marks his teeth had left on my neck. I looked at his back. He seemed to be breathing hard, his shoulders were heaving.

"Maybe you better take this back."

There was a small clatter and my pentacle landed on the black painted wooden floorboards before me. In stunned silence, I watched my fingers close numbly about it.

"Maybe you better leave, too."

I cringed at these words. I stared at his back for a long moment while I tried to desperately catch my breath and collect my thoughts.

I had to swallow a couple of times before I could trust my voice to speak.

"I can't do that," I finally shivered out.

He turned around and I looked down, unable to meet his eyes.

"I'm sorry I did that just now," I stammered out as best as I could. "But I had to know."

I watched his bare feet advance slowly up the stairs and approach me.

I huddled there on the floor shuddering, totally baffled at what to do next.

"And I'm not leaving," I said in a firm tone.

"Why not?" he asked in a husky voice.

My eyes flickered up and away. His face was shadowed and blank.

"Because I care about you just a little," I whispered.

He crouched down beside me.

"Why?" he asked again, insistently. "Because I'm a vampire?"

A smile flickered across my face.

"I'd like to say no," I began. "That would be the expected answer. But I've only known you as Mykhalo the vampire. I know no other way to relate to you. But whatever you are, I care."

There was a long pause.

"How much?" he said. "As friends or something more?"

I looked into his eyes at this. I saw a terrible regret swimming there for what he had just done. I also saw an aching yearning for something else.

"Is something more possible for someone like you?" I said.

It was his turn to swallow with difficulty.

"God, I hope so," he said.

My eyes locked onto his.

"Please don't ask me to leave again," I told him.

I fought it but I could feel the tears shivering on my eyelids.

"I'm sorry I got angry. I'm sorry I frightened and hurt you. I guess I too had to know," he said.

A fat tear rolled down my cheek to be caught by Mykhalo's cold hand.

I pulled back and turning away, got to my feet, dashing the tears away on my sleeve.

"Now look what you've made me do!"

I tried to laugh it off.

I sniffed and wouldn't look at him. I always hated anyone to see me cry, no matter what the reason.

He hesitantly took a step closer to me.

276

"I'm glad you thought me worth the tears," Mykhalo whispered into my hair.

There was a long pause between us.

"Zan, what do you believe me to be?" he asked. "Not the vampire. The person."

I swallowed hard and noisily as I composed my thoughts.

"Well…" I began in a tremulous voice. "I believe you to be a good person deep down inside, enslaved, and tormented by your predatory, dark side which we all have in us. But with you, that dark side is harder to control. I believe you have had to do many things you regret in order to survive. I believe your heart yearns for the friends you've lost and to have some sense of normalcy. I believe you desperately want to have friends even though you know having mortal friends is dangerous for them and you wrestle with this knowledge constantly. I believe you have a conscience. I believe you have a soul. I believe you are a dangerous person. And I believe you are a good person."

I could not look at him while I said this. But as I said the last sentence, I turned and peeped through the strands of my black hair to see what his reaction to my words would be.

His brows were wrinkled and his deeply shadowed face seemed on the verge of breaking down, fractured by some great emotion held just under the surface.

"Okay," I whispered to him. "Now your turn. What do you believe me to be?"

A smile softened his features and he turned his face away momentarily as he mastered his emotions.

"A fair question," he began hesitantly. It seemed now he was having trouble composing *his* words. He cleared his throat several times and made a few false starts before finally taking a deep breath and just going for it.

"I believe you are a woman capable of great things and comprehending things most people would not waste time with. Your mind is complex and intriguing to me and that's why I keep coming back for our little discussions. Of all the new-age witches I've encountered, you are the only one who seems real to me and I find that fascinating. I believe you to be a beautiful, spiritual woman, solid in her beliefs and loyal to her friends. You are a devoted and protective mother and yet not overbearing in her maternal instincts. You have raised an intelligent, strong-minded, independent daughter and that speaks very highly of you. Your beliefs are unshakable. I wish I had that kind of faith in spirituality. I feel faith has betrayed me. But then I look at you who have seen so little and yet are so strong in her beliefs and it inspires me and gives me hope. You speak your mind when others dance around the topic. I have always appreciated truthful people. I believe you to be a beautiful and complex person and that's why I love you."

I gasped and spun my head about to look him straight in the eye.

"Did you just say the 'L' word to me?" I said quickly.

Mykhalo immediately began to stammer nervously.

"I...I meant to say...that is one of the things I love *about* you," he hastily corrected himself. "That's what I meant to say."

"Now who is dancing around the topic?" I said, smiling smugly. "Typical male! Is the great Baron Mykhalo Von Ludwig afraid of the word love?"

But the look he gave me was a serious one full of apprehension and fear.

"I am *not* afraid of the word or the emotion!" he hastened to assure me. "I'm just afraid of the consequences of it on those I love."

I stepped closer to him.

"Everyone should fear the word love," I told him. "Not just you the vampire towards me the mortal. Love is a four-letter word. It can make women run back to the men who beat them and men stalk women who choose to escape them."

Mykhalo snorted derisively.

"That is not love!" he insisted. "That is control!"

"Yeah, well tell them that!" I said.

"And is that not what I'm doing to you?" Mykhalo put to me.

I frowned as I pondered his words for a long moment and then I uttered a long sigh.

"Whatever relationship we have, whether it stays as friends or makes the leap to something more, will always be dangerous, especially to me," I said. "Do you want to take that leap?"

His eyes met mine. For a long moment, he was silent. Then he forced himself to swallow and answer me.

"Yes, very much so," he said.

I smiled and stepped closer to him. I raised my hand and stroked the side of his face tenderly. He closed his eyes and leaned into my touch as if he had been waiting for the reaction for a very long time.

"Let's see if I can make you warm again," I whispered to him.

He clasped my hand but not to stop my touch.

"You already have," he said.

He bent his head to mine and our lips embraced.

## CHAPTER 29

I awoke in the dark hours of predawn, wrapped in silken sheets and caressed by the perfume of a spring night's breeze. The events of the previous night unfolded in my mind like a well-treasured book and I smiled in private satisfaction at the things I would never speak of, only remember fondly.

It had been a long time since I felt this peaceful.

And then I realized I was alone in this great canopy bed.

I sat up and looked about the bedroom. The windows were open and the drapes were flapping gently in the breeze. A shadowed figure stood beyond them.

"Mykhalo?" I called softly.

The figure moved and he stepped into the room lit by fluttering candles. He silently came to sit beside me on the bed. His face seemed very sad.

"What's wrong?" I said. I hoped he hadn't been disappointed in me!

"Nothing," he hastened to reassure me. "You are a beautiful woman. I never thought to be able to share such a moment with anyone again, safely. I thought it might end differently, to my grief."

"Has that happened before?" I said.

He was loathe to reply.

I crawled on my belly up to his side and wrapped an arm around his bare shoulders.

"Mykhalo, I'm not the jealous type, if that's what you're worried about," I said.

He gave me a surprised look and I laughed softly.

"I'm a realist, not a teenager!" I explained. "And you've lived nearly three hundred years! I'm sure there was some other woman you were interested in, probably several. I'm okay with that. I didn't know you and you didn't know me. Why fuss about water under the bridge?"

He turned his face into the shadow.

"The last time I tried this…it ended badly," he finally said and his voice was filled with regret.

"You killed someone you cared about deeply," I said.

He nodded not trusting his voice.

I sighed heavily.

"Given what you are, that's always a possibility," I told him. "I'm sorry for her pain and the pain you must have felt when it happened. And I realize there are no guarantees. The next time we do this, that might happen to me."

"There will be no next time!" he growled and pulling away from my grasp, stalked across the room. I saw his shoulders tense and then relax as he mastered himself.

"I will not take the chance of it happening. I want tonight to remain as it is a wonderful memory for both of us to treasure and hold onto when things are bleak."

He turned and looked out of the window. The moonlight sliced across his face and threw his features into shadow.

"Besides, I am running out of time," he whispered as if speaking to himself.

I shivered at his words and drew the sheets closer. I suspected he meant something else.

"What are you talking about?" I said slowly.

He turned to look at me. His face was now entirely in shadow but I could still see his eyes, glittering at me in the dark.

He came to the bed and sitting down beside me, took my hands in his.

"Zan, I need you to pay strict attention to what I am about to say," he said. "There are things you need to know for when I'm gone and things you need to do. I think I have prepared everything down to the last detail. You and Bree will be taken care of. But you must also take care of yourself. Because of what we did, you will become a magnet to other creatures of the night and not all of them will be friendly. You need to know how to sense them and especially how to avoid them. Trust your witch's instincts. Never turn them off! Avoid places with big crowds of people if you can. If you can't, I would invest in a good pair of dark sunglasses. Those predators seeking to harm you will be confused if they cannot see your eyes. Those who can be trusted will speak a word to you. That word is 'hoffe'. Remember that! Please don't forget it."

I pulled back, confused by what he had said at first.

"Wait a minute!" I stopped him. "What did you mean by time is short? How short? Why?"

He sighed heavily.

"Do you remember what your 'face of God' said when she tested me? She promised me my dreams. Unfortunately, I was selfish in those dreams. I only wanted to die. I did not wish to become mortal again."

My heart seemed to beat very slowly.

"I understand now what She meant," he continued. "I was to get my affairs in order. She was being generous by allowing this. Maybe even this night with you was in Her plans. But I don't think living out a mortal life married to you was."

There was a strange lump in my throat and my heart was acting odd.

"Time is short," I mumbled numbly and he nodded.

"How short?"

He paused and looked out the window and then back at me.

I screamed.

"*NO!*"

My cries were stifled by his tight embrace. He was murmuring something into my ear and stroking my hair but it all made no sense.

It wasn't fair!

I clutched tightly onto him as if he would be ripped away from me this very instant. This couldn't be possible. I wanted more time!

283

For years, I held myself at arm's length from being any man's love interest because I was still so devoted to the memory of my lost warrior love. Now this vampire had shown up and in only a few months' time, he had coaxed me into breaking all the rules of my heart. Taking him away now, just when I had relented, seemed too cruel.

What was Sekhmet thinking?

I hung on harder as the tears came fast and furious. I didn't want this to be the ending to the story. There had to be another way. I thumped his shoulder blade with a closed fist out of frustration. I sank my teeth into his shoulder in aggravation so hard I drew blood. I tasted his blood on my lips. I felt him wince slightly and chuckle softly.

"Now who is the vampire?" he whispered into my hair.

Abruptly I pulled away and took his face in my hands.

"If this is your last night, then I beg you, break your rules again. Just as I have broken my own," I demanded of him. "Just once more. Please!"

He sniffed in amusement and wound his fingers through my hair.

"You dare to tempt me with pleasure I thought I'd never experience again?" he said to me in a growl. His tone was hard but his eyes were soft.

I set my jaw with determination.

"Isn't that what the religious authorities have told you through the ages that we women were especially talented at? Ever the evil temptress?" I retorted as if it were a dare.

He laughed the comment off.

"I never believed much of what they said anyway," he replied.

He sighed heavily.

"Very well," he said, giving in. "I accept. I could never refuse you anyway. You command my heart."

And with this, he lowered me gently down to the mattress and flung the silken sheets over our heads.

## CHAPTER 30

I stood in front of the windows and watched the sky begin to lighten with a creeping dread deep within my heart.

Mykhalo came up behind me and wrapping his strong arms about me, kissed my shoulder.

"My dear, what was that you just did?" he said in amorous fascination.

I chuckled in a smug way and stroked his head from behind me.

"Just a little sex magic," I teased him. "Every woman knows how to do it. Most women are too afraid of their own power to go there."

I turned to face him and wound my arms around his body, trapping his form close to mine.

"You like?" I whispered.

He smiled and rocked me in his arms.

"Hmm. Very much so."

I purred and rubbed my cheek against his chest.

"I see you've never bedded a witch before," I mumbled. "Just imagine what you've missed!"

Then I noticed his bare arms were lit by the coming dawn. I became suddenly quiet and mournful.

"I don't want you to go," I whispered.

He sighed and hugged me closer.

"Hush," he consoled. "Death is not always evil. And I am long overdue."

I looked up into his eyes.

"Do you really want this? Now that we have taken this step, don't you want more for us?" I had to ask.

He sighed again and went to his knees before me.

"I will always want more for us," he said. "But can you not see this from my point of view? I want closure to my life. I hunger for the circle you live in that has always been denied me. I want to see my family again, yes, even my cruel, frustrating father! I want to see if reincarnation is true and if it is, then there's still a chance we may meet again someday and carry out a relationship in a less complicated and dangerous form."

He reached his hand up to my face to wipe away the tears which were starting to fall again.

"You said it yourself, there are no guarantees. If I ever did become human, there would be no assurance that we would live, love and grow old together. I would want the theater and the opera and you would want the drum circle and dancing around bonfires. We might end up hating each other. I could walk out the door and die of a heart attack or you could die in an auto wreck tomorrow. I want better for you than to love a creature of the night. You deserve to love a human. And I will never be that. If I truly love you, then I must go and complete the circle. And you must carry on. Bree still needs her mother. Do you understand?"

I stood there and tried not to cry. It didn't work.

"I'm trying," I replied as honestly as I could.

He nodded and rubbed my hands reassuringly.

"Never doubt my feelings for you," he went on. "I do love you, Susanne Miller and I will miss you. Never forget that. And please don't ever give up your faith. It's one of the traits about you that I love the most."

He rose to his feet and embraced me again. I clung like a frightened child.

"Now can you promise me something?" he said.

I answered too quickly.

"Anything!"

I felt him smile onto the top of my head.

"Your 'face of God' promised me that I would not burn. Do you know what that means?"

I shook my head.

"She meant that there would be a body to dispose of and a grave for you to visit after I am gone. Very generous of her."

He sighed.

"I know this is difficult for you to hear but you must listen to me carefully," he instructed. "I know you prefer cremation but I do not want that. I want to be buried in my family's churchyard in Bavaria between my mother and my wife. You will do this for me, yes?"

I turned my face upward to look at him.

"Okay, now I don't understand," I said. "I thought you said you hated the church."

He smiled apologetically.

"I hate the bureaucracy of Rome. Always have. It's always been very easy for me to hate bureaucracies.

"Be that as it may, I have nothing against the religion I was raised in which was Catholicism. I was never that religious a person until I was turned. Then the parish I was raised in, even the graveyard became poison to my presence. My father was very thorough at seeing that the family's graves would never be disturbed by any vampire. He filled the church and the cemetery with powerful wards against vampires. The church has some very old magic. Unfortunately, he never thought that in doing so, he might be shutting out his own son. I never wanted to get into any church so badly as when I suddenly couldn't, when it was forbidden to me."

I smiled in rueful understanding.

"Mother always said they should outlaw all religion and the schools. Then people would be dying to get in," I muttered.

He sniffed in agreement.

"Your mother was a wise woman," he replied. "I bet you stood at her graveside at her funeral. That honor was forbidden to me with my wife. Do you know what it is like not to be able to attend the funeral of your loved one? To get no closer than the cemetery gates and only to appear after dark? It is insulting! You feel like a leper!"

287

He looked into my eyes.

"You will attend my funeral. You will be the mourner of honor and stand at my graveside, not the gates and you will stand in the sun surrounded by spring flowers. Promise me that, Zan."

I gulped down my apprehension. I would rather be alone with my grief, not surrounded by strangers, in a strange land and in a strange church.

But this was his request, and I loved him so I agreed.

"I want a big Catholic funeral in my homeland," he went on. "The preparations have already been made and paid for. Can I trust you to see this through?"

The tears had dried up. I nodded numbly.

"I promise to see it through," I said to him. "But why between your mother and your wife?"

He chuckled softly.

"I adored my mother. She never died by my hand. She died of consumption when I was twenty-five. My wife, although I never truly *loved* her, we were great friends. She taught me what it was to be a friend with a woman and how to properly honor that bond. She taught me honor and respect and I am very grateful to her. I wish our friendship had ended any way other than it did."

I swallowed with difficulty.

"I will see that you are buried between your mother and your wife with a nice big tombstone to hold you down. I promise you that."

"Thank you," he whispered and squeezed me hard.

I felt numb inside.

"Dawn approaches. Come with me," he said and taking my hand, he led me out of the bedroom.

I followed him silently down the hallway of his great house and the immense, sweeping staircase to the porch outside. The birds were just beginning their morning songs. The tulip and daffodil heads were nodding in the gentle breezes.

Mykhalo led me to the bank of the Koi pond and stopping there, wrapped his arms around me and held me close. We watched the brightly colored fish dart about just under the mirror's surface.

"This is a beautiful place," he sighed. "I'm glad I got to share this with you."

I could say nothing. I stared at the fish flashing and flickering their orange and white scales beneath the water.

"Zan, do you have any idea how much death I have seen in my long life?" Mykhalo asked me.

"Probably too much," I mumbled.

"Yes," he said. "Do you know how many people I have had to kill to stay alive? Do you have any idea how much horror, despair, and grief I have caused and had to live with in all that time?"

I had to admit, this was a concept beyond my imagining.

"Dying here, with you, in this setting...it is not so bad. It is peaceful. This is how every life should end, peacefully. Do you see what I'm saying?"

I was silent for a moment.

"It is a fitting end for one who has seen so much horror," I whispered.

"Yes," he replied.

I looked up into the brimming rays of the morning sun. The wind ruffled my hair and gently swayed the hanging tendrils of the weeping cherry trees and the willows. The bullfrogs croaked their morning mating calls. Somewhere distance there was a splash as one jumped into the water, creating ripples which cut the reflections of the morning rays.

"Mother?"

I heard Bree's voice just behind me.

I turned to see my daughter standing behind us, dressed in red.

"How did you find us?" I asked.

She laughed and touched the talisman necklace I had made her during the ritual.

"Why shouldn't I find you?" she said. "I found you before. I *am* your daughter."

I gathered her in a warm embrace.

She kept the hug brief and then forcibly pushed me away. She turned to Mykhalo.

"I'm sorry it's me that has to do this," she said. "Please don't think I will enjoy it."

I looked from my daughter to Mykhalo.

He just smiled quietly.

"I'm not going to blame you," he told her. "And it's not really you who will be doing it, anyway."

The realization of what was about to happen was slowly dawning on me.

"I'm sorry I didn't get to know you better," Bree was saying. "It would have been kinda cool to have a vampire as a stepdad!"

She giggled like a typical teen.

"Not as 'cool' as you might think!" Mykhalo said earnestly. "But yes, I will miss getting to know you better. I'm sure you are just as intriguing as your fine mother here is. How could you not be?"

"No!" I stated aloud, suddenly interrupting. "This can't be the way it's going to happen! Not by my daughter's own hand!"

They both looked at me.

"Hey! Don't gripe at me! This is Sekhmet's idea," Bree said.

"Would you rather see me stabbed by some ego-driven religious zealot, or my head sliced off by some pompous vampire hunter? Or any myriad of other horrible ways I can think of?" Mykhalo interjected.

"This is really the most respectful way to handle it, Mother," Bree said. "And isn't that what you've always tried to teach me, respect and honor in all things?"

Mykhalo snickered.

"Out of the mouths of babes," he mused.

"What about, 'And it harm none'?" I shot back.

Bree sniffed.

"That's why *She* is going to take over," she said. "Besides Ma, you know I could never really *kill* anyone or anything without divine aide. That's not the way you raised me."

My eyes traveled down her wardrobe.

"Where is the dagger then?" I said.

I had noticed the Coptic dagger was not anywhere on her person.

"I was told it wasn't needed," Bree said. "Not for him."

Mykhalo sighed in relief.

"Thank you for that," he said.

I turned to look at Bree again and noticed her eyes were swirling, changing color.

Mykhalo immediately fell to his knees.

I remained rooted to the spot. I don't know why but I just couldn't kneel.

"Zan!" Mykhalo hissed at me.

He gestured to me to the ground with his eyes but I still couldn't obey.

"Hush, Nosferatu. It is all right." Sekhmet's deep voice purred to us both. "The little mother has been through much in these past few days."

I looked at Bree but she was no longer there. Instead, there was the towering form of the lioness headed goddess.

There seemed to be sympathy in her eyes as she strode to me. She took my jaw in her tawny hands. They were warm and welcoming as sun touched sand.

"I too know what it is like to be ruled by the heart and not the head. Love makes fools of us all at one time or another, even the gods. And I am in a kindly mood today. Be at ease. You are safe."

As she said this, she kissed me gently on the forehead. I closed my eyes and leaned into her maternal presence.

When I opened my eyes again, I was on my knees before her where I belonged.

"Do not be so sad. This is all as it should be. The broken circle will be healed this day. There is no harm in this. Let your troubled heart be at peace. There are no endings. Only beginnings," she purred softly to me.

She stroked my face as if I were a wayward kitten and smiled. All grief left me as I looked into her deep eyes. I would have agreed to anything right then.

She straightened slowly and made her way to Mykhalo.

"Did you enjoy your last night?" she asked him, smiling knowingly.

I saw his eyes flicker up and meet mine. He smiled and held my gaze for one long moment. Then he cast them back down.

"Yes, very much," he said. "It was magical. Thank you, Lady."

"And are you ready to take your leave of this place of existence?" she said.

Here, he raised his head and looked at her.

"All is prepared," he said. "I am ready."

She nodded.

"Very well then."

Sekhmet raised her hands before her and once again, they began to fill with some sort of liquid, but this time, it wasn't blood. It was golden and thick like beer.

"Drink from this sacred chalice and accept the gift I bestow upon you. So shall the line of your life be healed into a circle once more. So shall the splintered parts of your soul be mended together once again where they belong. So shall your true destiny be revealed. Drink and accept my gift, whatever form it takes."

Mykhalo reached forward and took her hands in his. He bent his head to drink but at the last moment, his eyes met mine. He paused and we stayed like this for a long moment which seemed frozen in time. There was no need for words between us. The emotions were too poignant for words.

He then bent his head to the golden liquid and drank deep.

I crept to his side on my knees and knelt beside him. I needed to touch him. My hand tentatively reached out and touched his arm.

Mykhalo drank until her cupped hands were dry. He then sat back on his folded legs and paused, considering.

"That was the best beer I've ever tasted," he said.

He looked at me and smiled.

"How do you feel?" I said in a trembling voice.

"Different," he replied slowly. "Complete."

He reached out and touched my face.

I gasped.

His hand was warm with life!

The sun crept above the horizon and lit his face in gold. He turned his eyes to take it in. He smiled again in amazement.

"It doesn't hurt," he told me. "The sun's light doesn't burn me. This is fantastic!"

He sighed.

"I've been cold for so many, many years. It feels good to be warm again."

He closed his eyes and drank in the newborn morning warmth, basking in this new, amazing sensation.

He took my hands in his and clasped them tight.

"I am no longer Nosferatu!" he said. "I can feel it!"

He embraced me tightly. I clutched him in return, happy for his new discovery but also full of dread.

He suddenly shuddered as if he had been shot.

"Mykhalo?" I said. "What…"

I pulled away to look into his eyes.

Through those two, beautiful, silver orbs, I saw the change taking place deep inside.

His newly returned soul was leaving.

"I feel heavy," he said and coughed. "Is this what it feels like to be old?"

My words choked on my lips as I said them.

"I don't know. I'm not there yet."

A smile flashed across his face in response to this.

He was suddenly racked with a fit of jagged coughing. I tried to hold him up as he doubled over with their force. But he was a big man and very heavy. I felt his form spasm and convulse in my arms. I struggled to hold onto him tighter.

In desperation, I looked up at Sekhmet. She was circling us slowly, chanting something in ancient Egyptian. I could feel the power of her soft voice rumble through the ground. I knew she would not stop this.

Mykhalo gave a huge gasp and fell over backwards into my arms.

"Are you in pain?" was all I could force out.

He shook his head in denial and answered in a husky voice.

"It's nothing!" he insisted. "Not compared to…it's not bad."

He swallowed with difficultly and stroked my face.

"Remember. This is what I wanted. Never blame yourself. It had to be."

His chest heaved as he struggled for breath.

"My love for you won't end. There is no end to love," he hastened to assure me. "She was right. This is no end but a beginning."

He coughed again.

Sekhmet knelt beside us and wrapped one arm about Mykhalo and one around myself. She was purring calmly, peacefully. Her touch was soothing and warm.

"Please promise me," he gasped. "That you won't stop living because of this. Take care of Bree. Your life is a circle. You need to continue. Promise me that."

I heard Sekhmet's voice echo his words as he spoke them.

The tears were coming hot and fast. But I managed somehow to choke out my promise to him.

He gasped struggling for one more breath.

"I will see you again," he told me. "I promise."

Again, Sekhmet echoed his words. I looked briefly into her fathomless eyes. Their color had shifted to black, shot with pinpoints of light like the night sky.

I turned my gaze back to Mykhalo. He was shuddering violently in my arms.

And then there was abruptly no spirit behind those eyes.

I clasped Mykhalo's face close to my heart and began to rock him as I sobbed. Some dim sensation told me Bree had come back and wrapped her arms around me tight.

I held Mykhalo, and she held me. And we wept in the light of a new day.

# CHAPTER 31

The constant hum of the airplane's engine thrummed its low-pitched sound to us as Bree and I watched the fluffy clouds pass outside the small window. I was lost deep in thought when I heard Bree's voice speak quietly to me.

"Mom, do you hate me for what happened?"

I turned to look at my daughter. She had removed her iPod's plugs from her ears and was staring at me, her green eyes wide as though she was expecting to be punished. I drank in her features for a long moment before I answered, noticing her bright red hair, her red, and black striped outfit and her pale skin. She was fingering the necklace and the talisman bottle which held a small lock of my own hair.

Automatically, my own hand went to the necklace of bloodstone around my neck and I stroked the bottle which held a lock of her shocking, red dyed, hair.

I smiled in return and gathered her into my arms as well as I could. The arm of the plane's seat made this awkward. She did not resist my hug.

"I never blamed you for any of this," I said as I kissed her soft, red hair. "Sekhmet maybe, but not you."

I felt her smile into my arm.

"Good, I'm glad," she said and her voice was slightly muffled. So I released her.

"It's just that you've been so quiet lately that I thought you were mad at me."

I sighed heavily.

"I'm sorry, Luv," I said. "I've just been a little preoccupied, that's all."

My thoughts went back to watching the airplane personnel load the large black casket into the cargo hold of the airplane.

I felt a lump come into my throat at the thought. With an effort, I forced it down.

Bree nodded.

"That's quite understandable," she said.

She inspected her red fingernails as if she had something more to say but was uncomfortable to broach the subject.

"I never hated Mykhalo, Mom," she finally managed to spit out. "From the first time I saw you talking at the convention, I liked him. I thought you two would be good together. Of course that was before I knew all the…"

Here she hesitated and looked about uncomfortably as if someone might be listening.

"…details about him," she said in a lowered voice. "But even after I knew, I still liked him. I didn't want to believe he was a bad person."

I felt the tears brim on my eyelids.

"What about Brittany?" I asked with difficulty. "You mean to say that you still don't blame him after finding out what he did to her?"

Bree's eyes dropped to her lap and she frowned.

"I don't blame him. I blame *her*!" she corrected. "In my opinion, Brittany still committed suicide, only Mykhalo was her knife. She used him to get what she wanted. She was hurting and wouldn't let anyone help her. She just wanted a way out. Mykhalo was a convenient way to get what she wanted."

Bree set her mouth and glared out the window.

"She was stupid!" she growled in frustration.

I looked at my daughter with new eyes. I suspected she meant more than she was really saying and it concerned me.

"I didn't know you were so angry at her. Were you jealous because she had a boyfriend and you didn't? She and Brad were dating for quite some time," I said.

Bree sniffed and rolled her eyes at me in disdain.

"Brittany was doing *something* but I'm not sure I would call it dating!"

I was my turn to stop and look her full in the face.

"But…she and Brad were together," I countered.

Bree waggled her head.

"Yeah, but he wasn't exactly marriage potential and she knew it when they hooked up. She was muttering to me about leaving him right before her grandmother died. Then, after that, well life seemed to go to hell for her," she confessed.

This made me fall into a thoughtful silence for a moment.

"Sounds to me like you two weren't very close in the end," I commented.

"We weren't," was her response.

Then she sighed heavily.

"Okay, look. I probably shouldn't tell you this. But a few weeks before you met Mykhalo, Brittany convinced me to sneak out and go to a party with her."

I froze all except for my heart which started to patter like crazy.

"You did *what*?" I said. I forced myself to be calm and take a deep breath.

"What kind of party was this?" I made myself ask, quietly.

Bree sniffed and one corner of her mouth tilted up in a wry smile.

"The wrong kind of party," she informed. "There were college boys there. They had a keg and people were smoking pot in the basement. Brittany was having a great ol' time and every one of the college boys was trying to dance with her or get her alone.

"Some of them went for me. One kept trying to spike my Coke to get me to loosen up a bit."

She sighed again and refused to look me in the eye.

"All you need to know about that night is I didn't like the party. I didn't feel comfortable or safe there. The first chance I got, I excused myself like I had to go the bathroom and I ducked out the back door and ran all the way home. It was a Friday night and I was in bed by ten trying to forget it had ever happened!"

She was quiet for a moment.

"The next time I saw Brittany at school, she made fun of me. Said that I didn't know how to party. I knew then it was the beginning of the end for our friendship. We were going in separate directions. She wanted to be the party girl and play with the jocks. I wanted to stay home, hang out with the nerds, and play Dungeons and Dragons. I felt safer being the only girl in a role playing game than I ever felt at that party!"

"And that's the truth?" I asked.

She nodded.

"I would have told you before about this but then her grandmother died, stuff with Mykhalo was going on and well…life got a bit crazy. I'm sorry, Mom. But please believe me, I never want to go to one of those parties again!"

I had no idea what to say. So I just hugged her tight. She hesitated and then hugged me back.

"You're such a smart girl even when you're being a brat," I whispered in her ear. "I'm so proud of you!"

And then I held her out at arm's length.

"And if you ever do such a thing again…!" I threatened.

Bree gave an uncomfortable laugh and waved her arms.

"I really don't think it's gonna happen. Once was bad enough!" she assured me.

"How can the 'smart kids' act so stupid?"

Bree was quiet for a moment before going on.

"I wish she would have talked to me more instead of shutting me out. I didn't know what to do to help her," she continued wrinkling her nose. "In any case, it still didn't convince me that Mykhalo was bad. He didn't feel that way to me."

"He wasn't really," I replied. "He was just a tormented soul who has now found the peace he deserved."

It took a monstrous effort to talk about Mykhalo in the past tense. Bree nodded.

"Mom?" Bree went on. "If you're not done crying, you know you always got me to lean on."

I laughed, touched by my child's sensitivity.

"For the time being I'm done. But I'm sure there will be more," I assured her.

"Well, be sure to let me know because I don't want you crying all alone," she demanded.

I laughed again but almost did begin crying all over again.

"Bree honey, do you know why I gave you the name Tempest?" I asked.

Bree's face wrinkled in confusion.

"Because of the girl that died?" she answered.

I smiled and stroked her red hair.

"Not entirely," I said.

My thoughts drifted away for a moment until I realized her eyes were searching my face, expecting more of an answer.

"I named you Tempest because I thought it would help you be strong enough to weather any storm."

I could see her mulling over my words carefully before she responded.

"Well, it certainly worked didn't it?" she said with a grin. "I…er…*WE* beat all those damn suckers now didn't we?"

I found myself laughing at her words before I could stop myself.

"My dear, life is full of storms. There are more battles yet to come. I hope you can weather those storms as well as what you have just experienced. Life is a roller coaster. Just remember to buckle up!"

"Like Storm Runner or the Big Bear?" she chuckled, referring to some of the wilder rides at Hershey Park she so loved.

I chuckled and let it slide.

"Hush, my little bookworm, and get some sleep," I told her. "We have a long flight ahead."

I wrapped the commercial blanket around her shoulders and let her snuggle against me as best she could with the damned armrest between us. Bree mumbled something about waking her when we got to Germany. I placed my arm over her and rubbed her back until I heard her breathing become even and deep. Then I turned my attention to the clouds outside the window.

Presently I too fell asleep, head leaning against the airplane's windowpane.

I dreamed. I dreamed I was standing in a beautiful green meadow with rolling hills which met the edge of a deep green forest. Above the forest stretched the awesome beauty of craggy, snow-capped mountains.

I knew the place wasn't anywhere in America. I assumed it was in Bavaria.

Mykhalo stood by my side, holding my hand. The wind teased his golden locks and the sun lit his face. I realized I had never seen him in the light of full day. He looked even more handsome than I remembered.

He looked at me, smiling, and I knew I was to stay. He let go of my hand and began to walk down the hill away from me and toward those beautiful mountains.

I heard a dog bark and glanced up. Over the crest of the nearest hill, a dog appeared followed by another. They were both Great Danes. One was silver gray the other was a harlequin with one blue eye. The gray dog saw Mykhalo first and woofed a greeting. It then began to wriggle like dogs do when they see someone they love. It pounced on its partner, delirious with joy and leapt down the hill at a gallop, the harlequin in hot pursuit. The closer the two came to Mykhalo, the harder a time they had running because their tails were wagging so fast. Mykhalo held his arms wide in welcome and both dogs smiled widely back. They pounced on him, knocking him over in their joy. I heard Mykhalo laugh loud and easily as the two dogs barked and wound their long bodies around him, frantic in the joy of his touch again.

I smiled in understanding. These must have been his favorite dogs. They had been waiting all this time to see him again.

And then I heard the sound of a horse's neigh.

A stallion had crested the hilltop. He was a dappled, liver chestnut in color and his mane and tail were white and long.

Mykhalo saw him and shouted something in German.

The horse squealed, half reared and tossed its head, causing its mane to dance like a wave. It plunged down the hill towards Mykhalo bucking and kicking in joy; the sun turned the brown of its flanks into a dark, brassy gold.

Drawing near, the horse checked its speed and waited, tossing its head as Mykhalo ran up, and threw his arms around his horse, and hugged him tightly. The stallion curled his neck around Mykhalo, returning the embrace.

I remembered Mykhalo's words from before, *"Horses panic around me now. So I don't go anywhere near them. It's a shame because I loved dogs and horses at one time."*

I realized how much joy Mykhalo had lost in becoming a vampire.

Then there was a shout.

Looking up, I saw a much younger Bill Gibson crest the hilltop, dressed in an old, World War II uniform. He waved and laughed and then called behind him. People I didn't recognize, all wearing clothes from different time periods, suddenly began to appear on the hilltop. They all paused in shock, seeing Mykhalo. I noticed many of those gathered bore a striking physical resemblance to him. Then there were shouts and screams of joy and they began to flood down the hill towards him with tears in their eyes and their arms open wide. They swarmed around him in an excited mass, all fighting to be the first one to hug him. The stallion trotted away to a safe distance. The dogs jumped about, barking in glee.

I felt tears of joy come to my eyes as I watched.

Mykhalo was no longer alone and in the shadows. He stood in the sun surrounded by love and his family.

"Mrs. Miller?" a voice at my shoulder said.

It startled me out of my thoughts.

I turned to see Bill Gibson standing by my side.

"You've done very well by Mykhalo. We are very glad to have him back. Thank you for your sacrifice," he said to me.

I bit my lip and nodded.

"It was all for the best," I said.

"Yes, it was," he replied. "I always knew Mykhalo had to meet you. Why, at the time, I didn't know. But it all makes sense now."

"Funny how that happens," I mused. "Things never make sense until later."

"Hmm," he muttered. "Mrs. Miller?"

"Yes?" I asked.

"You were permitted to see this at Mykhalo's request. But you are not permitted to stay. You've got some time before you need to come here. You must go back. Understand?"

I nodded again, casting my eyes down for a moment.

I looked up again, hoping to catch Mykhalo's eyes just once more before I left. But Bill Gibson stepped in front of me and all I could see were the medals on his uniform.

Then everything faded into the blackness of dreamtime.

* * *


My name is Susanne Joel Miller and I am a witch. I believe in God. I believe in a Goddess as well. I believe in balance. I believe the Divine that touches our lives, cares not what name you give it. Names are not important. Belief is. I believe that love is powerful and gratefulness is more powerful than we give it credit. I believe that people are inherently good until something happens to change them and that we can choose how to allow that change to affect us. I believe those good people that rise above the evil in their lives are heroes. I believe in soldiers and fighting the good fight. I believe there is a time to stand up for your beliefs and a time to stay silent about those beliefs. I believe in magic and miracles. I believe in the unshakable bond between a mother and her child. I believe that evil exists in the hearts of some wounded people. I believe that devils need to be human. I believe in vampires, and not just the psychic ones either!

And I believe that Mykhalo Von Ludwig, vampire or not, was one of those good, heroic people.

## THE END

Made in the USA
Middletown, DE
21 May 2023